KATE RHODES

The Winter Foundlings

A Novel

Minotaur Books
New York

THE WINTER FOUNDLINGS. Copyright © 2014 by Kate Rhodes. All rights reserved. Printed in the United States of America. For information, address St. Martin's Press, 175 Fifth Avenue, New York, N.Y. 10010.

www.minotaurbooks.com

Library of Congress Cataloging-in-Publication Data

Rhodes, Kate.
   The winter foundlings : a novel / Kate Rhodes. — First U.S. edition.
      p. cm. — (Alice Quentin series ; 3)
   ISBN 978-1-250-01432-0 (hardcover)
   ISBN 978-1-4668-6692-8 (e-book)
   1. Women psychologists—England—London—Fiction. 2. Serial murderers—England—London—Fiction. 3. Serial murder investigation—England—London—Fiction. 4. London (England)—Fiction. I. Title.
   PR6118.H48W56 2015
   823'.92—dc23

                                                    2014033908

Minotaur books may be purchased for educational, business, or promotional use. For information on bulk purchases, please contact the Macmillan Corporate and Premium Sales Department at 1-800-221-7945, extension 5442, or write to specialmarkets@macmillan.com.

First published in Great Britain by Mulholland Books, an imprint of Hodder & Stoughton, an Hachette UK company

First U.S. Edition: February 2015

10 9 8 7 6 5 4 3 2 1

The Winter Foundlings

Also by Kate Rhodes

A Killing of Angels
Crossbones Yard

For all the children cared for by the Foundling Hospital

'Death may be the greatest of all human blessings.'

Socrates (469 BC–399 BC)

The Winter Foundlings

PROLOGUE

Ella stands on the school steps, shivering in the cold. The playground's almost empty, and two girls from year six run past like she doesn't exist. They don't even notice her shoes glittering. Her granddad bought them for her on Saturday, and she can't stop admiring them – cherry red, shining like mirrors. It's the buckles she loves best, round and glossy as new pennies. She's longing to dance across the playground, tapping a bright red tune into the snow. One last boy passes through the school gates, dragging his satchel behind him, and then she's alone.

She's been waiting so long, the smile has frozen from her face. She scans the road for a glimpse of her grandfather's car. It must have broken down again. She'll have to walk home without him for the first time, but she doesn't mind. It will make him realise that she's almost grown up. She was ten last birthday, plenty old enough to walk a mile on her own.

Coloured lights flick on in people's houses as she sets off along the street. Christmas is only a few days away, and she's excited about the tree waiting in the living room. Tonight Suzanne will help her to decorate it with tinsel and baubles. She treads carefully on the ice, taking care not to slip. The street's quiet, apart from a man loading shopping into a van. His bags are too full, and one splits as she passes, pieces of fruit scattering across the pavement. He sighs as an orange rolls past her feet.

'Can you fetch that for me, love?' the man asks.

Over his shoulder, Ella sees her granddad's car arriving, then the man's arm catches her waist, his hand stifling her mouth. She's too shocked to scream as he bundles her into the van. The door slams shut and there's a scratching sound behind her. When she spins round, a ghost is hovering in the shadows. A girl in a white dress, her hair an ugly nest of rats' tails. She's bone-thin, knees pressed against her chest, her body tightly folded. Her dead-eyed stare is terrifying. Suddenly Ella's yelling for help, fists battering the door. Through the van's smoky window she sees her granddad rushing up the school steps, and one of her shoes lying on the snow, among the apples and oranges. When the van pulls away, her head knocks against something solid. The pain is a sharp white knife, separating her from everything she knows.

I

The chill attacked me as soon as I stepped out of the car. It made me wish I'd worn a thicker coat, but at least it made a change from the misery on the radio – weathermen predicting more snow, train services at a standstill, and another girl missing from the streets of north London. I picked my way across the ice, pausing to admire Northwood in its winter glory. Rows of dark Victorian tenements stood shoulder to shoulder, braced against the wind. My colleagues at Guy's thought that I'd taken leave of my senses. Why would anyone rent out their London flat and swap a comfortable hospital consultancy for a six-month sabbatical at the country's biggest psychiatric prison? But I knew I'd made the right choice. The British Psychological Society had invited me to write the first-ever in-depth study of the regime at the Laurels, home to some of the country's most violent criminals. The work would be fascinating, and provide an ideal subject for my next book, but that was just part of the reason. If I could handle six months in the company of serial rapists and mass murderers, it meant that I was cured. The suffering and deaths I'd witnessed during the Angel case hadn't left a scratch.

A mixture of curiosity and fear quickened my heart rate as I approached the entrance gates. The warning signs grew more obvious with each step – barred ground-floor windows, razor wire and searchlights. Dozens of reminders that the place was a prison for the criminally insane, as well as a hospital. The security guards gave cautious smiles when I reached reception: two middle-aged women, one tall, one short. Neither seemed overjoyed by their choice of career.

'Bitter out there, isn't it?' the tall one said.

The smaller woman gave me an apologetic look before turning my handbag upside down and shaking it vigorously. A flurry of biros, lipstick cases and old receipts scattered across the counter.

'I'm afraid mobiles aren't allowed,' she said.

'Sorry, I forgot.'

'You wouldn't believe the stuff people try and take inside. Drugs, flick knives, you name it.'

I processed the idea while she searched my belongings. It was hard to imagine anyone bringing weapons into a building packed with psychopaths, unless they had a death wish themselves. She led me to a machine in the corner of the room.

'The card's just for identity,' she said. 'Our doors open with keys or fingerprint recognition.'

I pressed my index finger onto a glass plate, then a light flared, and the machine spat out my ID card. The woman in the photo looked unfamiliar. She had a caught-in-the-headlights stare, cheeks blanched by the cold.

The site map the security guards gave me turned out to be useless. Paths narrow as shoelaces twisted through the maze of tenements packed tight inside the walls of the compound. The architecture was designed for maximum surveillance, hundreds of windows staring down as I wandered in circles, until the Laurels loomed into view. The building had been a cause célèbre when it opened five years ago, protesters outraged that it had consumed thirty-six million pounds of taxpayers' cash. It was a stark monument to modern architecture, surfaces cut from steel and glass. Walking inside felt like entering a futurist hotel, apart from the security measures.

Two sets of doors snapped at my heels as I crossed the threshold.

I felt apprehensive as I searched for the centre director's office. Dr Aleks Gorski had a formidable reputation. When a prisoner escaped from the Laurels the previous year, he had refused to take responsibility, blaming the government for cutting his security budget. Gorski went on the offensive as soon as the prisoner was recaptured, giving angry interviews to the press. His outspoken style had cost him some important allies. It was common knowledge that his seniors were longing to have him removed.

Gorski seemed to be fighting a losing battle with his temper when I found the right door. He was around forty, wearing a tight suit and highly polished shoes, black hair shorn to a savage crew cut. His smile was too brief to be interpreted as a welcome.

'Our appointment was at nine, Dr Quentin.'

'Sorry I'm late, the M25's closed. Didn't you get my message?'

He sat behind his desk, eyeing me across yards of dark brown mahogany. 'Your head of department says you want to write a book about us. What do you plan to focus on?' Gorski's speech was rapid and a fraction too loud, with a strong Polish inflection.

'I'm interested in your treatments for Dangerous and Severe Personality Disorder. I'd like to learn more about your rehabilitation work before release.'

'Very few of our men ever leave, but you're in the right place to study mental disorder. This is the DSPD capital of the world. The only reason our inmates are here is because the prison system spat them out.' He observed me coolly. 'Do you know how long our female employees normally last?'

'A year?'

'Four months. Only a few stay the distance; the ones that carry

5

on fall into two categories – the flirts and the lion tamers. Some are attracted to violent men, and the rest have got something to prove. It's too soon to guess which category you belong to.'

I gazed at him in amazement. Surely statements like that had been outlawed years ago? 'That's irrelevant, Dr Gorski. I'm here to learn about the welfare of your patients.'

'It's your own welfare you should worry about. Last summer an inmate attacked one of our nurses so savagely she was in intensive care for a week. These men will hurt you, if you fail to look after yourself. Do you understand?'

'Of course.'

He gave a curt nod. 'In that case, I'll give you a tour.'

By now I was yearning for my regular boss at Guy's. He was so chilled out that he had a sedative effect on everyone he met, but Gorski seemed as volatile as his patients. He would register a high score on the Hare Psychopathy Checklist, ticking all the boxes for aggression and lack of respect for social boundaries.

I inhaled a lungful of the building's smell as we crossed the corridor. It reminded me of all the hospitals I'd ever visited: antiseptic, air freshener, and something indescribable being char-grilled in a distant kitchen. An overweight young man was being led towards us. Two orderlies were flanking him, another following at a respectful distance, as if a backwards kick might be delivered at any minute.

'What's your staff-to-patient ratio?' I asked.

'We're short-staffed, but it should be three to one.'

'Is that level always necessary?'

He nodded vigorously. 'Fights break out all the time. Yesterday an inmate had his throat slashed with a broken CD case. He needed twenty stitches.'

The day room seemed to tell a different story. A cluster of grey-haired men were huddled in armchairs, watching *A*

Place in the Sun. From a distance they looked like a gang of mild-mannered granddads, dressed in jeans and tracksuits, sipping from mugs of tea. Female staff must have been a rarity because their heads swivelled towards me in perfect unison. Lacklustre Christmas decorations dangled from the ceiling, but everything else at the Laurels looked brand new. There was a games room for table tennis and pool, and a gym packed with running and rowing machines. The place even had its own cinema.

I saw a different side to Gorski as we wandered through the building. He spoke passionately as he explained the holistic approach he planned to adopt, if funding increased. Psychologists and psychiatrists would work alongside creative therapists, to create individual treatment programmes, and inmates would spend far more time outside their cells. At present the centre could only afford to employ one part-time art therapist. It was snowing again when we came to a halt beside a set of sealed windows.

'Do your patients ever use the main hospital facilities?' I asked.

'If they make good enough progress. I can show you an example.'

Gorski pressed a touch pad and the doors released us into the compound. I had to trot to keep up, brushing snowflakes from my face. Two male nurses were loitering outside the library, shivering in the cold. The building's high ceilings and stained-glass windows suggested that it had been the hospital chapel once, but the place had been neglected. Many of the shelves were empty, out-of-date books stacked in piles by the door. The choice of DVDs was limited to *The Green Mile, Top Gun* and *The Shawshank Redemption.* Apart from a librarian sitting on the other side of the room, head bowed over a pile of papers, the reading area was empty.

'Do you recognise him?' Gorski whispered.

On closer inspection I saw that the man's left wrist was handcuffed to the metal frame of his chair, and when I studied him more closely, I realised it was Louis Kinsella. He twisted round in his seat to face us, and his gaze had a disturbing intensity. He still bore an uncanny likeness to my father. Even his stare was identical, letting me know that I'd failed him without uttering a word. But he'd aged considerably since he'd filled the front pages seventeen years ago. His Eton-cropped hair had faded from brown to grey, and his features were more angular, with gaunt cheekbones and a prominent forehead. Only his half-moon glasses had remained the same. I'd been revising for my GCSEs when Kinsella's killing spree hit its peak, and his face had lodged in my mind, among the facts I'd memorised. Maybe he fascinated me then because my father was gravely ill. He was being cared for at home, but he'd lost the powers of speech and movement. While his physical powers waned, his doppelgänger had suddenly become Britain's most prolific child killer – a record that Kinsella still held after almost two decades.

His eyes followed me as we turned to leave. The chill felt deeper as we stepped outside, and when I looked down, I saw what had transfixed him. Snowflakes had melted into the red fabric of my coat, darkening it, like spatters of blood.

2

'Everyone reacts like that. Some of my staff won't even stay in the same room. It's the silence they can't stand.' Gorski gave a condescending smile as he watched me shiver.

'What do you mean?'

'Kinsella's choosy about who he communicates with. Most people get the silent treatment. He sends me written complaints occasionally, but he hasn't spoken in years. It's a protest, because his last tribunal failed – he wants to finish his sentence in prison.'

'He thinks he's cured?'

'Louis claims that DSPD isn't an illness. He says it's a personality trait. Now that he's learned to control his impulses, he should be released. His lawyer makes quite a convincing case.'

'But you don't agree?'

'Of course not. The only reason he hasn't killed recently is because he hasn't had the chance. You must have heard what happened at Highpoint?'

'He attacked someone, didn't he?' I remembered seeing a newspaper headline years ago, but the details had slipped my mind.

'He gouged out a prisoner's eye with his thumbs.' Gorski monitored my reaction, then turned away. He seemed determined to make my introduction to the Laurels as unsettling as possible.

The isolation unit was the next highlight on my tour. The windowless cells were padded with dark green foam rubber. If the intention was to pacify patients with subdued colours, the screams from a cell nearby proved that the strategy had back-fired. When I peered through the observation hatch, a young man was hurling himself at the wall, then scrambling to his feet and trying again, as though he'd located an invisible door.

'One of our new recruits,' Gorski muttered.

The combined effect of encountering Louis Kinsella, and watching someone ricochet round a padded cell like a squash ball was making me question my decision. Maybe I should have stayed at Guy's and committed myself to a lifetime of helping depressives lighten their mood.

Gorski came to a halt beside a narrow door, then dropped a key into my hand. 'This is your office; my deputy Judith Miller will be supervising you. She'll be at the staff meeting on Wednesday.'

I wondered how long Dr Miller had coped with life at the Laurels. Given her boss's unpleasant manner, I suspected she must be a lion tamer rather than a flirt. I twisted the key in the lock and discovered that my new office was no bigger than a broom cupboard. A narrow window cast grey light across the walls, and the desk almost filled the floor space, a threadbare chair pressed against the wall. Gorski's footsteps had faded into the distance before I could complain.

I spent the rest of the afternoon failing to launch my Outlook account. Someone had left me a pile of papers, including a list of therapy groups to observe, and dates of meetings with the care team. I searched through the pages, looking for familiar names, half expecting Gorski to have booked one-to-one sessions with his most famous psychopaths to test my nerve.

Northwood's staff common room was a million miles from the café at Guy's, which was always packed with talkative nurses. A handful of staff members were sprinkled round the room, staring thoughtfully into their coffee mugs, and I could understand why. They were on high alert all day, waiting for chaos to break out. A few people stared at me curiously as I crossed the room, before returning to quiet contemplation, and I tried to picture how they vented their repressed tension when they got home. Maybe they put on Nirvana at high volume and head-banged around their living rooms. I collected a drink from the vending machine and stood by the window. The view was another reason for the sombre atmosphere. Snow was still falling, security lights blazing from the perimeter wall, an ambulance waiting by the entrance gates. The place looked as secure as Colditz: a few patrolmen with bayonets and Gestapo crests on their caps would have completed the scene. I glanced round the room again, but no one met my eye.

On the way back to my office, I saw a prisoner refusing to follow instructions. He looked like a textbook illustration of mental disorder. Everything about him was ragged, from the tears in his sleeves to his unkempt beard.

'I shouldn't be here,' he yelled at a trio of male nurses. 'They're trying to kill me.'

The man's claw-like hands kept plucking at his clothes, and I wondered what his original crime had been. An orderly was struggling to grab his arm. From a distance it looked like he was trying to tether a scarecrow to the ground in the middle of a full-force gale.

It was dark by the time I left. Someone had cleared the paths, but the car park was still covered in snow. A van edged across the uneven surface, wheels spinning, before disappearing into the woods. My Toyota was groaning with cardboard boxes, containing everything I needed for the next six months, and I was keen to find my rented cottage. But when my key twisted in the ignition, nothing happened. The engine didn't even clear its throat. I drummed my fists on the steering wheel and breathed out a string of expletives. In my race to meet Gorski, I'd left the sidelights on. A gust of freezing air greeted me when I wrenched the door open, the hospital lights glittering on the horizon as I hunted in the boot for jump leads, cursing quietly to myself.

'Are you okay?' a voice asked.

When I straightened up, a man was looking down at me. It was too dark to tell whether he was concerned or amused.

'My battery's dead.'

'Stay there. I'll bring my car.'

He parked his four-wheel drive in front of my Toyota, and took the leads from my hands. I felt like telling him I could do it myself, but at least it gave me time to observe him. He was medium height and thickset, his cap so low over his forehead that I couldn't see his hair colour. All I could make out was the fixed line of his jaw, wide cheekbones, and his blank expression. It was hard to know whether he loved rescuing damsels in distress, or resented every second. He didn't say a word as the engines revved. Icy water leaked through the soles of my shoes, but he seemed comfortable, wrapped in his thick coat and walking boots. I got the impression that an earthquake would struggle to disturb his inner calm.

'You're the new recruit, aren't you?'

'That's me.' I nodded. 'I'm at the Laurels, doing research.'

'Lucky you. Up close and personal with our world-class freaks and psychos.' His expression remained deadpan.

'Are you on the clinical team?'

He gave a short laugh. 'God, no, I'd probably kill someone. I'm a humble fitness instructor.'

The man looked anything but humble. There was something

disturbing about his eyes, so pale they were almost colourless. The car purred quietly as he unhooked the jump leads.

'You're a life-saver. I owe you one.'

'Buy me a drink some time. Did anyone tell you what happened to Gorski's last visitor?'

'Not yet.'

'It's probably best you don't know.' He raised his hand in a brief salute then walked away.

I was so happy my car had revived that I didn't question his statement. He'd disappeared down the exit road before I realised he hadn't even told me his name.

Charndale looked like a ghost town. I didn't see a soul as I drove past a post office, a pub, and rows of small houses with picket fences. The minute scale of the place made me question how I'd cope with village life. One of my reasons for accepting the research placement had been to cut my umbilical cord to London. Since the Angel case I'd been partying too hard with Lola, trying to forget all the suffering I'd witnessed. The thing I needed most was to remind myself how to be alone, but the countryside was foreign territory. It was somewhere I visited on holiday, to go walking and eat hotel food.

The sat nav bleeped loudly, telling me to turn left down an unlit track, and my spirits sank even lower. It had been almost impossible to find somewhere to rent – maybe this was the reason why the place was vacant. I edged through the narrow opening and Ivy Cottage came into view. It stood by itself at the end of the lane, white outline highlighted by a backdrop of trees.

I left the headlights on to help me find my way, but the keys the agent had sent were unnecessary. The front door swung open the moment I touched it, as though the place was longing for visitors. The cleaner must have forgotten to lock up, which reminded me how far I was from the city. In London someone would have nicked everything that wasn't nailed down. The air in the hallway was only marginally warmer than the temperature outside, my breath forming clouds as I hauled everything in from the car. I found the thermostat and twisted it to maximum heat.

The rooms were a good size, but the decor was questionable, with lace doilies on the coffee table and headache-inducing swirls on the carpet. At least my new bedroom had an old-fashioned charm. There was an iron-framed bed, and rosebud wallpaper that looked like it had clung to the plaster for generations. I hung my clothes in the wardrobe then peered out of the window. All I could see were pine trees, and the clearest sky imaginable, the moon hazed by a blur of yellow light. The view was stunning enough to compensate for the cold. Back home I'd grown used to light pollution shrouding the sky, but from here I could make out whole constellations. The boiler interrupted my star-gazing with a loud groan. It sounded as if it was working flat out, but the radiators were only lukewarm.

There were very few comforts when I got back downstairs. I perched on the edge of the settee, still wrapped in my coat. The TV was an enormous black antique, with erratic volume control. A newscaster was describing how a girl called Ella Williams had been abducted, near her primary school in Camden on Friday. She was ten years old but the photo made her look even younger. The kids in Ella's class probably made fun of her cloud of brown ringlets, and the NHS glasses that shielded her bright, inquisitive eyes. The picture switched to her grandfather – a frail-looking grey-haired man, doing his best not to cry. Ella's disappearance was the fourth abduction from north London in the space of twelve months. Two girls had been taken a year before, their bodies found months later.

Then a third victim, Sarah Robinson, had vanished a few weeks ago, and was still missing. Her features had been blazoned across the front page of every tabloid. She looked like the archetypal Disney princess; the whole nation was familiar with her golden hair, turquoise eyes, and milk-white smile. I felt a twinge of professional regret as I studied her picture. I'd vowed to steer clear of police work, but in the rare cases when children were brought home alive, the satisfaction was incredible.

I looked at the screen again and my stomach lurched into a forward roll. Don Burns was standing outside King's Cross Police Station, wide shoulders set against the cold, almost filling the screen. He'd lost even more weight since we worked together six months ago, but he was still built on a monumental scale. He looked like a rugby player after a tough defeat. An irrational part of my brain wished the TV had a pause button, so I could see him more clearly. His skin was bleached by the cold, dark hair in need of a comb, but something about him made it difficult to look away. It made me wish that I'd accepted his dinner invitation after the Angel case, but I knew he wanted to compare notes, and I was still too raw to discuss the crime scenes we'd witnessed. By the time I'd recovered, too much time had passed to call him back. But now it was clear that his confidence had returned. His unflinching eye contact with the camera reminded me why I admired him so much. You could rely on him never to bullshit; he was always the truest thing in the room.

Burns had acquired a new deputy. She was a tall, dark-haired woman in an immaculate suit, and there was so little air between them, they could have been Siamese twins. An odd feeling twitched inside my chest. Either the cold was getting to me, or the memory of my last case with Burns was resurfacing. It had started with a man being pushed under a Tube train, followed by half a dozen of the worst murders I'd ever witnessed. At least this time I had the perfect excuse: my research at Northwood would leave me no time to help the Met.

I waited in the kitchen for the kettle to boil. So far it had been a day of mixed blessings: a flat battery followed by an unexpected rescue, a new home that felt like an igloo, and a night sky to die for. I heard a light bulb fizz, then the light failed in the hall. I floundered through the darkness to lock the front door, but the mechanism refused to budge. As I wrenched it open an owl screeched from a tree overhead. The call was so loud and pure, it was impossible to guess whether it was a greeting or a curse.

3

Ella's thoughts are a solid block of ice. There's no way of knowing how long she's been locked in here, without heat or light. The one thing she's certain of is that the room is made of metal. Flakes of rust litter the floor, scratching the bare soles of her feet, and the only sound is the click of her teeth chattering. It's so dark that her hand is invisible when she holds it in front of her eyes. The torch he left is beginning to fade, and Sarah hasn't talked for hours. Her breathing makes an odd sound in her chest, like liquid pouring from a bottle. In the pale torchlight her eyes are stretched open too wide, as though the roof has peeled back and she can count the stars. Ella tries not to flinch when Sarah's thin fingers grip her wrist.

'Smile at him,' she whispers. 'Don't scream, it makes him angry. Do everything he says.'

Ella squeezes her hand as Sarah's eyes close. The gurgling sound still rattles in her throat, like she's breathing under water. All Ella can do is carry on talking and holding her hand. She describes her estate, the meals her granddad cooks, and the way her sister believes in ghosts. But soon the cold freezes her to sleep, and when she wakes up, metal is scraping over metal as the door creaks open. The man reaches inside and grabs Sarah from the floor. When the bolt slams back into place, Ella can't help calling out. She yells until her throat aches.

It's impossible not to cry, because Sarah's gone and the dark presses in from all sides. Now the torch has died, there's no brightness anywhere. All she can do is wait and think, but only two ideas give her comfort. Last week her teacher said she was the smartest girl in school. The memory of her praise makes a light inside her burn for a few seconds. Sarah's advice repeats itself too, but it will be hard not to scream, because the sound keeps building in her throat. But next time he opens the door she won't make a sound. She'll widen her lips and try to smile; she can't manage it yet, but it's something she can practise.

Suddenly Ella's so cold, she has to find a way to warm herself. The crown of her head grazes the ceiling when she stands, but she flings back her arms, bare feet jittering on the metal floor. The sound of her footfall echoes from the walls of the box. She runs on the spot until feeling returns to her hands, and winter sunlight seeps through the crack in the door.

4

Someone had reached my office before me the next morning.
The man fiddling with my computer looked like a guitarist
from an obscure grunge band forced to dress like an office
clerk. Ill-fitting black trousers and a white shirt hung from his
gangly frame, dark roots visible in his bleached blond hair, a
network of fine scars across one of his cheekbones. He must
have been in his late twenties, and his smile was awkward, as
though I'd caught him trespassing.

'I'm Chris Steadman from the IT unit. You left me a
message.' His voice was so quiet I could hardly hear him.

'Thanks for coming, I couldn't get online.'

'That's because your modem's defunct.' He gave the box
a gentle shake, loose connections rattling against the casing.
'I'm afraid most of our kit's past its sell-by. I'll bring you a
new one.'

'Thanks, that would be great.'

'I heard about your car. Did you get home okay?'

'Eventually. It'll take me a while to adjust to Charndale,
though. Pretty sleepy, isn't it?'

His face relaxed into a grin. 'It's barely got a pulse. Give me
a shout if you get stuck again, I'll give you a lift.'

Steadman held my gaze for a beat too long, but it didn't feel
predatory. It reminded me of the way kids size each other up
in the playground. The dark smudges below his eyes suggested
that he might be a party animal under that shy exterior,

spending his weekends falling out of nightclubs. He gave another tentative smile then slipped away, the broken modem cradled in his hand.

At nine thirty I made my way to the art room on the first floor. At first I thought I'd come to the wrong place, because a burst of Erik Satie's piano music drifted along the corridor. I checked my information sheet. The name of the art therapist was Pru Fielding, and she was running a session for three long-term inmates. The music grew louder when I approached the open doorway. A woman with a cloud of blonde curls was lifting a piece of clay from a barrel, and laying it carefully on a table. In profile she looked around my own age, a Pre-Raphaelite beauty, with delicate features and an intent frown. She carried on smothering the clay with wet cloths until she finally spotted me and turned around. Shock made me take an extra breath; her disfigurement was so unexpected, it took a beat too long to replace my smile. At first I thought her face had been scarred by deep burns, but a second glance revealed that the discoloration was a dark red birthmark. The stain covered half of her face, extending down her forehead, cheek and neck, as though a can of paint had been flung at her.

'Are you the observer?' she asked.

'My name's Alice. Thanks for letting me visit today.'

'I'd shake your hand, but you might regret it.' She raised a clay-covered hand in greeting. 'The guys should be here in ten minutes. This music always calms them.' Her voice was breathless and high-pitched, and I noticed that she used her blonde curls for camouflage, locks of hair shielding her face.

'How long have you worked here, Pru?'

'Two years. I came here after doing an MA in painting at the Slade.'

'That's a long time in an environment like this.' Gorski's

comment about women at the Laurels being either flirts or lion tamers came to mind. She seemed too self-contained to fit either category, and I realised that the director's statement said more about his prejudices than the staff who worked for him.

'I like it here. And weirdly enough, there aren't many jobs for full-time artists, unless you're Tracey Emin.'

A grin illuminated Pru's face and I caught a glimmer of how attractive she'd be if she found some confidence. Her expression was clouded by the engrained anxiety I saw on the faces of abuse victims and recovering drug addicts. But it fascinated me that as soon as her clients arrived, her persona changed. An entourage of orderlies, security guards and psychiatric nurses filed through the door, but her assertiveness flicked on like a light bulb as she settled each man at his own table. There were no sharp implements available, only blunt plastic sculpting tools, and when I read the group's case notes, the reason was obvious. All three men had been prescribed anti-psychotics to control their violence. One of them had approached a stranger at a bus stop, chatted to him briefly, then stabbed him twenty-seven times. The other two had killed members of their families. I sat in a corner and watched the inmate nearest me. He looked too young to be imprisoned indefinitely, his face closed and inexpressive, as if his emotions were kept under lock and key. But after five minutes he was humming contentedly to himself as he shaped the clay.

Some of the group's sculptures were arranged on a shelf by the window, and one that caught my attention was a bust of a man's head and shoulders. It had captured his anatomy perfectly, skull bones prominent on his high forehead, but there was something odd about the model's features. His mouth gagged open, eye sockets hollow, with nothing to fill the voids. I went over to Pru while the men were busy working and pointed at the sculpture.

'That's incredibly lifelike, isn't it?'

She looked pleased. 'It's Louis Kinsella's. He's the best sculptor here.'

When she drifted back to her work I looked at the statue again. There was no denying how realistic it was, but no one would want it on their mantelpiece. It would be impossible to relax while that sightless gaze followed you around the room.

The phone was ringing when I returned to my office. It was one of the women from the reception block, her tone sharp with urgency, asking me to report there immediately. She rang off before I could ask why. Snow was falling again in large, uneven flakes as I crossed the grey hospital campus, but the police car by the entrance doors made me forget about the cold. The news must be about my brother. Will hadn't answered my calls for weeks: maybe he'd fallen asleep in a bus shelter somewhere in his worn-out coat, hypothermia catching him when he closed his eyes.

The woman waiting for me in the foyer looked around my age, primed to deliver bad news. Her lipstick was a glossy crimson, but she didn't smile as she rose to her feet, long legs slowly unfolding. It was rare to see a policewoman with such a chic haircut, her fringe bisecting her forehead in a precise black line. Relief washed over me when I realised it was the woman who'd stood beside Burns during his broadcast the night before. Any message she was carrying wouldn't concern Will.

'DI Tania Goddard.' She shook my hand briskly. 'Is there somewhere we can talk?'

Her accent was the opposite of her appearance, a raw, east London drone. She sounded like a native of Tower Hamlets or

Poplar, and she would have needed plenty of grit to break the Met's glass ceiling and forge a senior career. I got the impression that she'd taken no prisoners along the way. Her high heels tapped the lino insistently as we climbed the stairs to an empty meeting room. It smelled of urine and stale air and the woman's frown deepened.

'You're Don Burns's deputy, aren't you?' I said.

'For my sins.'

'What happened to Steve Taylor?'

'He got a security job in Saudi.'

I couldn't help smiling. A hot country would be ideal for Taylor's serpentine personality. He'd be happy as a sand-boy, and Burns would be thrilled to escape the thorn in his side. When Goddard reached into her briefcase, I noticed that her fingernails matched her lipstick, everything about her polished to a high shine. I buried my hands in my pockets, aware that my last manicure was a distant memory.

'What's brought you here, Tania?'

'You've heard about the missing girls, haven't you?'

I nodded but didn't reply, too interested in hearing her proposal.

'Burns thinks you can help the investigation.' So far her tone had remained neutral, never shifting to first gear.

'But you don't agree?'

'It's nothing personal. My first investigation was the Green Lanes case – forty-three rapes and eight murders. One of the bodies was so badly mutilated, even the photographer went off sick with stress. The shrink gave us the wrong steer. We'd have nailed the killer years sooner if we'd ignored him.'

I made no attempt to defend my profession, because she was right; the consultant on the Green Lanes case was struck off for malpractice. But it was Goddard's manner that fascinated me. Her calmness was impressive, but so far there had been no sign of warmth. It made me wonder what lurked under that slick surface. Perhaps her living room was a chaos of dirty wine glasses, takeaway cartons festering behind the sofa. Judging by the strength of her gaze, she was a woman on a mission, unwilling to let anything slow her down. I was so busy studying her that her next statement caught me unawares.

'We found Sarah Robinson's body last night.'

She pressed a photo into my hand. It was a close-up of a young girl's head and shoulders, her blonde hair thick with ice, lips frozen in a pale blue yawn. The Disney princess who'd starred in every news bulletin for days had become a ghost, puppy fat melted away, collarbones protruding from her skin.

'It's the same killer who took Kylie Walsh and Emma Lawrence,' she said.

'Are you sure? A committed serial killer wouldn't normally wait so long.'

'We're certain – there are too many connections. Both the first two victims were taken from Camden. He dumped Kylie's body in an alleyway, then Emma was found on waste ground nearby. They were starved to death, and he kept them in a freezer before dumping the bodies.'

I took a moment to absorb the fact that the killer had stored the girls' corpses before abandoning them. That degree of planning called for a rare level of self-awareness and premeditation.

'Who was the SIO when the first two were found?'

Tania's expression soured. 'He's retired. The Murder Squad were running the show, drafting specialists in from all over. A lot slipped through the cracks.'

'They didn't get far?'

'That's putting it mildly. Three months after Emma's body was found, the top man went off sick and got a payout to retire.'

My sympathy for Burns increased. It sounded like he'd inherited one of London's worst unresolved cases. I forced myself to focus on the pictures of Sarah Robinson's body. She was dressed in a long white nightgown, lying inside a cardboard box that fitted her as neatly as a coffin. Her reed-thin legs were arranged side by side, arms folded across her chest, like a statue on a medieval grave. My gaze settled on another photo of her bare feet. Her toes were raw with frostbite, and a tag had been attached to her right ankle. The number twelve was printed on it in thick black ink, as though she was a museum exhibit.

'Were the first two tagged as well?'

She nodded. 'And the dresses were the same.'

I closed my eyes for a second. By the time I was this child's age, I'd become an expert on hiding places: the cupboard under the stairs, behind the coal bunker in the cellar. I'd squeezed behind every wardrobe and under every bed, waiting for my father's rage to subside. But it was nothing compared to this.

'Was she abused?' I asked.

'We won't know till the PM. But he's getting more violent; she's covered in bruises.'

'How did she die?'

'Cold or starvation probably. They don't think she'd been in the deep freeze, but it looks like she was kept outside.'

I put down the photos. 'I still don't understand why you're here.'

Goddard's calm stare settled on my face. 'We'd like you to interview Louis Kinsella.'

'Why?' The idea made my skin tingle with panic.

'The killer's carrying on from the exact point where Kinsella stopped. Kylie was taken from the same street, on the same date as his last victim, seventeen years ago. Kinsella killed nine girls before he was caught, so the numbers on the tags give us another link. And the press have already spotted the connection with Ella Williams. She's a pupil at St Augustine's School, where he was headmaster.'

I looked down at Sarah Robinson's face and the pressure in my chest increased. It was impossible to guess how much the girl had suffered, or how many times she'd begged to be set free. If I refused to help, her image would tattoo itself on my conscience permanently.

'Where was she found?'

'On the steps of the Foundling Museum, around three this morning,' Tania replied.

I'd walked past the building dozens of times on my way to King's Cross, but never gone inside. It was right at the centre of Bloomsbury. The killer must either be crazy or completely fearless to carry a cardboard coffin through the heart of the city. I studied the girl's face again; her pale blue scream was impossible to ignore. Tania's strident voice interrupted my thoughts.

'We're so sure it's a copycat I've intercepted Kinsella's mail, in case the killer tries to contact him.'

'You know he won't talk to me, don't you? He only speaks once in a blue moon.'

Goddard's lips twitched in amusement or disbelief. 'Burns says you're a miracle worker. I'm sure you'll find a way.'

'You'd need the centre director's agreement.'

'I've already got it.'

The news didn't surprise me. Tania had probably left heel marks on Gorski's back when she marched all over him. She pulled a contract from her bag and talked me through her requirements with brisk efficiency. A consultant forensic psychologist from the Met was overseeing the case, but Burns wanted me to assist him and work directly with Kinsella. Once

26

I'd signed on the dotted line, Goddard scooped the photos back into a plastic wallet without saying another word.

I caught one last glimpse of Sarah Robinson's face. The photograph had been taken at such close range, it revealed a smear of dirt on her cheek, and a perfect set of milk teeth, but her eyes had lost their transparency. The irises were opaque, as though she was studying the world through a layer of frost.

5

The cottage had more surprises in store when I got back from work. It was a shock to discover that the WiFi worked perfectly, even though everything else was stuck in the twentieth century. A string of emails had arrived from friends at Guy's, reminding me that I'd taken leave of my senses, and Lola had sent a picture of herself, posing glamorously by an emerald green wall in her newly decorated lounge. She looked so smug, I couldn't help smiling. No doubt she and the Greek God had already christened every room of their rented palace. The next message was from my mother. She'd read a newspaper article about professional women struggling to find partners. Despite her spectacularly unhappy marriage, she seemed determined to find me a husband. She'd even attached a shortlist from Match.com, but her criteria differed from mine. The first man was a forty-five-year-old lawyer from Hunstanton. His hobbies included clay pigeon shooting and the music of Roy Orbison, and there was something alarming about his smile. Her next choice looked suspiciously like a drug dealer I'd assessed once in Brixton Prison. I deleted the message immediately. There was more chance of finding romance among the psychopaths at Northwood.

The thermostat was cranked to its highest setting, but the living room still felt chilly, so I collected a torch from the kitchen and went looking for the log store. All I could see was an expanse of snow, and an outbuilding at the far end of the garden. A pile of logs was stacked neatly inside the shed and I wondered why someone had bought a supply of fuel, only to leave it for the next occupant. Maybe they'd found somewhere warmer and decided to cut their losses. Something odd caught my eye as I trudged back across the lawn. There were footprints in the snow, which must have been recent as it had been snowing all afternoon. I ran my torch beam across the ground and saw that someone had circled the house. The tracks stopped by the kitchen window, then continued along the wall. I compared the marks with the imprints my size three boots had left. These were much bigger. I was still staring at the ground when something rustled behind me, and my pulse rate doubled. But when I swung round the garden was empty. I must have been imagining things; it was probably a fox hiding in the bushes. I hurried inside and slid the latch into place. There had to be a reason for the footprints. It was probably nothing more sinister than a neighbour, keen to say hello, but my heart rate took a while to slow down all the same. The footprints were a reminder of my isolation – there was no one to help me if I got into trouble.

I concentrated on getting the fire started. There were no matches, so I twisted a spill of paper and lit it from an electric ring on the cooker. After an hour it was finally roaring, and my phone rang as I was admiring the flames. When I turned round I realised that the noise was coming from my computer. Someone was Skyping me. I was expecting Lola, but when I pressed the reply key, a dark-haired, handsome man appeared on the screen. It made me wish again that I'd taken up his dinner invitation when I had the chance. Don Burns's gaze was as sharp as ever, a smile slowly extending across his face.

'DI Burns, long time no see.'

'I'm a DCI again these days, Alice.'

'Brotherton finally retired?'

'The invisible woman vanished, thank God.' He leant forwards and studied the screen intently. 'You look well.'

Burns's image flickered, then reinstated itself in another position. I've always hated video links. It's like communicating with astronauts, their messages stuttering back to Earth, with time delays lagging between sentences. I wished he would stay still so I could see him more clearly. It looked like he was calling from his flat. There was a bookshelf behind him and a brightly coloured painting. I was curious to see more, because I knew that he'd joined the police after being thrown out of art school. He acted like a Scottish brawler with his colleagues at the Met, but I'd always suspected he was concealing highbrow interests.

'Did Tania give you the details?' Suddenly he was so close I could see his five-o'clock shadow. I thought about his new assistant; she was as tough and remote as he was humane and accessible. His face twitched with outrage when he spoke again. 'Sarah Robinson was found by a poor sod walking home from his night shift, nineteen days after she was taken. The bastard got rid of her quicker than the first two.'

The statement hung in the air as his image froze, but he didn't need to spell out the facts. Ella Williams had been gone three days, and the clock was ticking. But where was he keeping her? Maybe she was trapped in a pen outside, like a farm animal. Or her body was already lying in a freezer in a lock-up somewhere. When Burns reappeared, he looked homicidal.

'Who's your consultant, Don?'

'Alan Nash. Scotland Yard's insisting on it.'

'They've pulled him out of retirement?'

'More's the pity. The commissioner's his best chum, but so far he's done nothing but whine.'

Burns had told me his opinion of Professor Nash on several occasions. In his view the man was a puffed up, self-seeking time-waster, more focused on writing true crime books than helping the Met. But his assessment wasn't completely fair. I'd noticed Nash's egotism when he trained me on my Masters course. He'd revelled in his applause after lectures, but he had genuine reasons to feel smug. He'd been a groundbreaker in the Nineties, and his expertise in interview techniques had sealed dozens of high-profile cases. When Kinsella was captured, it was Nash's skills that flattered him into a confession. His book *The Kill Principle* analysed Kinsella's mindset and gave new insights into the motivations of serial killers. It had been a bestseller and was still required reading on forensic psychology courses. But Nash was approaching seventy, and things had modernised since his heyday. Huge steps had been taken in geo-profiling and crime linkage software used to determine where serial killers would strike. His professional knowledge was unlikely to be up-to-date.

'If you've got the top man, why do you need me?'

'You're my link to Kinsella,' said Burns. 'Can you interview him tomorrow? Our man knows things about his MO that never got released. He's got to be a personal contact.'

'Kinsella hardly ever speaks, Don.'

His grin flashed on for a second. 'He'll sing like a canary when he sees you.'

I noticed that Burns looked calmer than before; the shadows under his eyes were absent for once. He leant towards me as he said goodbye, but he wasn't lunging at the screen for a virtual kiss. He was just reaching down to switch off his computer.

The silence grew louder after that. All I could hear were the logs hissing on the fire. I pulled back the curtain and stared at the empty lane, wondering who had been spying on me. Snow was falling again, but this time it was as fine as sand. Louis Kinsella's face appeared in my mind's eye then erased itself.

I'd taken every precaution to stay safe, locking my windows, and bolting the doors. But Ella Williams had no choice. She'd been gone for three days and nights, held captive by someone who enjoyed killing children, outside in the cold. I stood there for a long time, peering into the dark.

6

Dr Gorski seemed as tense as ever next morning at the team meeting. The group consisted of psychiatrists, guards and mental health nurses from the Laurels, and one ridiculously good-looking man who introduced himself as Tom Jensen, the head of the fitness centre. It took me several minutes to realise that he was the one who'd helped me start my car. He had unkempt white-blond hair, and looked like he'd stepped straight from the pages of a brochure advertising the health benefits of outdoor holidays. He seemed completely at ease, relaxing in his chair, pale eyes monitoring every gesture in the room. Gorski's bullying style didn't seem to bother him. He listened calmly while the director snapped at his underlings and issued endless instructions.

A woman on the other side of the room gave me a gentle smile. She looked around forty, slim and elegant, with chestnut hair scooped back from her face. Her eyes had a dreamy look, but it was her hands that drew my attention. Every finger was adorned with silver rings, heavy bracelets around her wrist. She gave me a wave of greeting, but her hand soon dropped back to her lap, burdened by the weight of metal. At the end of the meeting she caught up with me in the corridor.

'Sorry I missed you before. I'm Judith Miller, I've been away at the Mindset conference. How are you settling in?'

'Pretty well, thanks. I'm finding my way round.'

'Let me show you where my office is, in case you need anything.'

Her room was full of unexpected details that seemed out of keeping in a shrink's office. A set of Tibetan prayer bowls stood on her desk, wind chimes dangling from the ceiling. The shelves contained none of the standard psychiatric manuals, but I could see *King Lear*, *Paradise Lost*, and the poems of John Donne. The pin board beside her desk was covered with postcards and letters.

'They're from patients,' Judith said. 'I work in the main hospital too. They write to me sometimes, after they leave.'

I could see why she kept them. The letters were a reminder that mental health patients often recovered, even if the men in the Laurels could never go home.

'How long have you worked here, Judith?'

'Fifteen years.'

'That's quite an achievement.'

'Not really, I'm addicted to fixing things. It's the same at home; I never throw things away.' Her expression grew more serious. 'I hear the police have asked you to interview Louis Kinsella.'

'Don't remind me. I've already got stage fright.'

'There's no need. I treated him for years, until he stopped talking to me. He'll want to charm you.'

'Have you got any advice?'

Her calm eyes met mine. 'He's an expert manipulator, and he never forgets a personal detail. Don't give any secrets away.'

It seemed impossible that she'd spent more than a decade counselling the sickest men in Britain. The confessions she'd heard could melt paint from the walls, yet she emanated calm. The display of gratitude on her wall must be preventing her from throwing in the towel.

I spent the next hour in my office reading the Care

Quality Commission report on the Laurels. It supported Gorski's claims about a catastrophic lack of funding. The place was so understaffed that most inmates spent just ten hours a week outside their cells, and the staff team was suffering too. Workers at the Laurels had the highest rate of sickness in any UK hospital or prison. It wasn't surprising that Gorski was tense: there was no extra cash to get the Laurels back on course, and he'd only been given a year to turn the place around.

Outside my window it had stopped snowing, but there were no breaks in the cloud. It looked like someone had unrolled miles of grey cotton and pinned it to the sky. When I glanced down, Louis Kinsella was being led across the square. He walked with a straight back, hair combed rigidly into place. His deportment explained why his colleagues refused to believe that he was guilty of killing children. From a distance he looked like a textbook headmaster, with his military bearing and haughty expression. Even his gait reminded me of my father. I closed my eyes for a second, and when they blinked open again, Kinsella and his guard had disappeared into the maze of buildings.

I scanned the crime report Tania Goddard had given me. Kinsella's spree had lasted for two years and infiltrated every corner of London: Hackney, Kentish Town, Lambeth, and Hammersmith. Most of the girls' faces were still familiar; every other news story at the time had paled into insignificance. Several more girls had stories of lucky escapes. One had managed to run away, instead of being dragged into Kinsella's car. It was her testimony that finally put him behind bars. She had memorised his number-plate, and her grandmother phoned the police when she ran home, but nine families had been traumatised forever. Kinsella had used every possible trick to increase their suffering. He sent audio

35

tapes of their children screaming for their lives, and others had received photos of their daughters' mutilated faces. When the news broke, Kinsella's wife, Sonia, was working as a nurse in an old people's home in Islington. The press released pictures of a mousy-looking young woman shrinking from the glare of flashlights. After his conviction, she'd vanished from the public eye, and I hoped she was living quietly somewhere, undisturbed.

The consulting room looked nothing like the ones at Guy's. It had the obligatory box of Kleenex, and inoffensive still lifes on the walls, but the panic buttons were more plentiful. There was one on the desk, two either side of the door, and another in the middle of the wall. The window was barred, with cotton-thin wires threaded through the glass. Once the door was shut it would be impossible to smash your way out. The idea failed to comfort me when I heard Kinsella's footsteps. Someone must have done an assessment and decided that a female shrink was high risk, because he was handcuffed to his guard. I recognised the nurse who accompanied him; he'd introduced himself on my first day. His name was Garfield Ellis. He was a tall, heavily built black guy of around forty, with an appealing West Indian lilt to his voice. It was clear he took his job seriously from the careful way he arranged the room while a guard blocked the doorway. A third man waited in the corridor as Kinsella's handcuffs were locked to the chair.

Kinsella's likeness to my father was even more unsettling up close, and I had to swallow my panic. He had the same high forehead and ascetic features, but he exuded an energy I couldn't identify. He sat motionless, observing me through his reading glasses. The nurse didn't seem to notice my discomfort, but Kinsella had picked up on it immediately, his expression growing smugger by the minute.

'Thank you for agreeing to see me, Mr Kinsella.'

His mouth widened into a hawkish smile, and he manoeuvred his shackled hands to produce a notebook from his pocket. He was wearing black trousers and a brown corduroy jacket. With a little imagination, he could still have passed as a headmaster with a blameless reputation, dressed casually for the weekend.

'I'd like to ask you some questions, if you're prepared to answer.'

His expression changed to amusement, and I got the impression that he could have sat in silence all day, watching me. There was something mesmerising about his smile. Even though I wanted to ignore it, I couldn't look away. He seemed to be studying my eyes with particular interest. I tried not to think about the man he'd blinded at Highpoint. No doubt Kinsella watched the news with equal fascination, keeping track of every detail surrounding the girls' disappearance.

'The police have asked me to help investigate the abductions in London. They think the killer is someone you know. What do you think of that theory?'

Kinsella shook his head, then rested his bound hands on the table to scribble a few lines before shunting the notebook towards me. His writing was a spiky copperplate, every T sharply crossed.

A poor start, Dr Quentin, worth B minus, at best. Try some subtlety please. I've always hated crude overtures.

'Forgive me. I could have invented a pretext for our meeting, but you'd have seen straight through it. I've read your file. Your IQ's a hundred and eighty, isn't it? That puts you up there with Einstein and Garry Kasparov.'

Kinsella seemed to enjoy the flattery. His grin twitched wider as his eyes scanned every detail of my outfit, from my black dress and turquoise scarf to my scuffed suede boots. He even scrutinised the jacket I'd hung behind the door, as though he was making an inventory of my wardrobe. His eyes were a dark unblinking brown, and his gaze was like my father's in the moment before his mood soured. A drop of sweat chased down my backbone.

'I'll be honest with you, Mr Kinsella. The man we're searching for is an expert on your crimes. Any help you give would be gratefully received.'

His face registered no response at all. He carried on studying me intently, as though I was a laboratory specimen.

'I saw on your file that you're a jazz fan, but there's none in the library, is there? I've brought you a couple of CDs: Miles Davis and Jack Pescod. They're favourites of mine.' Kinsella reached again for his notebook, but I raised my hands before he could scribble another message. 'A clumsy bribe, I know, but you're not giving me much option. Ask for me if you decide to talk, Mr Kinsella, or send me a note. I can see you're a keen writer.'

He adopted the smile that teachers use to patronise dimwitted students, pointedly leaving the CDs on the table. The nurse gave me a look of sympathy as he led him away. Garfield must have seen dozens of psychologists flounder under the weight of Kinsella's silence.

My defeat rankled when I returned to my office. It bothered me that I'd failed to squeeze a single syllable out of him. But at least there was an email from Judith, inviting me to the pub in Charndale that evening. It would save me from sitting alone at the cottage, with the memory of Kinsella's gaze crawling across my skin like a colony of flies.

There were no new footprints when I got back to the cottage that evening, so I told myself that the problem had disappeared. In a village as small as Charndale, people were bound to be curious about new arrivals. Someone from a neighbouring house must have called by to introduce themselves. I grabbed a torch and set off for the pub. It was called the Rookery, and from the outside it looked uninviting. The sign showed an ominous blur of birds hovering in the sky. But when I opened the door, the place was heaving with Northwood staff, every table loaded with glasses. The volume of conversation was deafening as I pushed through the crowd. Judith was surrounded by companions, and I recognised some of the faces from the Laurels. Chris Steadman, the young man who'd fixed my computer, was quietly nursing his beer. He looked even more like a teen idol in his battered leather jacket, cheekbones too prominent, as though he existed on starvation rations and very little sleep. Pru, the art therapist, was beside him, listening intently as he spoke, hiding behind her mask of blonde curls. Away from the pressures of his job, Garfield Ellis looked more relaxed, but the group struck me as an odd assemblage. No one seemed comfortable in their skin. Perhaps we had all wound up at Northwood because we were running from something.

'What are you drinking, Alice?' Judith asked.

'Coffee, please. It's bloody freezing out there.'

I waited beside her at the bar, but my coffee never materialised. She ordered two brandies instead.

'You'll need this if you're going to survive at the Laurels.' She saluted me with her glass. 'How did it go with Kinsella?'

'Not great. He just scribbled in his notebook.'

'Count yourself lucky. He only gives notes to the chosen few.'

Judith's serenity was still intact, but she took a long gulp from her drink. The stress of the hospital seemed to be impacting on everyone. I followed her back to the table, and her openness made me warm to her immediately. She told me that work had dominated her life since her divorce, and she missed her kids terribly now they'd left home. Her oldest son was studying in the US, and her daughter was taking a gap year in Indonesia.

'Maybe I'll follow her,' she said. 'I could do with a month in an exotic health spa.'

The dreamy look on her face made me laugh. Out of the corner of my eye I saw Tom Jensen standing by the bar, a gym bag slung over his shoulder. Judith looked amused when she spotted him.

'The world's most over-qualified fitness coach,' she whispered. 'He's a sweetheart, but don't ask him about God, whatever you do.'

Jensen arrived before I could find out what she meant. He sat down beside me in the only empty chair, and embarked on a long conversation with the man opposite. Judith was busy talking to someone else, so I had time to observe him. His hair was so blond it was almost white, and he was wearing faded jeans and a shirt with a worn collar. I got the impression that although his good looks confronted him every day in the mirrors at the gym, he chose to ignore them. His accent was hard to place, either Home Counties or west London, each word perfectly pronounced. When he finished his beer he caught me studying him, but didn't seem fazed. People must have been admiring him ever since he was a lean, suntanned schoolboy, winning every trophy and dating the prettiest girls.

'How's the car?' he asked.

'Running perfectly. Let me buy you a drink to say thanks.'

Jensen's expression was difficult to read, his eyes studying my face. He looked so serious, I couldn't help smiling.

'What's funny?' he asked.

'Nothing. You're staring, that's all.'

'I'm considering your offer.'

'It's a beer, not a marriage proposal.'

'One thing leads to another.' The corners of his mouth twitched upwards. 'Go on then, twist my arm.'

He waited beside me at the bar while I bought a round, which was disconcerting. It had been months since I'd flirted with anyone.

'Did anyone tell you about Jon Evans?' he asked. When I shook my head, his smile vanished. 'He's a therapist. He was at the Laurels last year, working with Kinsella.'

'What happened to him?'

'Gorski found him locked in his office, talking to himself. He hasn't worked since his breakdown.'

'Jesus. I need another drink.'

His face gave nothing away. 'Are you renting locally?'

'Just round the corner, Ivy Cottage.'

'I know the place. It's been vacant for years; the locals say it's haunted.'

'Thanks for sharing that with me. My house is ghost-ridden and my predecessor went crazy. Got any more good news?'

He looked amused. 'You don't seem the type to scare easily.'

Jensen turned away to carry drinks back to the table, leaving me wondering why he'd tried so hard to unnerve me. The noise level in the pub had risen by a few decibels, Bruno Mars thumping in the background, the Northwood crowd yelling just to be heard. The place had a pressure-cooker atmosphere. If it got any wilder they'd be dancing on the tables, necking tequila straight from the bottle. I was about to pick up the tray of drinks when I spotted the TV above the bar. The picture must have been high definition, because I noticed new details when Ella Williams's picture appeared. There was a red daisy on her hairclip, almost hidden by ringlets, a rash of freckles scattered across her nose. I stood by the bar and studied her gap-toothed smile until she disappeared.

7

It could be a nightmare, but it never stops. It's worse than the ones that seized her when her mother died. And it can't be a dream, because pain is shooting through her feet and hands. Sitting on the metal floor, Ella rubs warmth back into her toes, but it only lasts a few seconds. It drains away when she stands up, every muscle twitching with cold.

Night-time scares her most. She's never known complete darkness before. At home the glow from the streetlights sifts through her thin curtains, but tonight the dark is absolute. It settles around her, locking the chill deep under her skin. Her eyes hunt for a speck of light. It's tempting to lie down on the freezing metal and let the dark claim her. But then she'll end up like Sarah, all her strength gone, struggling to breathe. Ella keeps hoping that the man has taken Sarah back to her family. Soon she'll look pretty again, like the pictures in the news-agent's window.

Her mouth feels like it's full of dust. It's been ages since she drank anything. The man opened the door and threw in a can of lemonade, and she swallowed the liquid in a few quick gulps, bubbles stinging her throat. Since then there's been nothing. She imagines the man standing there, and anger makes her lash out. Her hand grazes across the metal, leaving a trail of wetness. Drops of water are running down her skin. She kneels beside the wall, blindly collecting droplets with her tongue, the liquid sour and peppery. It takes an hour to swallow a few mouthfuls, but at least her lips feel comfortable again. She sits cross-legged, massaging warmth back into her feet. It's important not to give in to sleep. Her sister needs her. Suzanne is six years older, but she relies on Ella to keep her calm. She carries on rubbing the heat back into her toes, until her skin begins to burn.

8

My eyes felt too big for their sockets when I stepped onto the train at Charndale Station the next morning. I kept them closed as the carriage rattled through Berkshire, and by Paddington they were recovering. I knocked back a smoothie from a juice bar when I arrived, promising myself never to drink brandy again.

Burns arrived ten minutes late. I caught sight of him, pacing through the crowd. His wide shoulders strained the seams of his coat, but his clothes looked more expensive, and his thick brown hair was neater than before. He came to a halt by the arrivals board, checking his phone messages. When I tapped him on the shoulder he swung round to face me. I expected him to shake my hand but he leant down and kissed my cheek instead. His stubble left a graze as he pulled away. For an irrational moment I wanted to embrace him, but managed to stop myself, my face hot with embarrassment.

'You didn't have to collect me, Don.'

'The incident room's a nightmare. We can talk in the car.'

I followed Burns through the crowd, and it was clear that his promotion had restored his confidence. Even the discovery of another child's body on his patch hadn't removed the spring from his stride. When we reached the car park he headed straight for a brand-new Audi.

'Very swish.'

He looked embarrassed. 'The Mondeo finally bit the dust.'

Despite the upmarket car, Burns still drove like he was piloting a tank through a field of landmines. His Scottish accent came to the fore as he spoke, a sure sign that he was under pressure.

'Go on then,' I said. 'Give me an update.'

He glanced across at me. 'The press are on us, twenty-four/seven. The Murder Squad made a pig's ear of the double murder investigation for Kylie Walsh and Emma Lawrence. Some of the relatives weren't even interviewed, so we've been going back, filling in the gaps. I've chucked all my manpower at it since I took over. Uniforms are combing every street in Camden looking for Ella, forty detectives on the case.'

'Why isn't Alan Nash here? I thought he was overseeing the profiling.'

Burns grimaced. 'He says he hasn't got time for minutiae. Apparently he predicted this would happen in *The Kill Principle*. He won't get involved until we start interviewing suspects.'

'Hindsight's a wonderful thing,' I muttered. 'When was Sarah Robinson's PM?'

'Yesterday. She died of pneumonia. Her feet and hands were so frostbitten she'd have lost fingers and toes if she'd survived. But this time, he didn't keep her in a freezer. It looks like he dumped her soon after he killed her. She was starved and beaten, but there's no sign she was raped.'

'That's a surprise.'

'It's the only good news so far. Whatever he did to her, she lasted nineteen days.'

I gazed through the window at the snow heaped on the pavement, pedestrians swaddled in hats and scarves. If Ella Williams was being kept outside, she was unlikely to survive much longer.

The traffic had stalled and Burns was staring at the

hoardings, as though clues were hidden between the brand names and slogans.

'The lab's trying to work out where he's keeping them,' he said. 'The pathologist found fragments of rust under her nails and in her hair.'

'Meaning what?'

A muscle ticked in his cheek. 'She was probably kept in the back of an old lorry or a van.'

I closed my eyes and tried to imagine Sarah's last days. The vehicle could have been parked anywhere, while snow fell outside, the cold gradually weakening her screams. There were millions of houses in London with gardens big enough to conceal a van from prying eyes.

'Tell me more about Ella. Does she live with her parents?'

'Just her sister and granddad. Her dad cleared off to Spain the year after she was born, then her mum died of breast cancer two years ago.'

I gazed at the council estates we were passing on Pancras Way. It sounded like the Williams family had already dealt with too much bad luck, and when Burns pulled up outside Alan Chalmers House, my sympathy deepened. The apartment building had seen better days. It was six storeys high, bricks weathered to a dull brown, right beside the arterial road. The residents must fall asleep to a lullaby of night buses grinding south from Holloway. Freezing winds had flayed paint from the front doors, splintering the exposed wood. I followed Burns across a layer of ice. The snow had refrozen so many times we'd have been safer on skates. It was easy to tell which of the ground-floor flats belonged to the Williams family from the press camping outside. Photographers stood in gaggles, long-lens cameras dangling from their necks. In addition to their ordeal, the family would have to run the media gauntlet every time they went outside.

Burns marched through the crowd without responding to the reporters' barrage of questions. The flat was on the ground floor, and there was a mat by the entrance with the word 'Welcome' woven across it in bright red. He squared his shoulders when he rang the doorbell, composing himself like a method actor. Half a dozen cameras clicked in unison the moment Ella's grandfather opened the door. His skin was the colour of parchment, grey hair arranged in an untidy quiff, a cigarette dangling from his fingers. Two facts about his flat were inescapable as soon as we stepped inside: someone had conducted a colour experiment on every wall, and there was a fug of smoke lingering in every room. The atmosphere contained more carbon than oxygen, windows sealed against the cold.

Mr Williams led us along the fuchsia pink hall into the living room. His teenaged granddaughter was slumped on the settee, chestnut curls scraped back from her face. Her resemblance to Ella was striking. She had the same freckled complexion, eyes hidden behind round-framed glasses. Her eyes were so glazed she didn't seem to notice that two strangers had walked into the room. I noticed a Christmas tree standing in a bucket in the corner, still wrapped in plastic netting. The girl's eyes met mine for a second then slid away.

'Suzanne won't say much,' the old man said. 'The doctor gave her tranquillisers.'

I wondered how much Valium she'd swallowed. She was still in her dressing gown, struggling to stay awake. The lime green wall behind her seemed ridiculously cheerful, but the rest of the room was chaotic, with magazines and copies of the *Racing Times* piled on every surface. A mound of ironing on the table formed a haystack of crumpled T-shirts and jeans.

'Is there any news?' Mr Williams's eyes fixed on Burns.

It was the first time I'd seen him look hopeful. The prospect of his grandchild coming home had forced him out of bed that morning, and dragged him through the motions of a normal day, while Suzanne came apart at the seams. His face grew bleak again when Burns admitted there was no new information. The emotional roller-coaster he'd been riding since Friday was unimaginable.

'Could I see Ella's room please, Mr Williams?' I asked.

He stared back at me, and I could tell what he was thinking. Why should he let yet another official poke through the girl's belongings? But eventually he led me along the hall, and it was a relief to escape into cleaner air.

I'd been expecting another outlandish colour scheme, and clothes scattered across the floor, but Ella Williams's bedroom was immaculate. The walls were painted cream, with drawings neatly tacked to a pin-board. There was a desk in the corner, piled with school books, and a Philip Pullman novel on the bedside table. It looked like an adult's room with minia-turised furniture. I stood by Ella's desk and leafed through one of her schoolbooks. The pages were littered with ticks and gold stars, and her drawings were equally impressive. One showed a giant tree, taller than the skyscrapers around it, almost touching the clouds. The tree was incredibly lifelike, each leaf picked out in different shades of green, the gnarled trunk fractured with age. Very few ten-year-olds could have conjured up anything so beautiful.

When I got back to the lounge, Burns was dispensing comfort as usual, Suzanne crying quietly into one of his outsized hankies.

'You're very close to your sister, aren't you?' I said quietly.

'She's amazing. I always tell her she's got twice my brains.' Suddenly Suzanne's eyes regained their focus, glittering with panic. 'Please, you have to find her.'

The intensity of her stare disturbed me. The girl grabbed my hand so tightly I could feel her nails cutting into my palm.

'I'll do everything I can, I promise.'

Her gaze bored into me, as though she was testing my resolve. Burns must have sensed my discomfort because he asked her another question. 'Do you know anyone with a van or a lorry, Suzanne?'

'Just the caretaker at Ella's school, Mr Layton. Why?'

'We're checking out some details.' He gave a brief smile then rose to his feet.

When she realised we were leaving, Suzanne's shoulders slumped again, eyes half closed. Her grandfather showed us to the door with yet another roll-up dangling from his lip, puffing on it like a vital oxygen supply.

I turned to Burns as soon as we reached the car. 'Very clever, Don.'

'How do you mean?'

'Meeting Ella's sister won't help me profile her abductor. You brought me here to make me commit. Now I've seen her family, I can't walk away. You're turning into a shrink, aren't you?'

Burns held up his hands, making no attempt to deny it. A smile appeared at the corners of his mouth as he began to drive. The journey from Alan Chalmers House back to the police station took five minutes. He seemed to be gathering his thoughts for the team briefing, so I studied the shop windows, packed with tacky Christmas decorations. At least the view stopped me worrying about Suzanne Williams's fragile state of mind. It would shatter like a pane of glass if her sister wasn't returned home safe and sound.

Professor Alan Nash was holding court in the incident room when we arrived, and the smile he threw me was lukewarm.

50

His hair was greyer than before, but he hadn't lost his talent as a crowd pleaser. He was dressed like a country gentleman, his tweed jacket and dark shirt designed to hide a growing paunch. Nash was explaining the importance of his work with Kinsella – his approach had changed the nature of forensic interviewing forever. Most of the group seemed genuinely impressed, but a few looked sceptical. The Met has a low tolerance for bragging. Most coppers believe in keeping quiet and letting other people congratulate them when the job's done.

I recognised most of the investigation team. Pete Hancock, the chief crime scene officer, nodded at me. His black monobrow was still hovering half an inch above his eyes, making it impossible to judge whether he was thrilled or suicidal. Tania Goddard had already positioned herself so close to Burns that it looked like she had a secret to confide. Her appearance was as immaculate as before, her dress accentuating every curve. Millie, one of the family liaison officers from the Angel case, gave me a long-suffering smile as she greeted me. We chatted for a few minutes, then she nodded towards Burns and Tania and rolled her eyes.

'Those two couldn't care less about the case,' she whispered.

'I thought they were working flat-out.'

'They're too loved up to concentrate on anything. It's common knowledge they're seeing each other. She's all over him.'

I was too stunned to say a word; the idea of Burns starting a relationship with a cool customer like Tania took a huge leap of the imagination. Fortunately the briefing was just about to start so I didn't need to reply.

The atmosphere in the room felt tense. Cases that involve children always generate their own type of gloom: the media attention is relentless, and the victims' families are like a

Molotov cocktail. A single badly chosen phrase can light the touchpaper and trigger an explosion. Burns and Tania were standing side by side, like a well-rehearsed double act, but she receded into the background when he began to speak.

'Let's review where we are. Kylie Walsh was abducted eleven months ago, then Emma Lawrence three weeks later. The killer washed the bodies, dressed them in white, then hid them in a freezer before dumping them. Sarah Robinson was abducted from St Paul's Crescent in Camden on the thirtieth of November, around five thirty in the afternoon, on her way to the corner shop to buy bread for her mum. A neighbour on his way back from work saw a white van driving too fast along the street. We spent the next eighteen days on door-to-door, and going through the sex offenders' register. Her body was found early on Monday, outside the Foundling Museum, and that could be significant. The place was London's first orphanage.'

Tania carried on without a pause, as though the script was prearranged. 'Ella Williams's grandfather was late picking her up from her school in Camden last Friday. The school caretaker is our last eyewitness. He says he saw her from his window, waiting by the gates. One of her shoes was found on St Augustine's Road, close to the school. This time a white Ford transit was spotted on CCTV, with no number-plates.' A blurred black-and-white image of the van speeding down a car-lined road appeared on the wall. It had no identifiable dents or scratches, but the roof and bonnet were grimed with dirt, the driver's face hidden by shadows.

Burns rose to his feet again. 'There are strong links with the serial killer, Louis Kinsella. He took his last victim on the same day that Kylie Walsh disappeared, tagged his victims and dressed them in white. He was a trustee at the Foundling Museum, where Sarah's body was found, and he used to be headmaster at Ella Williams's school.' He paused to scan the room, then held up a transparent evidence bag containing a scrap of electric blue material, criss-crossed by a thread of yellow ribbon. 'This was sent to Kinsella on Saturday at Northwood psychiatric prison, from a central London post-mark. The lab's checking for fingerprints and DNA. The fabric was cut from the dress Sarah was wearing, and we'll know tomorrow if this is her hair.'

I looked more closely at the evidence bag and suppressed a shiver. The yellow strand pinned to the cloth was human hair, not ribbon. For the first time the killer had sent a love token direct to Louis Kinsella, letting him know his campaign was continuing.

'Two forensic psychologists are working with us. Professor Alan Nash is in charge, and Alice Quentin's working at Northwood. She'll be our main point of contact with Louis Kinsella.' Burns nodded at Nash, inviting him to speak.

Nash's body language reminded me of veteran actors like Jeremy Irons and Richard Gere, still sublimely convinced that they're sexy. He strutted to the front of the room, as though the women around him were hanging on his every word. And it's fascinating how potent self-belief is. Most of the faces round the table looked intrigued when he began to speak.

'Anyone who knows my book *The Kill Principle* will remem-ber that Louis Kinsella has always claimed that someone will continue his mission. He didn't give a date, but he did time at Pentonville, Brixton, and Highpoint before ending up at Northwood fifteen years ago. There's an outside chance that his follower is just a lonely obsessive who's done his research, but it's likely to be someone who's spent time in his orbit. You'll need to chase down every one of Kinsella's contacts since before his arrest.' Nash held up his hands and beamed,

53

as if he was embarrassed by so much admiration. 'I know it's asking a lot, but we have to use every fact at our disposal.'

'Thanks for that, Alan.' Burns was on his feet again. 'Would you like to add anything, Alice?'

Nash shook his head decisively before I could speak. 'I'm sure that won't be necessary at this stage.'

I was too stunned by his rudeness to say a word. Burns shot me an apologetic look and carried on with his briefing, but I seethed quietly as he gave out instructions. He wanted the school caretaker's Luton van checked, inmates from Kinsella's prison days interviewed, and checks run on former employees at St Augustine's School. I stared at the two items the exhibits officer had placed on her evidence tray: the scrap of material from Sarah Robinson's dress, and Ella Williams's red patent leather shoe, shining so brightly it looked brand new. I was still gazing at the objects when Alan Nash appeared at my side. His smile flicked on but there was no warmth behind it.

'I read the reviews of your last book, Alice; my star student seems to be making quite a name for herself. I'm looking forward to working with you.'

'Me too, Alan. But I'd prefer not to be silenced in future.'

He took a step closer, his smile unwavering. A waft of sickly aftershave enveloped me, and I noticed the veins littered across his cheeks like strands of purple cotton. 'You're my assistant on this case, Alice. I think it's important you remember that, don't you?'

Anyone watching us would have seen two colleagues exchanging pleasantries, but his stare was colder than the air outside. He strutted out of the room on a wave of arrogance, and I could guess why he was making covert threats. This was his last chance of glory, and he was hell-bent on establishing his reputation as the pre-eminent star of forensic psychology.

There was no way on God's earth that anyone was going to steal his thunder.

The room had almost emptied. Only Burns and Tania Goddard were left behind, and they were too absorbed to notice me. Her hand rested on his shoulder while they peered at a report, her face inches from his, and he was making no attempt to move away. Millie had been right after all – Burns had found himself a girlfriend. I stuffed my notebook into my bag, gave an excuse about an urgent meeting, then stumbled out of the door.

9

My head was still spinning when I got outside, which made no sense whatsoever. I'd missed my chance to get to know Burns after the Angel case, but hadn't regretted it at the time. Maybe that was because the case still gave me nightmares, and I couldn't face going back over old ground. But now it was obvious that he and Tania were an item, from the possessive way she touched him. My jealousy felt ridiculous. Relationships had always been my Achilles heel. Whenever someone came close, panic set in, and I backed away. I was thirty-three years old, but none of my relationships had lasted more than a year. Even if Burns was madly in love with me, the pattern would stay the same. But there was no denying that I wanted to be the one with my hand on his shoulder. It shocked me that seeing someone else touching him had unsettled me so much.

I found a window seat in a coffee shop nearby, hoping a dose of caffeine would restore my sanity. A flashing sign on the other side of the street was reminding shoppers that there were only four more days until Christmas. A woman traipsed past with her small daughter clinging to her hand, and my thoughts cleared instantly. There was no time for self-pity; my private life was unimportant, compared to finding Ella Williams. I leafed through the notes I'd made during the briefing, and decided to visit the Foundling Museum, where Sarah Robinson's body had been found.

I headed outside and trudged through the snow, into the

back streets of Bloomsbury. I'd always planned to explore London's literary district, but never found time to visit. The area still had a Dickensian feel, with handsome nineteenth-century townhouses clustered on both sides of the street. It would make the perfect set for *Oliver*. All it needed was a little more grime, some gas lamps and horse-drawn carriages.

The Foundling Museum was hidden on a narrow turning off Hunter Street. The crime scene had already been cleared away, and I stood on the forecourt, trying to picture the killer calmly depositing a child's body there, in the middle of the night. The Regency building was long and austere, with dozens of sash windows, dark grey bricks and a colonnaded front door. It had a direct view across Coram Fields, which local kids used as a football pitch in the summer. The square of parkland was empty now, apart from a few abandoned snowmen. When I walked inside, the interior was even grander than the facade, with panelled walls and chequered floor tiles. A sign explained that the Foundling Hospital had become London's first home for abandoned infants in the 1740s.

I was about to walk into the main hall when a tall, well-groomed man approached me. A silk handkerchief peeped from the pocket of his blazer, gold buttons gleaming. His face was so heavily lined that I assumed he must have been sixty at least, but his hair was dark brown, without a strand of grey. The badge on his lapel announced that he was a museum volunteer and his name was Brian Knowles.

'Have you been here before?' He gave a welcoming smile.

'Never.'

'Would you like a tour?'

I accepted his offer, but would have preferred to wander around on my own. Knowles had an unctuous manner, gazing down at me as though I was visiting royalty. But if I was lucky he might shed light on the reason why the killer was fascinated by the place, and it was obvious he took his role seriously. He launched into a history lecture before we reached the first exhibit.

'The Foundling Hospital was London's first orphanage. It cared for thousands of starving children over two centuries, but even more were turned away, because places were limited.'

The man spoke in a reverent tone, but it was doubtful that benevolence had made Louis Kinsella become a trustee. A row of small white pinafores and nightdresses hung from hooks in the main hall, replicas of the uniforms the foundlings wore two hundred years ago. The children's misery at being parted from their mothers must have seeped into the building's DNA, and Kinsella would have sensed it. The starched uniforms had probably inspired him to dress his victims in white.

'How long have you been a volunteer, Brian?' I asked as we climbed the stairs.

'Almost as long as I can remember,' he said, smiling widely, and I caught myself wondering if his teeth were real or false. 'I'm the archivist here, and a lot of local organisations visit us, so I'm always on the phone, arranging things.'

The first-floor exhibits were even more distressing than the uniforms. Glass cabinets were filled with the tokens mothers left with their children: brooches, scraps of fabric, and a few tarnished thimbles.

'These were used to identify the foundlings, on the rare occasions when parents came back to claim them. But disease and poverty meant that very few children ever went home,' Knowles explained.

I stared at the rows of tokens, neatly labelled and dated. There were buttons, matchboxes, and pincushions, but the one that touched me most deeply was a scrap of red fabric, cut in the shape of a heart. Every mother must have dreamed that her luck would change, and one day she could return to collect her child. I felt sure the killer had stood exactly where I was standing now. But the token he'd sent Kinsella had a different meaning. There was no tenderness in his gift – it was nothing more than a trophy, proof that a child had died.

'Tragic, aren't they?' Knowles was standing a little too close. 'Would you like to see the top floor?'

'I'm afraid I'll have to come back another day.'

He looked disappointed, but accompanied me downstairs, pointing out drawings of the foundlings displayed in the stairwell. When we reached the exit he pulled a camera from his pocket.

'Could I take your photo? I keep a record of visitors for our newsletter.' He took the snap before I had time to reply. 'Can you tell me your name and occupation too?'

'Alice Quentin, I'm a psychologist.'

'Fascinating,' Knowles murmured. 'An expert on the dark corners of our minds.'

There was something so creepy about him that I felt desperate to get away. 'Could I ask one more question?'

'Of course, anything at all.'

'Louis Kinsella was a trustee here, wasn't he? Did your paths ever cross?'

His unnaturally white smile vanished. 'That monster almost got this place closed down, and now his ghost has come back to haunt us.'

Knowles's manner had changed completely. His extravagant courtesy had been replaced by suspicion, so I thanked him and said goodbye. So many things about the man had struck a false note, including his dyed hair and veneered teeth. But maybe he'd formed the same impression of me. For all he knew I could be a journalist, looking for the inside story on one of London's grisliest crime locations.

★ ★ ★

I found myself thinking about Burns on the way back to Charndale. The train took forty-five minutes, rattling through the suburbs, then crossing miles of dark fields. The idea of his new relationship still smarted, but I forced myself to leave a business-like message on his phone, apologising for my quick departure. There was no way I could reveal my feelings. I knew how he'd react – comfort was Burns's speciality. He'd pat me on the shoulder, then lend me a hankie to weep into.

The cottage was freezing when I got back. The temperature had fallen even lower, so I laid a fire, then went outside to collect more logs. There were new footsteps on the snow and I felt a surge of panic. I collected a torch to look at them more closely. A fresh set of boot prints formed a necklace around the house. Someone had circled it, peering through every window. It crossed my mind to call the police, but they would think I was crazy to bother them with something so insubstantial. Surely there had to be a legitimate reason? If someone wanted to burgle the place they'd have done it by now, because it had stood empty all day. It was probably the letting agent, wanting to speak to me about my request to get the heating fixed.

When I got back inside I tried to quell my anxiety. I'd been afraid too many times in the last few years, and I was determined not to let fear dominate me again. I peered into the fridge, but my appetite had gone. The prospect of waiting an hour for the fire to warm the living room did nothing to improve my morale, so I made a snap decision to go out, hoping that the pub's hectic atmosphere would stop me thinking about Burns. I pulled on my boots and padded coat and set off, shining my torch on the icy ground. When I reached the end of the lane I looked back at the cottage. The downstairs lights glowed like beacons, warding off would-be thieves.

The Rookery was quieter than normal. I'd hoped to see

Judith but there was no sign of her, so I sat at the bar and studied the menu. Someone appeared beside me before I'd made my choice. It was Tom Jensen, and he was standing so close I could almost taste the cold air trapped in his clothes.

'Great minds think alike,' he said. 'I couldn't face cooking.'

'What do you recommend?'

'Nothing. Eating here's an act of desperation.'

I ordered pasta and a glass of wine, and Tom sat opposite me at a table by the window. Clearly we were sharing dinner, whether I liked it or not. I watched him take off his coat. He was wearing jeans and a black T-shirt, and he had a muscular tennis player's build, hard ridges of muscle standing out on his forearms. His good looks were undeniable but he was tough company. Long silences didn't concern him, and he made no attempt to fill the gaps between statements. Whenever conversation flagged he sat back and observed me. His interest only flickered into life when I mentioned my running.

'You finished a marathon?' he sounded incredulous. 'In what time?'

'Four hours thirty-nine minutes.'

His gaze skimmed across my body. 'Not bad. Do you still train?'

'Not much since the freeze started. I'm going stir crazy.'

'You should come to my lunchtime sessions. They're staff only.'

I shook my head. 'Treadmills don't do it for me. I need to smell the tarmac.'

Jensen ate the rest of his meal in silence. I couldn't work out whether my company bored him or the poor cuisine had spoiled his mood. The experience made me wish I was more like Lola. She'd have relished an impromptu dinner date with a gorgeous stranger, whether or not he chose to speak.

'What were you doing in London anyway?' he asked.

'Working for the police.'

'Really? Doing what?'

He studied my face closely while I told him about interviewing Kinsella, and my visit to the Foundling Museum. When he finally started to talk, he asked so many questions it felt like an onslaught, so I retaliated.

'Judith gave me some advice. She said it was a bad idea to mention God to you.'

His eyes snapped open. 'Mention anything you like. I'm a confirmed atheist, that's all.'

'I envy your certainty. I think having a faith would be comforting, but church services leave me cold. Everyone else looks so devout, but when I close my eyes there's nothing there.'

'That's how I feel these days.'

'But you were a believer once?'

'A long time ago.' His shoulders tensed and I wondered why the subject made him defensive. Maybe I'd met my match: someone else who hated anyone poking around in his private life.

'I think I'll get a coffee,' I said.

'That would be a mistake.'

'Really?'

'It's undrinkable.' He pointed at the window. 'See that building, set back from the road?'

'The old school house?'

'My flat's on the top floor, and I've got a brand-new Gaggia.'

I paused for a microsecond. 'What are we waiting for?'

The cold was breathtaking as we crossed the road, and I followed him up the steps. Jensen helped me out of my coat once we got inside, his hands skimming my arms. His living room reminded me of my flat in Providence Square: white walls, bleached floorboards, and very few personal items on display. The decor told me nothing about his personality, but his bookshelves were more helpful. His choice of literature seemed unlikely for someone who made a living from the body beautiful. The shelves groaned with novels by Goethe, Stendhal, and Zola, and three different versions of the Bible. I wanted to ask why a committed atheist needed so many copies of the good book, but his reaction earlier had shown that questions were foolhardy. He sat beside me on the sofa, so close that our elbows were touching.

'How did your chat with Kinsella go?' he asked.

'It wasn't exactly a chat. He didn't say a word.'

'After what happened to Jon, I was concerned.'

'Don't worry. I can take care of myself.'

'Is that why I found you freezing to death in the car park?' He studied my eyes and then my mouth, eyelashes so pale they looked like they'd been dipped in frost. 'You know, I wanted to invite you here that night.'

'Why didn't you?'

He gave a slow shrug. 'You didn't need a stranger hassling you on your first day. Would you like another drink?'

'Not yet, thanks.'

'You'd better choose your entertainment then.'

'What are the options?'

'Depends what you feel like.' He reached across and pushed a loose strand of hair back from my face. 'We could talk some more, or drink another coffee, or we could go to bed.'

I choked back a laugh. 'Are you serious?'

'Absolutely. But I have to be honest, I'm not looking for complications.'

'Neither am I.'

He didn't bother to reply. He was too busy tracing the outline of my mouth with his index finger, and I knew exactly what was on offer: a straightforward one-night stand, with no

63

intimacy whatsoever. My brain was advising me to say no. He was too predatory and Burns was taking up too much space in my head, but my body had already decided.

'I'll go for the third option,' I replied.

It was easy after that. The conversation stopped, and he kissed me instead. My head spun when he finally drew back. His bedroom was as sparsely decorated as the rest of his flat, but I didn't care, because I was too busy watching him undress. Ropes of muscle were stretched taut across his chest and abdomen. I was so mesmerised that I forgot to be scared, even though it had been two years since I'd slept with anyone. Maybe that's because the contract was so simple. Nothing emotional was on offer, so I only had myself to consider. And he was intent on giving me pleasure. The first time was over a little too fast, but the second was incredible. It had been so long since anyone had touched me that my skin felt sensitised, every inch gradually catching fire. I had to press my mouth against his shoulder when I came, to stifle my screams. His performance was the opposite of mine, far more controlled and watchful. I got the sense that he was grading me out of ten, but at least he seemed to relax afterwards, lounging back against the pillows.

'Was that better than staying home with your ghosts?' he asked.

'Definitely.'

He smiled then turned away to sleep, and I lay there watching the ceiling. My body hummed with contentment, but my mind was refusing to shut down. Something about Tom refused to make sense. Why was a man who was so great in bed in full-scale retreat from intimacy? I thought about the foundlings, then Suzanne Williams, burdened by too much grief, and Burns, in bed with his new girlfriend. Tom was already asleep, so I pulled my phone from the pocket of my jeans and took a photo of him for memory's sake, then set the alarm for five o'clock. I couldn't face the ice-cold cottage yet, but I wanted to be gone by sunrise. Tom had made it abundantly clear that he was the kind of man who preferred to wake up alone.

10

Gorski was the first person I saw at the Laurels the next day. He was clutching an outsized mug of coffee and I felt like advising him to detox – caffeine would make his temper even harder to control.

'My office now, please, Dr Quentin.' He strode down the corridor at his usual racing trot, and when he closed the door his expression was even more outraged than normal. 'I'm not comfortable with you interviewing Kinsella. You must have heard what happened to the last researcher who worked with him.'

'But you gave the police your consent.'

'If you get out of your depth, the press will be all over us.'

'I don't have a choice. The Met think Sarah Robinson's killer knows him; they're insisting on another interview.'

'And you think you've got special powers, do you? After years of saying nothing, he'll just open his mouth and confess.' Gorski's accent grew broader with every sentence, as if he might revert to his native Polish.

'What are you trying to say, Dr Gorski?'

He slammed his hand on the desk. 'You don't realise how dangerous Kinsella is. Even his silence could leave you traumatised.'

'Are you suggesting I sit back and do nothing?'

Luckily someone opened the door. When Judith's calm face appeared, I could have kissed her.

'Is everything okay?' she asked.

Gorski shut his eyes, clearly sick of looking at me. 'I've warned Dr Quentin that she's putting herself at risk. If anything goes wrong, she should remember that. You are my witness.'

'I'm supervising her, Aleks. That's what we agreed, isn't it?'

'Someone has to keep these people safe,' he muttered.

'I'll make sure nothing happens. Come on, Alice. We can talk outside.'

Gorski turned away abruptly, as if we'd ceased to exist, but the exchange had shaken me. The man seemed barely in control of his rage, as if anyone who countered him was in danger, but the source of his anger mystified me. He seemed to resent the idea of anyone trying to access Kinsella's secrets. Judith stood there, wearing a concerned smile.

'Don't take it to heart, Aleks is under a lot of pressure,' she said. 'By the way, Kinsella gave this to Garfield. I have to meet my trainee now, but if you want company when you read it, come and see me later.'

She passed me an envelope then set off for her meeting before I could thank her. My name was scrawled on the paper in jagged black copperplate, and a knot of tension twisted in my stomach, as though a set of poor exam results was hidden inside. When I got back to my office I took a deep breath and opened it.

Dear Alice,

I saw you from my window the day you arrived, picking your way across the ice like a ballerina. I noticed how small your waist is, the black buttons on your red coat, and the way your hair falls precisely to your shoulder. People assume that because I'm often silent, I no longer see or hear, but the opposite is true. I know everything about this place. I could tell you the history of each brick.

I have a strong suspicion about who may be carrying out these attacks. If I'm correct, the killer is more astute than either of us, with good reasons to continue. The killer under-stands that taking a child's life is sacred. Killing a child is not like killing an adult. No matter how much pain rains down on them, they never expect to die. The last expression on a child's face is always disbelief.

If we meet again, I promise to talk instead of scribble. And I hope you'll permit an old man like me to offer a compliment. You have the most extraordinary eyes – such a wonderful transparent green.

Yours,

Louis Kinsella

Pins and needles pricked the palms of my hands. I'd never been more horrified by a compliment in my life. On a rational level, there was nothing to fear – Kinsella couldn't lay a finger on me. But I knew too much about his crimes. I'd read Alan Nash's book and remembered what he'd done to those girls in the flat he'd customised, the bridesmaids' costumes he dressed them in before he strangled them. And now it was me, featuring in his fantasies. At five foot nothing, weighing a fraction over seven stone, I was probably the closest thing to a child that he'd seen in two decades. I stared at his signa-ture again. A graphologist would have had a field day, studying the horizontal line of his name. It looked like a heartbeat flatlining. I dropped the letter on my desk, reluc-tant to touch it again. Perhaps Gorski was right. I was already out of my depth, sailing into something too complex to understand.

The phone on my desk jangled and Burns started babbling immediately, as though we'd been interrupted mid-conversa-tion. 'You won't believe this, Alice. Our man took a black cab to the Foundling Museum. A cabbie dropped a bloke with a big cardboard box on Hunter Street around three a.m. His face was hidden by his hat and scarf, so the driver didn't get much of an ID.'

I tried to picture the killer calmly sitting on the back seat of a taxi with a child's body balanced on his knees. 'He's fearless, isn't he? That's what worries me.'

'Has Kinsella started talking?'

'Not exactly. He sent me a letter instead.'

Burns gave a low whistle when I read out the message. 'You're already his favourite girl.'

'He could be lying about knowing the killer. Manipulation's the only power he's got left.' I stared out of the window at the roof of the infirmary, slates glittering like wet steel. 'I'd like to see Kinsella's ex-wife.'

Burns sounded surprised. 'She's changed her identity. You won't get much of a welcome.'

'I'm not expecting one. But she might have something I can use to prise him open.'

'Leave it with me.'

I said goodbye and wondered how Burns would react if he knew about my reckless night with Tom Jensen. He'd probably stand there, rubbing the back of his neck like he always did when he was lost for words.

At five o'clock I locked my cubbyhole, then headed for the car park. I couldn't resist peering through the window as I walked past the gym. Jensen had his back to me, watching an inmate perform sit-ups. It looked like he'd been working out too, blond hair slick with sweat. I still had no idea why he worked at Northwood when he could have made a fortune as a personal trainer. There had to be a reason why he was making life hard for himself. Sleeping with him had restored my confidence, but although I felt curious about him, there was no flicker of emotion. It had been an act of mutual convenience, not the start of an affair.

Snowflakes whirled in a vortex in front of my headlights as I drove down the exit road. I've always loved snow. I could stand by the window for hours, watching it thicken, but driving through it is another proposition. My hands tensed around the wheel when I arrived in Charndale. The car slalomed across the road, executing a perfect 360-degree turn, coming to rest bumper to bumper with a stationary BMW. The near miss made my heart thump a quickstep rhythm at the base of my throat. Luckily no one else was crazy enough to venture out in the middle of a snowstorm.

Lola phoned as soon as I'd finished dinner. Her voice sounded even more upbeat than usual. She comes from a long line of theatricals, and Christmas with the Tremaines always involves high excitement and endless games of charades.

'What are you up to?' she asked.

'Not much. I just lit the fire. How's the Greek God?'

'Preening himself. He's got a part as a nurse in *Holby*.'

'That's brilliant!' Neal was thirteen years younger than Lola. Normally he played schoolboy roles or wayward undergraduates. 'Have you heard from Will lately?'

'Last week. He's still at that hostel in Brighton; he sounds happy enough.'

I gritted my teeth. It was a relief to know my brother was okay, but I wished he'd call me occasionally, instead of my best friend.

'You're still coming for Christmas, aren't you?' she asked.

'I can't, Lo. I've got to work.'

It wasn't strictly true. But drifting from party to party, then fighting Neal's cat for space on their sofa didn't appeal. I wanted to test my nerve and see if I could handle a Christmas alone. There was a dramatic pause at the end of the line while the idea sank in.

'What about your presents?' Lola sounded like a disappointed five-year-old.

'I'll come the day after Boxing Day, I promise.'

'That'll have to do, I suppose.'

When I put the phone down I felt a pang of guilt, remembering the first gift she ever gave me when we were twelve years old: a huge box of make-up from Woolworths. It kept us entertained for days. We spent most of the Christmas holiday attempting to make ourselves look like movie stars.

I was in bed when a text arrived from Burns. Kinsella's ex-wife had changed her name to Lauren French, and she'd agreed to see me, after some strong persuasion. I dropped my phone back onto the bedside table. Burns might have a new girlfriend, but his habit of working past midnight was still firmly in place. The wind picked up as I tried to sleep. It made an odd, howling sound in the chimney, the windowpanes rattling in their frames like teeth chattering. No wonder the locals believed the cottage was haunted. The place was full of inexplicable sounds.

11

The man's footfall crunches across the gravel, and the fear gnawing in her stomach grows even sharper. She never knows what to expect. He can be angry or laughing, or he leaves her alone, until the light fades from the crack in the door. Her smile makes him treat her better. Yesterday he brought gifts: two bananas, a bottle of water, and a dry blanket. The fruit made her stomach hurt, each gulp sticking in her throat. Already she's hungry again, but at least she has the blanket. It makes the chill less raw, the thick wool locking warmth close to her skin. She forces herself to beam at him when the metal door swings open.

'Still awake, Ella?' His eyes are invisible, his knitted hat pulled low over his forehead.

'I've been waiting for you.'

'You little flirt.' The man's laughing now, lips peeled back to reveal his straight white teeth. His laughter is more scary than his frown. 'I've got a treat lined up for you. I don't want you getting bored. Do you fancy coming out for a drive?'

'Yes, please.' Ella doesn't care where he takes her. Anything's better than being locked up alone in the metal box.

'Come on then, let's be having you.'

She tries to make her body relax as he reaches for her. If she screams or tries to run, he'll lash out, so she takes a deep breath then steps into his arms. It's the opposite of the way her grand-dad holds her, a quick hug before she goes to bed. The man throws her across his shoulder, blood rushing to her head. His torch trails a thin yellow line across the snow. The blanket falls to the ground but she doesn't let herself cry out.

The back door of the van is already open, the darkness inside waiting to swallow her.

'Can't I go in front with you?' Ella's shoulder hits the door as he pushes her in.

'What did we agree?' The man's eyes are round and black, like holes drilled into the ground. A scream rises again in Ella's throat, but she manages to silence it.

'You make the rules.'

'And never ask me for things. Remember that. People have ordered me around all my life. I don't have to take it from you.'

She kneels by the window as the van pulls away, rubbing her bruises. Streetlamps, trees, and unfamiliar buildings slip past as she stares through the dirty glass. After a long time the van pulls up behind a row of houses and the man shuts the driver's door softly behind him. At first Ella wonders why he's standing in the shadows, staring at the lighted windows. Soon the lights go out, one by one, but the man carries on standing there, gazing into the darkness.

12

The Laurels was like a ghost town when I arrived on Saturday. Most of the prisoners were confined to their rooms, because so many guards were on Christmas leave. The only sounds I could hear were the hum of a generator and cars churning up grit on the approach road. I logged onto my computer and opened Louis Kinsella's file again, looking for proof that Nash's theory about the killer was correct. Nash was convinced that he had to be an intimate contact from Kinsella's past, but the impact might have been momentary – a chance meeting that triggered an obsession.

Kinsella's crime file was longer than *War and Peace*, a catalogue of some of the worst acts of sexual sadism ever committed, yet his childhood and adolescence gave no hint of what was to come. His early years were a roll call of academic success. He'd won prizes at his public school, then studied history at Oxford. His tutors assumed that his rejection of a college fellowship to become a primary school teacher in London's inner city was due to youthful idealism, but his profession had given him the perfect cover for his paedophilia. After his murder trial, dozens of former pupils testified that they had been molested. The extreme violence only began in the Nineties, after he became a headmaster – Kinsella had been biding his time. He rented a flat in Camden, less than a mile from his house in Islington, then soundproofed every room and rigged a network of cameras.

A row of pictures confronted me. The girls he'd abducted were between the ages of eight and eleven, but there was no common denominator; they had different builds and came from a mix of races. Some beamed confidently at the camera, while others were too shy to smile. Their post-mortem pictures showed a different species. The faces were unrecognisable, deep wounds ruining their eyes. Kinsella had been questioned repeatedly about whether the girls were alive when they were blinded, but he refused to speak about the pain he inflicted on his victims. The coroner's report stated that most of them were subjected to days of torture before they died.

A dull wave of nausea welled in my chest and when I closed the file, someone had appeared in the doorway. It was the IT guru, Chris Steadman. He still looked like he'd been burning the candle at both ends, shadows hollowing his cheeks. Even his peroxide hair was more unkempt than before, long strands flopping in his eyes.

'Is your computer behaving itself?'

'Pretty well thanks, Chris. Shouldn't you be on holiday?'

'No such luck. I work shifts, right through the year,' he said, transferring his toolkit from one hand to the other. 'I'm having a party on Boxing Day – you'd be welcome.'

'I think I'll be in London.'

'That's a pity.' He pulled some Post-it notes from his pocket then leant over and stuck one on my desk. 'Here's my address, if you change your mind.' He gave an awkward smile then slipped away.

I made myself reopen Kinsella's file and study it for another hour. By mid-morning a headache was throbbing at the base of my skull. Either I was tired, or the horror of his crimes was taking its toll. I grabbed my coat and hurried back to reception. Burns's text had promised a car at eleven o'clock to take me to see Kinsella's ex-wife, but it didn't arrive until quarter past. The driver was called Reg and he was close to retirement age. I got the sense he would have preferred to be at home, eating mince pies and knocking back sherry.

'The roads are a nightmare,' he grumbled.

'How long will it take to get to Windsor?'

'An hour, with luck.'

Reg didn't bother to make conversation, which left me free to admire the view as we drove east. The fields were a clear, bluish white, almost matching the sky. Snow had converted the landscape into a blank canvas, with rows of stick-like trees marking boundaries between farms. I concentrated on the questions I needed to ask Lauren French, aware that the police's focus had been on culpability and involvement when Kinsella was arrested. She was bound to clam up if I revisited old ground, but I needed to discover the location of his Achilles heel.

It struck me as odd that she'd moved from London to the same county as her ex-husband's jail, even though she never visited him. In her shoes I'd have relocated to the Outer Hebrides. But Windsor seemed the ideal place to reinvent yourself. The whole town was ridiculously picturesque – full of cobbled walkways, and timber-clad medieval buildings. I caught a glimpse of the castle as we crossed the river. It looked like a fairy-tale illustration had been drawn on the sky, battlements outlined in the lightest graphite.

After a few minutes, Reg pulled up at the end of a street lined with small Georgian terraces. 'You'd better walk from here,' he said. 'The boss says the lady doesn't want police cars outside her house.'

I thanked him and set off in search of number twelve, already curious about the meeting. It would make me the envy of every tabloid journalist in the land. When Kinsella was charged, the papers had vied for an exclusive, trying to uncover whether she'd harboured any suspicions about her husband's crimes, yet she'd always refused.

Lauren French's front door was a vivid red, but her appearance was much less colourful, her outfit a tasteful blend of grey and black. She ushered me into her living room, which gave no indication that Christmas was only two days away. A large Chinese vase dominated the mantelpiece and a wooden crucifix hung above the bookcase. I gazed around while she was in the kitchen making coffee, but no family photos were on display.

When Lauren reappeared, I wondered whether she'd had plastic surgery. The mousy, thin-faced creature who'd cowered in front of the cameras seventeen years ago had been replaced by someone else. Her hair was two shades darker, and her face had filled out, her pallor masked by skilfully applied make-up. Only her expression had remained the same. It was so tense that she seemed to be preparing herself for the next attack.

'Did DCI Burns explain the reason for my visit?' I asked.

'To talk about Louis, of course. I refuse, normally. The press hounding me is the reason I left London.'

'But he told you what's happened?'

A flare of anger lit her face. 'The police only contact me when they want help. They didn't care when someone punched me outside the courtroom. Why on earth would I know about the missing girls? I haven't seen Louis since he was sentenced.' Her hands clutched together, trembling in her lap.

'I'm sorry, I know how difficult this must be for you, but the killer seems to be an expert on Louis's crimes. Anything you can remember will help us.' My apology cooled the temperature of our conversation slightly, some of the tension easing from Lauren's face. 'Do you mind me asking you how old you were when you met Louis?'

'Sixteen. He was almost twice my age.'

'Where did you meet?'

'At church, believe it or not.'

I smiled at her. 'Of course I believe it. Why wouldn't I?'

'Everyone called me a liar after the trial, but I told the truth. There were no signs. He was romantic, idealistic even, right till the end. He never forgot our anniversary. When we met, Louis wanted to do something good in his career, make his mark on the world. That's why I fell for him.' Lauren's expression was fervent, as though she was intent on changing my point of view.

'Can you tell me anything about the people Louis socialised with, before his arrest?'

Her lips formed a grim smile. 'He didn't have time for a social life. He ran the church choir, fundraised for a local charity, and helped the Foundling Museum.'

'Do you know why he volunteered at the museum?'

'I remember him saying that the place was special because it saved so many children's lives. People don't understand how caring he was, before the illness took hold.' Her voice tailed away. The irony of Kinsella's admiration for an organisation that cared for vulnerable children seemed to hit her with full force.

'Was he close to many colleagues at school?'

'Not really. His staff admired him, but he didn't have favourites.' She frowned in concentration. 'The caretaker Roy Layton put him on a pedestal. Louis said he felt sorry for him, he was such a loner. He came to the house almost every week, and they'd sit in his study, talking for hours. Louis told me he was persuading him to go to college. He said Roy was wasted in his job.'

'How long did Layton's visits go on?'

'It's hard to remember. About a year, I think. He'd come for dinner and stay all evening.'

'And there was no one else?'

'I don't think so.'

'Do you mind me asking whether your marriage was happy, before Louis's arrest?'

'Very happy. No one was more shocked than me.' Lauren's mouth trembled. 'Louis is the best communicator I've ever met. He could persuade anyone to do anything. I didn't have a clue about life until I met him.'

'I'm sure you had your own views, even at sixteen.'

She shook her head firmly. 'I came from a big family, and my parents were strict. We couldn't speak out of turn. I had to do as I was told.'

An elderly black and white cat appeared and settled at her feet, and I wondered how much comfort her new life contained. Meeting people would be a constant risk. Her fake identity couldn't shield her forever, and exposure would be dangerous. Some of the victims' families believed that she knew about her husband's attacks and should have been thrown in jail too. I swallowed a deep breath. The house seemed to lack oxygen; it was like a cocoon, vacuum-sealed to keep intrusion at bay.

'How long ago did you and Louis separate, Mrs French?'

Her face tensed. 'We're not divorced, I just changed my name after the trial. I'm Catholic, you see. It would be wrong to get an annulment without telling him face to face.' She looked down at her hands. 'It's partly my fault he lost his way, because our plans didn't work out.'

'What plans were those?'

Her eyes glistened. 'We kept trying IVF in the early days, but it came to nothing.'

'Surely you don't blame yourself?' I tried to keep the incredulity out of my voice.

For a moment she was too distressed to reply. 'There must

have been a trigger for what he did. He was in pieces when they told us it wouldn't work. There's always a cause, isn't there?'

'Not with this kind of illness. Psychosis can make people commit terrible crimes without any reason at all.' Lauren stared at me, glassy-eyed, as if she was having trouble focusing. 'Would you be prepared to visit Louis to help the investigation?'

A spasm of anxiety crossed her face. 'I've driven past Northwood hundreds of times, but I can't make myself go in.'

'I can understand that. Thanks for your help today.' I nodded and rose to my feet, but her eyes searched my face anxiously.

'Would it help the missing girl if I saw him?'

'I can't be certain, but it might do.'

Her gaze dropped to the floor. 'I'd have to think about it.'

My thoughts spun when she closed the door. Lauren still seemed gripped by regret, even though she'd done the world a favour by failing to bear Kinsella's children. Her statements explained why she'd chosen to live so close to Northwood. On some level she still saw herself as his wife, and the reason why Kinsella had chosen a juvenile bride was obvious. At sixteen she would have been easy to control, conditioned to obey her parents' commands without question. She still seemed to be in his grip. All the different terms for brainwashing slipped through my head: thought change; mind control; coercive persuasion.

I called Burns as soon as I got back to the police van. In the background I could make out the hum of the incident room – raised voices and a cacophony of phones.

'It's like it happened yesterday. She hasn't seen him in seventeen years, but she's still scared to criticise him.'

'Did she talk about people he knew?' Burns asked.

'She struggled with names, but she said he ran the local choir, and volunteered at the Foundling Museum most Saturdays – some evenings, too. The school caretaker was one of his closest contacts.'

'You sound distracted, Alice. Are you okay?'

'There's something odd about her. People don't often feel that depth of connection after so long apart. He must have controlled her completely.'

'Maybe she's just lonely.'

'It's more than that. It's like she wants to appease him, even now.' I stared out of the window as a scattering of snow drifted past. 'I should come with you tomorrow to see the caretaker.'

Burns sounded relieved as he said goodbye. Maybe no one else was crazy enough to volunteer to work on Christmas Eve. I watched the outline of Windsor Castle grow smaller through the rear window, and thought about Lauren French, still defending her husband's reputation. Her mindset fascinated me. If my husband turned out to be a murderous paedophile, I'd have invested in some intensive psychotherapy, then ditched my religious principles and filed for a speedy divorce.

13

I had to race through Covent Garden on Christmas Eve, because lateness would have resulted in an all-out war. The pavements were clogged with tourists queuing for lunch, weighed down by shopping bags, so I trotted along the road instead. My mother had booked a table at an eye-wateringly expensive French restaurant on Garrick Street, and the maître d' led me through the packed dining hall. She was alone at a table by the window. Even from behind, she was instantly recognisable – grey hair drawn into a chignon above the straight vertical line of her back. It was impossible to imagine her permitting herself to slouch.

'You're awfully flushed, darling. Is something wrong?' She kissed the air above my cheek, making me wish I'd stopped to fix my make-up.

'The train was late, I had to run.'

My mother has always believed in keeping up appearances; neatly combed hair and fresh lipstick are the sticking plasters that prevent the world from falling apart.

I studied the menu and saw that it was identical to the previous year. We'd been following the same ritual for so many Christmases, I could have placed my order blindfolded. Two Martini cocktails arrived at the table as soon as I sat down.

'How's the new job?' she asked.

'Interesting. But it's a steep learning curve.'

My mother's grey eyes assessed me coolly. 'I can't imagine what possessed you, Alice. Those men are monsters.'

'It's only for six months, Mum. Guy's was getting too comfortable.'

'What's wrong with comfort, for goodness' sake?'

Fortunately the waiter arrived before a row could get under-way. She ordered her favourite meal: lobster bisque followed by Dover sole, while I chose the full Christmas blow-out.

'How's your brother these days?' She took a minute sip from her Martini.

'Okay, I think. Still in Brighton, as far as I know.'

My mother pursed her lips silently. She had decided years ago that Will was my responsibility, blaming me for all his mishaps. 'And what about Lola?'

'She's on cloud nine. Her and Neal have found a flat in Borough.'

'They've bought somewhere?'

'You're joking. Banks don't give mortgages to actors.'

She gave me a meaningful look. 'At least she's found someone.'

I decided to ignore every brickbat. By now I should have been immune: she always found something to criticise, from my haircut and clothes to my work ethic and lifestyle. On a rational level I knew that she was hypercritical because her own mother had been exactly the same, but that didn't make it any easier to swallow. She explained what she'd been up to while we ate our starters. Her schedule hadn't changed since she retired: flower arranging at church, visits to galleries and lectures, and one day a week volunteering for Help the Homeless. I watched her as she spoke. Her appearance was a triumph of skilful make-up and expensive clothes. She still wore her wedding ring, even though my father died years ago. But when I looked at her hands more closely, I noticed something unexpected. They were trembling so hard that drops of orange liquid splashed back into the bowl when she lifted her soup spoon.

'Are you okay, Mum? Your hands are shaking.'

'It's nothing. Tiredness, probably.'

'But you're getting it checked out?'

'Of course. I've made an appointment.'

'I'll come with you, if you like.'

She looked exasperated. 'Don't be ridiculous, Alice. I've been overdoing it, that's all. I'm taking a holiday after Christmas.'

'With Sheila?'

'On my own this time. I'm going on a cruise. It starts in Cyprus, crosses the Med, then through the Red Sea to the Indian Ocean.'

I tried to disguise my amazement. Normally my mother took short holidays on the Greek islands with a friend from the library. She'd never mentioned a burning desire to circum-navigate the world.

'That sounds wonderful. How long will you be gone?'

'Three months.'

I watched her as she described each destination. The tremor was still there, and I flicked through a list of potential illnesses: a brain tumour, Parkinson's, multiple sclerosis. Until that moment I'd assumed that we had forever to fix our relationship. I'd made an effort to see her more often, hoping we'd reach a point where we could talk honestly, instead of our endless bickering. As a child I'd been convinced she was superhuman. No matter how hard my father hit her, she always got out of bed the next morning, styled her hair and dragged herself to work. The idea that she might be ill made my own hands unsteady as I lifted my glass. But she was avoiding the subject, picking at her meal, keeping the conversation inside safe limits.

My mother produced a thin package from her handbag as soon as we'd finished our main courses. Part of our Christmas routine involved exchanging presents while we waited for dessert. I watched her unwrap my gift: a charcoal grey scarf from Liberty's, with a simple Art Deco design.

'It's beautiful, darling.' She looked stunned that I'd chosen something so tasteful. 'Try not to be angry when you open yours.'

'That sounds ominous.'

I tore the wrapping paper and drew out a large gold envelope. It looked like the ones TV presenters use to announce Oscar nominees. I expected a voucher for a health spa, or some theatre tickets. But when I studied the company logo, I realised she had bought me a year's membership of a dating agency in Knightsbridge called Introductions Unlimited. I scanned the brochure quickly, trying not to look appalled. The pictures showed couples beaming adoringly at each other. All of the men looked athletic and confident, and the women's smiles must have required countless trips to Harley Street. When I reached the last page, I couldn't believe my eyes. My mother had left the receipt in the envelope – she was so desperate to find me a suitable husband that she'd parted with two and a half thousand pounds.

'This is too much, Mum. I can't accept it.'

'Nonsense. For the right person, it's worth every penny.'

I put down the envelope in a state of amazement. I'd never seen my mother cry, but her eyes were brimming. She must have spent days locating an agency that specialised in well-heeled stockbrokers. She blinked rapidly then looked me in the eye.

'You could still find someone special, Alice, if you'd only start looking.'

I wanted to tell her not to worry. My friends and my job

were enough to satisfy me, but she was too distressed to talk. When I touched her hand it was trembling, like a butterfly struggling to get away.

I spent the next hour in a frenzy of shopping. Retail therapy doesn't usually work for me, but it took the edge off my anxiety about my mother. I found the ideal dress for Lola in a vintage clothes shop, a cashmere scarf for Will, and some shocking pink coral earrings for my friend Yvette. At three o'clock I slogged through the crowds to Tottenham Court Road, catching a northbound Tube to meet Burns. His Audi was parked opposite the station, and a jolt of attraction hit me when I saw him, like an unexpected punch. I had to blink hard to ignore it.

'Has Alan agreed I can help interview Layton?' I asked.

'Of course. He wants you doing the legwork, then he'll swoop in when we start arresting suspects and collect the kudos.'

'And you're letting him get away with it?'

Burns rolled his eyes. 'The guy's spending Christmas with the commissioner, Alice. He's godfather to the top man's kids.'

There was no sense in labouring the point; his irritation with the situation was obvious. My main concern was that evidence could be lost in the yawning procedural gap between Nash and myself. I'd submitted a crime analysis report and entered the locations of all four abductions into the Home Office mapping software to create a geo-profile, but so far Alan had contributed nothing to the investigation apart from his eminence.

'Have you been investigating the staff at Northwood?' I asked.

'Not yet. The searches for the first two girls were local, and the leads in Sarah and Ella's cases centre round Camden.'

I stared at him. 'But the link to Kinsella's obvious, isn't it? It's likely to be someone who's spent time with him.'

'Northwood staff all have enhanced security, don't they?'

'That only picks up people with previous offences.'

Burns gave a brisk nod. 'I'll put it on my list.'

'What do you know about Roy Layton?' I asked.

'He's been asking too many questions. When my team searched the school, he was all over them.'

'That could just be natural curiosity.'

Burns frowned. 'There's nothing natural about him. He gave us permission to check his computers yesterday. I bet he thought he'd done a good job of cleaning the hard drive, but there are images of young girls on one of them.'

'Child porn?'

'The violent kind. The Sex Crime Unit's looking at it now. You can assess him, then he'll be taken to the station. I've got a warrant for a full search.'

'Is there anything else?'

'He's been caretaker at the school for thirty years, single, no previous convictions. I thought he seemed okay at first, but Tania reckons he's an oddball.'

Burns glowed slightly at the mention of his girlfriend, and I turned my attention to the council houses outside the window. Miles of Scandinavian forest must have been decimated to provide Christmas trees for so many front rooms. News footage of Louis Kinsella being led from St Augustine's flashed through my memory as we arrived at the schoolhouse, which was classic, red-brick Victorian. A hundred years ago, boys and girls would have been corralled through different entrances every morning when the bell rang. I peered into a small classroom. The walls were freshly painted, miniature chairs and tables in a range of primary colours, as if the place was determined to banish its dark reputation.

Police officers were swarming round the caretaker's house. It was a dilapidated building just behind the school, with tiles slipping from the roof, and a view of the playground. Yards of yellow crime-scene tape circled the perimeter, and a gang of SOCOs were erecting a tent over a white Luton van parked on the drive. There was a sour tang of damp when I followed Burns into the hallway, strips of woodchip paper peeling from the walls. The carpet pattern had been stamped into non-existence years ago. I fished in my bag for a notebook and a psychological assessment form. I'd filled them out so often that I knew the categories by heart: state of mind, evasiveness, and propensity for violence, with a sub-section for observations about whether the interviewee was lying or concealing information.

Roy Layton looked around fifty-five, but the years hadn't been kind. He was huddled over a two-bar heater, hands clasped over a sizeable beer belly. Buttons were missing from his brown cardigan and, apart from a ruff of grey hair above his ears, narrow as a monk's tonsure, he was completely bald. When we walked into the room he looked in my direction, but full eye contact was impossible. One of his pupils lit on my face, while the other scanned the ceiling for cracks. Burns loitered by the door, close enough to eavesdrop, but not to interrupt.

'Hello, Mr Layton, my name's Alice,' I said. 'Do you mind if I sit down?'

'You're the first to ask. The rest just barge in, without a by-your-leave.'

'Can I ask you a few questions?'

Layton's good eye assessed me nervously. 'It's a free world.'

The man's shoulders were hunched round his ears, but under his truculence I could sense his anxiety. His home, reputation, and livelihood could vanish in a blink.

'Can you tell me about your time here, at St Augustine's?'

I kept my head down and scribbled a few words on the back of my form. People are always more forthcoming when you're submissive. It interested me that Layton was manifesting the full range of anxiety gestures, tugging at his sparse hair, crossing and uncrossing his legs.

'Nine head teachers have come and gone in my time. The new one said she'd get this place done up, but it never happened.'

'You were the last person to see Ella Williams, weren't you?' I asked.

'So they say. I've been kicking myself – I spotted her through the kitchen window, I should have waited with her till her granddad came.'

'How did you know he'd pick her up?'

'I see the cars arrive every day. Are you having any luck finding her?'

'There are some strong leads.'

'But nothing definite?' His good eye fixed me with an intent stare while the other spun in its socket.

'Let's concentrate on the questions I need to ask you, Mr Layton. Can you tell me if you ever invite the schoolchildren into your home?'

His cheeks reddened. 'What do you mean? I've been CRB checked, you know.'

'Of course, but the police will search your house very thoroughly today. It's best to tell us now if Ella ever came here.'

'Never.' He shook his head vehemently. 'Sometimes I open the back of the van and let them play in there. That's as close as they get.'

'What made you choose this job?'

'Variety, I suppose. I'm a jack of all trades – a bit of maintenance work, some painting and decorating.' His voice faded into silence, as if he'd lost the gist of his argument.

89

'Did you know Louis Kinsella well?'

His face clouded. 'I know it's terrible, what he did, but it was right out of the blue. He did more for this school than anyone. He's the only one who treated me like an equal.'

The caretaker grew more confident as he spoke, and I saw Burns shifting in his seat. I waited a moment before asking the next question.

'The police have found some pictures of children on your computer, Mr Layton. Can you explain that for me?'

His good eye fixed me with an outraged stare, while the other whirled like a marble being sucked down a drain. 'You lot have got filthy minds. That's a second-hand computer. If you've found something dodgy, it wasn't me that put it there. This is a witch-hunt.'

Burns rose to his feet. 'Keep your voice down, Mr Layton. You can explain at the station.'

The playground outside looked identical to the one behind the primary school I'd attended, with a basketball hoop, swings, and a climbing frame loaded with snow. Burns peered over my shoulder as I scanned my notes.

'He's tense, and socially inept,' I said. 'And he's displaying a high level of anxiety in his patterns of speech and body language.'

'The bloke's pretty fond of Kinsella, isn't he?'

'It could be Kinsella's charisma he remembers, not the violence, but you're right to investigate him. I know he ticks all the clichéd boxes, a lonely misfit who prefers kids to adults, but stereotypes exist for a reason. Most paedophiles take a defensive stance at first interview stage.'

Burns looked satisfied. 'I'll see him again as soon as I get to the station.'

'Try and find out more about his relationship with Kinsella.'

Twenty yards away, Layton was waiting outside his house,

and I felt a twitch of sympathy, even though there was a possibility he was the killer. People must have shunned him for years. Mothers would drag their kids across the road, simply because of his appearance. His walk was shambling and he was wearing a duffel coat that looked twenty years old, faded trousers a few inches too short.

'I'll fax my report to you.'

Burns glanced down at me. 'How are you spending Christmas, Alice?'

'Doing as little as possible.'

'Lucky you. My place'll be mayhem.'

A half-smile appeared on his face. I could picture Tania wrapping his gift, then she'd arrive at his flat wearing something glossy to dazzle his kids.

'Can I give you a lift?' he asked.

'No, thanks. I need the fresh air.'

I'd expected the school to be in darkness as I walked past, but the art room was brightly lit. A pretty middle-aged black woman was loading packages into a cardboard box on one of the tables. She hurried to the fire exit when she caught sight of me through the window. Her hair was cropped short, revealing strong cheekbones.

'Can I help you?' she asked.

'I'm working on the police search for Ella Williams. My name's Alice Quentin.' I dug my ID card out of my pocket and showed it to her. 'I wasn't expecting to find anyone here on Christmas Eve.'

'I'm Ella's teacher, Lynette Milsom.' She took a step backwards to let me in. 'I just came to collect my grandson's presents; he always finds things I hide at home.'

I noticed a pile of paintings stacked on a table nearby. 'Did Ella's form do those?'

'Would you like to see them?'

'If you don't mind.'

She spread the papers out, taking care not to damage them. 'They were drawing outside last term.' Lynette gazed at the images, then shook her head. 'Ella's suffered too much already. I always tell myself not to have favourites, but she's the smartest kid I've ever taught. Her SATs scores are unbelievable.'

She seemed to be holding herself together by the skin of her teeth, staring down at the kids' pictures. Most of them featured skyscrapers and double-deckers, a few stick-limbed families beside garish houses with tumbledown roofs. But one of the paintings was in a league of its own. A sombre grey building filled the page, and I felt sure I'd seen the place before. It looked like the ideal residence for a family of ghosts.

'Is this Ella's?'

Lynette nodded. 'She drew it after our trip to the Foundling Museum.'

I held her gaze. It seemed an odd coincidence that children from Kinsella's old school were still visiting his favourite museum. 'Did the kids go there recently?'

'We always take them in September.' She gave a narrow smile. 'The head wants them to realise how lucky they are, but the trip affected Ella most of all.'

'How do you mean?'

The teacher's gaze made me feel like I'd missed something obvious. 'Because she's today's equivalent of a foundling, isn't she? Her father abandoned her, then her mother died.'

I studied the painting more closely. The place looked even more haunting than in real life, its windows grimed with shadows.

'I don't know what I'll say to her friends when term starts,' Lynette said quietly.

'Ella could be back by then.'

Her smile faded as she shuffled the children's paintings

back into a pile. When I looked out of the window, Roy Layton was being driven away, shielding his face with his hand. I left Mrs Milsom tidying feverishly, as though her life depended on an immaculate classroom.

It was already dark as I walked down the street in Ella Williams's footsteps. There was no one around, and curtains were already closing, Christmas lights glittered over people's front doors. It still seemed incredible that a child had been seized from the heart of the city, less than a hundred metres from her school.

14

It's been days since Ella ate anything; the hunger has become a dull pain that never stops. The man hasn't been back since he took her out in the van, and the box has felt smaller since then, stale air smothering her.

'Do you know what day it is, Ella?' the man asks when he unlocks the door.

'I can't remember.'

'Christmas Eve, silly girl.'

The torchlight settles on her face and she stretches her lips wider. Instinct tells her to shield her eyes from the dazzling light, but it's safest not to move a muscle. His shadow looms behind the bright wall of light. It's impossible to guess whether he's pleased or angry. Her hands are so cold, they can no longer move, fingers brittle as icicles. Maybe he'll put her in the van again, and drive around for hours. That would be better than staying inside the box; at least then she could watch the world passing, instead of staring at the dark. Tears seep from the corners of her eyes, but her smile doesn't falter.

'I've got you a present,' the man says.

'Have you?' Ella tries to sound pleased, but she's shivering so hard that her voice quakes when she speaks.

'Come here, I'll show you.'

He lifts her over his shoulder, and her arms flail, head lolling like a rag doll. The ache in her stomach is so intense that she wants to pound his back with her fists.

'Close your eyes,' he snaps. 'No peeking until I say.'

A door creaks open and Ella feels herself being lowered to the ground. She keeps her eyelids tightly shut, waiting for permission.

'Now you can look.'

The strip-light overhead makes her blink. She's standing inside a tiny room, with bare bricks and a stained mattress. There's a plate of food on a small table, sandwiches and a muffin, still wrapped in its plastic bag. Warm air gushes from a heater on the floor, touching her feet like a blessing.

'Do you like it?' the man asks.

For once her smile is genuine. 'It's perfect.'

'I hope you know how lucky you are. No one gave me presents when I was a kid.' The muscles in his face contort, as if he can't decide whether to laugh or cry.

'Poor you,' Ella says quietly. 'You must have been lonely.'

'You don't know the half of it.' His eyes crawl across her face. 'Remember, this is just for tonight. One foot wrong and you're back outside. Understand?'

'I'll be good, I promise.'

Her mouth's watering. She's longing to grab food from the plate, but the man's still standing there.

'Don't I get a kiss, princess?'

A wave of nausea rises in Ella's throat, but she forces herself to walk towards him, arms outstretched.

15

Loneliness and being alone are two different things. At least that's what I told myself when I woke on Christmas morning in an empty bed. The central heating was making ominous clattering sounds, and the air in my bedroom felt icy. So far the cottage had resisted every attempt to raise its temperature, but when I pulled back the curtains, I stopped caring. Edgemoor Woods had turned into the perfect Christmas card, the sky an empty shimmer of blue, lines of fresh snow balanced on the branches of conifer trees.

I hunted for my trainers in the bottom of the wardrobe, then stepped out into the silence. The city's roar had been second nature until now – ringtones and juggernauts, music blaring from open windows. But out here, there were no distractions. All I could hear was a hushing sound as the snow compacted under each footfall. I followed a bridleway at the end of the lane and set off through the trees. The rest of the village must have been sleeping, because even the hardiest dog walkers were absent. The woods were empty as I followed the track beside a frozen stream. After a fortnight without exercise, my hamstrings burned, reminding me that I should have warmed up more thoroughly before I set off.

The woods seemed to go on forever, the path unreeling like a spool of film, with no sign of a house or another human being. After twenty minutes I stopped to rest, my breath turning the air smoky and blurring my vision. I was about to turn back when a crackling sound came from behind me, but there was no one in sight. Maybe a branch had fallen under the weight of snow. The sound came again soon after, and this time it was nearer, twigs snapping under someone's feet. I didn't stop to investigate, setting off along the track at full pelt, white branches spinning past. I was convinced someone was floundering after me, a shadow moving between the trees. My imagination was so overheated that steam must have been coming out of my ears. My heart was still pounding when I reached the lane, but my panic was dwindling, because there was no sign of anyone. If I had been right, the person following me had veered away when we approached the road, but it was more likely I'd imagined the whole thing. I wondered why I'd let a few unexpected sounds get me so spooked. It was probably just another health freak taking an early walk to offset the Christmas excess. My nerves must be raw because there had been so much pressure recently. I felt embarrassed about racing through the woods as if I was starring in *The Blair Witch Project*, but at least my body was glowing from the exercise.

I stood under the shower afterwards, deciding how to spend the rest of the day. It was a choice between typing up notes about the treatment regime at Northwood, or relaxing on the settee watching reruns of *Harry Potter*. The doorbell rang before I could make up my mind. I hunted for a towel to wrap round my wet hair before running downstairs, but when I peered through the window, the porch was empty. A man was standing by the gate, back turned, peering into the depths of his rucksack. I yanked the door open, because the set of his shoulders and his dark blond hair revealed who it was instantly.

'Will!'

My brother swung round to face me. He looked almost his old self – tall and rangy, with no evidence of his injuries apart from a slight limp. Only his expression was different. Behind his sky blue stare, it was impossible to tell what he was thinking. The change unsettled me. I'd grown used to reading his body language, figuring out whether it was safe to approach.

'Happy Christmas, Al.'

His face stretched into a grin and I pulled the door wider so he could drop his rucksack in the hall. This version of my brother was clean-shaven and calmer than before, wearing trainers that looked fresh from the box. Six months ago he'd been a shambling mess, struggling through the days in my flat, dragging himself to Narcotics Anonymous meetings.

'It's great to see you,' I said. 'It really is.'

I tried not to look at him directly because eye contact always made him panic, but he pulled me into his arms. It was the first hug he'd given me in years. The rough fabric of his coat grazed my cheek like sandpaper, but I didn't care; I could have stood there all day. When he released me, the remote look was back in his eye.

'Have you had breakfast?' I asked.

'Not yet.'

'My fridge isn't very festive, I'm afraid.'

He rolled his eyes, but carried on smiling. 'I didn't come here for turkey and all the trimmings.'

'Thank God for that.'

My brother walked ahead of me into the kitchen and peered into the cupboards.

'I'll make something, if you want.' His words were delivered cautiously, as if he was selecting them from a dictionary before he spoke.

'Brilliant. I'll light the fire.'

My heart raced as I walked into the living room. In the three months since I last clapped eyes on him he'd metamorphosed into someone else. He still looked like Will, but he had

98

different boundaries. He could meet my eye and cope with being touched. When I returned to the kitchen he was busy chopping mushrooms. There was something unfamiliar about his gestures. He had always been a fidget, completing every action at lightning speed, but now he was methodical, dicing ham into chunks of exactly the same size.

'What have you been up to?'

'Not much.' He gave a brief smile. 'Living the life of Riley.'

I asked a few more questions, but his answers were either jokey or monosyllabic. All I could discover was that he'd hitch-hiked from Brighton the night before and waited in a bus shelter for the sun to rise. He wouldn't explain why he hadn't called to let me know he was coming. I could tell he had no intention of describing his new life, so I stopped probing and blathered about myself instead. He looked intrigued when I explained about my research, and the psychopaths at Northwood, minimising all the dangers.

'You're not still doing police work, are you?' Will put down his knife and turned to face me.

'Not as much as before.'

A deep frown appeared on his face. 'It's wrong for you, Al. You should tell them where to go.'

I bit my tongue. There was no point in explaining that I did it to help the victims, not myself. But I knew why he wanted me to quit forensic work. Two years ago he'd been caught in the crossfire during an investigation and ended up with compound fractures in both legs. He carried on preparing the meal, searching methodically through the cupboards for extra ingredients. After half an hour he'd created the perfect break-fast: French toast, omelettes with Parma ham, and mushrooms oozing with butter.

'Delicious,' I told him.

Will didn't bother to reply, too focused on his meal,

shovelling food into his mouth convulsively. I wondered how long it had been since he'd eaten. He'd lost his skeletal look, but his face was still dominated by his sharp cheek-bones. I was longing to know about his new life, but I was scared one more direct question would send him running for the door. Eventually the silence calmed him, and he volunteered snippets of information. He was gradually putting down roots. A housing project in Brighton had given him a room, and he'd found a job washing up in a pub in the centre of town.

'It faces the sea. I can watch the tide come in while I work.'

'Sounds like you've landed on your feet.'

I should have been more congratulatory about his first job in years, but the gap between then and now had engulfed me. I remembered tagging behind him at parties, girls chucking themselves at him from every corner of the room. His friends said he had the world at his feet. But he'd ended up in a half-way house, earning a pittance.

When he finished eating Will pushed back his chair and went into the living room, stretching out on the floor in front of the fire.

'You can rest here,' I said, offering him the settee.

'I'm fine.' He turned away and fell asleep almost instantly, his head cradled on his arms.

I curled up in the armchair and read a magazine, while Will shifted uncomfortably in his sleep. He must have been exhausted because he didn't wake again until that afternoon, and he seemed startled when he finally came round. I watched him reach into his pocket and pull out a strip of tablets. He swallowed a couple then buried them again. For once they looked like prescription drugs instead of the type you buy on street corners. He was finally taking his chlorpromazine, and I felt like hugging him, because medication was his best chance

of recovery. But I wondered how much he'd lost in the process. Patients who took anti-psychotic drugs often complained
that their lives became monotone. Things lost their glitter
without the manic highs and lows.

When he swung round in my direction, his face was tense
with strain, and I guessed that his anxiety levels were soaring.
The medication should have been taken hours before. A year
ago I would have backed away and waited for him to calm
down, but this time I stayed put. He stared at me, his jaw
tightly clenched.

'There's something wrong with this place, Al. Can't you
feel it?'

'I like it here.'

'There was a face in that mirror just now. It was horrible.'

The looking glass held a reflection of the empty window,
nothing visible outside except a grey patch of sky.

'Maybe you dreamed it,' I said, smiling at him. 'I haven't
seen any ghosts yet.' My brother gazed at the fire, thin hands
clasped around his knees. 'I almost forgot, I've got a present
for you.'

I ran upstairs, and the sound of his footsteps in the living
room drifted after me while I hunted for wrapping paper. His
present looked beautiful by the time I'd finished, decorated
with a plume of ribbon. I checked the spare room before going
back down. It was small but cosy, with fresh linen on the bed.
Hopefully he'd be comfortable there.

The living room was empty when I went back downstairs,
so I searched for him in the kitchen. My heart sank when I
saw that the fridge door was ajar. The only items missing were
a pint of milk and a block of cheese. I wished he'd taken more.
A blast of freezing air gusted from the hallway. The front door
hung open and Will's sleeping bag and rucksack had disappeared. I rushed outside, but there was no sign of him. All I

could see was the empty lane and my breath condensing in front of me. I stood there in foot-deep snow, clutching a Christmas present for someone who'd run away without even saying goodbye.

16

I fell asleep worrying about Will, and my nightmares took a long time to clear the next morning. A young girl was trapped inside a block of ice, screaming for help, fingernails scratching at the frozen water. Kicking and beating the ice made no difference; the solid wall of cold refused to break. All I could do was hurl myself at it, like the inmate I'd seen, bouncing from the walls of his padded cell. None of my efforts worked – the child was fading, her pale blue mouth gasping for air.

I launched myself out of bed as fast as possible, shivering in the cold. The boiler was groaning like a man in his death throes so I went downstairs to investigate. When I fiddled with the temperature dial, the pilot light went out and refused to reignite. I swore loudly to myself. The cottage seemed determined to make life difficult. The prospect of a freezing cold shower didn't entice me, so I packed soap and a towel into my gym bag before phoning the letting agent. Muzak blared in my ear, then an automated message informed me that the office was shut until New Year's Day.

I slammed the door hard on my way out, then drove to Northwood, with the temperature dial stuck on -5°C. One of the security guards gave a grudging smile as she nodded me through the turnstiles. Now that I had a valid ID card, I could have carried a chainsaw into the building without anyone turning a hair.

I picked up a newspaper on my way through the day room.

The photo on the front page was of Suzanne Williams clutching her grandfather's arm, so frail that a breeze would carry her away. The picture had been taken inside a church, hundreds of people packing the aisles, and I hoped the service had given them comfort. The memory of Suzanne's fingernails cutting my palm as she begged me to find her sister had stayed with me. No wonder she was clinging to her grandfather as if he was the only solid fact left in her universe. If Ella wasn't brought home soon, the psychological damage would be irreversible.

Louis Kinsella's letter lay in my in-tray, exactly where I'd left it. I pulled the paper from the envelope and studied it again: 'The killer is more astute than either of us, with good reasons to continue.' I let the sheet drop back onto my desk. The list of questions I needed to ask was as long as my arm, even though the chance of a straight reply from Kinsella was negligible. The prospect of seeing him made my skin crawl, but the photo of Suzanne was forcing me to try again.

Garfield Ellis was making himself a drink when I found him in the staff common room. The tension in his face suggested that he struggled to switch off, the pressure of his job trapped deep inside his skin. But even on a bad day he had the kind of physical presence that's hard to ignore; over six feet tall, muscular as a bodybuilder. His expression lightened for a moment when he saw me.

'Like one?' He held up the coffee jar for me to inspect.

'Thanks, I could use some caffeine.'

'How was your Christmas?' His voice sounded deeper than before; a rich baritone ideal for TV voiceovers, advertising chocolates and liqueurs.

'Quiet. How about you?'

'It was crazy. Fourteen of us crammed into the house – my kids screaming the place down.'

'Sounds like hard work.' I smiled in sympathy. 'Can I ask you a favour?'

'Fire away.'

'I need to see Kinsella.'

'Today?' His eyebrows shot up.

'You don't think he'll agree?'

'Of course he will. Seeing you was the highlight of his week. But you'll need Gorski's permission, won't you?'

I shook my head. 'He knows I have to see Kinsella on police business.'

'You want me to bring him to the therapy room?'

'Can you keep him there for ten minutes? I want to see his cell.'

Garfield looked uncomfortable. 'You'll get me fired. Only prison officers are authorised for cell searches.'

'It's not a search, just a quick visit.'

'No one's meant to see Kinsella without the boss's permission.'

I wondered why he was so afraid. Gorski's bullying seemed to have infected every corner of the Laurels. Maybe he had a history of firing anyone who stepped out of line.

'I'll take the blame if anything goes wrong, I promise.'

He walked away slowly, shoulders down, as if he'd completed a marathon.

There was no sign of Gorski when I went to inform him about the meeting. His assistant said that he was still on leave, which surprised me. It took a massive leap of imagination to picture him settling down with his family to watch *It's a Wonderful Life*.

I climbed six flights of stairs to the top floor where the long-term inmates were housed, pausing to take in the view. The hospital site was crammed inside a thick perimeter wall with only a hair's breadth between buildings, like a medieval city, the grey roof of the infirmary slick with ice. After a minute's wait, the guard pressed a touchpad and a sheet of reinforced glass slid back to admit me.

No one had warned me about the noise. A voice from a cell close by was wailing at ten decibels, while another chanted curses in an endless loop. The warden was relaxing in his chair, immune to the racket. He gave a mock-salute then returned to the sports pages of *The Sun*, and I glanced through the observation hatches as I walked down the corridor. Each cell was arranged differently. Some inmates had displayed drawings and posters above their beds, while others had left their walls completely blank. A face behind one of the hatches snarled like a caged animal, grey hair twisted into ragged dreadlocks. The noise level was increasing, the whole floor pulsing with knowledge that a woman had entered their domain. I felt thankful that the doors were made of four-inch-thick galvanised steel.

The guard unlocked Louis Kinsella's cell reluctantly, complaining that I should have brought a signed authorisation form from Gorski. The small room was immaculate. Black-and-white pictures of buildings were displayed on the facing wall, and when I looked more closely there was a cluster of London landmarks: Monument, the British Museum, statues in St Paul's Close. The only items on his desk were a laptop and some notebooks arranged in a neat pile. But it was the view from his window that interested me. From this vantage point he could see the approach road; he had probably watched Tom helping me jump-start my car. No one could arrive or leave without his sharp gaze monitoring them. As I turned away the wailing resumed, followed by fists thumping the wall, and I realised why Kinsella made his sojourns to the library. At least they guaranteed him a few hours' peace. My gaze landed on the largest photo on his wall. It was a view of the Foundling Hospital, placed directly opposite his bed. Its colonnaded entrance would be the last thing he saw before he fell asleep.

Kinsella's appearance was as pristine as his cell when I arrived at the therapy room. He was freshly shaven, and from a distance he could have been my father's body double, dressed neatly for a day at the tax office. Only the look in his eye was different. My father was easily distracted, always forgetting the names of people he'd met. But Kinsella's gaze was alert to every detail, lingering on the emerald green silk scarf around my throat. Garfield had already secured him in his chair, the other wrist still handcuffed to his own. I wondered how many hours each day the two men spent in close proximity. Perhaps the enforced intimacy explained why the nurse seemed over-loaded. I shunted the envelope I'd been clutching across the desk towards Kinsella.

'I'm afraid this didn't help me. The police want concrete proof that you know who's abducting the girls. They won't let me see you again unless you give solid information. And you promised to speak this time, instead of writing notes.'

His fountain pen flew across the page of his notebook, which Garfield passed to me. *I asked for a private meeting, Dr Quentin. Under those conditions, we can begin.*

'Garfield, could you wait outside while I talk to Mr Kinsella?'

The nurse grumbled about security protocols and being unable to guarantee my safety, but eventually he produced another set of handcuffs, so both of Kinsella's wrists were locked to the arms of his chair.

The energy in the room changed the moment Kinsella and I were alone. My pulse quickened as he prepared himself to speak. For an irrational moment I expected my father's voice to emerge from his mouth, still loaded with anger and disappointment, but his tone startled me. It was slightly dry from disuse, far more cultured than my father's. It had the cool intellectual certainty of a scientist explaining a complex process to a layman, and that's what chilled me. He could have convinced anyone that he was right. He sounded calmer and more rational than I did, perfectly in command of his actions.

'It disappoints me that you think I'd waste your time. In my situation, there's nothing to be gained from lying. Pretending to know the killer won't improve anything.'

'But it's getting you attention. Maybe you think it'll raise your chance of going back to jail.'

His almond-shaped eyes scanned my body as I crossed my arms, and I couldn't help remembering the parade of girls he'd dragged into his car. His gaze was so intrusive it felt like he was undressing me.

'I'm not naive, Alice. I know my campaign's unlikely to succeed. But if we become friends, I'll help you in return. It would be a welcome break from listening to the nurses' tedious gossip.' His hawkish smile flashed on for a moment. 'How much do you know about me?'

'I've seen your crime file. And I was still at school during your trial – it made compulsive viewing.'

The smile reignited. 'Hopeless misrepresentation by the courts of law. How old were you when I was arrested?'

'Sixteen.'

'Young enough to be intrigued.'

I nodded. 'The line between right and wrong is more hazy at that age. You're still deciding.'

'But now your moral code's set in stone, is it?' He looked amused.

My discomfort was growing. Somehow he'd derailed the conversation, and now he was trying to flirt with me. I forced myself to hold his gaze. 'I read *The Kill Principle* years ago. It was a set book on my Masters course.'

He gave a dismissive frown. 'It's pure fabrication. That book reveals nothing about me.'

'I visited one of your favourite places recently. The Foundling Museum – it's a real monument to Victorian misery, isn't it?'

'You're quite wrong. The orphanage was built for salvation: that's why the original trustees poured money into the place.'

His eyes glowered behind his half-moon spectacles, the muscles in his jaw starting to tense, and I couldn't summon a reply. Either Kinsella's illness included a spectacular lack of insight or he was being ironic. Very few child murderers spend their time championing an organisation that saved children's lives. Thankfully Garfield and the guard were still stationed by the observation hatch, ready to intervene if his temper flared.

'How long have you known the man who killed the three girls, Mr Kinsella?'

He blinked rapidly. 'What makes you think it's a man?'

'Are you telling me it's a woman?'

'I said in my letter that this is guesswork. I could be entirely wrong.'

'But if it's who you think it is, how long have you known each other?'

'Around twenty-four years.'

'Can you give me more details?'

'Only if you answer a question for me.' Kinsella leant forwards in his chair and I could see the surface of his skin. It had a grey sheen, slightly powdery, as though he was covered by a layer of dust.

'That depends on what you want to ask.'

'When you were sixteen years old, were you excited by my crimes?'

'Excited's not the right word. Horrified, or fascinated, maybe.'

His odd smile flickered back into life. 'That doesn't explain why I frighten you so much.'

'I'm a realist. You don't scare me while you're padlocked to a chair, but I'd put another bolt on my door if you ever broke out.'

A loud noise escaped from his mouth, somewhere between a groan and a laugh, as if I'd told the best joke in years. When he spoke again his voice was a dry whisper, forcing me to edge closer to him. Less than two feet of clean air separated us and I could smell his hair oil. It had a sour undercurrent, like citrus fruit picked too early.

'I hope you're listening, because I never repeat myself. The killer will take the next girl on the twenty-eighth of December. He will keep her for two days. Tell Detective Burns to look further north this time, and remember, Ella's been in his care a long time. He'll tire of her soon. Old toys lose their glitter.'

I was too shocked to reply, and Kinsella had transferred his interest to something else. His eyes narrowed to slits as he stared at the floor.

'What size shoes do you wear, Alice?'

'Three,' I replied without thinking.

'Child-sized,' he whispered.

The smallness of my feet had made Kinsella's day. The smile on his face widened into a rapturous grin.

17

Garfield was still tense when we walked back to my office. He was the opposite of the other psychiatric nurses I knew, who had witnessed enough distress to develop a thick skin. Despite his hulking stature, there was something vulnerable about him. He seemed terrified that the director would hear about my meeting with Kinsella, and he would receive the blame. Apparently Gorski took a dim view of people who broke his rules, but it still seemed odd that he provoked such fear. Garfield only calmed down when he'd got all his worries off his chest.

'Doesn't Kinsella's company get to you?' I asked.

'Not any more. I'm used to him by now.'

I wasn't fully convinced; his heavy walk made him seem loaded with burdens. 'How come you're his designated nurse?'

'I volunteered for the job. I thought it would be a new challenge.'

'You must have the patience of a saint.'

'Believe me, I'm definitely a sinner.' He laughed briefly, then his expression darkened. 'Louis likes a sparring partner. But it's water off a duck's back with me. Judith's the same – that's why he respects her.'

It surprised me that he considered Judith tough. She seemed to rely heavily on her wall of thank-you notes, pale with tiredness at the end of every day. Garfield's demeanour changed as he headed back to the day room. His walk had regained its swagger, as though he was unwilling to expose his frailties.

I left a voicemail for Burns when I unlocked my office, passing on Kinsella's cryptic remarks. The next hour was spent chasing central heating engineers. I lost track of how many begging messages I left, imploring them to call me back. Through the barred window in my office, the infirmary roof glinted in the last rays of sun. Gathering shadows made the buildings look bleaker than before, but at least my next call to Burns finally reached him.

'Did you get my message?'

'Slow down, Alice. I've been in a press briefing.' Burns sounded like he'd emerged from a long hibernation. I explained Kinsella's claims, and when Burns spoke again his voice was a low mumble. 'So he's known the killer twenty-four years, and the next abduction might be on Saturday. Except the whole thing could be nonsense.'

'Kinsella doesn't get any visitors, Don. Can you imagine how lonely that is? He knows he won't see me again if he lies.'

'But how would they communicate? Kinsella isn't exactly a free agent, is he?'

'He could be talking to someone in here.'

'Like I said, the staff at Northwood are CRB checked to stage two. There's no one with a criminal record.' The tetchiness in his voice forced me to drop the issue.

'How did the interview with Roy Layton go?'

Burns sighed loudly. 'He's got himself a smart solicitor. She insisted we let him go, pending charges, because the house search found nothing. The lab's still checking out his van and Hancock's taken boxes of stuff from his place to sample. We're keeping him under surveillance.' There was a ponderous silence before he said goodbye.

The last thing I saw before I left the office was Chris Steadman's address, still stuck to my desk on a yellow Post-it note: 21 Edgemoor Road. It had been weeks since I let my hair down, but my meeting with Kinsella had dampened my party spirit. The idea of facing a room full of strangers felt exhausting. I dropped the scrap of paper into the bin and immersed myself in diagnostic reports, keen to catch up on my research, because working for Burns had consumed most of my time.

Back at the cottage that evening, I trudged outside to collect more logs. There was no sign of footprints, which filled me with relief. My would-be burglar must have switched his attention to another property. I ate a hasty microwave meal straight from the container, standing in front of the fire. Afterwards I needed a glass of wine to wash away the salt and E numbers, then I settled down to study psychiatric profile reports on inmates at the Laurels. I don't know how long I'd been reading when something moved at the edge of my line of vision. When I looked again the room was empty, and I chided myself for being so jumpy that even a flickering light bulb could spook me. But next time I looked up, someone was outside, peering through the gap in the curtains. A kick of adrenaline brought me to my feet. The face belonged to Tom Jensen, and it flashed through my head that he might be responsible for the footprints, but the idea seemed ridiculous. My heart was still pounding as I opened the front door.

'You scared the life out of me.'

'It's your own fault. The doorbell's not working.'

I got the sense that he would have marched straight past me, even if I'd blocked his way. I caught a trace of his smell as he stepped inside, a whiff of pine forests and freezing cold air.

He looked irritatingly perfect, ash-blond hair spilling across his forehead.

'Do you want a drink?'

He shook his head. 'The party's already started. Come on, we should get moving.'

'I wasn't planning on going.'

'You'd rather stay here with your ghosts?'

'I'm not dressed.'

'You look fine to me.'

He was leaning against the wall, surveying me, and I felt irritated that he'd just assumed I'd have nothing better to do.

'Wait there,' I said.

I swapped my jeans for a short knitted dress and knee-high boots. My hair was beginning to curl, so I pulled it into a ponytail, then drew on a line of dark pink lipstick and hurried back to the living room. My papers from the investigation were stacked on the table, but Tom was standing by the fire, leafing through the pages of a Karin Alvtegen novel I'd left on the coffee table.

'Pulp fiction.' He sounded mildly disgusted.

'It's brilliant, actually. Reading foreign books satisfies my wanderlust; I never get time for holidays.'

A slow smile appeared on his face. 'You'll need one after the Laurels.'

The cold was breathtaking when we got outside, and I remembered that personal conversation wasn't Tom's forte. Eye contact ceased when I asked how he'd spent Christmas Day.

'I saw friends, drank too much. You know how it goes.'

'You didn't visit your family?'

He shook his head but didn't reply. His expression revealed that he had no intention of opening up, so I focused on tramping through the snow. After a few minutes he asked what I'd been up to, so I told him about Will's ultra-brief visit, and his inability to stay still. Tom came to a halt under a streetlight and gazed down at me.

'That can't be easy for him. I was like that for a while.'

The chill sliced through the fabric of my coat. 'How far is Chris's place?'

'We're already here.'

He pointed at a neat row of detached modern houses, each identical to its neighbour, with garages set back from the road. A beautiful vintage motorbike was parked on the drive outside number twenty-one. It made me wonder why Chris had left it in the open, when it deserved to be protected under lock and key. Music was flooding through the open front door, and most of Northwood's workforce seemed to be packed into the hallway. We left our coats in a side room and squeezed through the crowd. It was only ten o'clock but people were already dancing to old-style pop music in the lounge; two nurses were reeling drunk, propping each other up in the corner. It struck me again that Northwood's staff were a community of oddballs. Wallflowers were standing by themselves, swaying to the music, failing to interact with the other guests. An outsider could be forgiven for thinking that it was a boisterous Christmas party for psychiatric patients, not mental health professionals.

I bumped into Pru in the kitchen when I went looking for a drink. She was setting out bottles of wine and cans of beer, her movements so tentative she seemed to be longing for invisibility. Her curtain of blonde curls almost hid her birthmark, and I noticed that she was concealing her figure too, an outsized black shirt and faded jeans drowning her curves. The shrink in me wanted to tell her to get cognitive behavioural therapy to improve her self-esteem. When I said hello she gave me the terrified look of a child being forced to converse with an adult she'd never met before.

'Do you live in Charndale too?' I asked.

'Not far off. My place is in the next village.' She studied me from the corner of her eye. 'How's your research going?'

'Okay, thanks, except I keep getting distracted. What about you? Do you find enough time for your own work?'

'Not lately. The phone rings and my concentration's in bits.'

'What kind of paintings do you make?'

'They're hard to describe. I've never had an exhibition.'

'I wanted to ask how you find working with Kinsella. You have one-to-one sessions with him, don't you?'

Pru's shoulders stiffened. 'Not often. He came twice a week for a while, then he started going to the library instead. I haven't seen him for a month or two.'

'Does he speak to you much?'

She stared at me directly for the first time. 'Only when he's got something to say.'

I might have imagined it, but I thought she seemed angry. She helped herself to a can of beer, then walked away, as though mentioning Kinsella had upset her. She disappeared into the living room, leaving me to open a new bottle of wine. Chris appeared at my shoulder as I poured myself a glass. He looked more relaxed now that he was liberated from his work uniform. His bleached hair was carefully spiked, a few rips in his skinny black jeans.

'You made it,' he said, grinning.

'That's a great bike you've got outside.'

'She's a Triumph seven-fifty. I'll give you a spin some time.'

From anyone else the statement would have been a come-on, but his face was as guileless as a child sharing a new toy. I still couldn't guess his age – it could have been anywhere between twenty and thirty-five. The network of thin scars across his cheekbone was more noticeable up close. Maybe his passion for motorbikes had resulted in an accident, but the scars had faded to pale threads, as though he'd carried them for years. We chatted for a few minutes then he left me to go and welcome more guests. When I caught sight of him again, Pru had him cornered in the hallway, talking to him intently. For once she seemed unaware of her disfigurement, standing so close that he looked uncomfortable, his back pressed against the wall.

Tom was in the living room, flirting with a gorgeous dark-haired girl. Clearly now that we'd arrived, it was every man for himself, and it was a relief not to feel jealous. Being forced to watch Burns smooching with Tania would have been another matter. I swallowed a mouthful of wine and looked for someone else to talk to. Judith appeared before I could take another gulp. I was so glad to see a familiar face that I felt like hugging her. She looked stunning in a silver dress, smoky lines around her eyes making them even dreamier than normal. She turned to whisper something in my ear.

'Relax, Alice; switch off your inner shrink. Why aren't you dancing?'

I couldn't help smiling. Most mental health workers have the same attitude to parties: you're torn between the impulse to cut loose, or to sit back and psychoanalyse. I gazed around the room. The siege mentality was obvious; people had rushed here when their shifts ended, desperate to let off steam. I drained my wine glass then abandoned it on a coffee table.

'Go on then, I'm persuaded.'

The music was cheesy but great to dance to – a mix of vintage disco, house and Motown. Judith seemed to be in a world of her own, moving easily to a great song by To Be Frank, and I noticed that she had caught someone's eye. Garfield was standing in the corner, his eyes glued to her. There was a camera in his hands, as though he was waiting for the perfect shot, but Judith seemed oblivious. After we'd danced ourselves breathless, we flopped into some empty chairs.

'That's better. I need to sweat Christmas Day out of my system,' Judith said, laughing.

'It wasn't much fun?'

'With the kids away, it felt like the house was swallowing me alive.' She put her head on one side. 'I saw you and Tom arriving together.'

'It's nothing. He's moved on to pastures new.'

'Maybe that's just as well. You know he's trouble, don't you? I shouldn't say that, because he's a friend. But in romance terms, he's a disaster.'

'How do you mean?'

'He's got so much baggage, most people would collapse under the weight.'

I wanted to ask what she meant, but her expression suggested that she had nothing more to say, so I changed the subject.

'Pru seems keen on our host, doesn't she?'

She looked sympathetic. 'Poor thing. She's so good at her job and her paintings are amazing, but she's barking up the wrong tree. Chris has a new girlfriend in London who he's crazy about.'

Judith was on her feet again, and by now I was drunk enough to have a good time. I spent the rest of the evening chatting to people and dancing whenever a song I liked came on, my worries fading into the background. It was one o'clock by the time I noticed Chris collecting empty beer cans and the crowd beginning to thin.

There was no sign of Tom or the pretty brunette when I stumbled out to find my coat. He was probably making coffee for her, or maybe he'd skipped that stage in his routine and taken her straight to bed. I stood in the porch, but the cold was so bitter that I delved into my bag, trying to find my gloves. My eyes slowly adjusted to the dark and something glinted on the other side of the street; a sparkle of metal reflecting from a streetlight. I saw the silhouette of a couple, embracing in an alleyway. They must have believed that the shadows were deep enough to hide them, but I recognised Garfield's hulking shoulders instantly. It took me a moment to figure out who he was kissing. Then I realised it was Judith, the light catching on her silver bangles. Braving the cold showed how keen they were to keep their relationship secret, but it was their body language that interested me. They were so deeply entwined that a bomb explosion would fail to disturb them. Their kiss seemed to last forever, as though releasing each other was unthinkable. I felt a pang of envy, then turned up the collar of my coat, and launched myself into the cold.

I thought about Judith and Garfield as I walked home. She lived alone, but he was married with a young family, and she'd struck me as too wise to look for complications. The stress of working at Northwood made unlikely alliances spring up everywhere. Pru was the one I felt sorry for. She seemed like a child trapped in an adult's body, obsessed by her flaws and looking for affection where none was available.

When I reached the Rookery I set off down the unlit lane, dreading the prospect of wading through snow. I'd only been going a few minutes when I heard someone floundering behind me in the darkness. When I spun round, Tom was standing there.

'Why do you keep doing that?' I snapped.

'What?' He'd come to a standstill but it was too dark to see his expression.

'Scaring the shit out of me.'

'It's not intentional. Maybe you're too sensitive.'

'Sensitive? People normally say I'm hard as nails. You haven't got a clue about me, have you?'

'Guilty as charged.' He held up his hands in submission. 'I got bored, so I waited at home till you walked past. It's your turn to make coffee.'

'You're out of luck. I haven't got a machine.'

'It's too late for caffeine anyway.' The starlight reflecting in his eyes made him look more mercurial than ever.

I should have sent him away, but the Northwood virus had affected me too. I was thinking with my body, not my head. When I fumbled with my key in the lock, he was so close behind me that his breath warmed the back of my neck.

The fire's embers were still glowing so I piled more logs onto the grate, then he pulled me towards him, and for once I let myself stop thinking. I decided to be thankful for small mercies. A spectacularly handsome man was standing in my front room, taking off his clothes. When he leant down to kiss me, I realised I was a long way from sober. Closing my eyes made the world spin, so I kept them open. Up close his surliness was easier to ignore. All I had to concentrate on was his poreless skin and his intent stare. I kissed him back without worrying about the consequences. The sex was better this time, even though my hipbones took the impact of the hard floor. He communicated better with his body than words, every action precise and confident, like a gymnast completing a routine, but there was something mechanical about his performance. I made the mistake of looking into his eyes when he came: they carried no emotion whatsoever, except desire. If I hadn't been available, the brunette at the party would have suited him just as well. He seemed to approach sex like a workout – it improved your health, and quenched an appetite that the gym couldn't satisfy.

I half expected him to leave as soon as we'd finished, but he lay next to me on the sofa, the strain easing from his face. I had to remind myself not to stare. He looked like a photo-montage of an ideal man, with golden hair sprinkled across his chest and well-honed muscles, perfectly adapted for hunting in woodlands or swimming through fjords.

'Go on then, tell me your story, Alice.' He leant towards me, head propped on his hand.

'Another time. I'm half asleep.'

'But I don't know anything about you.'

'You don't need to. We're not getting involved, remember?'

'I'm intrigued, that's all.'

I rolled my eyes. 'I grew up in south London. One brilliant brother who crashed and burned. Father dead, mother alive. I studied hard, became a shrink, and hey presto, I'm here with you.'

'That's your entire autobiography?'

'It's more than most people get.'

He dropped a kiss on my shoulder. 'Give me more details.'

'Why?' I frowned at him. 'This is meant to be fun, isn't it? You never talk about your past because it makes you uncomfortable, so I don't pry.'

The mocking smile slipped from his face and he kissed me again. He was so good looking it was impossible not to respond as his knee pressed between my thighs, forcing my legs apart. This time there was no foreplay. He didn't break eye contact for a second when he pushed inside me, and I couldn't guess whether he was angry or just determined to watch me lose control. I tried to stay silent but it was impossible – I didn't yell the house down when I came, but I made enough noise to unsettle the ghosts.

Afterwards I fell into a deep sleep on the sofa, my body shocked by so much pleasure. When I woke up again, light was seeping through the curtains, and it was cold enough to make me shiver. I assumed Tom had gone home, but when I opened my eyes he was sitting at the table, fully dressed, flicking through my papers, and I tried not to move. If he thought I was asleep it would be easier to observe him. After a few minutes he turned his attention to my books, reading titles from the spines. He picked up a photo of Lola and me from the mantelpiece and studied it carefully, without making a sound. It felt like a spy had broken in while I slept, and now he was searching my house for something incriminating. When he slipped out of the room I half expected to hear him climb the stairs, to complete his inventory, but after a few seconds the front door clicked shut. All he had left behind was a blast of freezing-cold air.

18

There's a two-inch gap under the door, and in the morning light Ella can see a patch of wasteland. The snow is piled high, like icing on a birthday cake, and the metal box where he kept her stands beside a solid wooden fence. The box is bright red, with writing on the side, and rust flaking from the doors. It's the kind that lorries haul, keeping their secrets hidden inside.

She stands up again and scans the room. Every mark on the wall is familiar; it's been two days since the man left her here. She's terrified that he'll forget about her, leave her with nothing to eat or drink. Tears prick the backs of her eyes, so she forces herself to concentrate on playing a game. She counts the objects in the room: one mattress, two blankets, a chair with broken spindles, a loo that doesn't flush, and a ceiling light that never switches off. Warm air spills from the heater at her feet, and in the corner there's a pile of old newspapers and a cardboard box full of rubbish: a broken radio and a dartboard with no darts. The radio clatters when she picks it up, pieces loose inside the casing. She presses her ear to the plastic shell, and the hiss sounds like the sea. It reminds her of caravan holidays in Whitstable before her mum got sick, and Suzanne on the beach, throwing pebbles at the waves. She closes her eyes and concentrates as hard as she can. Maybe her sister will pick up her messages, like telepathy in Doctor Who.

The door swings open before Ella can rearrange her features and make herself look glad. The man's carrying a shopping bag and it's tempting to run past him, but the fence is too high to climb.

'Been waiting for me, princess?'

'Of course.' She stretches her lips even wider.

'You're better than the last one. The miserable little cow cried all day.'

Ella has to stop herself asking where Sarah's gone, because that would make him angry. 'Where've you been?' she says quietly. 'I miss you when you're not here.'

'I work miles away, but I'd rather be here with you. Look, I brought you these.' The man unloads a can of Coke and a chocolate bar from a plastic bag. Ella's mouth waters. The hunger pains are so sharp, anything would do.

'Thanks.'

'And here's something special.'

The man reaches into the other bag and pulls out a package. It's gift-wrapped in bright red paper. The man grins as he hands it to her. 'Open it, if you like.'

She tears back the paper and a piece of cloth drops into her lap. The white material is almost see-through, a dozen tiny buttons running from collar to hem. The dress is identical to the one Sarah wore.

'Put it on for me, princess.'

'Why do I have to wear it?'

'Because you're a foundling. I'm the one who takes care of you now.'

Ella's smile falters. She hates the dress. It's thin and papery as an old lady's nightie, but there's no choice. The man is standing there, waiting for her to turn into someone else.

19

The day after Boxing Day I caught the train to London to stay with Lola and Neal. Their flat was a five-minute walk from my place on Providence Square, and returning to the bustle and noise of the city felt like a homecoming, even though I could only stay a few days. I took a step back to admire Lola's apartment block. It was an upmarket warehouse conversion on Morocco Street, the bricks scrubbed to their original primrose yellow, every flat furnished with a steel balcony. A few months ago she'd been living in a grotty bedsit over an off-licence on Borough High Street. I couldn't help smiling to myself: Lola was the consummate survivor. Not only had she bagged a toy boy, she'd also found herself the perfect home.

Lola flung her arms round me when I arrived, as if I'd been away for years, travelling dangerous seas. She held me at arm's length, checking for signs of damage.

'Come in and get warm.' She galloped down the hall like an excitable red setter.

A transformation had taken place since my last visit. I'd helped her and Neal move in a month ago, when the flat was a blur of lacklustre walls and kitchen units, the air smelling of decay and stale food. All the rooms had been decorated since then, and the lounge was the *pièce de résistance*. Only thespians could cope with so much drama – emerald-green walls, and swathes of velvet hanging from the curtain poles, as though

125

Kenneth Branagh might step out at any minute to deliver a soliloquy.

'It's gorgeous,' I murmured.

She beamed at me. 'You wouldn't believe how much paint I got in my hair.'

The flat had been furnished with very little money but plenty of style. Lola had ransacked her parents' loft and haunted auction rooms for weeks. The place fitted her personality perfectly – a combination of wild flamboyance and a modicum of good sense. She left me reclining on an antique chaise longue while she prepared lunch, the radio blaring through the open doorway. The one o'clock news was announcing record low temperatures and more snowstorms; travellers were advised to stay at home. Outside the window, the sky was a solid bank of grey.

Lola kept me entertained throughout our meal, regaling me with stories about her teaching job at the Riverside Theatre and Neal's acting triumphs. I didn't have to speak at all, enjoying her nonstop flow of stories and impersonations. Eventually she asked about life at Northwood.

'How are the psychos treating you?'

'They're quite a bunch. One man's been inside longer than we've been alive.'

'What did he do?'

'He lured vagrants into his basement, then killed them. About two dozen, all told.'

Lola winced. 'Jesus. You have to work with someone like that?'

'Not yet. He stays in his cell most days; the guards have got him on suicide watch. If you make eye contact, he thinks you're after his soul.'

'God, I wouldn't touch it with a bargepole. His soul must be black and shrivelled as a walnut.'

'The Laurels wouldn't suit you, Lo. One guy killed every member of his family, then went out for fish and chips.'

She gaped at me. 'What's the attraction? Why go near people like that?'

I could have attempted a flippant answer, but she'd have spotted the lie instantly. 'They come from a different universe. When you meet them, they're terrifying and fascinating at the same time, and there's some amazing research going on at Northwood. Neuroscientists are close to finding a cure for violent psychopathy. Imagine how great it would be if we could delete it from our gene pool.'

'I still think you should let some other poor sod do the dirty work.' Lola hurried away to fetch dessert, and came back clutching a coffee jug and a plate of macaroons. Her skin was more flawless than ever, auburn hair gleaming with health.

'You look amazing. What have you done to yourself?'

'You won't believe it, Al.' She fell silent for a minute, building a dramatic pause. 'I'm eleven weeks pregnant.'

'That explains why you're glowing from head to toe.' I leant over and squeezed her hand.

'I've only told Mum and Dad. We're waiting till the first scan before we blab to everyone else.' Her smile widened by another inch. 'It was Neal's idea; he thinks we should have three at least. We want you and Will to be godparents.'

'Really? Are you sure?'

'Of course. Will's getting better all the time, he'll be perfect.'

'I'd love to. But I'm not the best nappy changer.'

I couldn't guess how my brother would respond. Lola had adored him since we were at school, but his godparenting style would be unconventional. He'd teach the child to believe in ghosts, and that clouds contain messages about your future. Only Lola was sweet enough to believe he'd be a good mentor for her child. When I looked at her again she was observing me closely, and I could guess her next question.

'What about blokes, Al? There must be some interesting ones at Northwood, apart from mass murderers.'

'Not really.' I took another bite of my macaroon. 'These are great, by the way.'

'Tell me, or I'll give you a Chinese burn.'

'Okay, okay.' I dug my phone out of my bag and showed her my photo of Tom asleep in his bed. 'It's purely recreational. He's a gym instructor and he's a bit of an iceberg.'

'Recreational's better than nothing. The man's beyond gorgeous.'

'I prefer someone else, but he's spoken for.'

'Married?'

'No, but he's definitely seeing someone.'

Lola raised her palms to the ceiling. 'All's fair in love and war.'

I pictured Tania's reaction if I tried to poach Burns from her grasp – she'd rip me to shreds with her immaculate talons. I put down my coffee cup and checked my watch; four hours had evaporated into thin air.

'I have to go out for a bit, Lo.' I made my excuses and promised to return in time for her dinner party.

London had a distinctly post-Christmas air as I walked to the Tube. A church bell was tolling above the drone of traffic, slightly off key, as if pollution had dulled its purity. I felt compelled to do something to help the investigation. Ella Williams had turned into an obsession; the portrait photos that filled the tabloids floated in front of me whenever I tried to relax. And Lola's news had wrong-footed me too. She'd make a brilliant, doting mother, but her relationship with Neal was six months old. All I could do was cross my fingers.

Blackened snow was heaped on the pavement when I

reached Russell Square, stained by smog and the footsteps of pedestrians. It was a different substance from the immaculate flakes that glittered on my windowpanes in Charndale. The temperature was plummeting, but I needed to see the Foundling Hospital again. I knew I'd missed something. The place had haunted me since Sarah Robinson's cardboard coffin had been left there like a macabre sacrifice, her body dressed in the foundlings' night-time uniform. It was clear that other people felt the same. Dozens of cards had been tied to the railings, and a sea of flowers, cards and cuddly toys had flowed across the pavement since my first visit.

The museum was still open when I arrived, but it didn't surprise me that the ground floor was almost empty. Any rational human being would be curled up at home watching *The Polar Express* instead of visiting the city's most disturbing museum. It was a relief not to bump into Brian Knowles, the volunteer who had given me a tour. Being alone made it easier to concentrate on the photo displays. The pictures were more than a century old, faded to a dull tobacco. Children's faces peered out through the brown haze. They were packed into a classroom, straight-backed and attentive, aware that the cane would be administered if they misbehaved. Another picture showed a long line of foundlings being marched across Coram Fields, for their daily exercise, the girls' pinafores streaming in the breeze. Their faces all looked the same, thinned by a legacy of hunger and anxiety.

I bypassed the first level and headed for the top floor. The gallery was filled with information about the hospital's founders. I was gazing at a portrait of the composer Handel, when someone tapped me on the shoulder and my heart sank. Brian Knowles was towering over me, beaming, as if we were old friends. He seemed to have forgotten the suspicion he'd shown the last time we met.

'Back so soon, Dr Quentin? You're my first visitor today. I've been stuck on this floor all afternoon.'

I tried to muster some sympathy, but felt like asking why he spent so much time locked inside a museum, memorising the names of every visitor. Maybe it was his loneliness that drove him out of the house. There was something unnerving about his immaculate appearance; hair so slick it looked like it had been coated with dark brown Shellac. He launched into a lecture before I could get away.

'Let me show you the portrait of our founder, Captain Thomas Coram.' He led me to a picture of a portly eighteenth-century gentleman in a powdered wig, with weather-beaten skin. 'When he retired from seafaring, he gave his riches to the city's poor. He was the Bill Gates of his day; his wealthy friends all supported London's first orphanage, and the charity was a favourite of King George II. Charles Dickens later gave generous amounts of time and money too, even though he had ten children of his own.'

Knowles's eyes glittered and I wondered why the place excited his passion. After listening for another ten minutes, I was an expert on Victorian philanthropy, but no closer to understanding why the killer had abandoned a child's body on the forecourt outside. Maybe he'd done it purely to impress Kinsella. When Brian finally stopped talking, he peered down at me expectantly, as though he hoped I would sign up as a full-time volunteer.

'Would you like to see our archive?' he asked. 'We keep all the original documents there.'

'Thank you,' I said, smiling.

He led me into a large, windowless office. The walls were lined with manila folders, carefully named and dated. 'We've got records of every single foundling from the 1850s onwards,' he said proudly. 'I spend a lot of time here; I'm writing a book about the place.'

The air smelled of dust, old paper, and obsession. It made me desperate to get outside into natural light, but Knowles looked regretful when I said goodbye. He peered down at my face, as though he was imprinting my features on his memory, and it was a relief to leave him fussing over his exhibits.

I spotted a stack of information sheets on the first floor, and when I scanned a paragraph about the hospital's history, my jaw dropped. Brian hadn't told me about the hospital's terrifying mortality rates. In the eighteenth century, seventy-five per cent of the foundlings died within months of arriving, from typhoid and scarlet fever. They were already sick when their mothers gave them up, and there were no antibiotics to treat them. When I reached the bottom of the page, the story grew even darker. Women had paid runners to bring their children to the Foundling Hospital, but hundreds never arrived. The infants were murdered, and their bodies sold to teaching hospitals for students to dissect. I shuddered as a vital fact slipped into place. Kinsella was bound to be an expert on the history of the place, the dead children fascinating him more than the living. That was why he gazed at the building every night before he went to sleep.

The dimly lit rooms were starting to feel airless, and I was in a hurry to leave, but I did a double take when I reached the exhibition hall. Someone familiar was standing by the window, his white hair unmistakeable. Tom Jensen was staring into one of the glass cabinets. He was so absorbed that he stood motionless, gazing at the tokens that had been left with the abandoned children. It took me a while to decide whether to say hello or sprint for the exit. He looked startled when I walked up to him, then his face relaxed into a smile.

'Alice, what are you doing here?'

'I could ask the same question.'

'I've been wondering about this place ever since you told me about it.'

'So you braved the big freeze and hopped on a train?'

He nodded. 'I'm meeting friends later, so I thought I'd do a tour. I've been to the British Museum too.' His gaze returned to the display of keepsakes. 'This place is amazing, isn't it?'

'Amazing's not the right word. I'd say sad or creepy.' When I looked at him again, a question slipped from my mouth before I could edit it. 'Why did you go through my things, Tom? I saw you looking through my papers at the cottage.'

He didn't even blink. 'I told you, I was curious. You never tell me about yourself.'

'All you had to do was ask.'

'That wouldn't help.' His smile wavered. 'You're worse than me at personal detail.'

'I'd better go. I should be at a dinner party.'

'Lucky you. I've got two hours to kill.'

I'm not sure why I let him tag along to Lola's. Maybe it was the shock of finding him in a foreign environment, or because sleeping with him was still fresh in my mind. Either way, he was in no hurry to leave. He took forever to examine a pair of child-sized gloves, pressed behind a layer of glass.

When we got outside, I realised I'd made a mistake. He strolled beside me wearing his enigmatic smile, and it seemed strange that he'd travelled through snow just to drink with friends and visit a museum. I picked up my pace as I marched down Coram Street. Until now the contract between us had been perfectly clear: sex with no questions asked. It irritated me that he seemed to be shifting the goalposts. No matter how gorgeous he was, I didn't need someone riffling through my belongings whenever I closed my eyes.

The look on Lola's face was priceless when she opened the door. I could tell she wanted to harangue me for being late, but Tom's good looks sent her charm mechanism into overdrive. She had managed to squeeze a dozen people round her dinner table, an array of school friends and actors, chatting at high volume. And away from the pressures of Northwood, Tom turned into someone far more sociable. He'd certainly piqued Lola's interest. She spent the next hour observing him from the corner of her eye.

Neal waited until everyone fell silent to make an announcement, tapping his wine glass with the tines of his fork.

'A toast please, everyone. After months of begging, Lola has finally agreed to be my wife.'

There was a collective hush, followed by loud cheers. Lola looked ridiculously glamorous as usual, dark red curls clipped back from her face, wearing the vintage dress I'd bought her in Covent Garden. The only sour expression in the room belonged to her drama-school friend Craig. Their relationship fluctuated between passionate commitment and disapproval. Craig had been uncertain about Neal from the start, but tonight their ages were immaterial. The couple looked like the definition of happiness – she was a young thirty-three and he was a wise twenty. I'd have staked large sums of money on their plans succeeding.

Tom announced that he had to leave before the main course was served.

'Stay,' Lola purred. 'Alice will sulk if you go.'

He gave an apologetic smile. 'I wish I could.'

His kiss goodbye felt cool as dry ice on my cheek. I heard Lola chatting to him courteously in the hallway, but she looked unsettled when she returned.

'Watch out, Al,' she whispered. 'If you can't melt him, no one can.'

I soon forgot her comment as the evening went on and Tom slipped from my mind. I was sandwiched between a beautiful

French actress and a mime artist, who entertained me with funny anecdotes. Fortunately no one asked me what I did for a living. Confessing that I worked with the criminally insane might have put a dampener on things. The rest of the party passed in a blur. I vaguely remember charades and spin the bottle, then a procession of people hugging me goodbye. After they'd gone I stood beside Lola at the sink, drying the glasses she handed me.

'Do you ever feel out of your depth?' I asked.

'All the time.' Lola's cat-like eyes peered at me, then she draped her arm round my shoulder. 'You can always come home, Al, if the psychos are getting to you.'

I squeezed her hand. 'I'll be fine in the morning. Go to bed. Let me finish this.'

She gave a grateful smile then raced away to join the Greek God.

When I settled down in the lounge, they were still cooing to each other in the bedroom next door, the rise and fall of their voices lulling me to sleep. But I woke before dawn, desperate for a glass of water. The chaise longue might have been the last word in elegance, but it was as hard as granite, and a car engine was revving at full throttle on the street outside. I stared at the digital clock on the table, its numbers glowing red in the dark. It was four a.m. and Kinsella's predicted date had arrived. If he was telling the truth, another girl would be taken today. I closed my eyes and tried to get comfortable, but shifting my pillows had no effect. Sleep eluded me for the rest of the night.

20

I made the call at ten the next morning. My mother sounded outraged when she picked up the phone, as though her worst enemy was bombarding her with nuisance calls.

'Alice, this is a surprise.'

'It shouldn't be. I left two messages, but you never got back to me.'

'I do have a life, you know. Things have been busy.'

'I know, Mum. I'm just checking how you are.'

'Fine, darling, absolutely fine. Why wouldn't I be?' The quake in her voice was still there, pulsing behind her rage.

'I'd like to come with you to your hospital appointment.'

'Don't worry about it, Alice. You've got your own life to lead.'

'Then let me drive you to the airport instead.'

'Don't be ridiculous. There's no need.' Her tone was cooler than antifreeze.

'I want to, Mum. Text me the date and I'll pick you up.'

My mother gave no indication that she planned to accept my offer, changing the subject abruptly to a concert she'd heard at Blackheath Halls.

'Fauré's *Requiem*. It was extraordinary, I cried from start to finish.'

Despite my mother's pathological reluctance to reveal her emotions, she could weep like Niagara Falls to a stirring piece of music, and it irritated me that the older I grew, the more her traits

135

became my own. If she was unwell, no one would ever know. She'd dealt with enough pain already – marriage to a violent alcoholic, then Will's illness. Independence had been her best coping mechanism; she'd pulled up the drawbridge so nothing could hurt her again. I pictured her standing on the deck of a huge ship, surrounded by families and couples, completely alone.

Lola insisted on dragging me to the shops that morning. The first thing I saw when we emerged from the Tube at Oxford Circus was a massive billboard, announcing that it was 28 December, the first day of the sales. A jolt of frustration passed through me – even though Burns had been chasing every lead, Ella Williams was still missing, and another girl could be gone by the end of the day. Lola was too focused on searching for maternity clothes to notice my state of mind. It felt bizarre to watch her selecting leggings with elasticated waistbands while she was still so willowy. The idea of her pushing a pram hadn't registered yet. Lola had always been joyfully irresponsible, but now she was trying on tops designed to accommodate her growing belly. I watched her admiring herself in a blue dress, patting her tiny bump, as if she was longing for it to grow. She grinned at me in the mirror.

'It'll be fine, Al. Trust me.'

'Sorry, I'm miles away.'

'Thinking about the wolfish new boyfriend?'

'Wolfish?'

'God, yes. He looks like he can't decide whether to ravish you or eat you alive.'

'Just as well it's going nowhere.'

Lola giggled. 'Pity. He's sexy as hell, isn't he?'

By one o'clock I was sick of queues and crowded dressing rooms. We ate a stylish but overpriced lunch at an Italian café on Chandos Street, then I left her to gloat over her bargains.

★ ★ ★

A crowd of journalists was camped outside the police station when I reached Pancras Way. Their faces were gloomier than the weather, as though waiting for a scoop was the toughest job in the world. There was no sign of Burns when I reached his office. Tania was gathering folders from his desk, black hair shimmering like it had been airbrushed. She gave me a nod of greeting then paused on her way out, clutching a stack of files. Her stare was sharp enough to spot a lie from a hundred miles.

'Can I ask you something?' she said.

'Of course.'

'What's your opinion of Alan Nash?'

I tried to gather my thoughts. 'He's been top dog for too long. He's still got a brilliant mind, but his approach is old-fashioned and he makes mistakes. Not that he'd ever admit it.'

'It's not just me then.' Her guard slipped for a nanosecond. 'I've never felt more patronised in my whole life.'

The idea of Nash putting her down surprised me; Tania looked capable of felling him with a single well-aimed punch. I felt an unexpected flicker of liking for her.

'Do you need a hand with those?' I nodded at the folders she was carrying.

'Thanks, I'm not going far. My room's across the way.'

Tania's office didn't match her polished image. A dozen plastic boxes were stacked against the wall, her desk littered with discarded papers. A look of embarrassment appeared on her face.

'There's been no time to unpack. The investigation kicked off the day after I arrived.'

I noticed a picture of a smiling dark-haired girl propped beside her phone. 'She's a beauty,' I commented.

For once Tania's face relaxed. 'My daughter, Sinéad. She's a nightmare most of the time – eleven going on twenty-one.'

I realised that having a daughter exactly the same age as the victims must be making the case even harder for her. Tania looked as though she was about to confide something, but the moment passed, leaving me with a sense of confusion. Until now she'd been easy to dislike – Burns's glossy, hard-as-nails new girlfriend – but now she'd revealed her human side. And she had far more in common with him than I did. They were both single parents, holding down the toughest jobs imaginable. It crossed my mind that maybe I should be grown-up about it and try to be happy for them.

Burns was back in his room when I arrived, his arms folded, triumph all over his face.

'What's happened?' I asked.

'We've arrested Roy Layton.'

'I thought he wasn't a suspect any more.'

'He wasn't, until the lab found Ella Williams's hair on a blanket in his van. I'm interviewing him now, you can do the assessment.'

'That's Alan's territory, Don. He wants to observe every major interview, remember?'

Burns shook his head. 'He's briefing the commissioner. I can't wait for him.'

'On your head be it,' I muttered.

We stopped in the incident room so I could collect an assessment form from Nash's table. It interested me that he'd set up his stall in the centre of the room, as if he was the lynchpin of the operation, but there was no time to admire his empire. Burns was already racing down the corridor.

We waited for Layton to be brought from the holding cells. The interview room seemed to be doubling as a store cupboard; a table in the corner was loaded with objects, hidden under a dustsheet. Burns's tension was beginning to show, his wide shoulders growing more hunched by the minute.

'At least no one's reported another abduction,' he said.

The clock on the wall showed that it was only five o'clock. If Kinsella was telling the truth, the killer had seven more hours to snatch his next victim. I kept my thoughts to myself, rather than adding to Burns's stress.

When the door swung open, a young officer led Roy Layton into the room. The caretaker looked more unkempt than ever, and he ticked all the tabloids' boxes for the textbook paedophile. Dark stains were splashed across his worn-out jacket, his ruff of hair projecting from his skull at right angles. Even his solicitor was keeping her distance. The well-dressed middle-aged woman had positioned her chair several feet away, as though poor grooming might be infectious. I watched Layton's reaction when the interview started. His good eye stared ahead, while the other spun in chaotic circles. He went on the offensive before Burns could begin, pointing an accusatory finger at him.

'You lot have made my life hell. I've had every kind of abuse since you took me in – hate mail and phone calls, dog shit through the letterbox.' Layton's hands twitched convulsively in his lap, and for the first time I could imagine his anger translating into violence.

Burns's face was impassive. 'Remind me how you spent the evening of the fourteenth of December please, Mr Layton.'

'Watching TV, like I said. I never went out.'

'Except your van was caught on film, heading down Sternfield Road.'

The caretaker blinked rapidly. 'I probably went out for petrol.'

'You said you stayed in, now I hear you went for a spin. Which one is it?'

'What are you accusing me of?' Layton's mouth gagged open.

'You were the last person to see Ella Williams, the day she was taken. What do you think I'm accusing you of?'

'I never touched her.'

'So why have I got forensic evidence that she was in the back of your van?'

Layton's mouth flapped open. 'I told you, the kids play there sometimes. They wanted to make a den, so I let them go in one playtime, a few weeks ago.'

The solicitor leant across to her client. 'Don't reply, Mr Layton. Say "no comment", if you prefer. Remember, there's no legally confirmed evidence against you.'

Burns ignored her pointedly. 'You were close to Louis Kinsella when he ran St Augustine's, weren't you, Roy?'

'He was my boss, that's all.'

'The kind of boss you have dinner with every week.'

'I couldn't exactly say no, could I? I still don't get why I'm here.'

'I'll show you.' Burns pulled back the dustsheet from the table, revealing a yellowing IBM computer. 'You recognise this, don't you? You let us remove it from your loft.'

The caretaker's gaze dropped swiftly to the floor. 'The school was chucking it out, I haven't used it in years.'

'I'm not surprised. It's a 1995 model, a museum piece these days. But the school's records match the serial number with Kinsella's name. The boss gave you this, didn't he?'

'Like I said, it was being chucked out.' The muscles in Layton's face tightened, lips pressed to a thin line.

'You did a lousy job of deleting the pictures, Roy. I bet he took them himself then scanned them onto the hard drive. Pretty inventive – he had his own gallery of violent child porn, way before the internet arrived. Kinsella showed you every picture, didn't he? You'd better tell me about your friendship with him.' Burns leant across the table like a drunk goading a bartender.

140

'You're threatening my client,' the solicitor snapped.

'That was a request, not a threat.'

Layton looked panicked. 'Kinsella sent me on a training course; he reckoned I should become a teacher. That's when it started.'

'What did you talk about?' Burns asked.

'I just listened most of the time. He was the smartest person I'd met – it was like he was educating me.'

The solicitor opened her mouth to speak, but a fierce look from Burns silenced her.

'You're saying he brainwashed you?'

'It wasn't like that. You're twisting my words.'

'Tell me what Kinsella said.'

'Normal stuff at first, about his childhood, how he started teaching and so on. Then it changed. I dreaded going there, but I couldn't say no. He showed me these pictures of kids with black marks where their eyes should have been. He'd crossed them out with a pen. He said that young girls can wrap you round their little fingers. They're more sexual than women. It's in their eyes when they flirt with you. He thought they deserved to suffer.' Layton came to a halt, like he'd suddenly run out of steam.

'Did he ask you to carry on if he ever got caught?'

'He mentioned something, but I refused, point-blank.'

'Is that right?'

'My brain doesn't work like that. I always said no.'

'Too much of a hero to get involved, were you?'

'I stored his computer as a favour, that's all. I'd never hurt anyone.'

Burns studied his notes. 'But we already know you've got a bad memory. Last time you said you couldn't remember what you were up to the nights Kylie Walsh and Emma Lawrence were abducted. Maybe your memory's let you down again; you can't remember putting Ella in the back of your van.'

'You're placing my client under unreasonable pressure,' Layton's solicitor snapped.

'All right,' Burns said, sighing loudly. 'We'll talk again later, Roy.'

The caretaker looked exhausted as he was led away, eyes wet with tears, which wasn't surprising. No matter what he'd done, his boss's secrets had been lodged in his head for twenty years.

'Self-pitying toe-rag. He wants sympathy for being Kinsella's little friend.' Burns's eyes darkened. 'I can't believe he's acting the victim.'

A muscle was working overtime in his jaw and I knew better than to advise him to calm down. If Layton was involved, Kinsella was to blame. The caretaker was another of his victims, dragged along in the wake of a stronger personality. Without Kinsella's influence, he would never have found the confidence to abduct a child.

'What do you think of him?' Burns asked.

'He's showing the typical signs a violent personality manifests when it's cornered: evasiveness, accusation, strident denial. But it's odd that he's got no history of child abuse. Most violent paedophiles start grooming kids in their teens. If it's him, he's either concealed his abuse so far, or he's a long way from the stereotype. Isolation would make him vulnerable to Kinsella's brainwashing. If his boss was his only social contact, every message would carry extra value.'

'He's staying here till after Kinsella's deadline. Hancock's lot are going over his house again with a toothcomb. We're checking everywhere he's been for forensic evidence. There's every chance he's got Ella in a lock-up somewhere, with a freezer in the corner.' Burns's state of mind seemed to have improved. The thought of tearing Layton's home apart brick by brick had restored his inner calm.

'How are you getting on with checking the Northwood staff for connections with Kinsella?' I asked.

'No overlaps so far. We're checking people from his church too.'

Tania strode into the room and asked for Burns's help, and he followed her without a backward look. I managed to ignore the pang of jealousy that threatened to knock me sideways and stayed focused on the job in hand.

I went to Burns's room to complete my assessment report after the interview. It took over an hour, because each sentence had to hold water in court if Layton was prosecuted. I had to decide whether or not he was capable of killing the girls, and it took me a long time to weigh the evidence. In psychological terms, his loneliness made him the ideal target for Kinsella's recruitment campaign. His social confidence had crumbled as soon as he started to justify his past, and his body language had been inconsistent too. Plenty of indicators suggested that he was either in a state of heightened anxiety, or he'd lied when he protested his innocence. In my final statement I concluded that he was a credible suspect.

Snow was still falling outside Burns's window. The cars parked on the street looked like they'd been sprayed with shaving foam, six inches of perfect whiteness balanced on every roof. When the door clicked open, I thought Burns had returned to collect my report, but Alan Nash stood there, glowering at me.

'Lucky someone's got time to daydream,' he sneered.

'I've been working for hours, Alan.'

I could judge his anger from the depth of his frown. 'Burns tells me you witnessed an interview.'

'He instructed me, I had no choice.'

'Why didn't you ask my permission first? I told you I would assess the suspects. You're jeopardising this investigation.'

'I followed procedure to the letter.' I thrust the report at him. 'If you're not happy, ask any question you like.'

Nash's small eyes were glazed with fury. Maybe I was the first person to face him down. 'This is gross unprofessionalism, Alice. What's wrong? Can't you cope with playing second fiddle?'

'Burns is the investigating officer. I take my instructions from him.'

'We'll see about that.'

The door closed with a resounding slam, and I knew that Nash would report my insubordination to his seniors immediately. His anger must concern his book deal – he could no longer claim sole knowledge of the investigation. If Layton did turn out to be the killer, he'd missed his big opportunity. It occurred to me that it might be safer to defer to his seniority, but I've always hated servitude. Hopefully he wouldn't get me removed from the case, because I was fully committed. I knew that Ella Williams might be past saving, but that didn't stop her appearing in front of me whenever I closed my eyes.

21

Ella's asleep when he comes back, her mouth parched with thirst. She's jolted out of her dream by the man's arms scooping her from the mattress. His face is so close she can see his eyes glistening.

'We're going for a ride,' the man hisses. 'Now keep your mouth shut.'

He sounds angrier than before, so she stays silent as he stumbles through the snow, the night air chilling her to the bone. He wrenches the back door of the van open and pushes her inside.

'I'm warning you, don't try anything stupid,' he snaps.

The man's different tonight. Words spill from his mouth like water gushing, and the door swings shut before Ella can reply. Then the van bumps across the rutted ground. She peers out of the window at rows of offices, every tree and post-box blanched by snow. Her jaw aches as she yawns, almost too tired to keep her eyes open, but it's important to stay awake. Maybe he's taking her home. She can picture Suzanne's face when the door flies open, and the thought makes her heart squirm inside her chest.

The van's travelling too fast, wheels skidding on every corner. It passes a parade of shops and an old man limping towards a bus shelter. His eyes stay glued to the pavement even though she waves frantically; he's too busy trying not to fall. The van is making its way along back streets, past ranks of unlit windows.

Ella's hands press hard against the glass. Surely someone will see her? But people are in bed, comfortable and warm, only a few metres away.

The van pulls up behind the same row of houses where the man parked before. Ella watches him pick his way down a narrow alley. He climbs the steps to the back door of one of the houses, then levers a window open and slips inside. The buildings are so near and yet so far. If she could open the door, it would take moments to hide in one of the gardens. Frustration makes her cover her face with the palms of her hands, trying hard not to cry.

When her eyes open again, the man's returning, carrying something in his arms, and when the door opens she takes her chance. Ella darts past him, screaming at the top of her voice. A light flicks on in the nearest house, but her foot catches on a tree root, sending her sprawling on the frozen ground. The man hovers over her, fist raised. The look on his face is so angry that her scream hardens into silence. He shoves her back into the van. But this time he doesn't care about the damage, releasing a punch that makes her ribs burn.

'Ungrateful little bitch.' His voice is hoarse with anger.

He throws the sack onto the metal floor, then the door slams again. Every breath hurts so much, Ella doesn't care what's inside, until the hessian starts to twitch. She can hear an odd mewing sound, and when she pulls back the fabric, a child stares at her, too terrified to scream. Her face is dark-skinned and delicate. She looks about five or six years old, and for a few seconds the pain in Ella's chest disappears.

'It's okay,' she whispers. 'I'll look after you.'

22

Lola's clock told me that it was two a.m. when my phone rang. I forced myself awake. Burns's Anglo-Scottish voice was mumbling too quietly for me to hear.

'Another one's been taken, hasn't she?' I asked.

'I'm going there now, I can pick you up.'

I gave him Lola's address and rushed to get dressed. The streets outside looked so clean and blameless, it was hard to believe that something evil had happened just a few miles away. Burns's car skidded as he pulled up, and he was too busy dealing with the road conditions to make conversation, but I gathered details from the radio blaring on his dashboard. The girl had been abducted from Kentish Town and dozens of officers were searching for an unmarked van.

The first person I saw when we reached the crime scene was an Indian woman standing motionless on the snow, so unnaturally still that she looked like a statue. She was wearing a thin cotton tunic, nothing protecting her feet except a pair of bedroom slippers. Pete Hancock's team was busy rushing in and out of her flat and she seemed to have been forgotten. I stood beside her, but she took a long time to notice me.

'I'm not going indoors.' Her voice was quiet but determined. 'I'll wait for her out here.'

'Can you tell me what happened?'

The woman turned to face me, blank-eyed as a sleepwalker, her words spilling out on a wave of panic. 'Something woke me around midnight, a noise from the street, but I went back to sleep. Amita's bed was empty when I woke again.'

'What's your name?' I asked.

'Usha.'

'And Amita's your daughter?'

She nodded. 'I adopted her two years ago.'

'Does she have contact with her birth parents?'

'They gave her up because of her diabetes,' Usha said, shivering. 'They couldn't afford medication. That's why I brought her back with me from India.'

'Why don't we go inside?'

'I told you, I'm not moving till she comes home.'

I asked one of the SOCOs for a blanket and she didn't even flinch when I draped it round her shoulders. She was too busy staring at the road.

When I looked back at the house, Burns was standing face to face with Tania, oblivious to everyone around them. She was thin as a mannequin in her expensive coat, and she seemed to be giving him a piece of her mind. I focused on Usha, still waiting beside me, refusing to move. The family liaison officer would need strong powers of persuasion to coax the poor woman back into the warm.

From a distance the house looked as though it had been refurbished recently; a tall Victorian terrace, windows and doors glossy with fresh paint. In this neighbourhood a flat in such a smart building would fetch half a million. I headed for the steps, hoping for a glimpse of the girl's bedroom. Two SOCOs were dusting a ground-floor window, which hung wide open, pale curtains flapping in the breeze. Tania drew herself up to her full height and blocked the doorway.

'There's nothing to see, Alice. You can stay outside.'

Her expression hovered somewhere between distress and anger. She barged past before I could reply, so I peered through the window into the child's bedroom. It was the picture of innocence. Daisies had been stencilled on the pale pink walls, a family of rag dolls clustered at the foot of the girl's bed. Her duvet had been flung back, as though she'd jumped out of bed in a hurry, keen to start the day. The only sign of an intruder was the splintered wood where he'd jemmied the window.

Burns reappeared, with his phone clamped to his ear. He didn't bother to look at me when he finally spoke. 'I'm going to the station. The press are waiting for me.'

I didn't envy him as I climbed into the passenger seat. The papers were already in a feeding frenzy. Their view seemed to be that losing one child was a misfortune, but more was a travesty. Now that a fifth girl was missing, they would be baying for a scapegoat. Their flashbulbs would catch every twitch of Burns's discomfort when he made the announcement. I caught sight of Usha as his car pulled away, still rooted to the spot, gazing blankly at the road.

'Tania's in a hell of a state,' he said. 'There's no point talking to her when she's like that.'

I got the sense that he was apologising on his girlfriend's behalf, and I didn't bother to reply. The only thing that mattered was tracking down the child. After a few minutes I changed the subject.

'You're still holding Layton, aren't you?'

Burns's jaw tightened as he nodded. 'For all we know there are two maniacs out there, stealing little girls.'

'But the number of child abductions by strangers in the UK is fewer than ten a year. It's more likely that Kinsella's telling the truth. He found a partner in crime two decades ago and pre-planned the whole thing.'

'If it's the same killer, he met his deadline with a few seconds to spare. Amita was taken just before midnight.'

I met his eyes. 'Layton told us Kinsella tried to brainwash him, but we don't know how many more people he worked on. Prisoners he met, acquaintances, relatives.'

'His family have all disowned him, except his wife,' Burns said.

'They would say that, wouldn't they? Specially if they're still following his instructions.'

'Is brainwashing people really that simple?'

'It's easier than you'd imagine. Think about how cults operate. The leader has to be a charismatic and brilliant communicator like Kinsella. Then all it takes is time and conviction. Once your followers are loyal, you just keep ramming your messages home. A weak personality can be persuaded to do anything.'

Burns was too preoccupied to reply. A crowd of photographers pressed forwards as we reached the police station, and he positioned himself by the doors, flanked by two press officers. There was complete silence when he began to speak, apart from a stutter of apertures.

'A five-year-old girl, Amita Dhaliwal, was reported missing from her home in north London at three a.m. this morning. We need to find her urgently. It's possible that she's being held by the same person who abducted Ella Williams. We want to hear from anyone who saw an unlicensed white van in the Caledonian Road area, in the early hours of this morning. Any information you give could help us find Amita.'

A few journalists called out to him, but Burns held up his hand. 'There'll be another briefing later today.'

The crowd gave a collective groan. My old nemesis, Dean Simons, was loitering at the back, the gutter press's worst offender. But the injunctions I'd taken out must have worked their magic, because he kept his distance as I headed inside.

The staff in the incident room looked shell-shocked. A row

of expressionless faces were manning the phones, a few more tapping information into computers, the rest huddled in groups, waiting for instructions. News of the girl's abduction seemed to be the last straw, while the investigation staggered from bad to worse. An image of Amita Dhaliwal had already been pasted to the wall. It was a passport photo that had been enlarged to poster size, flashlight bleaching her skin to a washed-out grey, and it was easy to see how young she was, her cheeks plump with puppy fat. She was giving the camera a trusting smile.

I was still studying the girl's face when Alan Nash swept into the incident room, and rushed past without acknowledging me. I focused on my notes for the team meeting. The girls' home lives had begun to interest me – none of them was being raised in a conventional nuclear family. Maybe the killer had planned their abductions systematically, choosing which victims to target. I felt certain that he was following Louis Kinsella's instructions to the letter, terrified of upsetting the master.

The briefing started as soon as Pete Hancock returned from the crime scene. He looked as taciturn as ever, taking his place in the front row without greeting anyone. Tania stood beside Burns with a pained expression on her face, as though she was desperate to go home. An audience of at least forty was packed into the incident room when the briefing started, and Burns's Scottish accent had broadened by a few degrees. His expression suggested that his smile had deserted him permanently.

'Amita Dhaliwal was taken from her bed in the middle of last night. She's small for her age, and in poor health. The adoptive mother, Usha, is an accountant, raising the girl on her own. She says Amita's diabetic. Without medication, she'll slip into a coma inside forty-eight hours.'

The room fell silent. It didn't take genius to guess that

everyone was imagining what the mother was going through. Soon Burns was issuing orders for house-to-house, checking CCTV cameras, and discovering whether there had been previous attempts to break in to the flat. Once duties were assigned to each team, he called for everyone's attention again.

'Louis Kinsella warned us this abduction would happen. He predicted the date, and he said that the location would be further north than the others. Tomorrow a team of you are going to Northwood. The directors have given us permission to set up a mobile incident room there, so we can find out what else he knows.'

Alan Nash walked slowly to the front of the crowd, savouring the attention, and I watched in fascination. Charismatics often commit unspeakable actions, yet they can still light up a room. He made a steadying gesture with his hand and everyone fell silent.

'Kinsella holds the key to these crimes, but so far we've failed to interview him correctly, and some of you have voiced your concerns. I can reassure you that from now on, I'll be leading the psychological work at Northwood.' Nash's eyes were black and glistening, willing me to challenge him. 'I promise to work round the clock to discover what he knows.'

At first I was too shocked to react, but then it sank in. Nash had gone out of his way to humiliate me. He was treating me like an incompetent novice, not a consultant psychologist who'd been practising for years. I felt like walking out immediately, but it wasn't an option. I'd given Suzanne Williams my word that I'd find her sister, and I couldn't let her down. I stared at Burns but failed to catch his eye. Maybe he agreed that I'd mishandled Kinsella and delayed the investigation. I sat there in silence, willing myself to keep calm.

23

The girl keeps screaming for her mother. Nothing seems to comfort her, and her face and hair are soaked with tears, fists flying in Ella's direction, as though she's to blame. All Ella can do is wait for the girl to finish yelling.

'It's okay,' she murmurs. 'We'll get out of here, I promise.'

At last the girl falls silent and sits down abruptly. Her head lolls forward, revealing her face for the first time. She's as small as the girls in kindergarten, wearing red pyjamas covered in teddy bears, the sleeves edged with braid. The girl yawns widely, tears still seeping from her eyes.

'What are you called?' she asks quietly. The girl meets her eye for the first time, but doesn't say a word. 'My name's Ella.'

'Amita,' the girl whispers. 'Please, let me go home. I want my mum.'

'He'll let us out soon, Amita. I know he will.' Ella covers the girl's bare foot with her hand. Her skin's so cold, it's like picking stones from a winter beach. 'Come here,' she says, holding out her arms.

Amita doesn't move at first, but slowly she crawls over and rests her head on Ella's shoulder. Her shivering is so intense that Ella wishes she had more to give than her warmth. The girl smells of home — the scent of bath-times, soap and clean clothes. After a few minutes she falls asleep, her head a heavy weight against Ella's chest, but she doesn't move her, hoping that rest will calm her down.

The man comes back before dawn, his boots making a shushing sound on the wet snow. Ella tightens her grip round Amita's shoulder and she stirs in her sleep. Lamplight wakes her as it spills into the van, and her scream is deafening. The man's face is furious.

'Can't you shut her up?'

'I'm trying.' Ella does her best to smile. 'I'm sorry about before.'

The man stares straight through her, then throws a parcel into the van.

'Get her into this,' he snaps. 'I'll sort you out later.'

Ella reaches into the plastic bag and pulls out a piece of material. This time the white dress is tiny, as though it had been made for a doll. The man's footsteps stamp away along the concrete path, and the girl's screams soften into dull moans as Ella whispers to her.

'Put this on, Amita. Then we can be twins, can't we?'

24

The first thing I saw at the Laurels next morning was Usha Dhaliwal's face. The eight a.m. news was blaring into the empty day room, and I paused to watch the bulletin. Shock had leached the colour from Usha's skin, and the coat shrouding her shoulders looked far too big. One of the uniforms must have given her his jacket, then positioned her in front of the camera without helping her prepare. Her face contorted as she gazed at the camera, and the pitch of her voice was higher than before, rising with despair.

'You can't do this. Give her back, whoever you are. You have to understand that my daughter's ill. She needs insulin. Let her go, please. She needs medical care.'

Her eyes screwed shut and someone put an arm around her, but the cameras carried on rolling as she wept. I jabbed the power button on the TV, and for once the day room fell silent. All of the victims' families must be gripped by exactly the same sense of horror, but the case was making no progress, and I was partly to blame.

Burns was the last person I wanted to see when I got to my office. It looked like someone had parked an Easter Island statue in the middle of the corridor, huge and immovable. The ability to stay still was one of his best professional skills. I'd seen him play dead during interviews, so completely immobile that it looked as if he was starting to petrify. Faced with so much blank passivity, his suspects had no choice but to talk.

'I owe you an apology,' he said quietly. Burns didn't seem to notice how minute the room was. There was less than a foot of clear air between us. I could have reached across and slapped his face with no effort at all.

'You let him walk all over me, Don. Nash hasn't lifted a finger since the investigation started. He's just swanning about, waiting to collect the glory. You can apologise till you're blue in the face, it won't change a thing.'

He looked embarrassed. 'Nash has got serious connections, Alice.'

'So he's a mason and he hangs out with the big boys. Why should I care?'

'We need to back down gracefully.'

I stared at him open-mouthed. Burns's interpretation of a graceful climb-down was my idea of a cowardly retreat, but there was no point in arguing, if the deal was done. 'What have you agreed?'

'I still want you involved,' he said quickly. 'The incident room's being set up in the Campbell Building, so we can be near Kinsella. Nash is seeing him today. I'd like you to observe the interview.'

'Kinsella will only talk to me.'

'He's sent a note to Dr Gorski, saying he wants to see Nash.'

'That's just a game. He hasn't forgiven Nash for writing *The Kill Principle* without his permission.' I felt like refusing to help. Without me to rely on, Nash would be exposed as hopelessly out of date. But it wasn't a competition – all that mattered was bringing the two girls home alive. 'All right, Don. I'm not thrilled, but I'll play the game. Let me know when you need me.'

He left straight away, clearly amazed to avoid another row, and when I looked out of the window Alan Nash was arriving with his entourage. Tania was striding across the ice in her spiked heels, clutching a box of papers. Three uniforms were scanning the rooftops, as if they were checking for snipers. As they reached the entrance to the Laurels, Gorski appeared, and I raced out of the office, fascinated to see the two super-egos collide.

The two men were so busy squaring up to each other that they didn't notice me loitering in the corridor. Gorski had a six-inch height advantage, and he looked as hostile as ever. Clearly it wasn't just me he objected to – even eminent professors received the same cold shoulder.

'I hope you'll follow safety protocols while you're in my department, Professor. You know the violence Kinsella is capable of.'

He gave a curt nod. 'It's good of you to brave the cold to welcome me, Dr Gorski.'

The professor swept past like he had no time to waste. His victorious smile indicated that he'd toppled an emperor from his throne, and Gorski muttered a string of Polish expletives. If we'd been on better terms I'd have bought him a coffee as a consolation prize. His irritation was still visible when he turned to me.

'I believe you're observing my parole board, Dr Quentin.'

'Thanks, I'd like to see your release procedures in action.'

'Follow me then. We're about to start.'

Gorski was silent as we walked to the boardroom. As usual I had to trot to keep up with his hectic pace, and it was obvious he was in no mood to talk. The other members of the board had already gathered in the meeting room. Judith smiled at me across a sea of papers, and I recognised two consultant psychiatrists from the Maudsley, and the head of clinical psychology from Rampton. Two parole requests were being considered at the meeting. One inmate was asking for a prison transfer, and the second was hoping for unconditional release.

When the first inmate arrived, I could tell his chances were slim. He'd been sentenced for assault eight years before, after knifing a man outside a nightclub in Sunderland, and he'd never expressed remorse. His schizophrenia had been diagnosed by a prison psychiatrist. He was fidgeting in his chair, scratching his face with talon-like fingernails. His hair was so lank, it couldn't have been washed for weeks.

'Tell us why you should return to prison, Neil,' Gorski asked.

'I don't belong here,' he snapped. 'My daughter shouldn't have to visit her dad in a nuthouse. Plenty of blokes in prison have done worse than me.'

'There's a note on your file, saying you've been threatening your guards. Can you tell us about that?'

The man's fists clenched in his lap. 'They've got it in for me, the whole lot of them.'

It took less than five minutes for the board to agree unanimously to reject his parole application. It would be considered again a year later, if he agreed to attend counselling sessions, and took a different course of anti-psychotics.

The next case was more complex. The man's name was Jamie, and he looked nervous when he arrived, eyes darting round the room, looking for sympathy. He'd been at the Laurels for five years, following two violent rapes. According to his notes he'd made significant progress. He was in therapy with Judith and seemed to be serious about tackling his issues; he had also elected to take medication to suppress his sex drive. The man answered each question calmly and thoughtfully.

'Do you still have violent sexual fantasies?' one of the consultants asked.

'Not for a year or more. I've learned to stop the thoughts as soon as they arrive,' he replied.

Judith tried to persuade the board that he was contrite and safe for release, but his application was rejected on the grounds that his violence could return if he was left unsupervised.

I flicked through my papers as they closed the meeting. Only one parole application from the Laurels had been granted in the last two years: an inmate had been released into the care of Brixton Prison to complete his life sentence. The company of crooks must have seemed preferable to the lunatic howls on the sixth floor, even though his living conditions would be far worse.

Judith approached me when the room emptied. She was wearing her usual array of jewellery, wrists burdened by bracelets that could double as handcuffs. I remembered how she'd looked at Chris Steadman's party, wrapped around Garfield Ellis like clinging ivy.

'Do you fancy a drink tonight?' she asked.

'God, yes. I could use one right now.'

We agreed to meet at the Rookery later and I felt glad to have bumped into her for two reasons. I was curious about her secret relationship, and the pub's noise would help me forget about Alan Nash.

A message had arrived from Burns when I got back to my office, inviting me to observe Kinsella's interview. I gritted my teeth as I put on my coat, knowing that Nash would be overjoyed that I'd been relegated to the sidelines. The air was so cold that it felt like stepping into a giant freezer, and I crossed the quadrangle at my quickest pace. The Met had been given a palatial interview suite on the Campbell Building's second floor. It had its own observation room, normally used by psychology trainees watching their supervisors carrying out assessments. The professor's voice greeted me when I arrived, ringing with false goodwill.

'No hard feelings, I hope, Alice?'

I took care not to blink. 'None at all, Alan.'

'Good.' His bouffant hair quivered when he nodded. 'We all want the same thing, don't we? And Kinsella and I are old acquaintances.'

I tried not to ill-wish him as he walked into the interview suite. When I gazed through the door, every surface seemed to be fashioned from glass, and two chairs faced each other, either side of a thick transparent screen. Clearly Nash wanted Kinsella's secrets, but had no intention of breathing the same air.

Burns was waiting in the observation room and I sat down beside him, forcing myself to concentrate on the task in hand.

'There's someone you should talk to,' I said. 'Brian Knowles has been a volunteer at the Foundling Museum for decades. He could tell you who Kinsella was close to when he was there.'

A light flashed on behind Burns's eyes as he scribbled the name in his notebook, then I turned away to look through the observation window. Nash's back was turned to us, and he seemed to be completing elaborate preparation rituals. He kept squaring his shoulders, and picking invisible threads from his jacket. When Burns's phone rang a second later, he listened to the message then groaned loudly.

'Kinsella says he's ill. He won't leave his cell.'

My panic rose even higher. Nothing would give the headmaster more pleasure than seizing power: gloating over the fact that the police were under his control, while the girls' suffering increased every day. If she was still alive, Ella must be hypothermic, and Amita was in danger of lapsing into a

160

coma. Only Nash was oblivious to Kinsella's act of manipulation. The professor was still sitting in his glass box, waiting for his nemesis, sublimely confident that he would be the hero of the hour.

25

Judith seemed gripped by anxiety when we met at the Rookery that evening. She took a deep breath, as if she was planning to dive under water for a long time.

'No one else saw me with Garfield, did they?'

'I don't think so.'

'Thank God for that. It's such a mess, Alice. Not long ago I was married and everything was normal.'

'But something happened?'

'My husband said I was a workaholic, but that was just an excuse. He'd already met someone.'

'How long have you and Garfield been seeing each other?'

'Two years. He's so paranoid about his wife finding out, I can't even phone him. Sometimes I think he'll crack under the strain – he's terrified of losing his kids.'

'But you're in love with him?' Judith didn't need to reply, her eyes glistening. 'I'm sorry,' I murmured. 'It sounds painful.'

Being a psychologist had stopped me making judgements about other people's love lives. I'd watched my clients suffer every emotional extreme for the sake of romance, from incest and desertion, to neglect and suicide. By comparison, Judith's fling with Garfield was a drop in the ocean.

'When the kids are older, he says we can live together,' she whispered.

Judith was dry-eyed and calm again, and I wondered if she genuinely believed his promises. Apparently Garfield's wife was a churchgoer with strong views on separation. She believed that people who deserted their children should be denied access, and the idea of losing his three daughters was more than he could bear.

'Everyone knows everyone at work,' Judith said. 'If word got out, she'd know in minutes. The place is full of Chinese whispers.'

I wondered if the stress of Judith's job had triggered the affair. Some people might argue that Kinsella had brought them together; she and Garfield had spent more time alone with him than anyone else at Northwood. When I looked around the pub, the place was heaving, the usual crowd of bedlam refuseniks milling by the bar, and it seemed like a good time to change the subject.

'Do you know Pru Fielding well?' I asked. The art therapist had stuck in my mind since Chris Steadman's party; it's an occupational hazard to worry about people who seem to be in psychological pain.

'Not really, she's a bit of a loner. We went for a drink before Christmas, and she let out a few secrets. I don't think she's ever had a serious relationship. Her crush on Chris seems to have started as soon as she got here.'

'She's liked him for two years?'

'Unrequited, sadly. Pity, isn't it?' Judith glanced at me. 'What have you been up to anyway? I hear the police are talking to Louis again.'

'Except he's not playing ball.'

A frown appeared on Judith's face. 'I'm not surprised – Alan Nash is Louis's worst enemy. When he first arrived, Nash paid regular visits. He promised him a prison transfer, but never followed through. I think he was just collecting details for his book.'

My thoughts slotted into place. The reason Nash wanted to

see Kinsella again was crystal clear. In his sequel to *The Kill Principle*, he could cast himself as the genius of forensic psychology. The only problem was that Kinsella despised him, and had nothing to gain from compliance.

'Did Kinsella make progress during your therapy sessions with him?' I asked.

Judith shook her head. 'He was unreachable. The only reason he came was to gain support for a return to prison, but I refused.'

'You think he'd hurt people there?'

She nodded vigorously. 'Violence and killing are the only things that make him feel alive.'

'But he never spoke about his crimes?'

'I steered him away from it. We focused on his childhood mainly: he was exiled to a boarding school in Kent when he was seven. His parents sent postcards from exotic countries while he got beaten up.'

'It sounds like you pity him.'

'Sympathy and understanding are different, aren't they? There's no justification for what he did, but his childhood gives it a context.' Judith's expression was so sombre, it looked like she'd witnessed every type of human suffering. But after a few seconds her face brightened again. 'Look who's arrived.'

Chris Steadman had walked into the bar, with Tom a few yards behind.

'Are those two close?' I asked.

'God, yes. The lost boys. They're thick as thieves.'

They were queuing shoulder to shoulder for drinks, and Tom was chatting animatedly for once. From a distance the two men looked like brothers. It was only when I studied them more closely that the differences were obvious. Tom was the picture of health, but Chris was skinny rather than slim, his peroxide hair an artificial copy of his friend's.

'An odd couple, aren't they?' Judith commented. 'Chris is happy-go-lucky, but poor Tom's a victim of his past. The only thing they've got in common is their IQ.'

'What do you mean?'

'They're both super-bright. Chris was a star student on his Masters course and Tom won a scholarship to Oxford. Don't be fooled by the physique – the guy's as sharp as they come.' She observed my stunned expression from the corner of her eye. 'Are you still seeing each other?'

'Not any more, relationships aren't my strong point. But how did Tom end up running the gym if he's such an intellectual?'

She gave an enigmatic smile. 'Ask him yourself. I'm not sharing any more secrets tonight.'

Judith carried on drinking whisky long after I switched to mineral water, and we stayed in the pub until closing time. It was clear that her relationship with Garfield gave her more pain than pleasure. At eleven o'clock I was relieved when she called a taxi, instead of trying to drive home. Her words were slurred when she leant down to kiss me goodbye.

'Thanks for listening, Alice. One day I'll return the favour.'

Through the window I watched her totter across the icy pavement to the waiting taxi. I finished my drink and steeled myself to go back into the cold. I was pleased to have avoided an awkward encounter with Tom, even though I couldn't help feeling intrigued by the mysteries that surrounded him. But when I reached the porch, he was standing directly in front of me, putting on his coat, blocking my escape route.

'I'd hate to think you were following me.' A slow grin dawned on his face. He seemed to be waiting for me to collapse into his arms.

'Maybe it's the other way round. You turn up everywhere I go.'

'It's just lucky timing.' His hand settled on my waist. 'Why don't you come back to mine?'

His offer was incredibly tempting. Even if it meant nothing, sleeping with him would wipe my mind clean as a new blackboard.

'I'd better not. Tomorrow's a busy day.'

'Another time then.'

When he kissed me I almost changed my mind. It took the entire walk back to the cottage to steady myself. Affairs seemed to be blossoming in every department at Northwood, people snatching at happiness to neutralise the madness and despair. I made myself concentrate on the patterns my torch made as I trudged down the lane, light bouncing across icy tyre tracks. When I reached the cottage there were new footprints in the snow. Someone had stamped all the way to the front door, then disappeared round the side of the house. I came to a halt, too frightened to move. The prints could have been there since that morning, because there had been no fresh snow all day. My pulse ticked faster at the base of my throat. Maybe Tom had come looking for me earlier that evening. When I got inside I paced from room to room, checking the locks on every window. Paranoid ideas kept intruding into my thoughts. The cause was probably completely innocent, but the idea that my visitor might be hiding somewhere in the dark garden refused to go away.

26

Amita's head rests heavily on Ella's knees. She looks like an angel in her white dress, but she's refusing to surface, even though morning light is flowing through the crack in the door. It shows how pale she is, her brown skin turning grey. The man's scraping around outside, but still she won't open her eyes. She mutters a few words when she hears her name, then sinks back into her dreams. The man's eyes are hidden behind thick sunglasses, and his scowl is frightening.

'What's wrong with her?' He's blocking the sunlight, staring down at the girl.

'She just needs more sleep.' Ella stretches her face into a hopeful smile, but this time it doesn't work.

The man shifts from foot to foot, his eyes burning through the thin cotton of her dress. It's a relief when he returns his attention to Amita. Her eyes are still closed, thin arms covered in goose bumps. The man lifts her hair from her face so he can see her more clearly, then his gaze settles on Ella, his fingers curling into fists.

'Which one do I choose?' He whispers the words to himself and suddenly his movements speed up, like a cartoon on fast-forward. He grabs Ella's wrists, then he's dragging her through the snow.

'Forgive me. I'm sorry.'

He keeps repeating the words under his breath as he strides towards the big house. Ella's hip catches on something sharp, her legs kicking against the cold, but she can't shake free. He doesn't even react when she screams. It's like she's already ceased to exist.

27

Press vans were clustered outside Northwood on New Year's Eve. A gang of photographers surrounded my car as I waited at the barrier, their long lenses making me yearn for tinted windows. Their presence didn't surprise me. One of the tabloids was promising fifty grand to anyone with information about the missing girls, while the rest of the country collapsed into panic. News bulletins kept reporting that parents were becoming paranoid, keeping their daughters locked inside, even though security had failed to help Amita.

The red light was flashing on my phone in the broom cupboard. But before I could check the messages, I noticed an envelope lying on the floor. The copperplate handwriting was instantly recognisable, each letter racing to its destination. Kinsella must have used Garfield as his messenger. I perched on the edge of my desk to read it.

Dear Alice,

I see you sometimes from my window, scurrying like a lost mouse. You'll grow smaller than your namesake if you carry on sipping from the wrong bottle.

I have some new information. The next girl will be delivered tomorrow, and this time, much closer to home. Everything's running smoothly in all bar one respect. But I mustn't grumble. It's an imperfect world, and there's already so much to celebrate.

Would you do me a favour? Tell your Scottish friend that I've changed my mind. You are the one I'll talk to, no one else. Professor Nash can return to his vulgar yellow-brick palace with its dreary, mock-Rococo garden. I look forward to seeing you this morning.

Affectionately,
Louis

I shoved the paper back in its envelope and set off for the Campbell Building without bothering to listen to my messages. The makeshift incident room was a hive of activity, and several dozen officers were busy inside. The note Kinsella had sent me earlier was clipped to an evidence board, beside a map marking the Foundling Hospital, and the sites of the abductions. I noticed Chris running a cable along a wall, hooking up some new computers. He looked more tense than normal, probably because he had enough work to do without the additional responsibility of sorting out the Met's IT.

Burns was working in an anteroom, crouched over a table that looked much too small for him, Alan Nash and Tania standing by the door. The professor recoiled when he saw me, as though he'd swallowed something sour.

'I think you should read this,' I said, dropping Kinsella's letter on the table.

Tania peered over Burns's shoulder as he read it. She looked awkward as she passed it to Nash. Maybe the insult about his home embarrassed her, but he seemed amused.

'My garden was featured in the *Sunday Times* recently. Kinsella's probably seething with jealousy.'

Tania shook her head. 'He predicted that Amita would be taken, and now he says one of the girls will be found tonight. We have to take this seriously, don't we?'

'It's likely she's dead already. We know he kept the first two in the deep freeze until he was ready to let them go,' Nash said.

Burns gave a reluctant nod. 'We've been searching waste ground inside his catchment. A man was seen dropping a cardboard box into Wenlock Basin, near where Kinsella used to live. A dive team are dragging the canal today.'

'You won't find anything. He leaves them where they'll be easy to see,' I said firmly. 'We have to assume they're still alive until he sends the next token to Kinsella.'

Nash looked contemptuous. 'We mustn't pander to his demands. It's best if I conduct the interview, despite what he says. Could you give me a hand, Tania?'

Burns remained hunched at his table after they left. He carried on staring at the letter, chin propped in his hands, mumbling quietly to himself.

'The *Alice in Wonderland* connection isn't surprising.'

'What do you mean?'

'Sorry, I was thinking aloud. I just meant you're blonde and very petite, aren't you? Like the girl in the story.'

I gritted my teeth, and didn't reply. People had been commenting on my size since I was five years old: school nurses advising me to eat more, kids in the playground calling me shrimp. The last thing I needed was Burns telling me I looked like a child.

He gave a sheepish smile, then launched into a description of the team's work since Amita went missing, as if he'd suddenly recalled that I was an adult after all. Usha Dhaliwal's family, friends, and colleagues at her accountancy firm had all been interviewed, and it was clear that the girl's abduction had been meticulously planned. The unmarked white van had only been caught once on CCTV.

'He knows north London inside out. Ether he's a local boy, or he memorised his route through the back streets.'

171

'Have you spoken to Brian Knowles yet?' I asked.

Burns's eyebrows rose. 'I ran his name through the box. The bloke's darker than you thought. He's avoided the sex offenders' register by the skin of his teeth. He was cautioned last year for loitering by a kids' playground. Uniforms have been to his flat twice in the last few days, but he's never there. It looks like he knew Kinsella well; Knowles used to be secretary to the trustees.'

The information took time to register. I had assumed that Brian Knowles was creepy but harmless, devoted to a good cause. His interest in the museum seemed more sinister than I'd realised.

Burns checked his watch. 'Kinsella's being brought over now, and you'll be the one doing the interview, not Nash.'

I waited in the observation room while he delivered the bad news. The professor was already facing the blank wall of glass, the room so brightly lit he seemed to be dissolving into whiteness. I watched the two men communicate but couldn't hear their words. Nash's arms flailed in protest, miming his displeasure. After a few seconds he exited the suite wearing an outraged expression.

In an ideal world I'd have fled the building too, but Kinsella was just arriving. His appearance was as irreproachable as ever, immaculately groomed, his half-moon spectacles poised on the tip of his nose. He still looked uncomfortably like my father. But this time his gaze was less benevolent, so focused it would scorch any surface it touched. It made me grateful for the inch of reinforced glass that protected me.

'Thanks for coming, Mr Kinsella.' The quake in my voice annoyed me – he was bound to capitalise on any sign of weakness.

'You know I enjoy our meetings, Alice. You're a sight for sore eyes.'

'Can you tell me what you miss most from the outside world?'

His eyebrows shot up. 'Everything. The freedom to follow my destiny, art galleries, good French food.'

'But you feel better now someone's finishing what you started?'

His hawkish smile widened. 'Do you really have time for small talk, Alice?'

'If you help us prevent another death, I can arrange a visit to one of those exhibitions you miss so much.'

He looked amused. 'In a charabanc, with five burly guards? Not really my style. But we can trade facts if you like, a truth for a truth.'

'If I can go first.'

'It's my turn – you've already asked a question.' He leant forwards until his forehead almost touched the glass, voice falling to a whisper. 'Who do I remind you of?'

'No one. I've seen so many pictures, in books and on TV, it feels like I know you.'

'You're lying, Alice. Remember those little girls, all alone in the dark.'

'You remind me of my father.' My heart thumped unevenly. 'Now tell me where they're being kept.'

'Near St Augustine's, but he's moving closer all the time. Did you love your dad, Alice?'

'Be more specific please, Mr Kinsella. What part of London are you talking about?'

'Did you love him?'

'Yes.'

'But he frightened you?'

I shook my head. 'Tell me the killer's name.'

'I'd rather hear about your father. He sounds much more intriguing.'

'Tell me his name.'

He gave an exaggerated yawn. 'My original theory may be wrong. It could be one of many. I was evangelical in those days, and they all got the same instructions.' His eyes bored into me. 'Tell me why your father scared you.'

'He was unpredictable, kind then cruel.' I returned his stare. 'Who are your disciples, Mr Kinsella?' He sank back into his chair, a sheen of perspiration covering his face, as though the effort of crawling under my skin had exhausted him. 'I met your friend Brian Knowles at the Foundling Museum. He's very devoted to the place, isn't he?'

Kinsella's eyes glittered. 'Dear old Brian. I wondered how long you'd take to catch up with him. He's a collector, you know. Ask him about it some time, I'm sure he'd love to tell you. But that's enough for today. I hope we'll meet again soon.'

His smile faded to nothing, and his skin grew even whiter. He made an odd gesture, a cross between a genuflection and a bow, before the guards led him away.

Burns looked concerned when I reached the observation room. 'There's more blood in a stone,' he muttered. 'Are you okay?'

'I'll survive.'

'You did well. He's starting to trust you.'

'It's just cat and mouse, nothing tangible.'

My legs were starting to feel weak. I couldn't explain what had upset me most: memories of my father resurfacing, or the way Kinsella had assaulted me with his eyes.

28

Burns must have seen the colour draining from my face because he pulled up a chair. 'Take a seat, Alice.'

'I'm okay, Don. It's not the best way to spend New Year's Eve, but I'll survive.'

He studied my face for a moment. 'Kinsella's mate Brian is at home now. Do you want to assess him for me? We could debrief in the car.'

'Give me a minute to collect my things.' Part of me questioned my sanity as I trotted down the stairs. I'd been working nonstop through the Christmas break, but slowing down wasn't an option until Ella and Amita were found.

I caught sight of Kinsella when I left the Campbell Building. Garfield was taking him back to the Laurels, with two security guards trailing behind. From a distance I could see Kinsella's lips moving rapidly. The two men were deep in conversation, which didn't match his reputation for silence. They were too far away for me to hear, but I made a mental note to ask Garfield what Kinsella had been saying next time we met.

I grabbed my briefcase from the broom cupboard before meeting Burns by the reception block. The sky was still leaden with snow, steam rising from the bonnet of his Audi into the freezing air.

'Where does Knowles live?' I asked.

'Hammersmith. We'll be there in an hour.'

'Go on then, tell me how's it's been going.'

A muscle ticked in his jaw. 'The team's done thousands of hours of overtime – scouring Kinsella's haunts, interviewing staff he worked with, the vicar and choir members, the Foundling Museum's trustees. We've re-interviewed all the relatives and contacts for each victim. It feels like I've spoken to every man, woman and child in north London.'

'What about the prisons where he did time?'

'He spent most of his stretch in solitary confinement, for his own protection. Hundreds of ex-cons have been checked out, with no links so far.'

I stared out of the window at the passing houses, every lawn a pristine expanse of white. 'It's odd that none of the girls come from a conventional family. They were all fostered, adopted, or being cared for by someone other than their biological parents.'

'And you think that's relevant?'

'Maybe he sees them as foundlings. In his eyes they're abandoned children, waiting for mercy, or to be cleansed from the streets.'

'But how would he know that before he takes them?'

'The abductions might not be random. Maybe he's got hold of records from somewhere.'

He looked uncertain. 'School registers, or medical files.'

'That's possible, but the foundling link's too strong to ignore. He's getting a kick out of dressing them up like Victorian orphans. The staging's for him, as well as Kinsella.'

Burns lapsed into silence, as though his mind was refusing to process any more theories. I stayed quiet and focused on the view outside as we headed east into the city.

Brentford Shopping Centre was lit up like a Christmas tree, as though the retailers were determined to milk a profit from the last dregs of festive good cheer. I waited until we reached Chiswick's expensive suburbs before asking another question.

'Do you know much about Brian Knowles?' I asked.

'He's sixty-two, widowed in his late forties, worked as a surveyor till he retired. He's been a volunteer at the Foundling Hospital since Kinsella's days. One of the trustees said they got on well, but no one mentioned it at the trial. He's got a clean record, apart from that caution for loitering by the playground in Richmond Park.'

We were pulling up outside a mansion block in Hammersmith, not far from the theatre where Lola worked. Each of the tall Georgian buildings fronting the river was worth millions, which meant that Brian Knowles must be extremely wealthy. It made me wonder whether his money was begged, borrowed, or stolen.

A squad car was parked on the double yellow line outside a block called Wentworth House. It was smaller than some of the others, but beautifully maintained. I waited in the car while Burns spoke to the two uniforms, then followed him up the stairs. The large building had been subdivided into at least a dozen dwellings. Knowles's flat was on the top floor and the climb explained why he was fit enough to march up the stairs at the museum. Burns was panting when we reached the landing.

'Let's hope it's worth the hike,' he muttered as he pressed the doorbell.

Knowles was still wearing his yachting blazer. It looked like he'd chosen Pierce Brosnan as style guru, his dyed hair carefully combed. When he caught sight of me his carefully prepared smile froze.

'What are you doing here, Alice?'

'I'm helping the investigation into the missing girls, Mr Knowles.'

'So you lied about being a psychologist. I thought you had a genuine interest in the museum, but you were just spying on me.'

I shook my head. 'Not at all. Everything you said was helpful.'

Knowles's expression was grudging as he admitted us to his flat, and it soon became obvious that he had traded space for a glamorous postcode. The place was minute, with a dining table wedged beside the sofa in his living room. But the view gave a touch of grandeur, showing the broad sweep of the river, surging east towards Hammersmith Bridge. Knowles stood by the window, eyeing us with suspicion.

'What do you want exactly? I told the other officers that I don't own a vehicle, and I was visiting a friend in Kensington when that poor child was taken.' Knowles touched the sharp pleat in his trousers, nipping the fabric tightly between his finger and thumb.

'I'd like to know more about your time at the Foundling Museum, Mr Knowles. You described Louis Kinsella as a monster, but he speaks of you as a friend.'

He adjusted his hair nervously. 'I thought he was an ally, that's why I was so disgusted. It's easy to be clever with hind-sight, but at the time he was a pillar of the community, the headmaster of an outstanding school. We shared a passion for the place.'

'He told me you're a collector, Mr Knowles.' I glanced around the room, but all I could see were antique vases, book-shelves stacked with local histories, and two Constable landscapes on the walls. 'Do you mind telling us what you collect?'

'I gather information. I've interviewed dozens of former foundlings; many are in their seventies and eighties. You could call it my life's work.' He pointed at a pile of folders stacked at the end of his table, at least a foot thick.

'Do you mind if I take a look?' I asked.

'Be my guest. I've got nothing to hide.'

Burns carried on talking to Knowles while I flicked through one of the folders, which contained dozens of interview transcripts. Underneath it was a plastic wallet marked 'Newsletter,' with a sheet of photos tucked inside. I did a double take when I saw my own picture, gazing unsmiling at the camera, with my name and occupation written underneath. Knowles had been very industrious, taking snaps of dozens of museum visitors, including schoolchildren, each one carefully labelled. Beneath that lay a copy of the previous month's newsletter from the Foundling Museum, the back page packed with faces that all looked as startled as mine. I returned to the armchair beside Burns.

'You seem fascinated by the orphans, Mr Knowles,' I commented. 'Do you mind me asking why?'

'The museum's our best source of history about their lives.' Knowles's lips parted in a tense smile. 'And I believe in its values. Children should be safeguarded, shouldn't they? Their innocence is sacred.'

'I can see that you hold children in very high regard.'

His face quivered as he spoke. 'That's why it disgusts me that we can't even admire them any more. If you so much as look at a child, they want you behind bars. They don't understand that if you're elderly and alone, it's uplifting to watch children happily playing together.'

Knowles's hands shook with outrage as Burns asked him question after question. He said that he had been travelling to Kensington by Tube at the time of Ella Williams's abduction, returning late that evening. He described himself as a gentleman of leisure, but his flat held little evidence of a man at ease. There was no TV, and the appliances in his kitchenette must have been there since the Eighties, holes worn through the lino by the sink. When we said goodbye, I caught only a fleeting glimpse of his unnaturally white smile before the door closed abruptly. Burns didn't say a word until we got back to the car.

'He's copying Kinsella, but without the bloodshed,' I commented. 'Collecting children's life stories and keeping them for himself. He's just a voyeur; he likes to watch children in the park, take photos of them at the museum. That's how he gets his thrills.'

'I'll check the CCTV at Hammersmith Tube, see if his story stacks up.'

'I'm sure it's not him, Don. Voyeurism's a passive condition normally; it's rare for it to escalate into this kind of violence.'

Burns met my eye. 'He may not be the killer, but you wouldn't want him for a babysitter, would you?'

The drive back took an extra half-hour thanks to a juggernaut jackknifing on the M4. Burns drove in an absorbed silence. I could almost hear his brain chunking through the information like a calculator working at full strength.

'Want to get a meal at the hotel?' he finally asked when we reached Charndale.

'I should probably go home.'

The Met team was staying at a hotel I passed on my way to work. Charndale Manor was a stately home that had fallen on hard times, with huge windows and decaying plasterwork, but I had no intention of spending the last few hours of New Year's Eve playing gooseberry among all that faded grandeur.

'Let's have a drink instead,' he insisted.

Burns pulled up outside the Rookery before I could argue. As usual the bar was packed with all the Northwood regulars, flirting and drowning their sorrows. He left me at a corner table then went outside to answer a call on his mobile, and I couldn't resist sifting through my notes. The more time I spent with Kinsella, the more certain I felt that anyone he'd met was in danger of succumbing to his messages, including Brian Knowles. I'd felt the draw myself. He had the negative magnetism of a whirlpool, pulling people towards him with the sole aim of destroying them.

Burns reappeared as I was poring over the updated HOLMES report he'd given me earlier. He was wearing his off-kilter smile, and I had to remind myself that we were spending time together for business, not pleasure.

'What are you drinking, Alice?'

'Pineapple juice, please.'

He rolled his eyes. 'Very festive.'

I watched him cut a swathe through the crowd, a foot taller and wider than the men around him. He didn't have to wait long to get served; the barmaid ignored the queue and poured his drinks instantly. When I looked up again, I spotted Garfield through the crowd. He was sitting by himself with two empty glasses at his elbow. His body language looked despairing, as though an invisible weight rested on his shoulders. I wondered if constant contact with Kinsella was making him depressed.

I felt a twitch of discomfort as Burns returned with our drinks. Tom had arrived, and he was watching me without a trace of a smile. He stared at Burns, then turned his head away and joined Garfield at his table.

'The connection has to be Northwood,' I said.

'What makes you so sure?'

'There's got to be a link between the Foundling Museum and Northwood. The killer knows all about Kinsella's obsession with the orphans. He understands subtle things about his style too; I'm sure it's a staff member.'

'You seriously think some doctor or nurse is abducting little girls, torturing them, then dumping their bodies in the snow?' He stifled a laugh. 'I thought mental health professionals were vetted before being let loose on patients.'

'And we're trained to resist manipulation, but Kinsella's different. Last year he reduced an experienced therapist to a breakdown. He's an expert, and he's got all the time in the world to indulge his passion for hurting people.'

'But no one spends time alone with him, do they?'

'Only a handful. I can give you a list tomorrow.'

Burns nodded, then gazed at me intently. 'Is there anyone else you think we should look at?'

'His wife still worries me. She wasn't much more than a child when they met, and she still can't acknowledge his crimes. How much do you think she knew at the time?'

'It's hard to tell. Kinsella protected her during his trial; he said he'd never told her a thing.'

'But she could have been his sounding board.' From the corner of my eye I saw Tom shooting me an angry look as he left the bar.

'Who is that bloke?' Burns asked. 'He's been giving you the evil eye all night.'

'A colleague from the Laurels. He runs the gym.'

'Looks like he needs to burn off some stress himself. What's his name?'

'Tom Jensen.'

Burns repeated his name silently, like he was committing it to memory, then concentrated on me again. 'How are you coping, anyway?'

'What do you mean?'

'Not everyone could handle talking to a freak like Kinsella.'

'I'm used to psychopaths, Don. I've worked with them for years.'

'You'd let me know if it gets too much?'

'I've been through worse.'

He held my gaze. 'I know. That's what worries me.'

Part of me felt like leaving before he dredged up the cases we'd worked on in the past, but instinct was telling me to stay. Sitting beside him gave me more comfort than sleeping with Tom had ever done. There was something reassuring about his scale, so monumental that only a natural disaster could knock him down.

'It's late,' I said. 'I'd better get home.'

We stood together on the pavement, Burns's shoulders blocking the streetlight.

'Let me give you a lift.'

'It's okay, I could use the exercise.'

He took a step closer. 'You'd better kiss me now then.'

'Sorry?'

'It's what people do on Hogmanay. It's a custom.'

I stood my ground, but the temptation to hurl myself at him was almost overwhelming. 'You're too early, Don. It's only half past eleven.'

'Pity.' He gave a rueful smile then slowly walked away.

Across the street, the lights were burning in Tom's flat, and I was struggling to think straight. Burns's request for a kiss was only a joke, but it had increased my confusion. I tried to wipe it from my mind as I trudged down the lane.

When I got back to the cottage, a minor miracle had occurred. The letting agent had finally responded to my phone messages. Someone had fitted a new lock – a heavy-duty mortise that had been left on the latch, the key posted through the door. When I tested it, the mechanism gave a satisfying click. It would be impossible to break, and sleep would come more easily now that the place was secure.

I peered out through the kitchen window at Edgemoor Woods. It was starting to snow, coin-sized flakes gluing themselves to the windowpane. That morning's meeting with Kinsella was still distracting me, and the frustration of making such slow progress was giving me indigestion. It felt like a pint of concrete was hardening behind my breastbone.

I'd silenced my worries about Burns, but the buzz of anxiety about the missing girls never left me. Even though it was past midnight, I sat down at the living-room table and started to write a list of those staff at the Laurels who worked one to one with Kinsella. I would need to check the contact sheet, but there had been individual meetings with Gorski and Judith. Garfield spent hours ferrying him round the building, Pru worked in the art studio with him, and Tom supervised him in the gym. But surely none of them was capable of killing children under the guise of caring for the mentally ill?

My phone woke me just after one a.m. I was slumped over the table, my cheek pillowed by my writing pad.

'Happy New Year!' Lola sounded effervescent as usual, as though she'd been sipping champagne through a straw.

'And to you, Lo. I hope you haven't been drinking.'

'Just cranberry juice, more's the pity. Where are you?'

'At home, by the fire.'

'We're in Trafalgar Square. You should be here, Al. There are loads of snoggable blokes.' Klaxons screeched in the background and off-key voices singing 'Auld Lang Syne'. 'Someone wants to talk to you, hang on.'

I expected to hear Neal, but the voice that greeted me was deeper and more gravelly.

'Will, this is a surprise.'

'I thought you'd be here. You're always with Lo for New Year.'

I couldn't explain that I was testing my independence, and giving her some space with her new man. Tinny music echoed in the background, followed by a loud caw of laughter.

'I hope it's a great year for you, sweetheart.'

When he spoke again, his tone sounded urgent. 'You should leave that house, Al. There are bad spirits in every room.'

'You think so?'

'Seriously. Find yourself somewhere else.'

After another blast of hardcore disco, the line cut out, and I scanned the lounge. It was shabby but comfortable, firelight landing on the worn-out furniture. If ghosts existed, they were busy haunting someone else tonight.

I was about to collect a glass of water when an unexpected sound came from upstairs, an odd, fizzing noise. The lights flickered then failed completely. Darkness pressed in on me, so suffocating that I could hardly breathe, and my mind flooded with panic. The new lock on my door meant nothing. Someone could have jemmied a window and hidden themselves upstairs. I listened for sounds, but all I could hear was my own frantic breathing. I fumbled my way to the mantelpiece for a candle and matches, but it took all my courage to leave the room. The candlelight wasn't helping. Shadows flickered across the ceiling, until the room seemed to be full of spirits.

I forced myself to climb the stairs, ears straining for sounds. It took forever to find the circuit box, but once I'd replaced the blown fuse, the lights blinked on immediately. My heart battered the wall of my chest, until I heard the grumble of a van's engine starting up in the distance. I don't know why the noise calmed me. Maybe it was just a reminder that there were real human beings out there, going home from New Year parties, while I grappled with my ghosts.

29

'No arguments, all right?' the man hisses.

Ella nods silently, too frightened to reply.

'Get in the front seat, and stay under the covers so no one sees you.'

The man drops a rough woollen blanket over her, and she takes care to keep still. Once the van begins to move, she shifts the fabric slightly, so she can glimpse through the window. Soon the city is replaced by villages and country lanes. Ella reaches down to see if the door's still locked, but the handle won't budge. She wants to pull back the blanket and ask the man about Amita, but he'll hit her if she speaks again. All she can do is stare through the narrow gap at the cottages slipping by. Soon the heat from the radiator sends her to sleep, and the next time she wakes, they're driving through woodlands, snow piled high on the sidings.

The van finally stops by an embankment, covered with trees. She hears the man get out, and pulls the blanket down a few inches. He stands in the headlights' beams, with a cardboard box balanced in his arms. The man's holding it so carefully, the contents must be fragile. He waits there without moving for a long time. Ella watches him lay the box at the foot of a tree, and when he returns to the driver's seat, he seems upset. The man puts the key in the ignition, then sits there, staring through the dark window. After a few minutes she remembers what her granddad says when she has bad dreams, and reaches out to touch his sleeve.

'You'll feel better when morning comes.'

She expects the man to be angry that she's pulled down the blanket, but he doesn't make a sound. His head bows over his knees, like he's saying a prayer. He takes a minute to recover then turns to look at her.

'I'm better than this, Ella. I'm doing what he wants because I owe him everything. I hate it, but I can't refuse. Do you understand?'

The man's voice is so fierce, she's too scared to reply. The only thing she can do to calm him is reach out and touch his hand.

30

The sky was a bright, deceptive blue when I peered out of the window on New Year's Day. Apart from the fresh fall of snow, it was a perfect counterfeit of a midsummer day. I took a sip of orange juice, but my appetite still hadn't returned. I was forcing down a piece of toast when my mobile rang. Burns sounded like he'd sprinted up a long flight of steps.

'We found her.' The bleakness of his tone warned me that he'd discovered a body, not a living child.

'In Camden?'

'She's in Edgemoor Woods. You know where that is, don't you?'

I stared at the snow-covered trees in disbelief. 'I certainly do.'

'Follow the path from Charndale till you reach the bridge.'

I locked the door and set off at a jog, turning left down the bridleway I'd taken on Christmas Eve, when I'd been convinced someone was chasing me. It looked like a battalion had marched through the woods, the snow trodden to polished ice, twigs stamped into fragments.

Burns was standing beside Pete Hancock; he was so much taller that it looked as if he was explaining something to a child. Hancock scribbled my name on his list, and I put on the Tyvek suit and plastic shoes he handed me before crossing the cordon.

'Are you ready to see her?' Burns asked.

His face was expressionless with shock as he led me deeper into the woods. A brown cardboard box lay at the foot of a tree, and part of me wanted to run back to the cottage. Children's bodies are always the worst. They linger in your nightmares for weeks. I wanted to ask which girl had been found, but my tongue had stuck to the roof of my mouth. A photographer was blocking our way, his flashgun releasing flares of yellow light into the thick shadows between the trees. Burns motioned for him to leave and, when I looked down, I saw that the girl inside the box was Amita Dhaliwal. She was barely recognisable, her black hair a mess of tangles, pinched face disfigured by bruises. I closed my eyes and thought of Usha standing in the cold, waiting for her adopted daughter to come home.

'When was she found?'

'Six this morning,' Burns replied. 'A woman was running with her dog.'

I knelt down to look more closely. This time the killer had taken less care. The cardboard coffin was too small for the child's body, her knees cramped against her chest. But the white dress was identical to Sarah Robinson's, a row of pearlised buttons running down from the collar. Judging by the wounds on her arms and face, she'd suffered more than the first victims. He was gaining confidence; if the series continued, his violence would escalate further.

'Why here?' I mumbled to myself.

'Good question. He's fifty miles west of his catchment.'

I stood up, wiping the snow from my knees. 'It's a tribute, isn't it? The woods border Northwood's grounds. He's left her on Kinsella's doorstep.'

It struck me that the child had been placed close to my home too. The roof of the cottage was visible above the line of trees and I was about to point it out to Burns, but he was staring at the snowy ground like he wished it would swallow him.

189

'What happens now?' I asked.

'Tania drives to London to inform the mother, the girl's body goes to the mortuary, and I get hung out to dry.'

Burns left me standing there while he supervised the team of SOCOs. Soon half a dozen officers in white suits were crawling across the ground, performing a fingertip search. I made myself look down at Amita's body one last time, and I had to swallow hard to suppress my nausea when I saw the ring of bruises around her neck. The bastard had stood over this child, fingers tightening round her throat, intent on watching her die. My hands balled into fists as I turned away.

When Burns drove me back to Northwood, it was obvious from the throng of press vans that the discovery had been leaked. A photographer sprawled across the bonnet of the car, taking snaps with a heavy-duty Nikon, his triumphant smile reflecting the fee he'd receive. The girls' disappearances were still the country's biggest news item, all the papers crammed with possible sightings. Every crank in the land was claiming to have seen Ella or Amita since they'd been taken.

'Fucking vampires,' Burns grumbled to himself.

It was unusual to hear him swear. In the old days he turned the air blue on a regular basis, but now he seemed determined to set a good example, and I wondered how he kept a lid on his stress. Someone yelled a question so loudly that we could hear it though the closed windows.

'How do you feel about another girl dying on your watch, DCI Burns?'

He stared ahead fixedly as we drove into the car park, hands clenched round the wheel, and I knew better than to attempt conversation.

The incident room smelled of anxiety and stale cigarette smoke. More staff had been drafted in from London, and spooky shots of Edgemoor Woods were already plastered across the evidence boards. The photos showed SOCOs in their white suits, flitting like spectres between the trees. Pictures of Amita in her disposable coffin were pinned beside ones of her beaming at the camera, exuberantly alive. Death had caught her by surprise. Her brown eyes looked startled, and I hoped someone would show enough decency to close them before her mother arrived.

Alan Nash glowered from the other side of the room, surrounded by young detectives who were vying to refill his coffee cup and polish his ego. When I looked up again, Burns looked more truculent than ever, preparing to address the crowd. Frustration had made his tone harsh and accusatory.

'This is where you lot live from now on. If we don't find Ella Williams soon, she'll end up in a box, just like Amita, and all of us will have failed. Every villager in Charndale needs a doorstep interview – you can bet your life someone saw that van arrive in the middle of the night.' His eyes blazed as he scanned the room. 'The girl's been gone twelve days. If Ella's still alive, she must think the whole world's forgotten her.'

The tension in the room increased as he gave his update. The Sex Crimes Unit had checked the offenders' register: over three hundred ex-cons with records of crimes against children had been accounted for. Only fifteen had passed through Wakefield Prison or the Laurels during Kinsella's stretch, and they all had alibis. Every member of staff at St Augustine's had been investigated too, but so far only Roy Layton had been arrested. He had been ruled out of the investigation because he was in custody when Amita was abducted. Several teachers had confirmed his story that he'd allowed pupils to play in the back of his van, which explained the presence of Ella's DNA. But he was still off work, facing a criminal prosecution for owning child pornography.

'The getaway van's still a mystery,' Burns continued. 'The

CCTV's being checked, but so far no unmarked vans came down the M4 yesterday. He could be using fake plates, or he took an indirect route. The camera on the main road through the village didn't clock him, so he could be back in London by now.' Burns hit a key on the laptop beside him and a photo of a child's white dress appeared on the wall.

'Sarah Robinson was found in this, and it looks like Amita's is identical. But there's a difference from the dresses that Kinsella's victims wore. He got a seamstress to make them; he said they were angel costumes for his school's nativity play, but these ones have been mass produced. You can buy them from any branch of John Lewis. It's a nightdress from their Victorian range, for girls aged five to thirteen. Small alterations have been made by hand – cutting out the labels and changing the collar from square to round, so they look like the ones the original foundlings wore. He's done his best, but his sewing's pretty crude.'

'What are you saying, boss?' A voice piped up out of nowhere.

Burns frowned. 'He's planned ahead. John Lewis sells thousands of these every year, which makes traceability a nightmare. We're looking at their credit card transactions, but chances are he's paying cash, and buying each one from a different store. Then he takes them home and customises them. Either he's making the alterations himself, or he's got someone untrained giving him a hand.'

There was silence as the information sank in. The idea of a serial killer patiently adjusting a child's nightdress with needle and thread was hard to absorb. This man, or woman, went against every known stereotype. Child killers normally murder their victims straight after raping them. But this one was the soul of patience. He'd waited nineteen days for Sarah Robinson to die of natural causes, and Ella might be suffering the same fate, the long delay adding to his sadistic pleasure. So far only Amita had died within hours of being captured.

The team melted away as soon as the meeting ended. Some officers were heading back to London to brief the team at King's Cross, and others were returning to the woods. The rest would search Charndale, street by street. The incident room emptied, apart from half a dozen detectives staring at computer screens. Burns beckoned me over to Alan Nash's table.

'We need to agree a strategy,' he said quietly.

Without his disciples, Nash looked diminished, an old man in need of a rest. 'I'm prepared to let bygones be bygones and interview Kinsella this afternoon.'

'Thanks for the offer, Alan, but he'll only speak to Alice.'

Nash's mouth flapped open but no sound emerged. The prospect of another tête-à-tête with Kinsella made the hairs rise on the back of my neck, but I kept my expression neutral and focused on my report. I'd tried every possible technique to work out where the killer lived: crime linkage, data analysis and geo-profiling. I'd used the latest Home Office software to map the co-ordinates of each crime scene. All five girls had been abducted inside a one-mile radius, but the team had searched the streets I'd highlighted and found nothing. Now the parameters would have to be redrawn. The killer had extended his boundary by fifty miles. Nash looked as frustrated as I felt.

'Kinsella told me in his original confession that someone would finish what he started,' he said, frowning. 'It's obvious that he trained someone before he was caught. Why aren't you looking harder at his old contacts?'

'Believe me, we are, Alan,' said Burns.

'I think we should increase the focus on the staff here at Northwood. He obviously knows this area, because he found the ideal spot to leave Amita's body,' I said. 'But the found-lings are at the heart of it. I'm sure the museum's part of his motivation. The killer's choosing girls he sees as orphans, which makes me wonder if he's an orphan too.'

Nash pursed his lips. 'Or the abductions could be oppor-tunistic; he's just seizing them where he can. The white dresses and the girl's body at the museum are a tribute to Kinsella, nothing more.'

'But why would he go to the trouble of altering the costumes himself?' I asked. 'The foundlings must have a personal meaning.'

The two men wore very different expressions. Burns looked open to persuasion, but Nash's eyes were glazed with contempt. We could have stayed in deadlock for hours, but thankfully a young officer arrived. He was panting, as though he'd sprinted a hundred metres.

'This just arrived, sir,' he told Burns.

The white envelope had been sent first class from central London, addressed to Mr Louis Kinsella. I watched Burns shake the contents into an evidence bag. There was nothing inside apart from a scrap of cotton, two inches wide, contain-ing a small red button. It was a direct copy of the tokens I'd seen at the Foundling Hospital, and when I looked more closely, the button was embossed with a teddy bear's face. All three of us stared at it in silence. The gift was as wide as my palm, and it had clearly been a labour of love. Someone had hemmed the pale pink fabric with dozens of minute stitches, and the shape of the token revealed the killer's feelings for Kinsella. It was a perfect, neat-edged heart.

31

Kinsella refused to meet me until five o'clock, so I had time to prepare myself. I let my gaze wander around the interview room to keep my mind occupied. Red security lights flashed above the doorway, a plastic chair behind the glass boundary, like a throne waiting for a king's arrival. The space was so pristine it could have doubled as an operating theatre, and even the smell was the same – disinfectant and anxiety. Hopefully the glass wall would prevent Kinsella from scenting my fear. The stakes had risen even higher since Amita had been found. The wire inside my blouse felt cold against my skin, and the recorder must have been picking up my rapid breathing and the judder of my heartbeat, Burns and his team listening to my discomfort.

Garfield led Kinsella to his chair then retreated. The headmaster wore the smug look my father adopted when he won an argument, flushed with pleasure at grinding his opponent's ideas into the dust. As usual his wrists lay handcuffed in his lap.

'I heard the news, Alice,' he said. 'My follower's showing extraordinary tenacity, isn't he? I thought they'd forget the rules I gave them, but so far not one's been broken.'

'The rules?'

He gave a nonchalant shrug. 'Call them guidelines, or a manifesto, if you prefer. It's amazing how many people love to follow orders. What about you? Do you enjoy being told what to do?'

'Only by people I respect. If not, I refuse point-blank.'

Kinsella gave a yelp of laughter. 'Your rebellious spirit is nearly as strong as mine, Alice.'

I pulled the token from its envelope. 'This arrived from London today to let you know about Amita Dhaliwhal. Either he killed her yesterday, or he sent it ahead of time, knowing that she'd be dead when it arrived.'

'Superb organisational skills.' He watched me expectantly as I pushed the scrap of material through the hatch in the glass screen. When it fell into his palm, it balanced there like a piece of gold leaf, the button glittering under the lights.

'You asked for a keepsake every time, didn't you?'

His expression remained neutral as he stared at the scrap of cotton, before lowering it gently into the hatch. 'Thank you for letting me see it. No one else in this place has an ounce of courtesy.'

'I need more details, Mr Kinsella. If you won't tell me the killer's name, you could at least say where he lives.'

'Poor Alice, always so keen to save everyone.' He leant forwards in his chair, until I could see the grey sheen of his five-o'clock shadow. 'Why don't you use those exquisite eyes of yours? It's at the centre of the whole affair. If you can't see where the girls were kept, you've got the wrong map.'

His disturbing grin flickered for a second, then the headmaster rose to his feet and nodded at Garfield to lead him away. I found myself gritting my teeth, and it was fortunate that the glass screen was in place – for his protection, not mine. Kinsella had got everything he wanted from our meeting, and his stare had been so intrusive it felt like he had X-ray vision. He'd seized the opportunity to make us all look like fools, because he was the only one who understood the rules of the game.

When the room emptied I turned to face the observation

window. All I could see was an expanse of opaque grey glass, but Burns was sure to be watching. I raised the palms of my hands in a gesture of apology. My relationship with Kinsella felt like a tennis match with a far stronger opponent, but the consequence of losing would be far worse than missing out on a trophy, and it was clear that I was already two sets down.

Kinsella's words rang in my ears when I returned to the incident room and studied the crime scene map, each one marked with a red drawing pin. I was still standing there, glassy-eyed, searching for a pattern between the dots of colour, when Tania sashayed across the room. Her expression hovered somewhere between professionalism and hostility.

'Burns said you'd give us a list of staff who see Kinsella one-to-one.'

'I'll finish it now.'

She turned on her heel and left me to it. The next hour was spent studying the staff rosters I'd collected from the HR department. They showed that Garfield saw more of Kinsella than anyone else. As his designated nurse, he was responsible for conducting him from his cell to the refectory, to meetings and therapy sessions. A physio treated Kinsella for back pain, and he had individual art and gym sessions to prevent other inmates from attacking him. At least one security guard always stayed in the room, but there would still be plenty of opportunities for whispered conversations. Half a dozen psychiatrists and psychologists had worked with him at Northwood, including Alan Nash, Gorski, Judith Miller, and a Jon Evans. I racked my brains to remember the name. I'd met so many new people at the Laurels that my memory was stretched to capacity. Then it came to me. He was the guy who'd worked with Kinsella the year before, the one who'd had a breakdown.

Finally I added the names of the security men who regularly guarded him, then went looking for Tania.

I found her in one of the anterooms, absorbed in a phone conversation, but she nodded a curt thank-you as I handed over the sheet of paper. It felt like a spectacular act of disloyalty to include Judith and Tom's names on a list of potential suspects, but I was sure that the killer had fallen under Kinsella's influence. Anyone who spent time inside his orbit was in danger of succumbing to his control.

By now it was seven o'clock and I was in need of a meal, but Kinsella's message still troubled me. He might have been lying about the map holding the key to the killer's address, but his expression had been unusually serious. He enjoyed the chase most when I was right behind him – it felt like he was offering me the chance to catch up. I opened my laptop and clicked on the map I'd created. It's a known fact that serial killers worked outwards from an axis, with their own home at the epicentre. Until Amita's body was found fifty miles from his patch, the killer had been working inside a tight radius. I stared at the screen again: three streets on the outskirts of Camden Town were flashing in traffic-light red. I was still hunched over the computer when Burns appeared in front of me.

'Found something?' he asked.

'You're sure that Willis Road, Orchard Row and Inkerman Street were all searched?'

Burns studied the map. 'We went through that area like a dose of salts.'

'I'd still like to take a look tomorrow.'

He stared down at me. 'You'd travel there, to look at streets we've already checked?'

'I'll be in London anyway.'

'I can meet you at midday. I've got to see the commissioner.'

Burns was gone before I could explain that there was no need. I was perfectly capable of exploring the neighbourhood on my own. I knew my hunch was unlikely to lead to anything, but Kinsella had planted a seed of doubt that would blossom into rampant anxiety if I ignored it.

32

It feels like days since the man locked her in the back of the van. Ella's back aches, and there's nothing here, except a bucket and a roll of toilet paper, and some torn overalls the man has abandoned. She's so hungry that her stomach hurts, her ribs covered only by a thin layer of skin.

When the door finally opens again, the light hurts her eyes, and the man's wearing his black coat, beaming at her. He helps her climb out into a small garage. The walls squeeze the sides of the van so tightly, there's hardly enough space to walk past. At the end of the garage she spots a large chest freezer and a pile of cardboard boxes – ten or twelve narrow cylinders, stacked inside each other. Ella wants to know what the boxes are for, but some instinct prevents her from asking. She remembers the man standing in the woods with a package balanced in his arms. His hand squeezes her shoulder as he leads her inside. The kitchen looks so like home that tears prick the backs of her eyes. Granddad's kettle is made of the same dull silver, and she can almost smell the smoke that trails after him wherever he goes. The man's grip is tight enough to leave a bruise as he pulls her down a narrow stairway.

'Like it down here, Ella?'

She forces the smile back onto her face. The room is tiny, with a window that's too high to see through, and it stinks of damp. Circles of mould stain the white paint. There's a narrow bed pushed against the wall, a small table and a chair with a broken back. Splinters needle her skin when she sits on it, waiting for him to leave. His woollen hat's so low over his forehead that his eyes are barely visible. But if she had to guess, the look he's giving her seems to be an apology. Boys give each other that stare in the playground when someone gets hurt in a game of tag, laughter draining away like a cup emptying.

Something odd is happening to the man's face. His cheeks twitch like he's trying not laugh. But when Ella looks again, tears are dropping from his eyes. Her gaze switches to the open door. If she had enough strength she'd push past him, but she can hardly stand. The man's head rests on her shoulder as he gulps out some words.

'I can't do it any more. They're bound to find us, and it's wrong, what I'm doing. The nightmares are killing me.'

'Can't your family help you?'

'I've got no one.' The man's voice is scratchy with tears.

'You've got me, haven't you?'

'And you'll never leave?'

'Never.' Ella shakes her head slowly. 'But I want to know why you chose me.'

'Because we're the same, you and me. We've lost everything, that's why we understand each other.' His stubble grazes her palm as he pulls away, but at least he's calmer. He drops a kiss on her hand then rises to his feet. 'You know you're my princess, don't you?'

She forces herself to smile, then the man steps out of the room. When he returns, he's carrying a plateful of food. A sandwich wrapped in clingfilm, fruit and a chocolate bar.

'All my favourites,' she whispers.

His eyes flick across her face as she eats. She's so scared he'll take the food away again, that she gulps down mouthfuls too fast, even though his gaze disturbs her. He seems to be counting each bite, keeping track of everything she owes.

33

The drive to London next morning took longer than I expected, the snow still causing traffic problems. My mother had been incommunicado for days, but she'd sent a text the night before reminding me to be on time. Snow fine as grit fell against the windscreen, but at least concentrating on the road helped me escape the pressures of the case for a few hours. It was seven fifteen by the time I reached Blackheath, and the view plunged me back into childhood memories. My eyes wandered across the heath land; a mile of pure whiteness, rolling away towards Greenwich Park. On a rational level I could see how beautiful it was – a pristine piece of countryside trapped inside the city limits. There's no explaining why it scared me so much. The landscape sent my internal clock spinning into reverse, as if my childhood might rise up from the ground and claim me again.

My mother was standing outside her apartment building on Wemyss Road, beside two huge suitcases. She was wearing a smart navy-blue coat and an outraged frown.

'You're twenty minutes late, Alice. Why didn't you call?'

I wrenched open the boot of my car. 'Then I'd have been even later.'

'I should have called a taxi.'

'Relax, Mum. You'll catch your plane, I promise. We can chat on the way.'

My mother's expression made it clear that chatting wasn't

an option. Her lips were so tightly pursed, it looked like they'd been sealed with superglue. After we'd been underway twenty minutes she seemed calmer, but her tremor was still in evidence, her hands jittering in her lap.

'How's the new job going?' she asked.

I considered telling her everything was fine, but I was too tired to lie. 'It's tougher than I imagined. In fact, it's the hardest thing I've ever done. Sometimes it's so upsetting, it makes me want to quit and do something normal like everyone else.'

My mother gaped at me. 'Goodness, Alice. That's the first time you've admitted to a weakness since you broke your arm at primary school.'

'I wonder where I get that from?'

A brief smile crossed her face. 'Have you been on any dates yet?'

'I will soon, I promise.'

My admission of vulnerability seemed to help, because she talked without pause for the next half-hour. Her voice was almost the same as normal, a slight quake making the words vibrate like notes from a cello. She told me about the cities on her cruise itinerary, and the lectures she could attend on-board. By the time we reached Gatwick, I was an expert on cruise ship etiquette and sites of interest in Dubrovnik and Marrakesh. My mother saved her bombshell until I'd unloaded her luggage onto the trolley at Gatwick.

'It's Parkinson's, by the way.'

'Sorry?'

'The neurologist says it's stage two. There's not much they can do, except monitor it.'

'How long have you known?'

'A few weeks. I didn't want to spoil your Christmas.'

I couldn't find a suitable reply, so I hugged her instead. It had been years since we'd embraced and I could feel how thin she was, the tremor running through her like a pulse. After a few seconds she patted my back firmly and withdrew.

'Don't, Alice,' she said quietly. 'There's no need to fuss.'

My mother has never believed in fussing, her feelings so firmly battened down, you could mistake her for an automaton. But I felt like making one on her behalf. If I'd lived with a man who beat me black and blue, then found myself gripped by a disease like Parkinson's, I'd have kicked every hard object in sight. But an emotional outburst would have been more than she could bear.

We set off together across the concourse and waited in silence to check in her baggage. She had two hours to wait for her flight to Cyprus.

'Shall we have a coffee?' I asked.

'No, darling, you've wasted enough time. I'll go to duty free and buy some sunglasses.'

'Enjoy it, Mum. Text me when you're on the boat.'

She kissed me on the cheek; when I glanced back, she was walking alone through the gateway, surrounded by families and couples walking arm in arm. From a distance she looked the same as ever, straight-backed and invincible.

The tears hit me when I reached my car. I don't know whether I was crying for my mother, the lost girls, or the knowledge that I was failing every day, but I bawled nonstop for twenty minutes. I remembered the symptoms of Parkinson's from my days as a medical student: muscle weakness, speech loss, paralysis. I was so deeply preoccupied on the way back that I hardly noticed the route as I cut north through the suburbs to Camden.

Burns was standing by his car looking disgruntled. The area seemed an unlikely spot for a serial killer's lair – Inkerman Street contained a row of prosperous 1930s semis, front doors glossy with Farrow & Ball.

'Are you all right?' he asked, gazing down at me.

'Fine thanks, why?'

'You don't look yourself.'

On the rare occasions when I cry, my nose glows like a Belisha beacon, eyes blurry and red-rimmed. Even though I must have looked like a train wreck, the urge to seek his comfort was almost irresistible.

'I've had some bad news, but I'm okay. Have you looked around yet?'

Burns shook his head. 'I brought the write-up from the house-to-house.' He pulled a computer printout from his pocket. 'Every address was checked, plus gardens, garages and sheds. Are you sure you're okay to do this?'

'Of course.'

I was beginning to feel foolish for wasting his time. We were standing at the centre of the killer's territory, but there was nothing here apart from a line of suburban homes that had all been checked. Willis Road was exactly the same. I was about to apologise when I came to a standstill on Orchard Row. The houses on the right-hand side had been demolished. Ten-foot hoardings lined the pavement, advertising a new housing development. Outsized photos of families sitting in show-home kitchens beamed at us as we walked past.

'There's nothing behind there.' Burns studied the printout again. 'Berkshire Estates have owned the site for eighteen months. Their building plans are on hold because of the downturn.'

'Did the search team go inside?'

He shook his head. 'The manager said it's patrolled regularly.'

We paused by a set of wooden gates, but it was impossible to see inside. 'It looks like someone's changed the padlock,' I said.

Burns turned the shiny new lock over in his hand and sighed loudly. It made a poor match for the rusty chain that held the bolt in place. 'Stay there, Alice. I'll take a look.'

He stepped onto the frame then swung himself over; but at five foot nothing, it was a harder climb for me. There was an ominous tearing sound as my coat snagged on a splinter. Burns looked unimpressed when I landed beside him on the icy concrete.

'What part of "stay there" do you not understand?'

I ignored him and gazed around the site. It was empty apart from a ruined two-storey building, with a few small outbuildings. There were no clues to explain what it had been used for originally, but I guessed it had been part of a Victorian hospital. The structure looked ready to collapse before the wrecking ball attacked it, glass missing from the windows, and holes gaping in the roof.

I left Burns peering through the doorway and skirted round the side of the building. There was a trail of indentations in the snow, and even though they had been buried by a fresh covering, it looked as if footprints were hidden underneath, and my pulse quickened. My eyes caught on a red metal container by the boundary wall, the doors hanging open. A powerful stench hit me when I peered inside. Soiled tissue paper littered the floor; there was a sodden blanket, and two buckets in the corner, reeking of urine and excrement. Maybe I imagined it, but another smell seemed to linger there: the sharp tang of adrenaline and fear.

'It's here, Don, quick,' I yelled.

I heard his footsteps, then a quick indrawn breath and he was on his mobile, calling for backup. The container explained why Sarah and Amita's skin had been grimed with rust. Flakes of orange metal were peeling from the walls, and I wondered how the girls had coped. Claustrophobia and terror would have overwhelmed me in minutes. I stared into the bleak interior and tried to imagine Ella cowering there. Then my eyes fell on a piece of cloth. It was almost unrecognisable; the cotton must have been white originally, but now it was pockmarked by dark brown stains. A foundling dress lay abandoned on the container's floor.

34

I was numb with tiredness by the time I got home. I'd escaped lightly because Burns had stayed at Orchard Row to deal with the influx of SOCOs, still fuming that the search team had taken the site manager at his word. He would probably be there all night while Pete Hancock's team searched for anything that held the killer's DNA. I sat by the unlit fire listening to owls dive-bombing the house, screeching at the top of their voices. I was about to go to bed when a text arrived on my phone. My mother had sent a picture of her cabin. I felt a twinge of jealousy. It looked so luxurious, I wished I could teleport myself there, and sit by her panoramic window for a few days watching the sea. It seemed like a good sign that she could muster enough energy to complain – apparently the ship was overcrowded, and the food plentiful but unimaginative.

When I finally crawled into bed, sleep dropped over me like a blackout curtain. But a few hours later, something roused me. I heard an unfamiliar noise, then slipped back into my dream. When it came again, it was much louder – a shattering sound, as if someone was hurling plates at the wall. My tiredness evaporated instantly, eyes straining in the dark. I crept out of bed in silence. From the window all I could see were acres of trees, their branches outlined in white. I was beginning to question my sanity. Maybe I'd imagined the whole thing – Will's bad spirits gate-crashing my dreams.

I was about to return to bed when there was a cracking noise, loud as a bullet, then a crescendo of glass shattering. I was too terrified to act rationally, dashing from room to room, hitting every light switch, hoping to fool the burglar into believing the house was full of people. The next sound was of footsteps floundering through the snow. But the road was deserted when I reached the front window. Whoever the intruder was, he must be hiding in the woods.

I pulled on my clothes and ran downstairs. The damage was obvious straight away. A brick lay in the middle of the hallway, a ragged hole through the glass pane in the front door. My heart juddered at the base of my throat. This time the burglar had meant business. He'd arrived in the middle of the night, intending to break in, and he'd almost succeeded. But the most frightening thing was that he knew there was little to steal, because he'd been here before, peering through the windows. It could only be me that he'd come for.

My hands shook as I phoned the police. I sat on the edge of the sofa, with an inch of brandy in a shot glass, but it failed to calm me. Louis Kinsella's face appeared every time I blinked. It felt as though he was the one terrorising me, even though he was locked behind a steel door. The hunch that he might be instructing someone at Northwood was getting stronger all the time. I kept busy until the police arrived, sweeping up broken glass, and tacking hardboard over the hole in the window. It was a relief when a squad car finally pulled up. A female copper and her elderly sidekick sat at the kitchen table. She was so young, it looked like she'd brought her dad along for the ride. He gave me an old-fashioned look when I explained about the footprints in the snow.

'The postman probably, trying to deliver a parcel. And Christmas is peak season for burglaries,' he said calmly. 'You should get an alarm.'

'I'm renting,' I replied.

His smile vanished, as if my temporary status explained everything. The young woman handed me the crime number on a slip of paper.

'You shouldn't be alone tonight,' she said. 'Can we give you a lift somewhere?'

'Yes, please.' The look on her face was so sympathetic I felt like advising her to become a social worker, before she grew as jaded as her sidekick.

At least I'd stopped shaking by the time we left, but my nerves were still jangling. It was unlikely that my would-be burglar was lurking in the woods, but I couldn't calm down. There was no one in sight as I looked out of the window of the squad car. The whole village seemed to be sleeping off the effects of a riotous New Year's party.

They dropped me outside the Rookery and I crossed the road to Tom's building with mixed feelings. I didn't feel comfortable about placing myself at his mercy, but the idea of bothering Burns at the hotel felt even worse. The main entrance was unlocked, so I let myself in. He arrived at the door to his flat wearing nothing except a pair of boxer shorts and a puzzled expression. His face was so inscrutable it was hard to know whether he was pleased or annoyed, but after a few seconds he stepped backwards to let me in.

'It's unbelievable,' he said. 'Nothing like that happens here.'

'There's a first time for everything.'

'And you say someone's been poking around?'

'Ever since I arrived.'

'Maybe you should find somewhere else to stay.'

I shook my head. 'I like the cottage. No one's going to scare me away.'

His cool gaze skimmed my face. 'Is this how you react to danger? Tough it out, and pretend it's not real?'

'What other choice is there?'

His hand rested on my shoulder for a second before he turned away, and I watched him moving round the kitchen, as he made me a drink. The physical facts were undeniable. His body was a thing of beauty, muscles taut across his back. The thing I needed most of all was a hug, but I stifled the impulse, knowing that we'd end up in bed. There was no point in complicating things – Burns was still stuck in my head like a bad tune.

'Who was that bloke you were with at the Rookery?' he asked.

'A colleague, from the Met. Why do you ask?'

'No reason.' He handed me a mug of tea and his expression softened. 'I never apologised properly for going through your things.'

'I wanted to understand why, that's all.'

'Every time I ask a question, you stonewall me, Alice. I've never met anyone more closed.'

My mouth flapped in outrage. 'You're not exactly open yourself.'

'At least I'm trying. Go on, ask any question you like.'

'Okay than,' I said, staring back at him. 'How do you get on with your family?'

I expected flippancy. I thought he'd say that his mother was overbearing, and his dad was lousy at golf, but his face was blank. 'That's hard to answer.'

'It can't be that difficult.'

'Believe me, it is.'

He looked so uncomfortable that I changed the subject. 'You don't seem like a fitness instructor to me. Judith said you went to Oxford.'

'Trust Jude to let that one slip.'

'You wanted to be an academic?'

'Do you really want an explanation? It's not that exciting.'

'It's okay. I won't flog your story to *HELLO!*, unless it's newsworthy.'

He put down his mug cautiously. 'I studied divinities. I was a believer back then, like I said, and I thought I had a calling.' He pulled a face, as though he'd told a lame joke. 'I worked as a priest for a few years but it didn't work out, so here I am, helping villains keep fit. A different kind of ministry.'

I gaped at him, shocked that I'd made so many wrong assumptions. 'What made you leave the church?'

He shook his head. 'That's enough revelations for one day.'

'Pity, it was just getting interesting. There was something else I wanted to ask. Does Kinsella talk to you when he's in the gym?'

'Occasionally, when he's running.'

'About his crimes?'

'He asks about my life. I guess he wants to hear about the world outside. Why do you ask?'

'I saw him talking to Garfield, nineteen to the dozen.'

'That's not surprising, is it? How would you cope with round-the-clock isolation?'

'Badly.'

He held my gaze. 'Feel free to come back if your door's not fixed tomorrow.'

'Thanks, but I'm sure it'll be okay.'

Tiredness was knocking me sideways, and Tom must have seen my adrenaline draining away, because his expression switched to concern. 'You should get some sleep.'

'I'll be fine on here.' I pointed at the settee.

Luckily he didn't try to change my mind. When he leant down to kiss me goodnight, my willpower faltered. It would have been easy to jump into his outsized bed, but I let him walk back into his bedroom alone. His revelation about having been a priest lingered in my head as he closed the door. It struck me as odd that his past was forbidden territory. I wanted to see him as a friend, because he and Judith were my only allies at Northwood, but the layer of secrets that surrounded him was too deep to penetrate.

I tiptoed round the room, scanning Tom's bookshelves. I had no intention of invading his privacy like he'd done when he riffled through my papers, but I couldn't suppress my curiosity. The rows of heavyweight novels on his shelves would have impressed a librarian: *Anna Karenina, Middlemarch, Mill on the Floss*. I couldn't have finished any of them – epics went beyond my concentration span. I was about to quit when I spotted a photo peeping from one of the books. I felt guilty for opening it but couldn't stop myself. The picture was fading, like a timeworn memory. It was a conventional portrait of a family enjoying their summer holiday. Tom stood on a beach, about twelve years old, beside a younger boy with the same lean build and white-blond hair. His parents looked relaxed and carefree. But Tom was wearing an expression I'd never seen before, beaming at the camera. There was no hint of the adult who'd become so adept at concealing his emotions. I tucked the picture back inside the book, then returned it to the shelf as a sound drifted through the wall. His footsteps were pacing the floor, as if he was completing one last work-out before he went to bed.

I fell into a restless sleep on the settee. Maybe I imagined it, but I thought I heard Tom's footsteps again much later, but this time they were tapping past me to the door. I surfaced for a moment and looked for him, but the room was empty.

35

The urge to cry is overwhelming. Ella conjures memories of home to lull herself to sleep. She imagines walking in the park near her estate. Tomorrow Granddad will drive her to school and nothing will have changed: the teacher's smile will be as warm as ever. Friends will sit at the same tables, voices swarming around her like bees. But when she wakes, the man has returned, his face twitching with tension. He perches on the edge of the bed and her backbone presses against the wall.

'Did you miss me?' he asks.

'I always do.'

His fingers close around her wrist. 'Why do you think you're getting special treatment, princess?'

'I don't know.' She struggles to sit upright, as his grip tightens.

'Because you're my favourite, of course. But he's told me I've got to stick to the rules.' The man stares at the ground and a few tears drop onto the grey concrete.

'Maybe it's time to break them.'

His head switches violently from side to side. 'I can't, Ella. I promised to obey him.'

He gives a long sigh then pulls her against his chest. His smell is sour as vinegar, but she can't escape. He's holding her so tightly she can hardly breathe.

36

I planned to tell Burns about my break-in the next morning, but there was no sign of him. Alan Nash was skulking in the corner of the incident room, and the discovery of the container on Orchard Row was keeping the rest of the team fully occupied. Tania strode towards me through the crowd, dressed in an immaculate pencil skirt and midnight-blue satin blouse, as though it was her duty to bring glamour to the investigation.

'You're flavour of the month.' She gave a brief smile. 'The tyre tracks at Orchard Row show that he drove his van into the site plenty of times. The lab's doing tests now, but they think all four girls spent time in that container, and in an outbuilding. But there are no adult fingerprints so far.'

'He wore gloves the whole time?'

'It looks that way.' She turned towards me, eyebrows raised. 'What kind of freak leaves a kid in the freezing cold with nothing to eat?'

Tania was called away before I could reply, which was just as well, because there was no easy answer. Either the killer was psychotic, or so profoundly disturbed that a child's suffering didn't even register.

I spent the next few hours in the broom cupboard, trying to concentrate on my research, studying the centre's drug regimen and going through case notes. When the phone rang at one o'clock, it was Burns, summoning me to the sixth floor.

I had a sinking feeling as I climbed the stairs. I could guess what lay in store. Burns was waiting on the landing with two junior detectives and a WPC. I could have told him about my break-in, but it was obviously the wrong time. He must have been working round the clock, five-o'clock shadow so well established that it looked like he'd abandoned his razor.

'I need you to talk to Kinsella again,' he said quietly. 'He won't come to the interview room, but he'll see you in his cell.'

My spirits fell even further: Kinsella's control of the investigation was growing stronger every day. The WPC handed me a listening device and I pinned it inside my collar.

'He'll only talk if you're by yourself,' Burns said. 'But don't worry, nothing can happen. We're just a few feet away.'

His reassurance meant nothing when the glass security door slid back. This time the noise was even louder, screaming and catcalls emanating from every cell. The whole floor seemed to know about my visit. The swearing, wolf whistles and chanted curses were all for my benefit. Faces leered through the observation hatches as I passed down the corridor, frustration oozing through the walls. My heart pounded as I approached Kinsella's cell, and I wished I'd worn different clothes. Suddenly my knee-length dress felt ridiculously short.

Kinsella was handcuffed to the metal chair in his cell. I made a rapid calculation. The chair legs were bolted to the floor, but he could still lunge at me. Two feet of clear air between us was the minimum I needed to keep me safe. I tried to ignore the fact that he was wearing a grey plaid shirt, identical to the ones my father used to wear. The cacophony from the other cells was audible, despite the thickness of the door. I perched on the edge of his bed and tried to look composed.

'Forgive my surroundings, Alice,' Kinsella murmured. 'The unquiet souls never rest.'

'Is that how you see yourself too?'

'Of course. And you know what I mean, you're unquiet yourself.' The look on his face was a mixture of pity and frank sexual interest. Even though I knew what he was capable of, there was something so powerful in his gaze that it was hard not to respond.

'Maybe you'd feel calmer if you told me about the killer. Why not get it off your chest?'

'I'd rather discuss something of interest, Alice.'

'Like what?'

'You, of course. You still haven't told me about your father.'

'There's not much to tell. He worked for the tax office, had a working-class chip on his shoulder, and he was an alcoholic. Most of the time he was so wrapped up in himself, no one else got a look-in.'

His lips parted in mock sympathy. 'Frustrating, for a daddy's girl like you.'

I forced myself to smile. 'Thanks for leading me to Orchard Row. You were spot on, it was right at the centre of the map.'

'Sometimes you can't see the orchard for the trees.' He looked amused. 'What did you think of my friend's old stamping ground?'

'It's hard to imagine anyone living there. Most of the houses have been pulled down. Why don't you tell me his name?'

'Like I said, it could be one of many. It might be a woman, not a man.'

'You know exactly who he is.'

He rubbed his temple. 'These conversations tire me. I can see you again tomorrow morning but, before you go, tell me, how is Alan Nash?'

'The same as ever.'

'A pompous, overbearing windbag, who lies through his teeth?' His grin flicked on again. 'Don't let him upset you, Alice. I'm sure he'd love to put you down.'

'Tell me something useful, Mr Kinsella. Or I won't come back.'

'You drive a hard bargain.' He leant forwards in his chair, and I caught the sharp scent of his hair oil again, cloves mixed with underripe limes, as he hissed at me. 'The next victim will be taken on Monday. And this time, he'll put out her eyes.'

Kinsella's warped smile lingered as I walked away, and I was so incensed that the catcalls from the cells didn't bother me. Burns was standing on the other side of the security doors.

'We're pandering to him, Don,' I said. 'All he wants is attention.'

'At least he gave us the next deadline.'

'He said Orchard Row was the killer's old stamping ground. Find out what that building was used for, then check every human being who went through its doors.'

I ripped off the listening device and dropped it into his outstretched palm.

I still felt embarrassed about snapping at Burns when I bumped into Judith later in the staff common room. Her mass of thin silver bracelets clinked as she nursed her mug of tea.

'I heard about the girl in Edgemoor Woods. Isn't that near your cottage?' she said.

'Right by it, and someone chucked a brick through my door last night for good measure.'

She looked horrified. 'God, you poor thing. Come to mine later, I'll cook you dinner.'

'There's no need. Lightning never strikes twice, does it?' I wanted to reassure her, but the break-in felt like a warning. Even though I was determined not to be driven away, returning to the cottage frightened me.

'If you won't visit me, I'll come to yours.'

I considered putting up a fight, but Judith was wearing a look of fixed determination. I was beginning to realise that she had an iron will, despite her dreamy appearance. I had no choice but to give in gracefully.

It was dark by the time I got back to my cottage. The porch light showed that the glazier had replaced the damage with a pristine piece of security glass, then posted the extortionate bill through the door. I went back outside, tracing the edge of the house gingerly, my nerves still jangling. Last night's adventure had left me with a sense of unease, as though someone might still be watching me. I inspected the ground carefully with my torch, but there were no fresh prints and my confidence revived. There had been so much fear in the past, I was determined not to let it dominate my life again.

Judith's car arrived just after seven and when I pulled the door open she was carrying bags from the Chinese takeaway.

'You didn't need to bring supplies.'

'It's a bribe.' She looked over her shoulder. 'I've got someone with me.'

Garfield was unfolding himself from the passenger seat of her car, and I raised my hand in greeting. I couldn't help pitying them. So far I'd never fallen for a married man, and his act of betrayal clearly troubled him. Judith trailed after me into the kitchen.

'This place is a time capsule,' she said, gaping at the brown tiles and patterned lino. 'Pure Seventies kitsch.'

'It's peaceful, though. No noise, except the owls.'

'Doesn't the isolation bother you?'

'Only when someone breaks down my door.'

Most days the silence still felt like a blessing. The city's roar is a constant when you live in London. You fall asleep to the chatter of cars, and by morning it's overwhelming. Traffic screams in your face when you step outside. Sometimes it's invigorating, but on a bad day you feel like an actor, listening to an audience yell their disapproval.

We found Garfield watching the fire in the living room. His face was so drawn that I wondered if the combined stress of concealing his affair and daily contact with Kinsella was pushing him to the edge. But as soon as we began to eat, I stopped worrying about him. Chinese food has always been a vice of mine. The mix of sugar and additives always gets me. Who cares if it triggers a sodium headache next morning? The flavours make it all worthwhile.

'How did you end up at Northwood, Garfield?' I asked.

He gave a half-hearted grin. 'I must have committed a crime in a former life.'

'Come on, I'm in the mood for a life story.'

He gave a sheepish laugh. 'I grew up in Tottenham, on a rough estate. My school pushed me to become a doctor, but I missed the mark and ended up nursing instead. Northwood pays better than most hospitals, so I found a job, got married, had kids. Now there's no going back.'

'You'd prefer to live in London?'

His reply was instant. 'I'd go tomorrow, if I could.'

'Not without me, I hope.' Judith's face held a mixture of amusement and concern.

The meal gave me time to observe their relationship. The chemistry between couples always fascinates me: it's so fragile, capable of tipping out of control at any moment. Judith was doing most of the legwork, but Garfield's eyes rarely strayed from her face. His attention only flickered in my direction when I mentioned that I'd be interviewing Kinsella again in the morning.

'Is he really that choosy about who he speaks to?' I asked.

Judith put down her fork. 'Absolutely. He's ignored me for years.'

'But he trusts you, doesn't he, Garfield? I saw you talking outside the Campbell Building.'

His shoulder twitched as though I'd struck him, and the bitterness in his tone surprised me. 'Louis was delivering one of his monologues. I couldn't walk away.'

'But you wanted to?'

'God, yes. I normally filter them out; most of what he says is poison.'

'What was he telling you?'

'He was moaning about Alan Nash. He's not his biggest fan.'

'Kinsella must be feeling pretty smug right now. He's holding all the cards.'

Judith's eyes fixed on me. 'Ask about his wife. It's the one thing he can't stand.'

The conversation switched to lighter topics after that, and I felt grateful that they'd sacrificed a whole evening to keep me company. It interested me that Garfield seemed addicted to Judith's calmness; she used touch to reassure him constantly, bangles clattering as her hand settled on his arm. At midnight I insisted that they left. Judith was reluctant to go, but I could see how eager Garfield was to have her to himself.

'I'll be fine,' I said. 'The village is crawling with police.'

After they'd gone I went upstairs to draw the curtains, and Judith's car was still parked outside. The moonlight was so strong I could see her staring into Garfield's eyes, cupping his face in her hands. He was frozen, as if her voice had placed him completely under her control. It passed through my head that the pair had spent more time with Kinsella than anyone else at the Laurels. My flicker of suspicion died out immediately; it was impossible to believe they could harm anyone. I glanced down at the car again, but it was such a private moment that I drew the curtains and walked away. Moonlight was pouring into the back bedroom, a white glow hovering above Edgemoor Woods. But when I looked more closely, my eyes were playing tricks on me. The SOCOs must still be guarding the clearing where Amita's body had been found. Arc lights had illuminated the sky like a stadium at night, bright enough to cancel out the stars.

37

It's dawn when the door slams again, light ebbing through the tiny window. Ella's head swims, but she's stopped feeling afraid. Right now all she feels is rage. The man calls her princess, then refuses to give her food. It takes all her energy to smile when he pushes open the door, but she can see that he's on edge. His lips are set in a grimace, revealing his sharp white teeth.

'We can't go on like this, princess. We need to think of a way out.' His hands tap an urgent rhythm against his sides.

'Maybe we could run away.'

The man's hands freeze. 'You think so?'

'That's a way out, isn't it?'

'You're right, Ella. Soon I'll have to leave him behind.' A cloud of fear crosses his face.

'We've got each other, haven't we?'

The man kneels down in front of her. 'Sometimes I think I'm going crazy, Ella.'

'Of course you're not. We're going to be fine.'

She forces herself to look into his eyes, but there's nothing there. It's like staring into an empty tunnel that goes on for miles. The man squeezes her hand so tightly that her knuckles burn.

'You're all I need, princess. You know that, don't you?'

38

Chris Steadman was parking his motorbike when I arrived at Northwood the next day, and I couldn't help feeling envious. Driving down the West Coast of America on a powerful bike has always been one of my dreams. I'd even taken my proficiency test the year before, more in hope than expectation.

'She's perfect,' I said, gazing at his vintage Triumph.

'Take her for a spin sometime, if you like.'

He hugged his crash helmet against his chest and grinned at me while I thanked him for his generous offer. Studying or partying too hard had left him dishevelled, stubble covering his jaw and inch-long roots showing in his peroxide hair.

Chris's expression grew more serious as we walked to the reception block. 'Have you been okay since your break-in?'

I nodded. 'I like the place too much to leave, and the damage is fixed now.'

'Give me a shout if you need anything.'

He gave a mock salute then hurried away, leather jacket draped over his shoulder, like a would-be rock star. It interested me that he'd already heard about the brick-throwing incident. The Northwood grapevine seemed to have a life of its own.

Burns was waiting for me in the Campbell Building, eyes burning with anticipation. 'We found out about the building, Alice. It was a care home, for kids up to the age of twelve, called Orchard House, and guess who fundraised for them?'

'Kinsella?'

'Spot on. He was involved with them for years.'

'When did the place close?'

'Eight years ago. There was some kind of scandal.'

I stared at him as pieces of information slotted into place. 'Kinsella said the place was the killer's old stamping ground. Maybe he worked there before transferring here.'

'We're having trouble getting hold of employees' details. Most of the paper records were thrown away when the place closed,' Burns said, studying me intently. 'Kinsella's here already. He says he's got something to tell you.'

Butterflies rioted in my stomach as I walked to the interview suite, but Kinsella looked as cool as ever. He watched me approach from the other side of the glass screen, not moving a muscle. I could feel a dozen sets of eyes gazing down from the observation room too, and the pressure made the muscles in my throat constrict. If I didn't get under his guard soon, the consequences for Ella Williams would be fatal.

'Tell me more about the Foundling Museum, Mr Kinsella. Your wife says you volunteered there most Sundays.' The mention of Lauren made him flinch, and he seemed to slip back behind his wall of silence. 'I'll tell you my theory. I think you love the place because hundreds of children died there. The doctors tried hard, but many of the orphans were dying when they arrived, of diphtheria, rickets, and polio. The mortuary was piled high with infants' bodies. But why's your follower so fascinated by the foundlings? Did he work at the kids' home on Orchard Row?'

Kinsella's reply was little more than a whisper. 'Your theories are reductive, Alice. I thought you'd learned to avoid crude conclusions. How is my wife? Did she ask after me?'

'She wanted to know whether you'd expressed any remorse, nothing else.'

His face hardened again. Judith had been correct – his wife was his Achilles heel. Despite so many years of separation, her opinion still mattered. Maybe he'd believed that he could carry on as Jekyll and Hyde forever; the model husband who slaughtered children in his spare time.

'She said she'd visit if you co-operate,' I said. 'You told me you knew the killer twenty-four years ago. I need to know if that's true.'

Kinsella gave a grudging nod and his gaze flickered across my charcoal grey dress, to the coral necklace round my throat, assessing every detail. The glass screen allowed him to study every inch of me.

'Are you listening, Mr Kinsella? Roy Layton and your wife both say you could persuade anyone to do anything. And that's what you've done, isn't it? You've brainwashed some-body into doing your work. There's a man out there who thinks he's ceased to exist; he's just an extension of you.'

He leant forwards, revealing the white line of his parting, straight as a surgical incision. 'These interviews exhaust me, especially when the cameras are rolling. But if you answer a question for me with complete honesty, I may help you.'

My heart rate doubled. 'Anything you like.'

His face pressed close to the glass, until I could see his pallor, sweat glistening on his upper lip. 'Were you in love with your father, Alice?'

A muscle twitched in my stomach. 'I spent most of my childhood loathing him.'

'Hate and love are so close, aren't they? Sometimes it's hard to tell them apart.'

'Tell me what you know about the killer.'

'Between you and me, I find it touching that he remembers the rules, after all these years. I think he plans to follow them indefinitely.' His eyes glittered with amusement and I wished the glass wall would dissolve, so I could administer the thumbscrews myself.

'If you want your wife to visit, write down every name, date and address you can remember. But one more question, before you go. Why did you choose silence for so long when it limits your power?'

He said nothing for several minutes, and the room filled with the hum of air conditioning, as his eyes burned scorch marks through my dress. 'Emerson was right about silence, Alice. If we listen to it carefully, we can hear the whispers of the gods.'

He pressed his index finger against his lips, as if he was counselling me to hold my tongue, and I stared back at him, unblinking. If deities existed, their message for Kinsella would concern damnation and nothing else.

Burns was replaying the interview when I found him in the observation room. I caught sight of myself on the screen, thin and insignificant in my high-necked dress. He looked up for a moment, then carried on scanning the film.

'All you have to do is keep going, Alice. He's in the palm of your hand.'

'I wish I had your confidence.' The thought of being Kinsella's favourite made me feel queasy.

'Someone called the helpline last night. An old woman saw a van in the woods, with a young girl in the passenger seat, but she couldn't describe the driver. I'm off to see her now.'

I could tell that he was pinning his hopes on the old woman providing useful information, and I didn't have the heart to remind him that most callers were unreliable. Too many murder investigations are derailed by lonely fantasists, longing for attention.

'Did you hear that someone broke into my place, the night after Amita's body was found?' I said.

He swung round to face me. 'Why didn't you say?'

'I tried but you were too busy. I reported it to the local force and got myself a new mortice lock.'

He opened his mouth to speak again, but his phone rang and he gave an apologetic look, before turning away to answer it.

I was so busy planning how to get under Kinsella's defences that I didn't notice Tom until we almost collided on the path outside. The high heels of my boots skidded on the ice, and he put out a hand to steady me.

'Your head's in the clouds,' he said.

'It feels like it's about to burst. I need to speak to someone who knows Kinsella, inside and out.'

'I know the right person. I'll come round later.' He was so sure-footed as he marched away that the ice didn't slow him down, even though it was slick as well-oiled glass.

I spent the rest of the day concentrating on my research. I'd promised a preliminary report to Northwood's governors, but my analysis had hardly begun. I studied the list of mental conditions suffered by inmates at the Laurels: affective disorders, schizophrenia, DSPD. The saddest case was a fifty-eight-year-old with hebephrenia, who'd spent forty years at Northwood, because he'd attacked a neighbour with a crowbar after persistent bullying. The victim only sustained minor injuries, but the inmate was still judged too dangerous for release. I shook my head in disbelief as I read his notes. Hebephrenia is the cruellest mental disease in the whole repertoire. It sends time into reverse before the victim reaches adolescence. People start to regress in their teens, becoming children again, locked inside adult bodies, and in some cases they retain enough awareness to understand the cruelty of their situation. The man's file showed a parade of annual photos and his pudding-basin hair gradually turned grey, but his confused expression had stayed the same for forty years. There were probably plenty more inmates at the Laurels who would be better suited to community care than a lifetime of incarceration. At five o'clock I jabbed the off button on my computer and pulled on my coat.

It was a relief to return to the cottage. I'd got into the habit of leaving the downstairs lights burning each morning when I left for work. No doubt it was costing a fortune, but it made me feel better. Fixing my eyes on the glowing windows made the freezing walk from the main road easier to bear. The place gave its usual shabby welcome when I opened the door, as though I was visiting an ancient relative who'd stopped decorating generations ago.

Tom's car arrived at seven. When I peered through the curtains, his expression was impenetrable, and I couldn't work out why he'd decided to help. He was so resolutely private that connecting with people seemed to distress him.

I studied Tom's profile as he steered his Jeep over the drifts of snow. He looked like the archetypal action hero. It was easier to imagine him enduring an Arctic mission than wasting energy in a gym. Once we'd cleared the lane, the car swung left onto the main road.

'Where are we heading?' I asked.

'We're going to Sedgefield, to see Jon Evans. It's half an hour from here.'

The name was still fresh in my mind; it had been on the list of people who'd worked with Kinsella at the Laurels. 'The therapist who had a breakdown,' I confirmed.

'That's him.' Tom kept his eyes fixed on the road. 'He was a gym user, so I got to know him pretty well. He's staying at his mother's place. I've seen him a few times since he left, and he says he's happy to talk to you.'

I looked out at the dark woodland, a sprinkling of houses peeping through the trees. It seemed strange that Evans had lived with his mother for more than a year. Maybe his breakdown had been so radical that he couldn't cope alone. I distracted myself by examining the contents of Tom's glove compartment. There was nothing there apart from a pair of leather gloves and his iPod. I scrolled down his list of albums. One or two of the artists were familiar, like Matthew P and Chase and Status, but most had complicated European names. I listened to a couple of tracks and the music was orchestral, sombre cellos carrying the melody. It provided another reason to be friends, not lovers. The beauty would soon wear off if I heard it regularly, revealing the sadness lurking underneath.

When we arrived at Sedgefield the neighbourhood was much more prosperous than Charndale. Handsome eighteenth-century homes were clustered around a green, and in June the village would transform into the archetypal picture-postcard. Evans's house had a peaked roof, gabled windows, and a Hansel and Gretel atmosphere; the kind of place where nothing could go wrong.

The man who answered the doorbell was thin to the point of emaciation. The hallway was too shadowy to see his face clearly, but he looked around fifty years old, and his eyes were open a fraction too wide. He reached out to shake our hands.

'Good to see you again, Tom.' The spooked look disappeared when the man smiled, but returned the instant he relaxed. 'And you must be Alice. Come on in.'

Under the bright lights in the kitchen, his frailty was obvious. His red hair was cut as short as a conscript's, and from the side he looked thin enough to slip through a letterbox. I tried not to stare as he busied himself making drinks.

'How've you been doing?' Tom asked.

'There are good days and bad.' Evans sat down opposite me. 'Tom tells me you're working with Kinsella.'

'I'm following in your footsteps. They've given me your old office too.'

'I don't envy you; the job was desolate. Or maybe it was fine, and I was the desolate one.' He gave a gentle smile, and I wondered how many jokes he cracked at his own expense.

'Can you tell me about your time at the Laurels?'

'Why I cracked up, you mean?' His gaze settled on the wall behind me. 'I'd just got divorced, incipient depression, pressure of work. Plenty of reasons that don't include Kinsella.'

'But some that do?'

'Of course. He sent letters every day. According to him, we were kindred souls.' His dark eyes widened again and his thousand-mile stare reminded me of the faces of veterans returning from battle zones.

'Don't do this if it's too much, Jon.'

'It's probably therapeutic,' he said, blinking rapidly. 'I'd been commissioned to write a clinical study, and Kinsella co-operated at first, then he fell silent. He said he'd write down answers to my questions, but his letters never addressed them. He described killing his victims, over and over, in unbelievable detail.'

'Did he say that his campaign would start again?'

Evans nodded vigorously. 'He called it the reawakening. His followers were out there, primed to kill on his behalf, using his set of rules. He never said who they were; I thought it was just a fantasy.'

'Did he ever try and justify himself?'

'Never. He thinks his world-view is correct, it's the rest of us who're blind. He made the same three points over and over: young girls are innately evil, they're tainted before they're born, you can see it in their eyes.'

His face wore a stunned expression, as if a barrage of memories was hitting him with full force, and I could see why he'd broken down. Kinsella had twisted his love of killing into a warped narrative of blame. Reading about his delusions could send anyone with a depressive tendency over the edge. I was about to ask another question when an elderly woman appeared in the doorway. She made a beeline for Jon and settled her hand on his shoulder.

'That's enough, darling. You mustn't tire yourself.'

Evans looked irritated for a moment, like a teenager being told to turn his music down, then a wave of relief crossed his face. Thinking about Kinsella must have forced him back into territory he'd fought hard to escape. Jon's mother smiled politely as he led us back along the hallway, and I turned to him again as we stood in the porch.

'Can I ask where the letters are now, Jon?'

He nodded. 'Judith kept them when I left.'

The idea refused to sink in. Judith's consulting room felt like an oasis of calm, yet an archive of the world's sickest correspondence was stored there. The thought stayed with me as we said goodbye. It seemed unbelievable that I'd asked her for help in understanding Kinsella's mindset, yet she'd never mentioned his letters. The openness that I'd admired in her might be nothing more than an act. What reason could she possibly have for hiding Kinsella's sick messages from the world?

39

Tom's mood had darkened when we got into his car.

'Jon's lucky to have a mother like that,' he commented. 'She's so supportive.'

'Isn't your mother the same?'

'She died when I was thirteen.'

'I'm sorry, that must have been terrible.'

He stared at the dark road as if he was searching for something. When he spoke again his voice was almost too low to hear. 'There was a plane crash in Germany, in the Nineties. Did you hear about it?'

'I don't think so.'

'It was flying from London to Hamburg. I was on a football scholarship in Germany that summer. My mother was collecting me. She wanted to see the Black Forest before we flew home.'

'She was by herself?'

'My father and brother were with her. No one survived.'

I was too stunned to reply. I pictured the photo of his perfect blond family, all gone in an instant. Patients had described horrifying losses in the safety of my consulting room, but rarely on that scale. It explained why he kept their picture hidden inside a novel, so no one could pry. His hands twitched on the steering wheel.

'Why don't you pull over?' I said.

'There's no need.'

'Do it anyway, Tom, just for a minute.'

He stopped on the hard shoulder and I waited in silence. It was a technique I'd used for years. Once a revelation begins, all you need do is sit still and let it finish. His voice was a quiet monotone, as though he was reporting someone else's tragedy.

'The metal was torn in pieces like paper, a crater on the beach where the fire took hold. The investigators said the impact was so quick, no one would have suffered. The pilots ditched on purpose to avoid the town.'

'What happened after that?'

'My grandparents raised me in London. It was a struggle for them; they weren't the most demonstrative people in the world. After the funerals, they hardly ever talked about what happened.'

'And they took you to church?'

He shook his head. 'They were atheists. I went by myself, but it started to feel hollow after I became a priest.'

'Do you want to tell me about your family?'

'It's too long ago,' he murmured. 'I can't remember.'

It was obvious that he was lying. He must remember them every day, blasts of unresolved grief hitting him from all sides. At least his coping mechanisms would help: constant exercise, one-night stands, the adrenaline rush of working in a danger-ous environment. The story explained his fear of intimacy – no one ever got close enough to pry, his survivor guilt shap-ing every nightmare. I wanted to ask whether he'd received counselling at the time, but the question would have sounded patronising. When I touched his shoulder he jumped, as though he'd received a hundred volts. I'd forgotten that he could only accept intimacy that he initiated himself.

I still felt shaken when we set off, but at least Tom was less morose. Maybe it had done him good to open up.

'What did you think of Jon?' he asked.

'It's like he's spent too long staring at the sun.'

He choked out a laugh. 'Kinsella isn't exactly sunny, Alice.'

'You're right. It's more like peering into a black hole.' I looked across at him. 'Did you know Judith had kept Kinsella's letters?'

Tom shook his head. 'If he sent me one, I'd use it for a bonfire.'

It was still early as we approached Charndale, but the houses were already sealed, curtains closed to lock out the cold. When we reached Ivy Cottage, Tom left the engine running, hands balanced on the wheel, like a taxi driver desperate for his next fare. It was so obvious that he wanted to be alone that I thanked him quickly and said goodbye. I watched his Jeep navigate back to the main road, snow flying as it piled through the drifts.

I made three calls as soon as I got back inside. My brother didn't pick up, so I left a message saying how much I missed him and that I planned to visit Brighton soon. Then I had a short, breezy chat with Lola. She told me that her waistline was already two inches bigger.

'No way, Lo, it's too early. You've been overdoing the chocolate.'

'I could ask someone else to be godmother, you know.'

'Too late. I've got a verbal contract.'

'So sue me,' she purred. 'When can I see that haunted house of yours?'

'Next week?'

'I'll text you a day. Night, night, sweetheart.'

There was no reply when I called my mother. She was probably in bed already, but I preferred to imagine her on deck, cocktail in hand, gazing at the sea.

The fire had almost expired, but I sat on the sofa and watched the cinders glowing in the grate. The evening had given me too much to consider. Jon Evans's discomfort was easiest to understand. His breakdown had robbed him of his job and left him dependent on his mother's protection. But Tom's revelation had caught me unawares. Maybe his grief was so unmediated that the smallest memory could open the floodgates. The thing that angered me most was Judith's secrecy.

There was no point in going to bed while my mind was still racing, so I dug out my research notes and started to work. It was a small consolation that I would be able to dazzle Northwood's governors with a polished presentation, even though my interviews with Kinsella were going nowhere fast.

40

Judith looked like the ideal therapist when I found her the next morning – relaxed but attentive, clear-sighted enough to spot any symptom. Patients would assume that her life was perfectly balanced. I noticed that the vantage point from the window of her consulting room was even better than Kinsella's, allowing her to monitor every arrival and departure at the Laurels.

'Are you okay? You look distracted.'

'I need your help, Judith.'

She closed the case file she'd been reading. 'Of course, fire away.'

'Why didn't you tell me you'd kept Kinsella's letters? You know I need to get inside how his mind works.'

Her serenity evaporated, bangles clicking frantically as her hands fluttered. 'I thought about destroying them, but Jon might need them some day, for his research.'

'That's not likely, is it? His contact with Kinsella triggered his breakdown.'

She shifted awkwardly in her chair. 'Alan Nash would get access if I put them in the archive. Kinsella wrote the letters as part of his treatment; we have a duty of care to keep them confidential.'

'You're trying to protect him?'

'It's my job to safeguard his rights, as I do every other inmate's at the Laurels.' The look on Judith's face set my alarm bells ringing. She had come out fighting to protect Kinsella, her softness replaced by ferocity, but maybe she would have done the same for any of her patients.

'Would you let me read the letters?'

She stood by her filing cabinet, arms folded. 'Why? They didn't do Jon much good, did they?'

'It might help the investigation.'

'And you won't tell anyone they're here?'

'I'll try. But if there's anything important, I'll have to share it.'

She gave a grudging nod, then unlocked one of her cupboards, revealing a plastic box, crammed with sheaves of white paper. The sight was daunting. Over the course of a year Kinsella had written the equivalent of several novels, his spiky handwriting zigzagging across hundreds of pages. Judith looked tense as I sorted through them.

'Can I take them to my office?'

'If you think they'll help.' She spoke again as I was about to leave, and it fascinated me that the harshness had left her voice. 'Do you want to meet for a drink later?'

'Can I call you? I don't know how long this'll take.'

The letters felt heavy in my arms as I walked away, and when I got back to the broom cupboard my breath quickened as I sifted through them. At first I felt squeamish about handling the pages, but soon I was too immersed to care. The dark complexity of his world fascinated me. Kinsella was so erudite that quotes from poetry and philosophy littered his stories. But the most disturbing thing was the breezy, matter-of-fact tone he used to describe his crimes.

I feel more alive while others are dying. I'm sure you've tasted that pleasure yourself, when you drive past an accident on the motorway or a friend describes the death of a relative.

Someone has yielded their life, to allow you to glow more
brightly. Imagine the intensity of that feeling when you are
responsible for the killing. Birds of prey have no qualms about
attacking weaklings, and I follow the same principle. My
crimes have made me nine times stronger than before.

The letters all contained the same mixture of fantasy and false
pride, and my brain was protesting about being force-fed
such vile information. A headache was pounding at the back
of my skull but I made myself open the next folder. I was so
deeply absorbed that I almost jumped out of my skin when
someone knocked on my door.

'Come in,' I called.

Tania Goddard stood there, frowning. The wide belt of her
suit cinched her figure into an enviable hourglass. 'I came
looking for you earlier.'

'I've been here all morning. Is Kinsella ready to see me?'

She shook her head. 'I've got some news about him.'

'Let me guess. He won't come out of his cell?'

'He's out of his cell all right.' Tania's eyes locked onto mine.
'He's had a cardiac arrest. The doctors say it's touch and go.'

41

'I've got a treat for you, Ella.'

The man's hand locks around hers as he leads her into the living room. Ella has to bite her lip to stop herself crying. There's a widescreen TV just like the one at home, a packet of biscuits on the coffee table. The room is empty and white-walled, long rows of books on the walls.

'Damn,' the man hisses under his breath. 'I forgot to buy milk.'

'Doesn't matter.'

'I wanted to make you hot chocolate.'

She touches the man's sleeve, but he's too agitated to notice, shifting his weight from foot to foot.

'The shop's only five minutes away.'

'That's okay,' she murmurs.

'You won't do anything daft, will you?'

'Course not,' Ella replies, smiling up at him.

Her heart pounds too quickly when the man leaves. She waits for his footsteps to crunch across the snow, then she flies around the room, twisting door handles, hunting for a phone. Her hands flap against the locked window, but there's nothing heavy enough to break the glass. Her chest aches as she slumps back onto the settee, but she feels better when the TV screen brightens. It's a relief to see different faces. She flicks through the channels until a blonde woman appears, her cheeks slick with make-up.

'And now a quick round-up of the news. Hopes are fading for Ella Williams, who's been missing for two weeks. The bodies of four young girls, abducted from the same part of London, have already been found, and the Metropolitan Police are increasing their search.'

Ella's breath forms a solid lump in her throat. Faces flash across the screen – two girls she doesn't recognise, then Sarah and Amita, and an Indian lady crying into her hands. Her thoughts are whirling. She's the only one left and, any day now, the man could change his mind. Her gaze jitters around the room and settles on a chest of drawers. There's nothing inside except tablecloths, reels of cotton, and a stack of photo albums. The man's footsteps are returning along the passageway, and it's only when she reaches the last drawer that something useful falls into her hands. A pair of kitchen scissors. The man's closer now, so she slips them inside her white dress.

'Mission accomplished,' he says, brandishing a carton of milk. 'Hot chocolate for my princess?'

'Yes, please.'

She gives her best smile and he disappears into the kitchen. The scissors are wedged tightly under her arm. The metal blades feel cold, the points snagging against her skin.

42

Tania marched beside me to the Campbell Building, the light already starting to fade. I tried to find out more about Kinsella's health since he'd been rushed to the infirmary, but she was rationing her words, her chic haircut glinting under the security lights. If I'd had to compare her to a substance, it would have been obsidian; the black gemstone favoured by Victorian widows, hard as granite and polished to a high glitter. It mystified me that she'd chosen someone as sensitive as Burns.

I followed her into an office on the second floor, detectives marching past us towards the incident room. Tania gazed at me as though I belonged to a different species.

'We need to improve your home security,' she said. 'Burns told me your place is near where Amita's body was found, and you've had a break-in recently. From tonight you're staying with us at the hotel.' Her face was hard with certainty, and I wanted to protest, but knew there was no point. It struck me again that she had many of the qualities I admired: resilience, style, and zero tolerance for bullshit.

I went straight to the infirmary after seeing Tania. The building was grey and imposing, two hundred years old, but the interior had been updated to the standards of a modern hospital. There were signs for pathology, physiotherapy, and a day centre for outpatient care. The registrar who met me at reception had a youthful face, but she was white-haired and slightly stooped, as though her job had aged her prematurely.

I explained that I was working with the police on Kinsella's case and she nodded calmly.

'He'll get the same care as the rest of my patients. If they're sick, I try and fix them, no matter what they've done.'

Her name badge told me she was called Moira, and her voice had a soft Irish lilt. I wondered how many rapists and mass murderers she'd rescued from the brink of death during her long career.

'Can you tell me what happened?'

'Louis was brought in with chest pain, extending through his jaw. His trace shows an irregular heartbeat. He may need an angiogram or bypass surgery at a specialist unit, but I can't move him.'

'No?'

'He's refusing treatment.' She gave me a searching look. 'The outside world must seem daunting after all this time.'

The theory struck me as unlikely. Kinsella had spent years campaigning to return to prison. He probably fantasised every day about Northwood's gates swinging open to release him.

'Can I see him?' I asked.

She led me upstairs, and I peered through the observation hatch into Kinsella's room. I did a double take when I saw Judith sitting by his bed. The rise and fall of her voice was musical and rhythmic. She seemed to be reading poetry from a book resting on her lap. The alarm bells I'd heard when she'd defended her reasons for keeping Kinsella's letters a secret were ringing even louder. Either she was closer to him than she'd claimed, or her supply of sympathy was never-ending.

It was doubtful that Kinsella knew he had a visitor. He looked years older, lines carved deeper into his skin, and he was hooked to a cardiogram. The numbers on the monitor were too distant to read, but the bleeps were erratic, the intervals between heartbeats much too quick. He seemed to be in a light sleep, eyelids fluttering, and his wrist was handcuffed to the metal bed-frame. Even in his weakened condition they were taking no chances.

I was surprised to find myself shaking. If Kinsella died, he would take his information about Ella Williams with him, but there was a more personal reason too. He looked like my father after his stroke. I'd found him lying on the kitchen floor when I got back from school, gasping for air. When he returned from hospital my mother employed a full-time nurse to feed and bathe him. She spent her evenings at her prayer group or at the theatre, while his wheelchair stayed in front of the TV, and he couldn't complain, because he'd lost the power of speech. It was the opposite of Kinsella's spells of silence, which only increased his strength – my father must have longed to scream his frustration at the world.

Moira reappeared as I headed for the exit. She spoke gently, as though I was a distressed relative. 'He'll recover, if he takes our help. But he's written a note asking not to be treated.'

'Is he allowed to refuse medication?'

'The governors say we'll have to intervene if his condition becomes critical.' She gave another gentle smile. 'At least he's popular. He's already had plenty of visitors.'

I checked the visitor log on my way out. The list of names started with Garfield Ellis, who'd rushed Kinsella to the infirmary that afternoon, but some of the others surprised me. Gorski, Alan Nash, Tom and Pru, as well as Judith. The infirmary's smell of sickness, damp woollen blankets and bleach seemed to cling to the air. Or maybe it was the memory of Kinsella that made me want to scrub my skin. I ducked into the nearest toilet and reached for the soap, but then an unexpected sound came from one of the cubicles. A woman was crying bitterly, ragged breaths between each sob. I was drying my hands when Pru Fielding finally stepped out. She didn't see me at first, too busy wiping her eyes. The livid birthmark that covered half her face looked even darker, her eyes bloodshot, as though she'd been crying for hours.

'Are you okay?' I asked.

She looked startled. 'I didn't think anyone was here.'

'I've been to see Louis Kinsella. Is that why you came over too?'

She shook her head. 'A man from my art class has got pancreatic cancer, but he still likes to draw, so we meet here one-to-one.'

'Is that why you're upset?'

'He hasn't got long to go. God, this place is bleak, isn't it?'

Maybe it had only just dawned on her that most inmates at the Laurels would never be freed. Tears carried on leaking from Pru's eyes as she hid her scar behind a paper towel.

My mind was whirring as I crossed the hospital campus. It interested me that the staff at the Laurels felt so much compassion. All I'd taken from my meetings with Kinsella was a blast of pent-up fury, and the memory of his eyes crawling across my skin. Alan Nash's visit was easy to interpret. It was pure self-interest; a deathbed confession would increase his book sales out of sight. But I wondered what Tom had gained from sitting beside Kinsella's sickbed. Perhaps it was a hangover from his days as a priest – a need to comfort the afflicted, whatever their sins.

When I got back to the broom cupboard, I switched on my laptop and checked the encrypted files Burns had given me, containing the HR records of every staff member at the Laurels. Judith's CV showed that she had spent her career specialising in treating violent offenders, and she had excellent references from her previous employers. It seemed odd that she had started at Northwood in the same year Kinsella arrived, but I knew I was just being paranoid. There was nothing to indicate professional malpractice or over-involvement. If she had fallen under Kinsella's spell, surely she would have restarted his campaign years sooner? My main ally at Northwood seemed to be blameless. Relief washed over me as I got ready to leave.

The solemn policeman who'd driven me to Windsor to interview Kinsella's wife was waiting beside my car, his gloom heightened by the cold. 'DI Goddard sent me,' he said. 'You're to leave your car here, then she wants you to pack a bag and go straight to the hotel.'

I gritted my teeth. I'd accepted that I had to leave the cottage, but people's efforts to help have always irritated me – you could describe it as independence or the worst kind of stubbornness. I tried to be civil, but my tone of voice was a fraction too curt.

'It sounds like Tania's got my future all mapped out.'

Reg gave me a bored stare, but maybe I was doing him a disservice. For all I knew, he spent his idle moments contemplating the nature of existence. A few personal details leaked out on the drive to the cottage. He came from Muswell Hill, he supported Arsenal, and he'd spent thirty-two years in the Force.

'The job's changed out of sight,' he said. 'Too many chiefs, not enough Indians.'

'The NHS is the exactly same.'

Reg smiled briefly to himself, clearly pleased that we agreed about the decline of public services, and in the end I was grateful for his lift. There had been a fresh fall of snow, and the van passed down the lane with ease, saving me a hike through the cold. I scanned the path outside the cottage for fresh footprints but the snow was unmarked.

After I'd packed my holdall I stood by the bedroom window. The sky was perfectly clear. Miles of black velvet, littered with sequins. Perhaps it was the surfeit of beauty that triggered my anger. My work for the Met had taken over my life again. I should have refused to help Burns, then I could have completed my research in peace and spent my evenings stargazing, but now I was too deeply committed. My mind defaulted to Ella Williams whenever I relaxed. The only way to regain my freedom was to work nonstop until she was found. I took one last glance at the moon, haloed by a fuzz of brightness, then marched back downstairs.

'Ready when you are.' I left the hall light burning, even though it was unlikely to help. With a little determination, anyone could smash a window and step inside.

The drive to Charndale Manor took less than ten minutes, and I studied the building as Reg parked the car. The hotel was built on a grand scale, with floodlights picking out Gothic turrets and leaded windows. It would make the ideal venue for murder-mystery weekends, the guests competing to be Miss Marple or Hercule Poirot.

My room was on the second floor. The curtains had seen better days and cigarette burns were dotted across the carpet; a couple in the room next door were having a row, the wall reverberating with each insult. I dropped my bag on the bed and escaped downstairs.

'A double espresso, please,' I told the girl behind the bar.

It was ten o'clock but my chances of sleep were minimal until my neighbours calmed down. The best option was to load up on caffeine and get on with some work. The hotel bar was a cavernous tribute to Queen Victoria, mahogany-lined from floor to ceiling, wall lights struggling to penetrate the gloom. I recognised some faces from the incident room. Pete Hanson was killing time further down the bar, browsing through his newspaper, but I couldn't face making conversation. Luckily there was a private bar, which turned out to be small, empty and warm.

I felt better once I'd engaged my brain. Tania had given me a printout of the latest HOLMES report, detailing every contact and witness statement since the investigation began. My phone rang before I'd reached page six. I considered ignoring it, but it was Lola. We'd sworn never to blank each other when we were twelve years old and, given my current run of luck, I couldn't afford to jinx myself.

'Pregnant women need extra sleep,' I said. 'Why aren't you in bed?'

'I had my first scan today.'

The idea jumped like a needle on scratched vinyl. 'It still doesn't feel real, Lo.'

'I've got evidence. The baby's going to be a giant.'

'Text me the picture, can you?'

There was a pause before she spoke again. 'Is something wrong?' One of Lola's best skills is clairvoyance. She can mind-read from a thousand miles, so there's no point in keeping secrets.

'Not wrong exactly. My cottage is out of bounds, that's all.'

Lola listened to my explanation then tutted loudly. 'I'm still coming for the weekend.'

'That's not a great idea.'

'Of course it is. I'll stay at the hotel.'

There was no sense in arguing. Once Lola makes up her mind, she's an unstoppable force.

I put my phone on mute afterwards, espresso fizzing in my bloodstream as I scanned the printout. The Met team had certainly been busy. They'd spent the last week monitoring parks, playgrounds and routes used by the girls, and analysing hundreds of hours of CCTV. I studied the section that profiled the registered sex offenders who'd been interviewed. One of them had seemed like a contender, but the thread was dropped because his alibi was rock solid. I stared at the page until the script blurred. It was possible that the abductions had nothing to do with sex. The killer had simply targeted the most vulnerable children he could find: motherless, fostered, or adopted. In his eyes they were the poorest wretches in society. Maybe he believed that he was exterminating street urchins, or being cruel to be kind. So far there was no clue about how he had tapped into records of the children's home lives. One of the things that concerned me most was the length of time he had kept his first victims. The post-mortem report on Kylie Walsh showed that her body had lain in a freezer for weeks. Serial killers who retain the corpses of their victims tend to become addicted to killing. They're so friendless and isolated, they're reluctant to part with their victims, as though they were lovers or relatives.

Despite all the evidence, I still had a hunch that Ella Williams was alive. No token had arrived for Kinsella, and her teacher described her as the smartest kid she'd ever taught, dragged prematurely into the adult world when her mother died. If she'd found a way to play him, then all I had to do was work out her method. Ideas were shifting into place when I heard the door opening. Burns was standing there, clutching a shot glass in each hand.

'Pete said you were here, so I got you a nightcap.' He dropped onto the seat beside me. 'Do you always work this late?'

'Why? Do you always drink whisky at midnight?'

'Once in a blue moon.' His mouth twitched into a smile, and I tried to quell the surge of attraction that arrived whenever I saw him. 'What have you been looking at?'

'The people who're close to Kinsella: Pru Fielding, Tom

Jensen, Judith Miller and Garfield Ellis. And the records say that Aleks Gorski had solo meetings with him before his tribunal.'

'You seriously think the centre director's involved?'

I shrugged. 'It's got to be someone in a position of trust. He's spent plenty of time in Kinsella's company.'

'Run me through your suspects.'

'Pru Fielding's the most vulnerable, she's the art therapist at the Laurels. Tom Jensen runs the gym. He's a loner, with no family. Garfield's Kinsella's nurse and he sees more of him than anyone else. Judith Miller used to be his counsellor – she defends his rights a bit too strenuously.'

'I'll take a look at them.' Burns scribbled the names in his notebook.

'Did you find any more evidence at Orchard Row?'

'Nothing.' He gazed at his whisky, swirling in its glass. 'We've got DNA from all five girls, but not a trace of him, apart from the tracks of his van. It's like he lured them there, then disappeared into thin air, like the Pied Piper.'

I returned my attention to my pile of notes, and my thoughts finally clicked into place. 'That's it, Don. You've hit the nail on the head.'

'I'm not with you.'

'We've been looking in the wrong direction. Kinsella was the Pied Piper. This is about kids, not adults, and Ella's found the killer's Achilles heel. She's found a way to mother him.'

'How do you mean?'

'Ella's playing the adult role. It's someone who's never progressed beyond the emotional state of childhood. He was probably less than ten when he met Kinsella. Kids are more suggestible than adults – given enough time and effort, you can brainwash them to do anything.'

'Like child soldiers,' he murmured.

'Exactly. Train an eight-year-old to use a machete and he'll kill for you, without asking why.'

'So it's a pupil from St Augustine's, not a teacher.'

'Not necessarily. It could be a boy from his choir, or any child he saw regularly. That would make Judith and Garfield too old to be the killer, and put Tom and Pru in the right age bracket. Maybe other kids Kinsella groomed have followed him to Northwood as well.'

The familiar obsessive look was back on Burns's face. Any second now he'd be banging on people's doors, rousing his team from their well-earned sleep. Over his shoulder I saw Tania standing in the doorway and felt a pang of discomfort. Our body language must have looked incriminating; her boyfriend huddled beside me, sharing a nightcap. She shot me a look of pure loathing then turned away.

'There's Tania,' I said. 'You should go after her.'

'You're right, she needs to hear this. You're a wonder, Alice.' He leant towards me, face glowing with excitement, and it would have been easy to make a complete fool of myself, so I forced myself back onto my feet.

'I'll see you in the morning.'

I scooped up my papers and headed for the stairs. When I got to my room, my neighbours had resolved their argument. Rhythmic grunts emanated through the wall, accompanied by the squeal of bedsprings. I went into the bathroom and peeled off my clothes then turned the shower to full blast. I stood there until the water ran cold, letting the torrent drown every sound.

43

The scissors are hidden inside the base of the chair, but the man pushes the door open so fast, there's no time to grab them. A wild grin is spreading across his face.

'I've got something to show you upstairs.' The man steps closer, but Ella doesn't feel afraid. She's been scared for so long, her body has stopped reacting.

'No, I'm staying here.'

'What's wrong?' He kneels down, his eyes brimming with feelings she can't identify. 'Don't let me down, princess. Not now. Please.'

'Why can't you tell me your name?'

'I told you, it's against the rules.'

'The rules don't work any more. And I want my old clothes back, I'm sick of this dress.'

The man's eyes darken. 'You have to wear it, because you're an orphan, like me.'

'I'm not. I've got granddad and Suzanne.'

The punch arrives out of nowhere. His fist catches her shoulder and sends her tumbling to the floor, and this time the exhaustion's too great. Tears flood from her eyes before she can stop them.

'I'm sorry, princess. You scare me when you talk like that.' The man lifts her back onto the bed, then kneels in front of her, unable to meet her eye. 'Can you forgive me?'

'Of course.' Ella forces herself to reach out and touch his face.

Soon his smile reappears, his white teeth sharp as the blade of a kitchen knife. 'Come and see my surprise.'

Ella's eyes blink at the raw brightness of the strip-light in the kitchen. It's dark outside and the clock says that it's two fifteen. A piece of white fabric lies folded on the living-room table, beside a box of pins and a cotton reel.

'I've finished the collar, so it matches yours.'

The man holds up a new white dress for her to inspect, and Ella's heart rattles inside her chest.

'When's the next one coming?'

'Saturday. Kinsella's chosen a real beauty this time, Ella. You can see a photo if you like.'

Ella nods silently, unable to speak. The man passes her an envelope and a picture falls into her hands. There's a glimmer of blonde hair, shiny and golden like Sarah's, then she slides the girl's face back into the envelope to keep it safe.

44

Forty sets of eyes blinked at me the next morning. I'd been dreading the briefing, because too much caffeine, booze and adrenaline had kept me awake for hours, but Burns looked considerably fresher. Only the creases in his shirt made me wonder if he'd gone to bed at all. Alan Nash shot me a disdainful glare from the back of the room, so I smiled sweetly in reply. Extreme courtesy has always been my preferred antidote to bullying.

'Some of you are going back to London today with DI Goddard,' Burns told the packed room. 'I want you to trace every pupil who attended Kinsella's school during his time there, the kids from the home on Orchard Row, and the ones in his choir. We need to rule out any child who was in close contact with him. Do you want to give us some guidance, Alice?'

A sea of faces gawped at me. 'It's likely that Kinsella brainwashed one of the children he cared for. Up to the age of eight or nine, kids are like litmus paper. They struggle to sift right from wrong. They absorb everything we say. If the child is vulnerable, and the guidance comes from an authority figure, it can be hard to forget.'

One of Nash's followers threw a question from the back of the room. 'You reckon some bloke's waited twenty years to start killing just because Kinsella chatted to him at primary school?'

'It's possible. Children lay down their deepest memories between the ages of five and ten. If you show a child violent images, violence becomes normalised. History gives us plenty of examples: the Hitler Youth, African child soldiers, Chinese kids during the Cultural Revolution. We know Kinsella tried to brainwash adults like Roy Layton by showing them violent child porn. Maybe the kids in his care got the same treatment.'

Some of the faces winced. A few clearly thought I was a crackpot, leading their DCI astray, and it was a relief when Burns started talking again.

'The rest of you are staying here, following local leads. Kinsella's wife is visiting him this morning, and she'll be wearing a wire.' He came to a halt and frowned at his audience. 'If I hear about anyone giving this less than a hundred per cent, you'll be back in uniform quicker than I can say snow.'

Burns dismissed the room with a nod, his expression slowly reverting from thug to gentleman, and I set off to collect Lauren French from reception. It surprised me that she had agreed to risk her peace of mind after so many years, and the shrink in me was excited about witnessing her meeting with Kinsella.

From a distance Lauren looked perfectly in control, wearing muted but expensive clothes, chestnut hair neatly styled. But at close range her fear was visible. She must have spent hours applying lipstick, foundation and mascara, as though war paint was her only psychological protection. I reached out and touched her arm.

'Thanks for doing this, Lauren.'

Her face trembled when she smiled. 'The detective said it might be my last chance to say goodbye.' Her pace slowed as we crossed the quadrangle, the infirmary roof glittering in the distance.

'I know how tough this must be, but did Louis ever mention any special pupils at St Augustine's? Any favourites that kept cropping up?'

'I don't remember.' Her gaze stayed fixed on the icy pathway. 'It's so long ago, I'm sorry.'

'Just ask him who's carrying out the attacks. You don't have to spend long in there.'

She nodded but didn't reply. By the time we reached the infirmary, she was shaking like a leaf. When I led her to a bench she hunched forwards, eyes staring, like she was memorising the pattern on the lino.

'Take your time, Lauren. Wait here till you feel ready.'

'I'll never be ready.' Her eyes flashed like a warning light. 'I just want this over and done.'

A WPC fitted the listening device in the observation room next to Kinsella's, helping Lauren to clip the wire inside her blouse, but she still looked terrified. I heard her murmuring quietly, giving herself a final pep talk. She crossed herself before setting off, as though she was leading a crusade.

The monitor showed her entering Kinsella's room. The camera above Kinsella's bed showed his prone body, and the crown of his head. But it was Lauren's face as she saw her husband after so many years apart that interested me most. Her eyes stretched wide as she stared at him, like it was a sin to blink. She stood a few metres from the bed – clearly she had no intention of going within touching distance. Kinsella's whisper was too quiet for the microphones to catch, but Lauren's voice was perfectly audible. Tension had raised its pitch by half an octave.

'I thought I'd feel something, but I can't even remember why I married you,' she said. 'You only wanted me because I was still a child. A nice little trainee nurse to cover for you. I blamed myself for missing the signs, but you were so convincing, Louis. You should have been an actor.'

The wire picked up an odd, strangulated sound from Kinsella, somewhere between outrage and an appeal for help. His wife's voice grew even louder.

'Promise me you'll tell them what you know, Louis. You pretended to be a Catholic once. If you confess, I might even pray for you.'

'Piety doesn't impress me, Sonia. You knew exactly what I was doing. You guessed months before the trial. I could see it in your eyes. All that violence excited you, didn't it?'

'You know that's a lie. Why don't you tell me his name?'

'What makes you think it's a man?' Kinsella hissed. 'Your sex is capable of evils that men can only imagine.'

When she stood up to leave, her final gesture shocked me. She twisted her wedding ring from her finger and threw it onto the bed.

'My priest has agreed to annul our marriage. I just came to say goodbye, Louis.'

Lauren walked away without looking back. But her strength expired when she reached the corridor. She was trembling so badly she could hardly stand, so I got her a coffee from the vending machine and loaded it with sugar.

'I made a mess of that, didn't I?' she whispered.

'Not at all. You did exactly what I asked.'

Tears seeped from her eyes. 'His voice used to be the best thing about him. Is he really dying?'

'I don't know. He's stable at the moment, but he's refusing treatment.'

Lauren blotted her face, leaving a blur of mascara under each eye. 'I thought of something after your visit. Louis used to send me letters at the start. They were censored, but a few lines slipped through.'

'And they stuck in your mind?'

'He said the foundlings would come back, one by one. None of them would forget.'

'What do you think he meant?'

She shrugged her shoulders. 'No one uses the word "foundling" any more, do they? We call them orphans nowadays.'

'Did you keep the letters?'

Her face hardened. 'I tore most of them up without reading them.'

We walked back to reception together. I didn't envy her the return trip to Windsor, with only her cat waiting to comfort her. Even her make-up had let her down, foundation smeared across her collar. Hopefully her bravery would carry its own reward; facing her worst fears might lighten her burden.

Kinsella's letters were still waiting for me when I got back to my office. The room smelled of panic and stale coffee, and even though it was freezing outside, I flung the window open, and a blast of cold air hit the back of my neck as I studied them. It was easy to see why Lauren had thrown hers away. Anyone with a depressive tendency could be persuaded that evil existed everywhere you looked – even in the souls of children. I carried on reading for the rest of the day, Kinsella's mindset growing clearer with each letter. Female children harmed everyone in their orbit. The youngest and sweetest looking were the most evil. I tried to suppress my anger at the excuses he'd fabricated. The worst thing about his narrative was the rapture he felt when he committed the murders.

At five o'clock I shoved the letters back into the box, bile rising in my throat. My mind flooded with pictures of his victims' ruined faces, and I just managed to reach the toilets at the end of the corridor before spewing my last cup of coffee down the drain. Afterwards I splashed my face with cold water and avoided looking at myself. I caught a glimpse of a blonde-haired ghost in the mirror, eyes hollow from lack of sleep.

I went out to the car park to wait for Reg, hoping the cold would revive me. There was still no sign of a thaw. Security lights poured across half a kilometre of whiteness, picking out the razor wire fences in the distance, designed to contain the bravest escapees. I was so distracted that I didn't recognise the man's voice calling my name, until I saw Chris Steadman. His bleached hair was falling into his eyes, crash helmet cradled in the crook of his arm.

'You look thoughtful.'

'It's an act, Chris. My head's a vacuum.'

'I have days like that. The best cure is to jump on a motorbike and go like the clappers.'

'Sadly I don't have one.'

'Take mine.' He dangled his keys in front of me. 'You've passed your test, haven't you? And the roads have just been cleared.'

I don't know why I accepted the keys. Maybe it was because his grin was a direct challenge. He seemed certain I'd be too scared, so I walked over to the huge Triumph.

'Go to Charndale and back,' he said. 'And don't get done for speeding.'

I turned the starter key and the bike roared into life. When I rode towards the exit gates, I felt as if I was turning into someone else. Someone braver and more adventurous. Steadman's crash helmet smelled of hair gel and cigarettes as I raced through Charndale. The engine throbbed from a purr to a roar, and I didn't care about the chill slicing through my coat, or that my thin trousers would offer no protection if I crashed. It was tempting to chase down the motorway and never come back.

45

Ella stands by the bed, listening for sounds. The walls muffle every noise, but occasionally she hears a lorry grinding down the road, or the stop-start of a postman's van. She's waiting for the door to slam, letting her know the man's come back, but there's something else, so faint it could be imaginary. A woman's voice singing. At first Ella's too shocked to react, then she realises it's coming from close by. She fills her lungs with air and starts to scream. The sound bounces from the walls; when silence returns, the singing has stopped. Maybe the woman is phoning the police. Ella screams again, even louder this time, her whole body pulsing with energy. But the singing starts again. The woman has no idea that she's locked underground.

Desperation pushes her to take a risk. She lifts the chair cushion, fumbling for the scissors, then forces the blade into the keyhole and twists the handle. It refuses to budge, but she keeps trying. Just when she's ready to give up, the lock clicks open and she runs upstairs. There's no view through the kitchen window except the high wooden fence. The woman must be behind it, singing to herself. Ella screams until her throat is raw, but still no one comes. Her heart ticks too fast in her chest, like a clock that's overwound.

Ella attacks the back door lock with the blade, but this time the trick fails. The handle feels like it's been set in concrete. The man has hidden the key somewhere. She searches in every cupboard, then her eyes catch on a photo album, fat enough to hold hundreds of pictures. The first pages are filled with newspaper clippings, yellow with age. Someone has written the word KINSELLA at the top of the page. They all show the same man's face. His hair is short and neat, but his eyes are frightening. They stare across sharp cheekbones, black and penetrating. Then there are pictures of little girls in their white dresses, eyes closed. Ella recognises Sarah and Amita, then her own name printed at the top of the next page. There are enough pages to hold forty or fifty more girls.

A car door slams in the distance and Ella shoves the album back in the cupboard. She races downstairs and pulls the door shut, jiggling the blade frantically in the lock, until it clicks tight. Now there are no sounds at all. The only thing Ella can hear is her heartbeat, drumming with panic, refusing to slow down.

46

The wind roared under the visor of the crash helmet, freezing my grin into place, yet I'd never felt freer. Concentrating on the road had helped me forget about Kinsella's warped fantasies. Eventually I forced myself to do a U-turn, because Chris would be fretting about his pride and joy. I slowed down to a sensible speed, the engine humming softly.

Chris had turned up the collar of his leather jacket when I got back to the car park, blowing warm air onto his hands. When I finally handed over his keys, he seemed amused.

'That was amazing. I feel like a new woman.'

'Go for a burn whenever you like.'

'You're a trusting soul. I could sell her to the highest bidder.'

'I'll risk it.' His gaze lingered on my face. 'Listen, Alice, I've been meaning to say something, about Tom.'

'Have you?'

'People read him wrong. They think he's cold, but he isn't at all. If you give him another chance, you'll find out.'

I blinked at him in surprise. He didn't seem the type to offer relationship advice, but it was obvious he was being sincere. 'Did he ask you to say that?'

'God, no. He'd kill me if he knew I'd spoken to you.'

'Don't worry, I won't tell him.'

Chris gave an awkward grin then climbed onto his bike. I watched it speed along the exit road, and I found myself re-evaluating him. At first he'd seemed edgy, but he was just ultra-sensitive, attuned to every emotion in the room. And he'd ignited my sense of guilt about Tom. If he had feelings for me, I was in no position to return them. Desire seemed to be the only emotion we had in common.

'Have you finished playing Evel Knievel?' Reg looked furious as he walked towards me. 'I've been waiting ages. It's brass monkeys out here.'

'Sorry, Reg. That was the chance of a lifetime.'

He scowled. 'Don't talk to me about chances. I've had one hell of a day.'

'How come?'

'DI bloody Goddard chewed my head off on the way to the station. According to her, my driving's lousy, and so's my attitude.'

'Poor you.'

My sympathy was genuine. I was probably increasing Tania's rage. On top of working on a harrowing case, she thought I was after her boyfriend.

The press had multiplied when we reached the hotel. News vans from Sky and ITV were blocking the hotel entrance, a few hardy photographers braving the cold. Most of the journalists would be propping up the bar by now, trying to buy details from the team for the price of a drink. I thanked Reg for the lift then hurried upstairs.

At least my room felt peaceful. Either my neighbours had gone out for the evening, or the state of their relationship had worsened, and they were locked in a grim silence. I picked up the phone and ordered room service, then spread out my papers. A photo of Ella Williams slipped from my folder. She looked at me expectantly, and I studied her again. Her eyes shone with curiosity, and she seemed to be studying the cameraman, figuring out how he composed his shots.

'What's different about you?' I muttered. 'Why's he keeping you alive?'

I looked at the timeline for the investigation. Ella had been gone almost three weeks. If she was still alive, she must have realised that there was a frightened child locked inside the man who was terrorising her. I gazed down at the last date on my list. In forty-eight hours another child would be taken, and this time Kinsella had claimed that she would be blinded before she died.

When my meal arrived I was immersed in crime-scene analysis. The waiter made a production of unloading dishes from a silver tray, but the food hardly seemed worth it. The vegetarian lasagne had seen better days, cheese sauce congealed into tasteless lumps. But I was too hungry to complain, flicking through reports as I ate. I was still unclear why the killer had shifted so far west from his original patch, apart from a desire to place his tributes closer to Kinsella. Maybe he'd been unnerved by dozens of uniforms pounding the streets, from Euston to Kentish Town.

By ten o'clock my head was throbbing. I'd leafed through every page of the HOLMES printout, and picked over my notes about the Foundling Museum, but the information had stopped making sense. I hesitated for a moment before picking up my phone. Burns sounded like he'd spent the evening smoking cigars, his Scottish burr even more pronounced than usual.

'I need a drink, Don.'

'Downstairs is crawling with hacks. Come to 311.'

Burns's room was directly above mine, but considerably bigger, the sitting area furnished with leather sofas. I glanced around while he reached into the fridge, selecting miniatures. His room was the direct opposite of Tom's pristine flat. It could have doubled as an artwork by Tracey Emin, with his whole life on display. A framed photo of his boys on the cabinet, clothes spilling from his suitcase, a book about Jackson Pollock on his bedside table, and a half-eaten meal abandoned on a tray. His evening had obviously followed the same pattern as mine, except the papers on his coffee table were stacked even higher. When he sat beside me, it was there again – the physical draw I always struggled to pin down. It certainly wasn't inspired by his clothes. He was wearing a faded black T-shirt, worn-out jeans, and trainers that Tesco's flog for a fiver.

'I'm glad you rang,' he said. 'My brain's imploding.'

Burns rubbed the back of his neck with the palms of his hands, and it would have been the easiest thing in the world to touch him while his eyes were closed. I folded my arms tightly and made myself concentrate.

'I keep thinking about the foundlings,' I said. 'The links are everywhere. The victims' bodies are tagged, just like the mortuary assistants numbered the corpses at the Foundling Hospital. And Kinsella said the foundlings would come back to him.'

'If he thinks the foundlings are going to return from the grave, he's even sicker than we thought.' Burns met my eye. 'I'm afraid Alan Nash has got wind of those letters you've been reading. He's asking for access.'

'So he can write another book, to titillate the copycats?' I shook my head firmly. 'Have you found any Northwood staff with childhood links to Kinsella yet?'

'We're still having trouble getting records, but so far we haven't found anyone from St Augustine's or Orchard House. The whole thing's pretty hard to believe, Alice. All two and a half thousand staff have been vetted, they're all squeaky clean.'

I shook my head firmly. 'The only way Kinsella's disciples can come back is by visiting the hospital, or getting a job there.

The guy's obsessed, isn't he? A job in the same building as his hero would be his dream come true.'

'They'd be breathing the same air,' he murmured.

We batted theories back and forth for half an hour but didn't seem to be getting anywhere. The ringing of Burns's phone broke into our conversation and I realised suddenly that I would need some sleep before I could bring clarity to the proceedings. I waited to say goodnight, but he was too busy issuing complicated instructions into his mobile. He touched my shoulder in gratitude as I headed for the door. A mix of emotions was visible in his eyes: panic, guilt, and something too raw to identify. Disbelief, probably, that five girls had been stolen in front of his eyes.

When I got back to my room, his footsteps were still pounding the floorboards above me, and my phone was buzzing on the coffee table. The first message was from Tom – a terse invitation to go to a party on Monday night. The next was from my mother, describing that day's trip to a lace museum in Nicosia. The final text contained a miracle. Lola had sent the picture from her scan, and I stared at it for a long time. My godchild shimmered against the black background, a half-moon of tiny silver bones, preparing to take the world by storm.

47

My brother rang at noon the next day. I was in the broom cupboard, poring over the last of Kinsella's letters. At least the call gave me an excuse to ignore the piles of yellowing paper.

'How are you, sweetheart?'

'Not bad. I'm waiting for my bus.' Will's voice was lower than before, as though a weight was resting on his chest.

'What have you been up to?'

'The usual fun and games. Scrubbing floors, stacking the dishwasher.'

'At least you've got a sea view.'

He made a sound that was somewhere between a sob and a laugh. 'Listen, Al, are you still in that cottage?'

'Not at the moment. Why?'

'Promise me you won't go back. I saw a cloud yesterday, over the sea. It was by itself, and it blew apart. When I looked again, the sky was empty.' His voice was rising with panic.

'It's okay, Will. I'm fine, honestly. And you'll see me soon, won't you?'

It took forever to calm him down. I reminded him of the date when we'd agreed to meet at Brighton Pavilion to go for dinner, and his voice was steadier when we said goodbye. Outside my window it was snowing again, the flakes so fine and powdery that walking through it would be like facing a sandstorm.

I tried to concentrate again on Kinsella's letters; the last ones described the killings from start to finish. Each child had been given the chance to repent, but Kinsella was never satisfied. The victims went through hours of torture. One was beaten, cut, and abused over a whole weekend. Yet he claimed repeatedly that the foundlings would return; there would be a reawakening.

'It doesn't make sense,' I muttered to myself.

I stacked the letters in their box and locked my office. The engaged sign was displayed on Judith's door, so I waited in the corridor. Five minutes later, the Shenfield Strangler emerged, handcuffed to his guard. I couldn't help taking a deep breath. Kinsella's crimes paled into insignificance compared to his, and there was something startling about coming face to face with such a prolific killer. He was smaller than I'd imagined, too weak to strangle anyone now, his messy black hair shot through with grey. Only his fierce expression reminded me of the newspaper portraits from the day of his sentence. His eyes refused to yield even a glimmer of light.

It surprised me that Judith looked brighter than normal; forty-five minutes in the company of one of the most dangerous men alive hadn't dented her happiness. Either she'd learned to separate her emotions completely, or her endless well of sympathy never ran dry.

'You're a miracle, Judith. How do you keep going?'

Her eyes looked dreamier than ever. 'Garfield stayed at mine last night. I had him all to myself.'

'And you still haven't come down,' I said, returning her smile. 'I brought back the letters.'

'Did they help?'

'There's a lot of fantasy in there. Did Kinsella ever talk about the foundlings coming back in your therapy sessions?'

She shook her head. 'Most of the time he talked about the past, not the future. Who are the foundlings anyway?'

'It's a long story. I'll tell you another time.'

'Are you coming to mine on Monday? I'm throwing a birthday party for Tom.'

'I didn't know it was his birthday.'

'Trust him to be secretive. You'll come, won't you?'

'Of course.'

I watched her hide Kinsella's letters again in her cupboard. It still mystified me that she could live with a testimony of the worst kinds of human evil right beside her chair. The bangles on her wrist clattered merrily as she waved goodbye.

Alan Nash was the first person I saw in the Campbell Building. His tweed jacket and corduroys were more suited to the Chelsea Flower Show than a psychiatric hospital, but he made an effort to look welcoming.

'I was just on my way to see you, Alice.' His thousand-watt smile flashed on for a heartbeat.

'Then I saved you a journey.'

'I hear you've unearthed some of Kinsella's letters.'

'One or two. They're part of an archive.'

'How do I get access?' Pound signs were flashing in Nash's eyes. He'd be sitting on a goldmine if he could print original materials in his book.

'You'd need permission from Dr Gorski.'

Nash's face flushed with anger. I didn't know why I'd headed him off at the pass. Probably because the letters were so toxic. Why release them into the world, if the sole reason was to swell the professor's bank balance?

A rugby scrum of detectives had gathered around the coffee machine in the incident room and, when I looked more closely, Burns was at the centre, calm as the eye of a storm. One of the detectives gave me a knowing smile, which made me wonder if someone had seen me leaving his hotel room the night before. The intent look on Burns's face filled me with anxiety.

'Has something happened, Don?'

'Kinsella wants to clear his conscience,' he said.

'He hasn't got one. Deathbed confessions don't apply with psychopaths.'

'It's you he wants to see.'

My stomach churned like a concrete mixer grinding into action. Reading Kinsella's letters had revealed the full depravity of his world-view, and the idea of spending more time with my father's ghost was more than I could face.

48

Ella can't guess how much time has passed since the man brought food or water, but her mouth's so dry her tongue is starting to swell. Every day it's harder to believe that she'll escape. She used to imagine running down the street into Suzanne's arms, but now when she closes her eyes, all she sees is a wall of blackness. She's forgotten how to dream.

The man's footsteps stomp across the wooden floor and he's talking to himself again. Sometimes Ella pities him. He's like the boy in her class who wears the wrong clothes: the others avoid him, but she can see how much he needs a friend, someone to laugh at the same jokes. The key scratches in the lock and when the man walks in, he looks triumphant.

'What do you think of this, princess?'

The dress is balanced on the palms of his hands. Ella takes a step closer and studies his stitch-work on the collar, buttons shining like mother of pearl.

'It's perfect.' She reaches out to touch the material, but the man yanks it away.

'Don't,' he snaps. 'Your hands are filthy.'

'That's not my fault. You should let me use the bathroom.'

The man stares at her. 'You always take over, Ella. I don't know why I break the rules for you.'

'It's so beautiful, I wanted to hold it.'

He relaxes slightly. 'Sorry, I'm on edge, that's all.'

'Why do you make us wear white?'

'That's obvious, isn't it? White's the colour of purity. If you wear it long enough, your sins will be wiped away.'

'What sins?'

The man looks away. 'I've got to go to work now. But when I get back you can have a bath. All right?'

Ella makes herself kiss his outstretched hand and the man's face softens. He kneels down until their eyes are level.

'Don't worry about the new girl, princess. It'll always be you and me. No need to be jealous.' His stubble chafes her skin as he kisses her cheek, and his breath encloses her in a cloud of sour air.

49

Kinsella was white-faced, propped up his on pillows, but still capable of staring me down. His gaze was intense enough to etch a pattern on my skin.

'Thank you for indulging me, Alice.'

I mustered a smile. 'You didn't give me much choice, did you?'

'I'm sure you had the opportunity to refuse.' Kinsella's pallor made him look even more ghostly, every bone visible under his skin.

'Before you say anything, you know this room's wired for sound and vision, don't you?' I pointed at the tiny cameras hidden inside the light fitments.

'Honest to the last. It's an admirable quality.'

'I wouldn't lie to you about the state of play, Mr Kinsella.'

'Surely you can bring yourself to use my first name?' The ghost of a smile trembled on his lips.

'Tell me what you want, Louis.'

'I thought I'd better confess. My wife fears for my immortal soul.'

'You're not dying. The registrar thinks you've got angina; if you see a consultant, it's treatable.'

His eyes glittered with amusement. 'My illness can run its course, for all I care. But I'd like to impart a few home truths first.'

If Kinsella genuinely believed he was at death's door, the

prospect didn't seem to bother him. His wrist was still hand-cuffed to the metal bed frame but even that couldn't disturb his calm. His eyes burned when he spoke again.

'The killer's enjoying Ella's company so much that killing her will be more difficult for him in the long run. In every other respect he's following the rules, but I'm afraid he's formed the wrong impression about us.'

'In what way?'

'He knows about our meetings. It's a simple case of jealousy.'

Nausea welled at the back of my throat. If he was telling the truth, the killer was out there somewhere, seething with resentment about my intimacy with his guru. 'Is he still planning to take another girl tomorrow?'

Kinsella nodded, but his voice was losing strength. 'This time he'll stay in the delightful county of Berkshire.'

'How are you two communicating?'

'We don't need to. I taught him everything twenty years ago.'

'He works here, doesn't he? It's one of your pupils from St Augustine's.'

'Close, but not entirely accurate. You struggle to think laterally, don't you, Alice?' His smile widened. 'How are you enjoying your stay at Charndale Manor?'

'Tell me who he is, Louis.'

'Send Alan Nash tomorrow morning. I'll tell him the name, I feel I owe him a favour.'

'You brought me here to tell me absolutely nothing?'

'So much rage, Alice, and so near the surface.' His eyes narrowed as he observed me. 'Your father must have cut you to the quick.'

I resisted the impulse to slap his face. 'He hurt himself more.'

Kinsella's words rattled round my head as I left the room. My hands were shaking – with anger, not fear. Manipulation was his only reason for summoning me: he loved being the puppet master while Ella's life slipped away.

'Let me see the tape,' I snapped at Burns when I reached the observation room.

I've always hated watching myself, but this time it was essential, because I knew I'd missed something. Kinsella's enjoyment was evident as the film replayed. Getting a straight answer from a sadistic psychopath is a clinical impossibility, because lying only increases their pleasure. He might have been physically weakened, but all the intellectual power lay in his hands. My fists clenched as I listened to his voice.

'Water-boarding was invented for people like him,' Burns muttered.

'He knows I've moved to the hotel. Someone here must have told him.'

'Not necessarily. There's a TV in his room, and bulletins have been filmed there. He's probably seen you going in.'

I didn't reply, but I thought he was wrong. No one knew that I'd left the cottage apart from my contacts at Northwood. I tried to remember who I'd told. I'd let Gorski's office know. Apart from that, I'd only spoken to Judith, Garfield and Tom, but news seemed to spread around the hospital like wildfire.

Burns reached past me to turn off the computer, and something about his bulk made me want to touch him, in the same way that it's tempting to caress statues in museums. His scale was so monumental, it looked like he'd been chipped out of granite. 'You did what you could, Alice. He never had any intention of helping us.'

His statement finally explained why I was so attracted to him. It wasn't just his physical draw, although the depth of his gaze appealed to me, and the way he held himself. It was his capacity for fairness. I'd worked with Burns for three years and never heard him lie. I listened to him explain why the team was struggling to identify Northwood staff who'd lived at Orchard Row. Records only went back fifteen years and the local authority couldn't access their archives.

'So far there are no matches,' he said.

He looked so bleak that I could guess what he was thinking. Maybe Kinsella's claim that the foundlings would return to him like homing pigeons was pure fantasy. My theories might be responsible for wasting hundreds of hours of police time.

Alan Nash barged past as I left the room and I gritted my teeth. Someone must have told him about Kinsella's request for a meeting the next day, because he wore the smug look of an actor who's trumped an audition and stolen the lead role.

50

Bubble bath scents the air like candyfloss, and Ella's whole body aches to climb into the warmth. Her hands are grimed with dirt and so is her white dress, the collar turning grey. She wishes there was a lock on the bathroom door, because the man is moving around outside. It would be stupid to let herself relax. When the bath is half full, she climbs in without taking off the dress. The warmth soothes her skin and she sinks backwards, letting herself submerge. All she can hear is the song of the water, the man's footsteps drowned into silence. But when she opens her eyes again he's sitting there, on the edge of the bath.

'Enjoying yourself, princess?'

She stretches her lips into a smile, then starts to rub shampoo into her hair, but the man refuses to vanish.

'We need to talk,' he says. 'You know the new girl's coming tomorrow, don't you?'

Ella nods just once, keeping her mouth closed.

'There's no need to get upset. It won't change things between us.'

'But we're happy as we are.'

'I know.' The man's face looks strained. 'But I have to follow the rules. This is the last time, I promise. They'll find out about us after that.'

'What are we going to do?'

'We can get across to France – run away, like you said. You'd like that, wouldn't you?'

Ella forces herself to nod, but all she can see is her granddad and Suzanne waiting for her at home.

'From tomorrow you'll live up here with me until we leave.' The man's smile exposes the sharp points of his teeth. 'Listen, I have to go out soon. Give me your dress and I'll put it in the tumble-drier.'

Ella wants to refuse but the man is holding out his hands. The water splashes as she pulls the shift over her head, wet cotton pressing against her mouth, making her panic. She slips back under the suds as fast as she can, but the man's still standing there, his eyes round and glassy, holding her dress in his hands.

51

I stayed at the Laurels longer than I'd intended. The broom cupboard's stale air was preferable to the hotel's odour of furniture polish, desperation and burnt food. I spent half an hour scribbling down the names of everyone I'd met at Northwood. Logic told me that someone in my immediate circle had told Kinsella that I'd left the cottage, and if he could persuade them to share details about me, maybe they were following other instructions as well. The list turned out to be extensive. I was on first-name terms with psychiatric nurses, doctors, administrators, the regular drinkers at the Rookery, and half a dozen guards who monitored Kinsella whenever he left his cell. By seven I'd lost track of time, still gazing in disbelief at the names on my list. When the phone on my desk jangled into life, I almost jumped out of my skin.

'Where are you?' Reg sounded as irate as ever.

'Sorry, I'm on my way. Give me five minutes.'

He sighed deeply when I apologised, as though my failings were too numerous to mention. I piled my notes into my briefcase and set off at a brisk trot, excess adrenaline coursing through my system. In an ideal world I'd have gone for a run, releasing pent-up energy through the soles of my feet, but it was pitch dark and a foot of compacted snow covered the ground. The hotel offered even less chance of exercise, because the complex was hunkered beside a main road. I made a mental note to go to the gym the next morning. An hour on the treadmill would be better than nothing.

When I reached the car park, Reg fixed me with a disapproving stare.

'How was your day?' I asked.

Driving conditions had been atrocious, and he'd been ferrying people around without so much as a thank-you. On top of that, his other half kept phoning to ask when he'd be home.

'At least she misses you.'

'Don't bank on it,' he grumbled. 'All she wants is a lift to the shops.'

Reg took ten minutes to vent his spleen, which gave me the chance to look out of the window. Part of me wanted to escape when we passed through Charndale. No matter how many ghosts Will had seen at the cottage, a night alone by the fire still seemed appealing. When we reached the hotel I thanked Reg for the lift and he thawed for a moment.

'At least you've got manners, Alice. You're not going out again tonight, are you?'

'I don't think so.'

He breathed a sigh of relief. My nonexistent social life meant that he could spend his Friday night watching TV. He marched up the stairs with renewed energy, clearly looking forward to slouching on the sofa with a beer.

The bar was heaving with journalists and detectives, standing in cliques, women in the minority. The noise was almost as overwhelming as the testosterone, and it seemed understandable that alcoholism was rife in both professions. They did so much waiting around – in their shoes I'd have been guzzling beer by the litre too. I edged round the side of the crowd to the members' bar, desperate for a cup of coffee, but when I reached the entrance I heard Burns's low Scottish drawl. Through the crack in the door I saw him sitting beside Tania.

His arm was slung around her shoulders and her glossiness had vanished. She was weeping silently, rivulets of mascara coursing down her cheeks. My feet rooted themselves to the spot. He was murmuring something, doing his best to offer her comfort. Eventually I stumbled back to the main bar, the cacophony of voices even louder than before.

'Can I get you something?' The barmaid eyed me with concern.

'Double brandy, please.'

The raw alcohol scoured my throat, but it had the desired effect. A few minutes after knocking it back, I was comfortably numb.

I sat down on the bed when I got to my room. At least seeing Burns and Tania together had put an end to my fantasies. It was time to move on. The couple next door were yelling at each other like banshees, but it didn't seem to matter. I unloaded my briefcase onto the table, even though there was little more I could do for Ella Williams. I'd combed through every detail of the case and given the team my advice. Whether or not another girl was abducted lay beyond my control. I might as well try and relax for the evening.

My phone rang as I was choosing between *The Matrix Reloaded* and *Good Will Hunting* on the movie channels. Tom Jensen's voice sounded as cool as ever when he greeted me.

'What are you up to, Alice?'

'Not much, to be honest.'

'Me neither. Do you fancy a drink?'

'I was planning to vegetate.'

'Come to the Fox and Hounds instead, it's near your hotel.'

'Can you give me a lift back?'

'No problem.'

When he rang off I had mixed feelings. A few hours spent admiring his good looks would improve my mood, but the last thing I needed was more confusion. I changed into jeans and a black cashmere jumper and reached for my leather jacket. On the way out the mirror threw back a glimpse of a thin-faced twelve-year-old, drowning in clothes she'd stolen from her big sister.

Reg was furious when I called for a lift. He reminded me that I'd promised to stay indoors. He could catch pneumonia because of my last-minute arrangements. When we reached the pub he insisted on writing Tom's name, address and phone number in his notebook.

'Text me when you get back from your hot date,' he growled as I got out of the car.

Reg's transformation into the world's most conscientious father-figure set my teeth on edge. Something about being blonde and five foot nothing makes men assume you're in dire need of protection, and there's nothing you can do, except stand your ground.

Tom was queuing at the bar when I arrived; the pub had a different vibe from the Rookery. There was a murmur of conversation instead of a blaring jukebox and, judging by the Barbours and Wellingtons, the county set had arrived for the evening. A well-behaved red setter was guarding its owner at the end of the bar. Tom and I settled on a narrow bench, backs leaning against the wall. I'd chosen orange juice instead of wine, in an effort to keep my head clear.

'Work's taken over,' I said. 'It's like a tsunami.'

His pale eyes examined me. 'The police were crawling everywhere today. They even came to the gym.'

'Really?'

'They asked me about Kinsella, but there wasn't much I could say.' His fingers tapped out a rhythm on his beer glass. 'He's only spoken a few times. The last time he asked about my family.'

His statement tailed into thin air and I remembered his revelation about the plane crash. The vulnerability he'd shown didn't match his image. He'd have made an ideal action hero, his face raw-boned and immobile as Daniel Craig's. Endless sympathy after the air crash must have forced him to hide his weaknesses deep inside his skin.

'Let's not talk about work tonight,' I said.

'You want to make small talk? That's not like you.'

'It's legal, isn't it? Tell me about your favourite books.'

His knowledge of literature was encyclopaedic. It made me wish I'd brought a notebook, so I could make better choices next time I visited Waterstones.

'You're wasted in that gym,' I said.

'I don't agree. Exercise is the highlight of the week for most of them.'

A flicker of missionary zeal crossed his face, and we spent the next hour discussing our career paths. Mine was more straightforward: I'd started out training to be a medic, but the mind interested me far more than the body. His work had travelled in the opposite direction. He'd started out ministering to people's souls, and ended up helping them to improve their health. When I checked my watch again, it was almost eleven.

'They'll send out a search party if I don't get back soon.'

'There's something I wanted to say, Alice.' He was twisting his glass between his hands, as though he was reshaping it. 'Guess how many relationships I've had.'

'That's tricky. I'd say not that many, three or four long ones, maybe?'

'Wrong. The answer is zero.'

I stared back at him, open-mouthed. 'How come?'

'A couple lasted a few months, but that's my limit. I was just drifting along.'

He made it sound like he'd been floating in the dark with nothing to navigate by, and I knew how he felt. My longest relationship had lasted a year, which didn't fill me with pride. But I'd finally met my match – someone who feared commitment even more than me.

'You don't need to explain, Tom. Being friends suits me fine.'

'Does it?' A muscle in his jaw ticked with anger. 'It's not friendship I'm after any more. I thought we could take it slow and see where this takes us.'

I was starting to feel confused. A minute ago he was explaining that commitment was impossible, and now he was canvassing for a relationship. 'That's the opposite of what you said at the start. And we're too similar, aren't we?'

His eyes darkened to a glacial blue. 'So why did you sleep with me?'

'You persuaded me, remember? And I don't make a habit of it. The last time was two years ago.'

He slammed down his empty glass loudly enough to make the woman at the next table flinch. The drive back to the hotel was so tense, I felt glad it was only a short distance. When he pulled up in the car park, I was eager to escape, but he leant over and kissed me while I fumbled with the seatbelt, the pressure of his hand on my shoulder heavy enough to hurt. His anger was still visible when I pulled away. I felt a twinge of guilt for sleeping with him, but a relationship with someone so troubled would be impossible. It was a relief to watch his Jeep spin away across the rutted snow.

52

The sound of the man returning wakes her, and this time his footsteps sound different. Normally he moves slowly, but tonight his feet jitter like he's tap dancing. She pulls the covers over her head but the sound refuses to stop. The man crashes down the stairs and light needles through the blanket.

'Are you asleep, princess?' the man whispers. His hot breath travels across her cheek. He smells of beer, like granddad does when he comes back from the pub. Sweet as toffee apples and caramel, with something sour under the surface, like milk on the turn. 'I've got something to tell you.' He pushes her shoulder until she has no choice but to open her eyes.

'What is it?'

'I did a practice run, everything's sorted. It'll work perfectly tomorrow.'

'That's good.'

'I know how to pick her up without anyone seeing.'

'But I like having you to myself. We don't need anyone else.'

'It's not my choice, angel. I've got to do what he says, one last time. Then he's setting me free.'

'Is he?'

He nods excitedly. 'He says I can go wherever I want after that. My duties are finished.'

'Am I coming with you tomorrow?'

'Not this time, princess. Someone from work might see us;

you can wait for me here. I'll say goodbye to him, then I'll pick her up.'

It's his stare that frightens her, his eyes wide and comfortless. She resorts to the method that always works best, twisting her mouth into its biggest smile.

53

The dining hall was empty when I woke up. It was only half past six but I was hungry from skipping dinner the night before. I'd planned to order room service but my row with Tom had changed my mind – nothing kills your appetite faster than a dose of unadulterated guilt. I scanned the sea of white tablecloths, and spotted Tania in the far corner, which gave me a dilemma. I could snub her by choosing a different table, or join her for a full English. I helped myself to coffee, and when I turned round she gave a half-hearted wave. It wasn't exactly an invitation, but at least she'd acknowledged me. I poured another coffee and made my way over.

'Mind if I join you?'

'Be my guest.' She gave a thin smile as I placed the cup in front of her.

Tania's image was firmly back in place, even though it was the crack of dawn. She was wearing scarlet lipstick and an emerald green silk shirt. It made me wish we were on better terms so I could ask her where she bought her clothes.

'How's it going?' I asked.

'Too slow for my liking. I'm not even sure we're going in the right direction.'

I wondered why she'd been crying the night before. Maybe they were tears of frustration over all the blind alleys the investigation had chased down. When the waitress finally arrived, Tania ordered grapefruit juice and a bowl of skimmed milk porridge. She looked nauseous when I asked for a bacon sandwich.

'Sorry, are you vegetarian?'

She shook her head. 'My appetite's gone. A lot's riding on this case for me. There was an incident at Hammersmith last year; I had to make a sideways move.'

'Was it something serious?'

'I thought so. Being professionally undermined isn't my idea of fun.'

I gave her a sympathetic look and tried to regain my balance. Candour was the last thing I'd been expecting.

'Did you hear that Nash is seeing the headmaster at nine?' she asked.

'Good luck to him. Kinsella's enjoying himself too much to give away any secrets.'

She glanced at her watch. 'I hope you're wrong. The next deadline's almost here.'

'People must be keeping their daughters under lock and key.'

'Locks don't work on mine, my mum's keeping an eye on her.' Her phone buzzed loudly on the table. 'I'd better deal with this. Thanks for the coffee.'

Tania picked up her cup and marched away, leaving me none the wiser about what had upset her the night before. Perhaps it was nothing more than a dispute with Burns. I tucked into my unhealthy breakfast and tried not to think about it.

It was obvious that Reg was under the weather when I met him in the car park. Either he was nursing a hangover or he was still sulking about being dragged into the cold. He gave a grudging nod when we reached Northwood and I headed for the infirmary. Alan Nash was already there, preening himself in front of a group of sycophants.

'God's gift to humankind,' Tania whispered, rolling her eyes.

The last of my animosity went up in smoke. It wasn't her fault that she was having a relationship with someone I cared about. She busied herself with preparing for the interview, and she did it all with calm, professional grace. Even Alan Nash submitted to her instructions without criticism. I stared down at the monitors, which were still channelling pictures direct from Kinsella's room. Garfield was sitting at his bedside, eyes half closed, as though he was fighting to stay awake, while a drip fed clear liquid into Kinsella's arm. He must have agreed to take medication at last. Behind his half-moon glasses his gaze had regained its intensity.

I watched the professor adjusting his wire, as a whine of feedback buzzed through the speakers. Once the settings had been adjusted he gave a mock salute and left the room. Kinsella didn't move a muscle when Nash arrived. But, through the monitor, I saw his eyes keeping track of his visitor. My attention must have wandered, because everything had changed by the time I looked up from my notes. Tania's voice was rising to a shout.

'Someone get him out of there,' she yelled.

The computer screens didn't help, because the security guard's back had blocked my view. All I could see was Kinsella's hand clutching the air. A wailing sound came from the corridor, and when I got outside Alan Nash was on his knees, hands covering his face. Blood oozed between his fingers, and a nurse was leaning over him, checking his wounds. Moira came towards us at a brisk trot.

'Come on, Mr Nash. Let's get you to triage.'

He moaned softly into his cupped hands, and when I caught sight of his eye, shock brought me to a halt. His eyelid had been sliced in two. So much blood was gushing from the wound I couldn't tell how badly his eye was damaged. I felt a surge of sympathy, even though there was little I could do. I slipped back into the observation room and replayed the film. Every movement was so seamless, Kinsella must have visualised the scene a hundred times. His free hand ripped the needle from his arm and swiped it across Nash's face, a gout of blood spraying the air. Afterwards the headmaster gazed directly at the camera, completely at peace. The sharp lines of his bone structure made him look as otherworldly as a monk at prayer.

Burns's body language revealed that he already knew about the attack on Alan Nash. He was standing in the incident room, his mobile pressed to his ear, shoulders rigid with tension. He thrust a sheet of paper at me then turned away to finish his call. The page was blank, apart from two names printed in block capitals.

'Take a guess who they are.'

'I'm not a clairvoyant, Don. You'll have to enlighten me.'

'Northwood staff who went to St Augustine's or lived at Orchard Row. We're missing a few years' enrolments, but records came through for these two last night: a trainee chef and the art therapist you told me about.'

I studied the page again: Steve Higham and Prudence Fielding. I was so used to hearing her referred to as Pru that I'd forgotten it was an abbreviation.

'Pru Fielding went to Kinsella's school?'

Burns shook his head. 'The bloke went to St Augustine's but her record says she spent years at Orchard House. We can't track her down, it's her day off.'

I felt a kick of sympathy. Pru's birthmark was the least of her worries, compared to years of childhood neglect. 'Have you spoken to the chef?'

'Higham's in the meeting room now. Can you do an assessment? His boss says he's a bit of a loner.'

'You're worried about him?'

He nodded vigorously. 'The uniform who took his details says he can't remember where he was on the dates of the abductions.'

I rooted around in my briefcase for an EF1, the psychological assessment form that's used at first interview stage. The young man waiting in the interview room was staring fixedly at the window, as though he was guessing how many injuries he'd incur if he took a running jump. He looked about twenty-five, black hair tied in a thin ponytail, and he was wearing the checked trousers and jacket worn by professional chefs. It was hard to believe that he worked in a kitchen because he looked malnourished, a rash of acne on his cheeks and the pallor that comes from spending every waking moment indoors. Burns greeted him in a pleasant tone of voice.

'Thanks for coming by, Steve.'

'There's nothing wrong, is there?' Higham was fiddling with his ponytail, twisting it between his fingers.

'I don't think so. You're just helping us with our enquiries.'

He gave a nervous laugh. 'That's okay then. You had me worried.'

'When did you start working here?'

'Two years ago. I was cleaning at first, then they put me in the kitchen. I'm halfway through my training.' Higham's voice had the singsong quality of a child trying to explain something complicated.

'Your boss tells me you've asked for a transfer to the Laurels.'

'It's not just me. Everyone wants to go there.'

'Really? I'd pay good money to avoid those guys. How well did you know Mr Kinsella when you were at St Augustine's?'

He blinked rapidly. 'Not at all. I only saw him at assembly.'

'So it's just coincidence that you left London to work here, and you've been angling for a job in his building?'

Higham's small eyes bored into Burns's face. 'All the big names are over there, aren't they? I grew up seeing them on the news.'

'Your heroes are mass murderers?'

'They interest me, that's all. It's not a crime, is it?'

A minute's silence unfolded before Burns asked his next question. 'Have you got a girlfriend at the moment, Steve?'

'No, why?'

'What car do you drive?'

'I haven't got one. I get the bus.'

'But you used to drive a van to work.'

'It cost too much to run. I sold it last year.'

'You've got proof, have you?'

'The papers are somewhere at home.' His gaze trailed towards the window again.

'Listen, Steve, I'd like to do something called a warrantless search on your flat. Would you agree to that?'

'You want to go through my things?' His eyes widened in outrage.

'If you agree, you can sign a consent form for me now.'

'What's the alternative?'

'You wait here until I get a warrant, then I go ahead and do it anyway.'

A single expletive escaped from Higham's lips. 'And if I sign, I can go back to work?'

'Straight away, if you like.'

Higham fished in his pocket then dropped his keys on the table with a sullen frown. Burns gave a low whistle when the door shut behind him.

'Some people would describe that as coercion,' I said. But

292

he was already striding away to sort out the search, leaving me to scan my assessment form. Higham had manifested acute anxiety right from the start, his body language changing from open to defensive as soon as Kinsella's name was mentioned. Burns had good reason to be concerned.

'Are you coming with us?' Burns had reappeared with the senior SOCO in tow.

The drive to Steve Higham's address took twenty minutes. Pete Hancock sat in the passenger seat while Burns drove, leaving me free to watch the snowy fields slip by. Higham lived beside the main road to Reading. From a distance the tower blocks were no better than the grim municipal estates that had sprung up everywhere in the Sixties, but at least the planners had shown a touch of irony; the hulking blocks were named after spring flowers. Higham's rented apartment was on the eighth floor of Primrose House. The balconies that hung from the concrete monolith looked purely decorative, too frail to sustain more than a pot of geraniums.

The flat was unusually tidy for a bachelor pad. Every wall was drenched in magnolia paint, as though the landlord had seen too many episodes of *House Doctor* and opted for complete neutrality. From the bedroom doorway I noticed that Higham had even found time to make his bed that morning. Pete was sorting through his cabinets, drawer by drawer; when I tried to cross the threshold, he growled so loudly that I backed away.

The kitchen looked blameless too, washing up lying on the drainer, surfaces clean enough to shine. I found Burns in the living room, scanning Higham's DVD collection.

'There's enough porn here to keep him happy for months.' He brandished one of the cases at me. A model in a school-girl's outfit was straddling a chair, her pigtails tied with scarlet ribbons.

'She can't be sixteen.'

'This one's geriatric compared to the rest.' He carried on inspecting the shelves.

Higham's books revealed a different range of interests: Formula One, extreme sports and true crime. Books about the exploits of Doctor Crippen and Harold Shipman were sandwiched between *Surf Hawaii* and *Learning to Hang-glide*. When I reached the last shelf I spotted Alan Nash's book on Kinsella, *The Kill Principle*. When I handed it to Burns, his eyes glittered with relief.

'Unbelievable,' he murmured.

'But it's not evidence, is it? It's too good to be true: an isolated young man with poor social skills, obsessed by sex and violence. It's like he's staged it, to make himself seem like the perfect serial killer.'

Hancock appeared before he could reply, with a set of keys dangling from his hand. His black monobrow hovered half an inch above his eyes, making him look sterner than ever. 'These were in his cupboard, with an MOT certificate for a white Luton van. There's no evidence it's been sold.'

'That's good enough for me.' Burns shoved the book back onto the shelf.

'Do you want me to set up a cordon?' Hancock asked.

Burns's eyes were strained a little too wide. 'Leave everything be. He's coming back tonight, so we can keep watch. If it's him, he's only got till midnight to take the next girl.'

54

The man's left her upstairs with a list of things to do: wash the dishes, scrub the kitchen floor, clean the sink. But now the tasks are done, it's hard to settle, and he's hidden the remote control. Eventually she finds it in the kitchen, concealed behind a stack of bowls.

Ella keeps the volume low, knowing he'll be back any minute. She flicks past game shows and soap operas until the news channel appears. A dark-haired woman is wearing a serious expression. She explains that an oil spill in the North Sea is causing damage. Pictures of seagulls appear on the screen, feathers rigid with black glue. Tears cloud Ella's vision. She blinks hard to clear them, and when her eyes open again, her own face has filled the screen.

'The Metropolitan Police have issued another warning. Families across the UK are advised to take every precaution to keep children safe for the next twenty-four hours. Ella Williams is still missing, and her family has made another appeal.'

Her grandfather peers out from the screen. He's wearing his one smart jacket, hands shaking as he reads from a sheet of paper. There's a pleading sound in his voice, and she reaches out to touch him, but her fingers bounce from the cold glass, and her tears drip onto the white cotton of her dress. For once she doesn't care if the man finds her crying. She wishes she could kick through the brick wall, then run down the street, yelling for help.

A new sound starts in the distance. The woman is singing again, the tune bright and happy, like she's had a good day. Ella wipes her eyes then rushes to the window. She hammers her fists against the glass, until her wrists begin to bruise.

55

Information buzzed from the radio when we got back to the car.

'Tania says Pru Fielding's back at her house. We can go over there now.'

Burns's tone suggested that he would prefer to hunt for evidence that might hang Steve Higham out to dry. I'd seen that fervent look on his face before – he was convinced that he'd got his man.

'She's worth a visit, Don. Pru comes over as a troubled soul.'

He still looked unenthusiastic as we set off, but Hancock was oblivious, hunched over his folder, filling out a crime-scene report. My mind flitted across everything I'd seen. It was possible that Steve Higham was Kinsella's disciple, but his flat seemed too sanitised for a killer's lair. There was no evidence of a disordered mind, only of a lonely man's unfulfilled desires. When the SOCOs carried out a finger-tip search they might find a trace of proof, or a memento from one of the killings, but so far there was no certainty that he was the killer. He seemed to live through vicarious thrills – reading about villains and dangerous sports, but too fearful to put himself in danger. If Kinsella had selected him from the ranks of nine-year-old schoolboys, it would have been because he was unimaginative and eager to please. It would take hours of careful interviewing to discover whether Higham had been groomed. I closed my eyes and pictured Kinsella sitting by a computer with a small boy. The child's tolerance for violence would have grown day by day, as he was exposed to images that grew steadily more horrifying.

By now we were pulling up outside Pru Fielding's house. It was in the village next to Charndale, an old-fashioned bungalow, hidden behind a Leylandii hedge. Hancock stayed in the car while Burns and I walked towards the property. The garage doors were in need of paint, window-frames beginning to splinter.

I did a double take when the front door swung open. For a split second I thought that Pru's birthmark had vanished. Her blonde curls were swept into a ponytail and there was no sign of a blemish on her face, but when I looked again I realised that I was mistaken. This woman's eyes were a different shade of blue. She must have seen my confusion, because she gave a short laugh.

'You thought I was Pru, didn't you? I'm her sister, Denise. Come in, she's in her studio.'

I smiled in reply, but couldn't help wondering how Pru felt about her sister's attractiveness. She must have spent years resenting it. Burns followed me along the corridor, studying the oil paintings that lined the hall. I had no idea whether they showed any talent, but he lingered in front of each one, and I remembered his art school background before he joined the Met. The landscapes were depicted in muted browns and greys, hardly any sunlight filtering through the clouds.

'Beautiful,' Burns murmured. 'They're so atmospheric.'

Denise turned to him, smiling. 'Pru won prizes at art school, but she never exhibits. Her work's changed since she did these. You'll see for yourself.'

Pru's studio was in a large outbuilding in the back garden.

When Denise opened the door she swung round to face us, and I tried not to stare at the paintings that hung from the walls. Dozens of children stared out from each canvas, so real that you could see their freckles and gaps between their teeth. They frowned down at us, and some of their faces were daubed with scarlet paint, as though they were spattered with blood. It felt like we were surrounded by child warriors, each one primed to attack. I heard Burns swear under his breath.

Pru was wearing an apron to protect her clothes, blotches of colour spattered across her boots. Her curtain of hair almost concealed the dark stain that bisected her face.

'I'm sorry to disturb your work, Pru,' I said. 'We'd like to ask you some questions about Orchard House.'

Her eyes widened. 'Why? The place closed down years ago.'

'I know. But we need to find out if Louis Kinsella had contact with any of the children there.'

She dropped eye contact, her arms folded tightly across her chest, as if her whole body was in lockdown.

'If she won't tell you, I will.' Denise was still standing in the doorway.

She led us back into the house, and we sat around the kitchen table. Pru was still refusing to look up, but Denise seemed determined to set the record straight. 'Pru was twelve and I was thirteen when Mum had her breakdown. Kinsella had gone by the time we arrived at Orchard House, but we heard about him. The older kids were still in shock. He used to take them on outings; most of them couldn't believe what he'd done.'

'So you never met Kinsella when you lived there?' Burns asked.

Denise shook here head. 'We had other things to worry about. Do you know why the place closed down?'

'There was an abuse scandal, wasn't there?'

'It went on for years. Even senior staff were in on it: there was violence, bullying, sex. Me and Pru got off lightly, because we had each other, but we saw everything. The other kids had no one to protect them.'

Pru's silence continued. She was studying the splashes of paint on the backs of her hands.

'I'm so sorry,' I said quietly.

Denise gave a brief smile. 'There were plenty of apologies, when the story came out. They gave us twenty grand in compensation. That's how we raised our deposit for this place.'

'It's a joke,' Pru said bitterly. 'Money doesn't fix anything.'

I didn't reply. It's tempting to console the survivors of abuse, but it never works. The best thing you can do is help them learn how to console themselves.

'Why did you apply to work at the Laurels, Pru?' I asked.

Her voice faltered. 'I thought facing men like that would make me feel more confident.'

'I have to ask you this. Is anyone else from Orchard House working at the Laurels?'

Finally she looked up, eyes glazed. 'No one I recognise.'

Burns checked the sisters' alibis, then thanked them quietly and rose to his feet. He said very little as we walked away, but his expression was sombre. I'm not sure whether he was contemplating the years of abuse the two women had suffered, or how to nail Steve Higham.

'They arrived the year after Kinsella left Orchard House. There's nothing to link Pru to the girls' deaths.'

I thought about the warrior children in Pru's studio, prepared to fight anyone who came near. 'I think you're right, but I'll have to recommend she goes on sick leave until she's had a psychiatric assessment. Right now she's too vulnerable to work at the Laurels.'

Burns's eyes widened as he turned to me. 'It's hardly surprising. I wouldn't fancy those girls' nightmares, would you?'

56

It was five by the time I got back to the broom cupboard. I considered phoning Reg for a lift to the hotel, but decided to call at Judith's consulting room first. Her face lit up when she opened the door. She grabbed my wrist as though she had no intention of letting me go.

'You're in luck. I finally got my percolator fixed.' Her office still felt like an oasis. Even her plants were flourishing, a cheese plant's leaves brushing the ceiling.

'Did you hear about Alan Nash?' I asked.

'It shows you can't take chances, doesn't it? There are dozens of attacks here every year.' Her tone was matter of fact, as though vicious assaults were to be expected. 'How are you getting to mine tonight?'

I'd forgotten all about Tom's birthday party. After our row in the pub I was probably the last person he'd want to see.

'I'll have to cry off. Getting a lift back would be tricky.'

'Stay over. I've got plenty of room.'

'Are you sure?'

'Of course, you can help me get things ready.'

It was clear she wouldn't let me off the hook. When she described the catering arrangements, it sounded like she'd plundered Sainsbury's for their entire stock of party snacks.

'I'll need to call at the cottage for something to wear.'

She sprang to her feet immediately. 'Come on then, we'd better get moving.'

Judith's car turned out to be a substantial black Volvo, with a collection of bohemian scarves tangled on the back seat. I sent Reg a hurried text as she started the engine and got a terse reply, asking for Judith's address and phone number. I fired off another message then dropped the phone into my bag.

'How long do you have to stay at the hotel?' Judith asked.

'Until the investigation's over.'

'Poor thing.' She sounded as sympathetic as ever. 'At least you can let your hair down tonight.'

Snow was falling again as we drove, large flakes littering the windscreen, but my heart lifted when the cottage's silhouette appeared between the trees. The temperature inside was colder than before, and when I reached the ground-floor bathroom it was easy to see why. The window had been forced open, freezing air spilling through the gap. I held my breath and listened. The only sound was the drone of Judith's car revving on the drive. My intruder must have vanished a long time ago, but I was still shaking as I made my way upstairs. I paused in the bedroom to catch my breath. It looked as though nothing had been taken, my jewellery box still sitting on the dressing table. But part of me was afraid that he might still be lurking behind a closed door, so I flung a dress and some high heels into a bag and ran back downstairs. The living room looked untouched too. I went back to the bathroom and pulled the window shut. Judith was tooting her horn, eager to get home. Phoning the local police could wait until tomorrow. I reminded myself that – compared to Alan Nash's injuries – a break-in was nothing to complain about.

Judith talked about Garfield constantly on the way to her house, so keen to air her fears that I didn't mention the broken window or my visit to Pru's studio. She still seemed convinced he would leave his wife, her voice full of artificial brightness.

It would have been cruel to say that the odds were poor; her face lit up whenever she mentioned his name.

The snow had eased by the time we reached her house, and I realised why she missed her family. The place was a huge Georgian rectory, sandwiched between a graveyard and a church, ten minutes from the nearest village. It would have made a great boutique hotel, but it seemed like a daunting home for someone living alone.

'It's stunning, Judith.'

'You think so?' She wrinkled her nose. 'My husband had delusions of grandeur when we bought it. These days he shares a flat with his juvenile girlfriend.'

She raced around like a whirlwind when we got inside, tidying up and preparing food. Her flagstoned kitchen was so vast that I had to raise my voice to be heard on the other side of the room. We spent the next twenty minutes preparing the buffet, putting mini-quiches on plates, and scooping salads into bowls. Judging by the number of wine glasses she put out, she was expecting a small army.

'Let's get changed,' she said. 'Then we can chill before they get here.'

Judith's bohemian chic permeated the whole house. My room on the second floor had a lit-bateau bed and drawings of Indian gods and goddesses hanging from the walls. I admired them while I got ready. They were the opposite of Pru's warrior children, their faces so tranquil that nothing could dent their serenity, headdresses traced in gold. Judith was singing to herself in the room next door. It reminded me of my grandmother's favourite torch songs, Dusty Springfield or Billie Holiday, deliciously mournful. I inspected myself in the mirror and realised that my dark red dress needed an accessory.

I tapped on Judith's door then entered her room. It felt like

I was visiting an art museum, crammed with artefacts. Every surface was filled with Asian statuettes and carvings, and Judith was almost hidden among the furniture, finishing her eye make-up. She laughed when she saw me gazing around the room.

'Relics from too many holidays. I can never resist bringing something back.'

'It's like Aladdin's cave in here. Have you got a necklace I can borrow?'

'You came to the right place.' Her jewellery box was the size of a small trunk, bracelets and beads hanging from hooks on the lid. 'Take whatever you like.'

I chose a heavy silver choker that fitted snugly against my collarbone.

'It looks valuable. Are you sure you don't mind?'

'It's perfect for you.' Judith looked dreamier than ever, in a floaty pale grey dress, eyes outlined with kohl.

When we got back to the kitchen she poured me some wine and began to unwrap a large birthday cake.

'You've really gone to town,' I commented.

'Tom needs people to make a fuss of him.' She studied me carefully. 'Have you been seeing him?'

'Just as friends.'

'That's probably just as well. I think he finds relationships tough. He saw a nurse from work for a few months last year, but things got out of hand.'

'In what way?'

'I'm not sure. Rumours were flying everywhere, but I ignored them. The girl ended up leaving her job.'

I gulped down a mouthful of wine. The more I heard about Tom, the more it seemed I'd had a lucky escape.

57

Gorski arrived on the stroke of eight. He was clutching a bottle of wine, and he'd abandoned his suit in favour of jeans and a jacket. Only his sharp-toed shoes and forbidding expression were carried over from his daytime uniform. Judith scurried away to greet the next arrival when we reached the kitchen, and it was clear that I'd have to work hard to start a conversation.

'Do you live near here?' I asked.

'Pretty near, but my house is less palatial.' Gorski almost managed a smile. 'Do you see now why I warned you about the Laurels? What happened to your colleague today could happen to any of us.'

'Of course. It's the last place you can let down your guard.'

We made halting small talk for the next few minutes, but he seemed relieved when the room filled, because it allowed him to retreat into the shadows. Social gatherings seemed to cause him so much discomfort, I wondered why he'd bothered to come.

Tom arrived fashionably late with his sidekick in tow. Chris Steadman raised his hand in an awkward wave, and I felt certain that he knew about the argument at the pub. But at least the birthday boy looked more relaxed. He stood chatting to people on the opposite side of the kitchen. Most of the guests were from the Laurels, only a few from other parts of the hospital. As the conversation rose in volume I heard

Kinsella's name being mentioned repeatedly, everyone bursting with gossip about the extent of Alan Nash's injuries. He had been rushed to Reading Hospital for a corneal graft. It struck me that working at Northwood made people immune to the suffering of others, but maybe that was inevitable. Witnessing so many suicide attempts and brutal attacks would harden anyone after a while.

Judith seemed intent on being the perfect hostess, but even she couldn't keep Tom amused. He looked preoccupied while a gorgeous red-haired girl used every trick in the book to claim his attention. I helped myself to some pâté and got chatting to a woman who turned out to be a great storyteller. Her name was Michelle and she'd been a nurse at Northwood for over a decade, developing a repertoire of hospital humour. She told me about an inmate who had dangled another by his ankles from a fifth-floor window, and it didn't matter whether the incident was fact or fiction. She turned the incident into a comedy sketch; it was a relief to laugh helplessly at her jokes.

My phone buzzed as Judith was unloading desserts from the fridge, and I slipped out into the hallway. The latest message was from Burns, a cryptic 'so far so good', letting me know that Kinsella's warning had come to nothing. Lola had sent a text too, reminding me to meet her at Charndale Station the next afternoon, and I couldn't help smiling. Despite my warnings about the lacklustre hotel, she was still determined to visit.

When I got back to the kitchen, Tom was blowing out the candles on his cake. The redhead's simpering had gone into overdrive, but he seemed unaware of it. Part of his appeal lay in the fact that he rarely noticed people's admiration – all of his gestures were simple and matter of fact, and he never flaunted his good looks. I felt a tug of regret, but knew a relationship was a non-starter. We were far too similar and, unlike

Burns, he carried his feelings deep below the surface, burying his intellect in a job that never challenged him. There was a wistful expression on his face as he watched Judith cutting the cake. He must have longed for family parties as a teenager, his adolescence marred by loneliness. Any partner he chose would spend a lifetime compensating for all his losses.

People drifted into the living room when the food started to run out. The room looked like the interior of a shabby chic French hotel, sofas covered in delicate embroidered throws. Chris was kneeling by the sound system, preparing the soundtrack for yet another Northwood party. By the time Judith reappeared, Emeli Sandé was purring quietly in the background.

'You're doing it again,' she whispered, 'observing people. Go and talk to Aleks, will you? He needs cheering up.'

Gorski was by himself, staring intently at a painting on the wall. He raised his eyebrows when he saw me approaching. 'Judith sent you, didn't she? That woman's biggest flaw is taking care of everyone but herself.'

'Isn't altruism meant to be a virtue?'

'Not when it takes over. Too much care for others is self-annihilating.'

'Spoken like a true shrink.' I grinned and raised my glass.

Eventually I coaxed a potted biography from him. He'd left Warsaw as a child, trained at Bart's in London, then worked his way through the ranks at Northwood.

'Why the Laurels? Your life would have been easier in general psychiatry.'

Gorski frowned. 'Because it's the last frontier. Nowhere else deals with such severe psychosis – everything we do is cutting edge.'

The frontier analogy rang true. Interviewing Kinsella was like interpreting a foreign language, a mile-wide gulf between us. When I looked up again, Judith was beckoning frantically, and I was about to make my excuses when Gorski spoke again. I'd never seen him smile before. His teeth were sharp-edged and unnaturally white, and there was something disturbing about the intensity of his stare.

'I made my mind up about you, by the way.'

'Sorry?' I gave him a confused smile.

'You're a lion tamer, obviously. I should have realised on day one.'

I remembered our first conversation and wanted to ask what he meant, but Judith was still trying to get my attention. The party was in full swing as I made my way over, the noise of people's chatter rising steadily. When I got closer her face was shining too brightly, like a light bulb just before it fails.

'Garfield's on his way here,' she said.

She sounded jubilant, and I felt a pang of sympathy for his wife, pining for him at home. But there was no time to worry, because things swung into fast forward. An influx of guests arrived from the late shift at Northwood, with offerings of beer. The knowledge that Garfield was on his way had released Judith's inner party animal. She circulated the room, chivvying guests onto their feet. Soon people were dancing in front of the fire, and the atmosphere reminded me of the Rookery, with plenty of flirting and discreet joints being smoked in the porch. The redhead was still clinging to Tom's side, and I found myself dancing to my favourite singer, To Be Frank, while Michelle and another nurse performed a reel. Chris appeared beside us. His dancing style was chaotic, but he seemed to be enjoying himself, a broad grin plastered across his face.

'Where's the new girlfriend?' Michelle teased him.

'Coming over next weekend. She doesn't do parties, she's the studious type.'

'I haven't even met her yet.'

He let out a laugh. 'That's what scares me, Michelle. You'll eat her alive.'

A few songs later I caught sight of him on the other side of the room, but this time Pru Fielding was beside him. She must have arrived with the latecomers, and she was making up for lost time. She was fiddling with her hair nervously as she tried to monopolise Chris's attention. I felt a pang of guilt about my decision to recommend that she be given a psychiatric assessment, but I knew I'd made the right call. Someone that vulnerable shouldn't be surrounding herself with so much torment.

It was after midnight when Garfield finally arrived. Through the open doorway I saw Judith rush to him. The crowd was thinning and I wished I had a lift back to the hotel instead of cramping their style. Gorski was still in the kitchen, talking to a bearded man with an earnest expression, and my head was starting to throb.

'Come on everyone, a drink to welcome Garfield,' Judith insisted.

She looked so radiant, I didn't have the heart to say that I'd rather curl up in bed and let the party finish without me. But Garfield seemed in need of a pick-me-up, his wide shoulders hunched, as though the day's burdens still weighed on him. By now Tom was alone, studying the fire. He looked far too sober for someone celebrating a birthday. Judith insisted on refilling everyone's glasses, even though Chris was obviously over the limit. He was leaning heavily on the mantelpiece, as if he was willing himself to stay upright. When the toast finished, Gorski gave Judith a brisk kiss on the cheek, then strode towards the door. Moments later I heard his car engine choking into life outside.

I sat on the sofa nursing my untouched wine, with no

intention of drinking it. The room was already blurring at the edges – lamps and coffee tables swaying dizzily towards me. When I opened my eyes again, Tom was beside me, his pale gaze monitoring my face.

'Are you okay, Alice?'

'A bit tipsy, that's all.'

'More drunk than tipsy, I'd say.' A brief smile crossed his face. 'I can drive you to the hotel if you like.'

I didn't reply, because the room had stopped swaying and begun to spin, which seemed odd, because I'd paced myself all evening, drinking more water than wine. Garfield loomed over me, and I heard his smooth voice instructing someone to help carry me upstairs.

The rest of the evening was a blur. I remembered the humiliation of being laid on the divan, and Judith's voice echoing from the landing. Tom's face was the last thing I saw. He leant over me, and for some reason I felt afraid. Relief washed over me as soon as the door closed. The scent of lavender clung to the sheets as I struggled to get comfortable. I drifted in and out of sleep, wishing the furniture would stop shuffling across the floor. My mouth felt dry as sawdust, but I was too weak to go hunting for a glass of water. Someone else was restless too. Footsteps passed on the stairway, slow and quiet, determined not to wake the other guests. I buried my head in the pillow and forced my eyes to close.

58

When I woke again there was a freezing draught around
my feet. My tongue rasped across the roof of my mouth,
and the sheets were scratching my skin like sandpaper. An
odd chemical taste hit the back of my throat, bitter as diesel.
The bed was rocking violently from side to side, and a wave
of panic hit me. I was no longer in Judith's guest room. I
was lying on cold metal in the back of a van. It was rattling
across the tarmac, streetlight falling through a smeared
window. The most terrifying thing was that my limbs were
refusing to follow instructions; I couldn't move a muscle. It
was impossible to surface and I was so terrified that I lost
control, a flood of urine gushing down my leg. When the
van juddered to a halt my body slid sideways, head crash-
ing against the wall.

The impact must have knocked me out, because my skull
burned when I came round. My surroundings had changed
again, and the panic rose even higher. Yellow light ebbed from
a lamp behind me, the room almost as small as the broom
cupboard. I tried to move but nothing happened. My hand
remained flat on the mattress, heavy as lead. My eyes were all
I could rely on as I dragged stale air into my lungs. The room
was silent and windowless; nothing to explain where I was, or
how I'd got there. All I knew for sure was that I was lying on a
bed, staring at whitewashed brick walls, a patch of damp
spreading across the ceiling. The air smelled of mushrooms

and fresh sweat, and my skin felt like it was on fire, perspiration soaking through my dress.

Shock or exhaustion must have sent me back to sleep. It was the sound of a man's quiet voice that woke me; the room was empty but I could hear someone whispering. His tone was refined and courteous. It sounded like he was standing outside the door, trying to comfort me. I called out for help, but even my voice had stopped working. Sentences formed perfectly in my head, but the noise I produced was a raw moan, like an animal in pain. After a few minutes the man's voice grew louder. I could make out individual words, the sound tender and hypnotic, as though he was crooning a lullaby.

'I wish I could be with you, Alice, but let's not waste time on impossibilities. I'll explain what happens next. My helper will arrive soon, to set up a camera. He found your address book at your cottage, and the film will be sent to your mother and your brother. I knew this was your destiny the moment I looked into your eyes. Purity comes from despair, Alice. You will see a whole world of pain, before you find joy and release.'

My heart rate tripled, but I was too weak to scream. Every atom in my body fought to propel me to my feet, but I still couldn't move. The voice belonged to Louis Kinsella, and it was fixed on a permanent loop. All I could do was lie there, listening to him repeating my death sentence. I was so terrified that my eyes darted around the room, looking for distractions, and I caught sight of a row of images taped to the wall. Girls' faces blurred then came back into focus: Kylie, Emma, Sarah, and Ella. The last one was of me, staring back at the camera, resentful about having my image stolen. I knew immediately where the picture came from. It was the one Brian Knowles had insisted on taking when I visited the Foundling Museum.

59

Ella's locked in the attic. It's the first time she's stood inside a room like this, thin beams holding the roof in place, the window too high to see through. Early light drifts over the bare floor-boards, and she stands in a patch of sun, letting it bathe her. It feels like months since she went outside. When she glances down again, her white dress looks even dirtier than before, the fabric blackened by dust.

The room is filled with tables, bookshelves, and crates. There's no escape route, and the handle on the trapdoor refuses to twist. She spots an air vent in one of the walls, a square piece of concrete punctured with holes. When she peers through she can see into another room. It must belong to the house next door. The vent shifts slightly as she pushes her finger into one of the holes, releasing a cloud of mortar. Ella wants to scream for help through the opening, but the man's feet are tapping on the steps of the ladder, so she waits by the trapdoor, preparing her smile.

'Get down here, Ella. I've got a job for you.' He's babbling so fast it's a struggle to understand. 'Listen, princess, we need to be quick. We can leave as soon as we're done here.'

'Did you catch the girl?'

The man ignores her question. 'I can't do it on my own. You've got to help me.'

'I'll do whatever you say.'

'I have to go out for an hour. You can clean her up in that time, can't you?'

'Of course.' She shows him her smile again.

He leads her to the kitchen and an unfamiliar voice echoes up the stairs, static hissing between the words. She wants to ask why he's left a radio playing, but the man pushes her through the door so forcefully that she lands on her knees. The key scrabbles in the lock as she recovers.

Her eyes struggle to adjust to the semi-darkness. A girl is lying in the middle of the mattress, blonde hair tangled across the pillow. It looks as if she's asleep, because she's so still, but her eyes are wide open. Ella's breath catches in her throat. This one is nothing like the others; lines of black eye make-up are smeared across her cheeks. The creature in the torn red dress is a woman, not a girl.

60

I didn't recognise her at first; her frizz of curls was all that remained from the photos on the news. Ella had lost her puppy fat, and her cheeks were pinched with hunger, round-framed glasses smeared with dirt. There was a look of fierce concentration on her face as she stared down at me. I opened my mouth, but nothing emerged except a rush of air. My thoughts were clearer than ice, even though speech had deserted me, and I knew I'd been poisoned. The toxin had brought on fever and paralysis, but left my thoughts intact. The panic in my chest was increasing by the minute. Feeling was returning to my hands and feet, but not movement, so I focused all my energy on trying to speak.

'I've been looking for you, Ella. My name's Alice.' My words were so slurred I was afraid she wouldn't hear, but she came nearer, listening intently. 'Your sister sends her love.'

I thought she might cry, but her self-control clicked back into place instantly. When she looked at me again it was like gazing into an old woman's eyes.

'He wants me to get you ready. This is your dress.' She pointed at a length of white cloth draped across the table and my heart pounded.

'He'll kill me if I wear it. You know that, don't you?'

She stood completely still. 'I have to do what he says.'

'Not any more. I'll take the blame, I promise. Do you know his name?'

'He won't tell me. It's against the rules.'

She looked so anxious that I tried to give her a reassuring smile, but even my facial muscles had stopped working. She looked deep in thought, weighing her loyalties.

'You've been so brave, Ella. But you'll have to be even braver now. Have you tried getting out of here?'

She gave a quick nod. 'The door opens sometimes, but the other locks don't work.'

'Try them all. Go upstairs and break a window. If you don't, he'll kill us both.'

'But I've got to stay with you.'

'Forget what he told you. When d'you think he'll be back?'

'Soon.'

'Suzanne's waiting for you, Ella. You have to do this.'

She vanished from my line of vision and at first I couldn't work out where she'd gone. Then I saw her attacking the lock with a pair of scissors, jaws clenched with determination. It seemed incredible that she was just ten years old.

'Keep going, sweetheart,' I hissed under my breath. 'You want to go home, don't you?'

Ella hesitated, then her thin fingers gripped the handle. She twisted the blade into the mechanism, again and again.

61

The door swings open suddenly, and she's on the threshold, unsure whether to stay or go. The man will be back any minute, and the woman on the bed is trying to speak. Her mouth trembles, like she's attempting to smile.

'Find a way out, Ella,' she whispers. The woman is in the same position, red dress torn to the waist, arms limp at her sides. It feels wrong to leave her, but her eyes are blazing.

The idea of home drives Ella upstairs. She gulps down a deep breath and tries to think clearly. Thumping her fists against the kitchen window has no effect – the glass doesn't even vibrate, so she runs to the next floor. The first room is empty apart from a bed and a wardrobe, the frosted glass window locked tight. Then she spots a bathroom with a small window set high in the wall. Ella stands on the cistern to reach it, and when the glass drops open, cold air breezes past her face, goose bumps rising on her forearms.

It's a sheer fifteen-foot drop to the snow-covered ground, but the woman's quiet voice echoes in her head. She pushes her shoulders through the narrow opening, and all she can see is whiteness, stretched out below like a carpet. She crouches on the sill, bare feet starting to freeze. The whine of a car engine passes and her heart ticks louder in her chest. She grips the window frame even tighter. It would be impossible to climb back inside, she hasn't got the strength.

The wind tugs at Ella's dress, trying to wrench her from the face of the building. Then she hears the sound she remembers: a voice singing, each note drifting on the breeze. She knows there's no other choice. Ella keeps her eyes wide open as she launches herself into the air, aiming for the deepest pile of snow.

62

Kinsella's voice seemed even louder after Ella left. There was a minute's reprieve between each message, and I tried to shut out his words, desperate for a sound from upstairs, but there was nothing except the rush of blood pounding in my ears. Either she'd escaped, or the killer had caught her red-handed. I couldn't believe that the man behind all this was Brian Knowles; he'd seemed like nothing more than a lonely fantasist with a creepy manner. I gritted my teeth and tried to lift my right arm above my head. My hand fluttered a few centimetres into the air then dropped down again.

My mind was working overtime. How had I ended up here? Last night I'd drunk no more than three glasses of wine, yet I'd fallen into a stupor. Someone had waited until the middle of the night before coming for me, strong enough to carry me downstairs to his van. The killer had to be someone I knew.

Suddenly the house fell silent. All I could hear was a car door slamming, and music playing in the distance – proof that the rest of the world was going about its business, while I waited for some freak to attack me. By now Kinsella's words were so deeply engrained that I could recite them: purity and despair, a whole world of pain. He was intent on breaking me, even in his absence. It was like Chinese water torture, droplets falling on your forehead, slowly driving you insane. My only defence was to stay calm, instead of melting into hysteria. I tried not to remember the pleasure on Kinsella's face when he warned me that the next victim would be blinded. I blocked out his words and pictured images from the past: kids I'd known at primary school; my father, relaxed and handsome, before the drink took hold; Lola taking her first bow.

A new sound filtered through the floorboards. Someone was walking around above my head, the footsteps much heavier than Ella's, and a jolt of panic travelled through me. The killer had returned and I still couldn't move a muscle. I gathered my strength to lift myself from the bed, but the effort overwhelmed me. The light faded from yellow to black as I lost consciousness.

63

Ella pitches forwards and pain sears through the heel of her foot. The low drone of the man's van is returning, but there's nowhere to run. He'll see her from the kitchen window. She searches the garden frantically, but the fences are too high. Then her eyes catch on a wheelie bin and she drags it to the boundary wall. The first time she falls backwards into the snow, but on the second attempt she manages to climb up onto the lid. Raw bricks graze her hands as she scrambles over the wall and drops to the ground.

At first she's too scared to move, because the man could be a few steps behind, but the singing is closer now. A radio's playing, the woman's voice following the tune. Ella can see her through the French windows, running a paint roller across a wall. The pain in her foot is growing worse, and it takes forever to wade through the snow. She smashes her hands against the glass, and when the girl turns round, Ella sees that she's not much older than Suzanne. The girl's roller drops to the floor, streaks of yellow paint splattering her clothes. Ella's breaths come in ragged spurts, waiting for the man to grab her from behind, and drag her back over the wall. The girl stares at her ragged dress, mouth open in amazement. She makes no attempt to open the door.

'Please, you have to help me,' Ella calls through the glass.

The girl still doesn't move, and part of Ella feels relieved. If she rushed over too quickly or tried to touch her, it would be more than she could bear. But she can't forget the woman in the torn dress, lying there, unable to move. Ella presses her hands against the glass, and when she looks over her shoulder, the red smear of her footprints is daubed on the snow.

64

The prickling feeling under my skin was still there when I came round. There was a loud rasping sound above my head, as if he was dragging something heavy across the floor. I could squeeze my fingers into fists, but that was the extent of it. I was locked inside a useless body, and the thing that scared me most was that Ella might already be dead. Her body could be lying in its cardboard coffin, and once he'd finished with her, I was next.

My mind spiralled around the killer's identity. A sea of faces swam at me, and all I could hear was a throng of voices, as though I was back in the Rookery. I could even smell the odour of beer and exhaustion. I remembered Garfield sitting opposite me at the pub. He was the closest person to Kinsella, and his mellow voice was the only relaxed thing about him, as though he carried secrets too important to share.

Kinsella's message was tattooed on my memory, even though the recording had stopped playing: soon his helper would arrive, and the film of my torture would be sent to my family. I screwed my eyes shut and tried not to imagine Will's reaction. Sweat poured from my skin; pent-up terror escaping through my pores. My mind flashed back to Gorski, his behaviour a master class in passive aggression. Then my thoughts scrambled into place. Maybe Tom was the person wandering around upstairs. All of his unresolved grief had flipped over into psychosis. He could have been lying when I saw him at the Foundling Museum; he'd pretended it was his first visit, but he might have gone there dozens of times.

Footsteps thundered down the stairs and I tried to prepare myself. My vision was still blurred, but I recognised Tom's white-blond hair immediately and shut my eyes, unwilling to meet his frost-coloured stare. But when I looked up again, the man leaning over me was Chris Steadman, peroxide hair sticking up in messy spikes. His eyes were stretched a centimetre too wide, muscles twitching like he'd overdosed on cocaine.

'Where's Ella?' he hissed.

'She escaped, Chris, the police are on their way. It's time to stop this.'

His jaw clenched as he stared at me. 'It's your fault Ella's gone. She wanted to stay with me.' He was already setting up the equipment, pointing a camera directly at my face. My only chance was to keep him talking.

'You could leave now, get a head start. How did Kinsella contact you, anyway?'

His hands shook with fury. 'My master key opens every door. We talk every day.'

'But you can't follow through, can you? He told you to mess up the girls' faces.'

'Shut up,' he muttered, colour draining from his cheeks. 'I promised to do this for him.'

'Without his blessing you'd be too weak to hurt anyone.'

He grabbed a knife from the floor. 'Carry on talking and I'll slit your throat.'

A green light flashed on the camera, and I made one last effort to move. My arm flopped onto the mattress, completely useless. But I forced myself to hold his gaze. Instinct told me that it would be hard to blind someone who was staring straight at you. I kept willing myself not to pass out as Kinsella's

325

message rattled around my head: pain and release, purity and despair. There was no way to silence it, even though the tape had stopped. The kitchen knife in his hand was poised inches above my right eye, light glinting from the steel.

'I can help you, Chris. You don't have to do this.'

A flicker of doubt crossed his face, then the knife lurched towards me. There was a tearing sound as the blade sliced the fabric of my dress, snagging the skin on my breastbone. He started to force me into the foundling costume, yanking my rigid arms through the sleeves.

'It won't fit,' I hissed. 'I'm not a child.'

He paid no attention as the fabric tightened round my shoulders. He'd begun his killing ritual, eyes set in a hypnotic stare. It wouldn't matter how hard I screamed. Only Kinsella could reach him now.

'Ignore him,' I whispered. 'Don't let him control you.'

The knife flew at me again, grazing my scalp. There was a sickening noise as it carved into the pillow, and when I looked up again, he was weeping uncontrollably. It took a herculean effort, but I managed to reach out and touch his hand.

'I'll take care of you now, Chris. You're a foundling, aren't you? That's what this is about.' A muscle jumped in his cheek and I was terrified he'd attack me again. 'Where did your mother leave you?'

Tears spilled from his eyes. 'In a phone box when I was two days old; that's how I met Louis. He gave me extra lessons at Orchard House.'

'And he showed you his pictures.'

He nodded slowly. 'He made me feel special. That's why I followed him.'

'Did you stay at the home your whole childhood?'

'I was fostered, but the families always sent me back.'

'Because you cut yourself, didn't you?' I studied the thin

scars on his cheek. 'You hurt anything you could find: insects, animals, other kids. You wanted them to feel the same pain as you.'

A car was pulling up outside, then the loud slam of a door.

'They're here now, Chris. Go out the back way. Ella's waiting for you.'

'Do you think so?' Hope lit up his face.

'I'm sure of it.'

The tension in his face eased, and when I opened my eyes again, the room was empty.

65

Ella's sitting on the back seat of the patrol car, and at first the policewoman doesn't seem to be listening, then she leans closer and talks very slowly.

'It's all right, sweetheart. You're safe now, we'll take care of you.'

An ambulance pulls up on the other side of the road, blue lights whirring.

'I don't want to go to hospital,' Ella pleads, 'just take me home.'

'You'll be there soon, love, but you've hurt your foot, haven't you? The doctor can bandage it.'

Her hand reaches out, and Ella shrinks from her touch. It crosses her mind to open the door and run, but she knows she wouldn't get far. Blood from the cut on her heel has soaked through the towel the woman gave her, and suddenly it's hard to tell where the pain begins and ends. Ella's mind explodes with memories: Sarah lying on the metal floor, staring at invisible stars, Amita's head resting on her shoulder. All the empty smiles she gave, to stop the man hurting her. When the policewoman speaks again her voice is gentle.

'That's right, love. You have a good cry.'

Ella scrubs the tears away with the ball of her hand. 'Can I use your phone?'

The woman looks startled. 'Of course you can.'

When someone finally picks up, there's no sound at all, but

Ella knows who it is immediately. She recognises the pulse of her breathing.

'It's me, Suze.'

Suzanne makes a strange yelping noise, then Ella hears her screaming for granddad to come to the phone. When she closes her eyes, her breathing steadies. She can picture her sister in the hallway, pacing on the spot, clutching the receiver with both hands.

66

I was terrified that Steadman might come back to finish what he'd started. If he did, I wouldn't stand a prayer; I could still hardly move. When the police battered the door down I tried to yell for help, but they were with me in seconds. Burns arrived first, followed by Tania and three uniforms. The relief that washed through me was as potent as the anaesthetic still circulating round my veins.

'He went out the back, it's Chris Steadman. Check the house first.' My speech was breathless and too fast, but at least it had impact. The uniforms scattered immediately, racing up the stairs.

Burns looked horrified, and the reason was obvious. The nick from Steadman's knife had bled copiously, a six-inch circle of blood drenching my white foundling's dress. Tania leant down and squeezed my shoulder.

'Keep your eyes open, Alice. That's it, try and stay awake. The paramedics are on their way. Do you know what he's given you?'

'Some kind of muscle relaxant.'

She turned away, bawling commands into her phone. My head swam, as if my thoughts had been soaking too long in hot water. When Burns crouched beside me, the urge to touch him was stronger than ever. The shadows under his eyes looked like they'd been sketched with charcoal.

'You look terrible, Don. You should take better care of yourself.'

He choked out a laugh. 'Did that bastard hurt you?'

'He bottled out. You can watch the movie.' I gave a weak nod towards the camera.

'Jesus,' Burns muttered, rushing over to switch it off.

Elation was giving way to cold. Suddenly my feet felt icy, my whole body shaking as though I'd spent a night lying in the snow. The paramedics swaddled me in blankets but it made no difference. The ride to hospital felt like rattling around inside a fridge, an oxygen mask choking each breath.

A doctor confirmed that Chris had spiked my drinks at the party, then a nurse came and advised me to get some sleep, but the chance never arrived. When I opened my eyes again, the room smelled of smoke, and an old man was sitting beside my bed. Ella's grandfather looked older than before. The lines under his eyes were grooved more deeply, his skin grey as cigarette ash. Even his quiff was unravelling, but his expression was transformed. His eyes were bright as a child's.

'I had to come and thank you,' he said.

'There's no need. Ella's the hero. She got me out of there alive.'

His smile trembled. 'She's not saying much yet. The lass won't let anyone near except me and Suzanne.'

'Give her time. She's been incredibly brave.'

A deep frown appeared on his face. 'None of this should have happened to her.'

The old man's head bowed, as if his thoughts were too heavy to carry. I couldn't think of anything comforting to say, so I reached out to him. His skin felt dry and papery, and I don't know how long we sat there in silence, hands entwined, because I must have drifted back into sleep.

When I woke again, Mr Williams had been replaced by Judith. She gave me her calmest smile but I could tell she'd been crying.

'Your friend Lola's downstairs. She says she's not leaving till she can take you home.'

I smiled weakly and pitied the nurses. Lola's protests are always high volume, and she never backs down.

'I feel terrible, Alice. I couldn't even keep you safe in my own home.'

'It's not your fault.'

She shook her head. 'Of course it's my bloody fault.'

The next statement emerged from my mouth without any conscious thought. 'You should destroy Kinsella's letters, Judith. Put them through a shredder.'

'They're clinical evidence, Alice. Someone might want to study them one day.'

'Alan Nash will publish them when he recovers, and the victims' families will suffer all over again.'

She looked uncertain. 'Let's talk about it when you're better.'

'Does Kinsella know his plan backfired?'

Judith nodded. 'He hasn't got cardiac problems at all. Chris gave him amphetamines to make his heart race. He's still in the infirmary, refusing food. They'll have to intubate him if he keeps it up.'

I tried to imagine Kinsella's state of mind. From now on his privileges would end. There would be no more trips to the library to escape the barrage of noise, and all his opportunities to manipulate people would be removed. Without his *raison d'être*, it didn't surprise me that he wanted to die. Oddly enough, the idea didn't fill me with jubilation. Five girls had lost their lives because of his brainwashing, and there was no way of knowing how many more children he'd groomed. But at least Ella was safe; my promise to her sister had been fulfilled.

67

No one bothered me again until the next morning, which was just as well, because Steadman's poison had given me an appalling headache. I tried to tidy myself up, but combing my hair was a step too far. My scalp felt like it was being attacked by red-hot needles. Someone had made a mercy mission to the hotel – a fresh set of clothes lay on the chair, beside a bar of chocolate. The prospect of food tempted me, but I gave up after a couple of squares, because it tasted bitter instead of sweet. By the time Burns arrived I was fully dressed, although my hair was a mess of ugly tangles. He stood by the window blocking out the light.

'They say you can leave, provided you're supervised.'

'Who's supervising me?'

'Yours truly. I'll drive you to the hotel.'

'No way.' A stab of pain jerked through my temple. 'I'm going back to the cottage.'

'You're kidding. That place is in the middle of nowhere.'

'I'll get a taxi if need be, on my own.'

'God almighty,' he said, rolling his eyes. 'Stubborn as a mule.'

Burns didn't say much on the drive to Charndale, which gave me time to look through the window. Nothing seemed to be moving. The sky was still loaded with snow, and the landscape looked like it had been whitewashed, no fences visible between the fields.

'This place is freezing,' Burns grumbled, when we reached the cottage.

'Light the fire then. There's plenty of wood.'

The journey from the hospital had exhausted me. All I could do was sit and watch him struggle with the matches. When the fire finally lit, I could tell he was dying to ask questions, so I made a pre-emptive strike.

'Have you caught him yet?'

Burns's face darkened. 'He was spotted twice yesterday, on the M4, then we found his bike near Reading Station last night. He walked in front of an express train, killed outright.'

A picture of Chris appeared in front of me, smiling as he offered his keys on the palm of his hand. 'Did you know he was a foundling?'

'He changed his name by deed poll; he didn't like the one the nurses gave him when he was found. Apparently he was abused at Orchard House. The only thing he had to look forward to was Kinsella making a fuss of him.'

'Was he there when Pru and Denise arrived?'

'He'd already left. We found a load of stuff at his house this morning: he was on the Foundling Museum's mailing list, so he got Brian Knowles's newsletter every month. I bet he showed it to Kinsella, so he could choose the victims. And he'd hacked into the local authority's website, to get the girls' addresses and find out which ones were fostered or adopted. He had a load of foundling dresses at the house, and there's a chest freezer in the garage. Forensics think he kept the first girls' bodies there.'

I shook my head in disbelief. 'How did he get me out of Judith's?'

'After he spiked your drink, he waited till everyone was asleep then got on his motorbike and went back to Charndale to collect his van. He left Judith's door on the latch so he could get back inside. He must have carried you down to the van.'

'Is Ella okay?'

'She's talking more. The trauma counsellor's pleased, but she's refusing to be examined.'

'That's not surprising.'

'We still don't know if she was abused.'

'She was the only survivor, Don. There has to be a reason.'

'Let's hope we're wrong.' He kept his eyes fixed on the fire. 'She's got more guts than my whole team combined.'

'When can I visit her?'

'Next week probably. The counsellor says she needs time with her family, before she sees anyone else.'

Burns told me the whole story over the course of the day. Steadman's job as IT guru had given him the perfect camouflage. If he carried his toolkit he could access every room in the building. Staff assumed he was fixing something, because the IT system was always breaking down. His colleagues saw him as a hard worker, highly committed to his job, which left him free to roam the infirmary, stealing handfuls of drugs. All he had to do was re-programme the passwords on the electronic locks.

'Higham's been filling in some of the gaps,' Burns murmured. 'Apparently Kinsella told the boys he groomed to follow him, like the Pied Piper. Get as close as they could and wait for his instructions. Chris is the only one who actually followed through.'

I gazed back at him. 'He was hurting kids like himself, as an extension of his self-harm.'

Burns's frown deepened. 'It's the other kids from Orchard House and St Augustine's who worry me. We'll have to interview the ones who spent most time with Kinsella and see who needs counselling.'

By midday I was exhausted; either I was on information overload or the fire had hypnotised me. I was stretching out on the sofa when my mobile buzzed in my pocket – there were twenty-seven unanswered messages, and the most recent one was from my mother, updating me on her cruise. She was spending the next day in Athens, exploring the Acropolis. The fact that she was enjoying herself filled me with so much relief that I could have wept, but I closed my eyes and slept instead. The flames were low in the grate when I woke up. It was already getting dark outside and Burns was still there, feet resting on the fireguard.

'What time is it?' I asked, rubbing my eyes.

'Nearly five.'

'Shouldn't you go? You've been here all day. Tania'll be waiting for you.'

'She's in London dealing with the press.' He looked crestfallen.

'Have you two had a row?'

He stared at me round-eyed, then stifled a laugh. 'We're not a couple, Alice. She's been a mate for years; we were at Hendon together. She's had a lot of crap lately – her ex is suing for custody of their daughter.'

Something loosened in my chest, like a knot untying. That explained why Tania had been so tetchy. It had nothing to do with me or Burns; her life was coming apart at the seams. I felt stupid for assuming the worst and believing the rumours. I got up to look out of the window, stalling for time, but the sky gave me no help whatsoever. There was nothing there apart from a black expanse of cloud. Burns was on his feet too, standing behind me as though he expected me to fall. Maybe he felt the same, half tempted to bolt. I kept my back turned when I spoke again.

'Are you staying here tonight?'

'What do you think? I promised to supervise you for the next twenty-four hours.'

I turned to look at him. 'Didn't Lola offer?'

'I sent her packing. I said there'd be questions for you when you came round.'

'What questions?'

He took a step closer. 'They've slipped my mind.'

'Don't worry. I've got plenty of time.'

His shoulders looked wide enough to support small towns, and when the sound came from outside, he didn't even flinch. It was loud and high-pitched as a siren, an owl hovering above the house. The next call was quieter and more plaintive, but Burns's expression was unchanged. There was a mixture of shock and anticipation in his face as he gazed down at me.

EPILOGUE

I arrived at Judith's house clutching a bunch of flowers. She looked tired, but her smile was welcoming when she opened the door.

'It's not your birthday, is it?'

She shook her head. 'I've got a surprise for you.'

Her garden was a riot of spring flowers, spears of iris and gladioli standing tall under the trees. Two deckchairs stood beside a brazier, which was already crackling. It seemed odd because the afternoon was so warm.

'Are we having a barbecue?'

She shook her head. And when I looked again, a large plastic box caught my eye.

'Kinsella's letters,' I whispered.

'I told Alan Nash they were lost, but he's bound to come looking one day.'

'Let's get to work then.'

I threw the first handful of envelopes into the fire and watched the flames consume them, the paper dissolving into long orange flames. Judith didn't join in; she stood beside me, studying her phone.

'What are you doing?'

'Getting rid of Garfield's messages. He's moving back to London next week. If we're having a ceremonial burning, I should let him go too.'

I put my hand on her shoulder as she pressed the delete

button, and her face slowly brightened as the flames rose. We gathered batches of envelopes and hurled them into the brazier. Kinsella was still alive, locked in his cell at Northwood, but his words had become an inferno. A plume of black air sailed high above the roofline as his credo went up in smoke.

ACKNOWLEDGEMENTS

I would like to thank my agent Teresa Chris for her unstinting encouragement and Ruth Tross for being such a wise and insightful editor. Nick Sayers deserves to be mentioned here, because he continues to be the kindest man in publishing and the most convivial. Karen Geary and Rebecca Mundy are also due much gratitude for publicising my work so tirelessly. Many thanks are also due to Andrew Martin at Minotaur, Hope Dellon, Dave Pescod, Miranda Landgraf, Penny Hancock, Sophie Hannah and the 134 club for their readings and sound advice. The helpful staff of the Foundling Museum gave me invaluable guidance on the history of the Foundling Hospital and allowed me to trawl through their archive. Thanks to the media teams at Broadmoor and Rampton Hospitals for advice on protocols at high security units. Thanks as ever to DC Laura Shaw for her excellent guidance on police matters.

Note: most of the locations in this book are real, but many are imaginary. Apologies for changing some of London's geography and street names; my motive is always to tell the best possible story.